TESSA M^CWATT

This Body

HarperCollins*Publishers*Ltd

For Faye, Greg, and in memory of Marsha

I love this body
made to weather the storm
in the brain, raised
out of the deep smell
of fish and water hyacinth,
out of rapture and the first
regret.

From "Anodyne" by Yusef Komunyakaa,
in *Thieves of Paradise*, 1998

PART I

CHAPTER ONE

Tomatoes

༺༻

I miss being dead, she thinks as she stares into the palm of her hand, examining the criss-cross of lines. Her thighs and buttocks leak through the spaces between the wooden slats of the bench, her flesh bulging like a lean rump roast tied with string at the butcher's. She adjusts her right buttock with a flick of her fingers. That's better.

Victoria is seated on a bench across the road from the Royal Albert Hall, just inside the gates of Kensington Gardens. She stands up and walks to the front of the spired monument in the square. Tilting her head back, she looks directly up at the loins of the prince consort. She shakes her head in disbelief. Will you look at that? A radiant effigy in gold, the Albert Memorial is a monument to grief. Or so they say. But grief never looked like that. Grief is grey and damp, and it gives time stubs where it used to have wings.

She steps closer to Albert. It's that grey, stubby feeling she misses now. "Laud, gimme strength," as her daddy used to say; then "Laud, forget me strength, gimme peace," when he wanted time to stop. But time didn't stop for her; it just clobbed along after Kola disappeared. And even now, so many years later, she can feel how time's limping allowed her to dismiss her once slim waist and gently curving hips. Ignoring the pulse of muscle along her thighs, she roamed the streets of Toronto looking for him.

And all the while, time was hollowing out small holes in her. But the slap of dough, the dicing of onion, the frying of rice filled the holes just a little.

She's never taken a good look at this statue, but now Victoria inhales deeply and absorbs the sight, twenty metres up, of a golden man posed under a gilt four-poster canopy surrounded by virtues, seraphim, and other nubile attendants. Another ten metres above the frescoed canopy protecting the prince, a gilt Gothic spire rises, topped by a bejewelled, golden cross, like those of the most ornate churches. Golden angels guard the cross, their arms outstretched, their wings spread. She wants to shout Hallelujah! but that would be inappropriate. She holds her breath. Below Albert are marble carvings of artists, poets, and their nubile muses. Lower down, guarding each of the four corners of the prince's coquettish boudoir, are symbols of his lady's empire, depictions in marble of all that desire can conquer. Tamed beasts—bull, camel, elephant, buffalo—are burdened with the empire's humble servants. Behind them, riches overflow from the barges of industry. Sculpted before her are fragments of the entire world captured in lust.

And the man himself? Robust as the first night he lay with his queen. Francis Albert Augustus Charles Emmanuel of Saxe-Coburg-Gotha, prince consort, immortalized in a manner more splendid than Nelson or Disraeli, or even Queen Victoria herself. Bigger than politics. Bigger than ideas. As big as appetite itself.

No, this has nothing to do with grief. This is a monument to sex. Victoria exhales.

Her affinity with that queen has always been in name only, but now, as she examines the queen's husband, she feels surprisingly jealous. This is a statue to love, unlike anything else in this city of statues. Eros, in Piccadilly, is a tribute to indiscriminate life instincts, and, as central London's most conspicuous meeting place, it is altogether too inclusive. This statue is to love specific: a singular, consuming love for one man.

The damp air succumbs to drizzle. Victoria's eyes roam the well-developed calves and thighs of the prince, but her keen examination is impeded by the golden cloak that drapes over his left leg, designed to hide his crotch from a modest public. A woman in the hospital kitchen where Victoria works told her that Prince Albert was reputed to have a member as long as his forearm, which necessitated a way to keep it in place inside his trousers. The story goes that his member had been pierced with a small ring, through which it was then strapped to his thigh, and the conspicuous organ could be kept as discreet as possible in the tight breeches of the day. The Prince Albert. Blimey. No wonder there's a statue to him. Victoria grins at Albert and shakes her head again. Your lady did you proud, she thinks. What a woman—to commission and erect a statue of her beloved, and to put it on display for all to adore and covet. And his own parlour: Royal Albert Hall, looking from here not phallic but safely domestic. Victoria sucks her teeth. All because a bloke is a good shag. Had the mad accident of birth placed her otherwise, it might have been Victoria Layne who erected a statue to her love. The Kola Memorial. Royal Kola Hall. Kola for the world to see. Kola for the love that left. Kola for belief. Kola for hope. Kola for dead.

She stands up and walks north through the park. As the wind tosses up a flounce of rain as it would a skirt over a subway grate, she senses something that has not quite formed into a thought: that love is something you lose, then worship.

And what now?

Now she has the great sexuality of memory. The slobbering, grunting, humping carnality of loss. And the boy. And food. These three things are the triptych of the present, the holy trinity of Victoria Layne, aged sixty-one. Blimey, blimey, blimey. Amen.

Weighted with her bags, Victoria decides to take the bus from Marble Arch towards Lenny's house off Edgware Road. When she arrives at Lenny Brown's front step, she has to stop and take another breath. Everything about her tingles since the boy arrived, as if blood was returning to numb limbs. That's why Kola is back—these vivid memories of a man she loved and lost more than thirty years ago. Forced to rise from the dead, she has to look after the boy and tell him things she's stored up during the deep sleep of her self. To resurrect the family intimacies that have eroded in the clumping time of the past three decades, and to tell the boy all the things he needs to know. 'Cause she's all he's got now.

She runs her hand through her salt-and-pepper hair, then reaches for the door handle. She no longer knocks on Lenny's door; she enters the house as though it's her own. In the cream-coloured hallway, she rests her bags on the floor and listens. These past few weeks she's learned to discern the presence of a seven-and-a-half-year-old. Tiptoeing into the kitchen, she expects to catch stray lids off jam jars or a trail of milk droplets along the kitchen counter. But the counters are clean and clear. The double ovens are in use, and the smell of pastry is like a leak of pleasure from a voice. Lenny has been working hard today, good man, filling orders for their baked goods.

She lifts her hand to the wall and runs her forefinger along a grease stain. The white walls are beginning to show signs of her labour. It was she who had insisted on white. When they first started all this, she made noises about the pale blue walls and the clutter in his kitchen, almost as a way of stalling this long haul towards financial stability she has been on to supplement her NHS-controlled income. She told Lenny that if she had to spend her early mornings here baking, she needed the absence of colour and knick-knacks. The walls were not to have any say in the hue or texture of her inventions. Obediently, he dismantled the oak cabinet in the corner where his wife had proudly displayed a collection of china teacups copied from original eighteenth-century East India Company designs. He made sure all counter surfaces and walls were white, and purchased a new, industrial-sized oven, which he installed where the china cabinet had been, assuring

Victoria that his wife would have admired the oven just as much. That was more of an offering of love than she has ever dared to acknowledge.

At Victoria's home things are very different. There is little she can do with the rooms she and Derek share, as they are lodgers, not owners. She has grown so used to the presence of old chairs, framed Edwardian prints, and carpets stained from the spills in other people's lives that she can't imagine waking up without them.

When Derek first arrived, she had to find a place for him in her private landscape. Ambushed in her own room, she'd turn to find him behind her, wide-faced and waiting for food. The strawberry birthmark that circles his right eye made him seem otherworldly, out of place within her walls. But she's more used to him now. She recognizes the clunky movement of things and the shuffle of feet that are growing faster than she wants to imagine. Listen. She can hear the sound of voices from Lenny's sitting room and can imagine the jittery twitch in Derek's legs as he sits watching television.

"Len?" she calls towards the basement, where he must be, perhaps hauling up supplies. Lenny appears at the top of the stairs with a ten-pound slab of organic butter, which they order on a monthly basis from a farm in Devon. "Oh, dear," she says under her breath, feeling guilty for not having helped him much in the last few weeks.

"Hello darling," he says in his soft voice.

"Did you find them?" she asks.

"Sure did, they're packed up and ready for you to take home. I gave him lunch, and if you hurry he can make it in time for the afternoon bell." Lenny drops the butter on the butcher block and it lands with a thud. A strand of his thin hair flies up, revealing scalp, then falls across his forehead. He brushes it back and turns towards the sitting room in an urgent step that reminds Victoria of a speed walker. She knows that Lenny's speedy but precise movements are why he can eat the pastries they bake and she can't. Nothing stays on Lenny for long.

He fetches Derek and hurries the boy's jacket on. He hands him the Marks & Spencer's bag with his new school clothes and ushers them out the front door before Victoria is able to thank him. At the door she turns to him with gratitude that falls into the chasms of unshared sentences between them. He gives her a wink, pats Derek on the head, and waves them off.

Walking along Edgware Road with the boy, she feels a small sense of triumph in today's accomplishments. Food, school clothes for Derek, and a bit of exercise. Is this where a mother's satisfaction comes from? Having isolated herself for decades from anything that smacked of kinship, Victoria's natural reaction to this feeling of achievement is resistance. Irritation takes over. She readjusts the plastic bags in her hands and walks faster, head down in the face of the chilly drizzle.

When her young sister got pregnant, something moved inside Victoria. Something disobedient, not unlike a child might become. But it was not living, this thing in her. It had no soul. It was just a moment—breathless and finite—the kind of moment you know you'll never have again. It gave her a good swift kick with its disappearing heel, flashed a reminder of missed opportunities, and then waved goodbye. She had considered it her first intimation of motherhood, but today, she thinks perhaps this blend of irritation and satisfaction speaks more to what mothers have.

She'd never agreed with the sperm bank idea of Gwen's—all those fatherless children running about with no idea through whose inherited eyes they were seeing the world. But now the poor squab is fatherless *and* motherless, and she feels more like an ageing woman who'd once felt life in a slow creeping foot along her spine.

Maybe that's why they're together now, she and the boy: he's the kick she felt, the one that grew, phantomlike, within her as a reminder of everything she's ever left behind. When she first saw his open, pensive face in a photo sent by Gwen, she had the urge to talk to him, to tell him things she'd never told anyone, but he was just a baby.

She takes Derek's hand as they cross Hamilton Terrace and head towards Abbey Road. Hesitation is in his fingers. He raises one shoulder, then the other. She wants to ask him not to squirm at her touch, and to tell him that she's trying to cope with the feel of his soft skin in her hand and the tingling sensations she's been experiencing. He drops his hand on the other side of the road. The abandoned look of the Bluebird of Piccadilly comes to her mind—the crimp of her eyebrows, the folds at her chin.

The woman Victoria calls the Bluebird would be grateful for the touch of anyone's hand. But more likely she'd want someone to rub her till she uncreased like an ironed sheet on whatever foul-smelling bed the poor old bird must lie in each night. Always dressed in her robin's-egg-blue shag coat, the Bluebird circles the statue of Eros at Piccadilly Circus for hours, as though, like everyone else there, she has a scheduled rendezvous. She's a big, black Caribbean lady, like Victoria's great-grandmother. Tourists notice her, but she stares ahead. When Victoria first saw her, she watched for someone to meet the Bluebird, and perhaps he eventually did, but that was three years ago, and the woman still circles daily. Victoria returns periodically to be assured of her presence, because on that first sighting the Bluebird became both a source of comfort and a caliper she used to measure the gradations of her own survival. She last saw her in June, and even then the Bluebird was wearing her coat.

It's that coat Victoria likes: full-length, like a blue shag-carpet hide. Victoria would never have bought herself a coat like that, and that's one of the reasons she admires the woman. Poor old gal. Circling back from the encroaching ambush of her life: her bad teeth, her callused feet, her matted hair. Signs of the inevitable betrayal of the physical container. The woman's eyes are sharp, though, despite the reddish ring—a shade of red that makes Victoria think of tomatoes. Not the hard pigskin, beef-blood gene experiments in the supermarkets today, but tomatoes as they should be, like the ones her father grew.

Derek walks quickly, slightly ahead of his aunt, and she allows this distance between them, knowing the cramped space they are returning to. Are there tomatoes in the fridge? She considers a stew, or a sauce for brown rice, or perhaps a ratatouille.

In Guyana, her family had the best tomatoes in the region, thanks to her daddy, who grew them in their yard in Kitty. When Victoria came home from work after a long day of cooking for a well-to-do family in Belair, her baby sister, Gwen, would say, "Vic, come quick, Daddy has tomatoes growin' undaneat he fingernails." Covered in soil and sweat, Daddy would be sitting on a chair in the kitchen, hunched over, elbows on his knees, cleaning the dirt from his nails with a pick. Three-year-old Gwen would stand by and watch, horrified by the dirt as it curled up on the pick like a scoop of black ice cream. Her father's nails would be left framed in white. Her squeal would be of both disgust and delight.

By the time they reach the top floor of the house on Blenheim Terrace, Victoria is out of breath, but there's no time to rest. She has to get Derek ready. She unfolds the shirt and burgundy cardigan that Lenny picked out and hands them to her nephew. She watches him. He is a master of the art of dawdling, and it takes him far too long to change. She glances at the clock on the bedside table as she draws Derek to her. It's close to one.

"Let me fix your shirt, the collar's curled under and these English people are fussy about those things." As she says this she realizes how untrue it is and that, as a child in Georgetown, Victoria was caned for wearing the wrong socks at the convent. "Oh go ahead, squirm, it doesn't matter," but she keeps a grip on his sleeve. She hasn't perfected how to talk to the boy yet. "You'll have to go sooner or later, you know. It's the last space they have, and Year 3, not 2, think of that. I'll let you off today, with this rain, but this week, you'll have to show up in that classroom, little man. I know it's hard—hard on me, too. But your mommy wanted you to go to school. I know she did. She wanted the best for you." Rest her soul.

Victoria doesn't know how she'll manage Gwen's birthday when it comes around. Gwen loved to celebrate anything. She'd dance around the kitchen table if their daddy told them he'd take them to the cinema. Her birthday was the day that Victoria would telephone Georgetown to catch up on a year's worth of family news, an annual conversation that would wrench her out of her self-satisfied isolation. Gwen would tell her of trips she had made to the countryside, or of picnics by the seawall, and Victoria's memories would rush forward to fill in the details. The good memories first, but in subsequent days, the bad ones followed, so that the pleasure associated with Georgetown ebbed as the year wore on.

Gwen passed her driver's test late, at the age of twenty-six, and her upcoming birthday would have marked twenty years of safe driving; Victoria still cannot reconcile herself to the image of the crumpled car from which her sister was pulled, too late. The police report said the driver lost control, swerving away from an overpacked minibus—twenty-five passengers in a fifteen-seat van—that was turning onto the road at a high speed. Gwen's car hit an oncoming fuel lorry, head on. There was much ado in the report about the fortunate fact that only the car ignited on impact, and that the lorry's cargo of fuel did not catch fire and explode. Each time Victoria thinks of the report, *she* ignites at the callous editorial comment.

Gwen had been a good driver. Unlike Victoria. Their father had been obliged to buy Victoria's licence from the examiner in Georgetown, and all the years in Toronto, she had neither need for nor access to a car. When she came to England at the age of thirty-nine, no one asked her to take a test. She presented the licencing office with her Guyana licence, and they presented her with an English one. Her boss at the hospital sold her his red Austin Mini; its engine was damaged in Victoria's first crash. After the Mini there was a Rover bought in mint condition from a used car lot; the sideswipe was not her fault, but she couldn't afford to repair the damage. Finally, the Renault, her favourite, had been brand new. It lasted longer than the others, but after a total of twelve accidents, the licencing authority won't let her drive anymore.

Victoria wonders if the Bluebird of Piccadilly is allowed to drive.

Derek has unbuttoned his school cardigan and is slipping out of it carefully—an almost imperceptible movement that will free his shoulder from the burgundy knit and release him from his aunt's grip. The grip is urgent, but he knows, after almost a month of living with her, that if she's mumbling to herself it will slacken, just slightly. This usually gives him a chance to escape. She talks under her breath, and up this close her breath smells livery. She's fussed with his collar, buttoning it up high so that he can barely breathe. Next she'll get his hair, he worries, and try to glue it down in a straight fringe to make him look proper for school. But Derek has decided never to go to school, and now his arm is free.

Ain goin back there, uh, uh, not me. He doesn't dare say this to his aunt, who looks at him sternly with her Chinaman slits. They share the same almond-shaped eyes that the schoolboys back home used to tease him about. Back home he could bear the teasing—to the point of encouraging it—because he gave as good as he got. And he knew the other boys were jealous of his beautiful mom and his mystery of a father. But here, teasing comes like the rain, cold and sapping. On the first day at George Eliot School, a square-shouldered boy with dark skin and thick, straight, black hair approached Derek and stood staring at him. Derek smiled nervously. It was only then that the boy seemed to have found what he'd come over for—one small fact to pronounce throughout the schoolyard. "Mind the gap . . . Mind the gap," the boy honked in an automated tone. He laughed and returned to his mates in triumph, leaving Derek feeling queasy in his stomach, with no idea as to what had transpired, but relieved that the boy had not mentioned his birthmark.

Only much later in the day did he twig as to the source of the reaction. As he smiled and opened his mouth to ask another boy his name, the boy announced in a robot drone, "Mind the gap, mind the gap." Derek realized they were referring to the wide space between his two front teeth. At home that afternoon he told his aunt what the boys had said. He watched her face lighten with a secret recognition that seemed to bar him from ever understanding this awful country. She told him about the space between the platform and the subway carriage in the London Underground, and the recorded announcement to remind passengers to be careful. No, it would be impossible for him to ever return to school.

He's been to school only twice since he arrived in Inkland, between faked, doubled-over stomachaches and invented sore teeth and throat. *Inkland*. In Guyana, if a boy at school went away to visit London and returned using fancy words, the other boys would tease him and tell him to learn to talk or go back to *Inkland*. Inkland: for the place where every word you say dries on a page to be read by someone else far away. London, Inkland.

But when Derek was leaving Georgetown, the boys didn't tease him. In fact, no one said a word to him, because he didn't go back to school after his mother died. His mom's friends kept him at home. Frances and Lata; Mabel and Rohini; June and Rosie—pairs of women at a time, cooking, cleaning, sleeping in the house at night, watching over Derek as though to catch him out crying. But he didn't cry in front of them. He wasn't going to have them pawing at him, so he only cried when he was in the bathroom. While the men phoned England and made plans for him, the women forced him to speak, to make sure he wasn't becoming a mute idiot they'd have to find room for in an institution. The only boy he saw was his neighbour, Thomas, who didn't open his mouth for the whole two weeks before Derek left for London, except to say to his mother, on their way out of Derek's room, that he felt sorry for Derek. But Derek did not want sympathy, so he kept Thomas at a distance. The women fussed around him, forcing food down him, treating him like a baby by insisting he lie down in the afternoons. The only advantage to having these strangers look after him was the unlimited time he was allowed to spend in front of the television. The old people left him alone then, as they made their plans, whispering, and weeping when they turned their backs. A new stream of visitors would enter his room daily, stare at him, walk slowly towards him as he slouched in the armchair, and their eyes would grow wider. They'd shadow him, bend over, then cup his chin in their palms, forcing his head up: *Derek, you're such a brave boy. Brave as a knight.* Sure. How would they know how brave a knight would have to be to lance a dragon?

Derek has lanced many a dragon in the space of his short life. The first was the red dragon that shimmered into view, tail-first, through the window of his bedroom as it backed away from its rampage on Roebuck Street, where it had burned down the movie theatre. The following visitations were less transparent and shimmery. The iron dragon at school made all the boys who weren't first or second in class do lessons every afternoon with the math tutor. Derek sliced off its head. Then there was the crystal dragon . . . *I slay thee crystal dragon, in the name of Guenevere . . .*

All of these creatures he'd slain with the sword his mother had given him on his sixth birthday, but which he'd only recently retrieved after she started to read him tales from the Knights of the Round Table and King Arthur. His mother was like the fair lady in the tales he wanted to save. The opposite of what happened. The horrible opposite.

His mother would have let him stay home from school in Inkland, he knows that. If only he'd stopped the killing sooner. Too many dragons lying splat out on the pavement of their car park in Kitty. Too much destruction, and now he will never become a full knight.

Derek has escaped Victoria's gaze, and he stands at the entrance to his new room in Inkland, blinking the furniture into focus. The room is a grey ice cube, the curtains drawn against the wind and rain outside. The two rooms he and his aunt share are on the top floor of a house on a quiet cul-de-sac off Abbey Road. They have a makeshift kitchen in the hallway, but share a bathroom with two others. Beyond the fire door to the adjoining house are their fellow lodgers—a Slovakian beautician and a German musician—and below them live the retired parents of Sonia and Martin, the couple who own this sprawling double house that hums like a hive, serving individual and collective needs. People come and go, and Derek isn't sure how to address them, so he merely smiles and nods when he encounters someone on the stairs. His aunt told him that the owners are kind, and kind was always the highest of praise from his mother. But his aunt has lived here for over two decades, and Derek wonders how anyone could survive that long without heat. It's not that heat doesn't come out of the radiators, it's just that it seems to pour from them directly outside, through the gaps between the window and its frame. The heavy curtains are an attempt to seal off the draught, but the resulting darkness is chilling in itself.

By this time in the afternoon in Kitty, the sun's harsh light would have been almost mango-coloured outside his bedroom window. The Kiskadee bird that woke him in the morning would have sung its part and bowed off the day's sound stage to make way for the afternoon performance of the God-bird that hopped along the fence. Its upturned tail and its cheery song of a trill and three long notes suited the yellowish light. Sometimes the God-bird would sit on the sill of his window, as though waiting for him to answer its final note.

His new room in London looks out over a well-tended garden. Crossing the room to the window, he pulls the curtain back slightly to peek outside. The garden is asleep. This is winter, he thinks with a shiver, and lets the curtain fall closed. He flicks on the light to keep his studies of Inkland limited to this room, with its square, dark, and musty-smelling furniture. But if he looks up, there is a different life going on above. The high off-white ceilings are adorned by mortar twirls in the four corners. Carved mortar faces peer at Derek in much the same squinty way his aunt does. Before Auntie Victoria puts on her eyeglasses in the morning, she senses her way about the room like a mole. But the sculpted heads on the moulding don't need glasses; they see everything. Derek sits on the bed. He feels twitchy in his legs, so gets up again.

He crosses the hall and stands in the doorway to his aunt's room to stare at the computer. The only computer he has ever touched was in his classroom in Kitty, where four PCs had been donated to the school by CIDA, a Canadian organization devoted to assisting developing countries. One monitor had arrived broken, and the other three machines were constantly in demand, so there was never time to play on them. His mother told him that one day she'd buy him his own computer. He hasn't yet found the courage to ask his aunt if he can play on this one. The screen is on. Trapezoid patterns skate around each other, linking up, and then pulling apart. He stares at the patterns and moves into the room. His forefinger presses a key. The patterns disappear, revealing the alert desktop icons, ready for someone who knows what to do next. But that's not him. Heart beating, he backs away and turns, expecting to see his aunt. He can hear her rummaging through the chest in the hallway. Quietly he moves to the doorway and watches her squatting in front of the chest, removing letters and documents, turning them over, examining them, replacing bundles, searching for something else. Above her a strip of wallpaper has peeled away from the wall like a jeering tongue. Stepping back into the room, he stares at the screen and its indecipherable icons. He stares and stares, not knowing what else to do. His heartbeat slows; time slows then quickens. Suddenly, the trapezoid pattern reappears. A sigh of relief. The shapes circle one another again, and the screen is alive. He can barely believe it. His first miracle. He breathes in deeply and returns quietly to the hall.

"Ahh! God!" Victoria's voice is high and angry as she spins around and faces him. "What are you doing sneaking up, child? Jesus Lord!" She catches her breath and stands holding a letter tightly over her heart.

Derek faces her, horrified. "What are you up to? . . ." But she hears her tone and stops, feeling ashamed of her crotchety manner. The boy is completely cowed. "You gave me a fright, is all," she says more softly. She folds the letter towards her and closes the chest. Derek stands rigid, his eyes wide. "I'm busy now. You run along for a few minutes," she adds, reminding herself that children are treated differently now than in her day.

Brave as a knight. Again. He hadn't meant to scare her, just to ask her if he could touch the computer, make the trapezoids dissolve into icons again. But now he can't open his mouth, even to say sorry, oh sorry. He has frightened her, and now she too will die like his mother, like the dragons, the way everything he frightens disintegrates. He couldn't bear another disintegration. He will have to atone for all of it, to take up a new quest, to bring them all back somehow. Gwen, fair Guenevere, the beautiful lady of Camelot. . . .

Miami

Dear Victoria,

It worked. I have a child in me. He was there on the ultrasound this morning. I heard a heartbeat other than my own.

This clinic is good, full of helpful nurses and the latest equipment. I didn't even have to bribe them to get proper treatment, like we have to do at home. And they know the doctor at the sperm bank. My obstetrician says that with only one functioning tube I'm lucky I didn't have to do in vitro. And I'm younger than Mummy was when she had me, so I won't have the scares she did, worried all the while that I'd turn out damaged.

I feel like I've finally done something that's my own. I'll soon tell

Mummy, and one day I'll have to tell the child himself. But there's little to tell, except to explain that he's all I ever wanted, and to give him the number—1119. It will be hard to tell the child his father is a number on a vial and that he wanted it kept so. On the form donors fill out before they are accepted, they can select to be traced when the offspring is eighteen, but this one has not consented to contact. Most of them don't.

I'm frightened, Vic, but I'm more excited than ever before in my life. I feel four years old again. I've "caught a baby"! Do you remember? Before you left for Canada, we used to lie in your bed at night and you used to tell me where babies came from. The tomato garden, you said. All the women in Georgetown came to Daddy's tomato patch late at night to pick ripe tomatoes from the vine before they fell to the ground, because those were the tomatoes that God sent babies in. But the women had to catch them just as they were falling, and that is why they would lie under the plants waiting for the fruit to drop. You were wicked to tell that to a four-year-old. After you left I used to wake in the middle of the night and sneak out to check if there were any women in our field. It wasn't until years later that I figured out that you were telling me about Daddy's women and a neighbourhood of bastards. I believed you for so long. Even a few months ago, when I thought all hope for having a child of my own had run out, I looked out in the patch and thought of the story.

You were right to escape, Vic, and in my own way maybe I too have escaped the bush. Miami is mad but spectacular. Guyanese who can afford it come here now to shop for everything under the sun, because things are so much cheaper here than back home, where prices have at least doubled in the last two years, and the corruption is worse than ever. And now I have my son. Vic, it's a miracle!

That was it. Kick, kick, right in Victoria's belly when she read that letter the first time. The feeling that something had moved and in the next second completely slipped away. Something gained and lost in one. Her resentment surfaces again, as she remembers Toronto, and the taxi driver she met at the restaurant—what was his name?—Harry, with whom she got drunk and who took her to bed. Harry said he could pull out, but Harry didn't know a woman from a parking bay, so Victoria ended up seeing a doctor a couple of months later, having to convince him that a child would be the death of her. "Money," she said. "I have no money," and the doctor checked something off on his chart. What she didn't tell him was that no one was going to be her family if it wasn't Kola, and he'd left years before. She kept that locked up, and freed herself from the taxi driver with a simple surgical procedure.

Enough of that now, she has work to do. She takes the letter with her to the kitchen and places it on the counter as she picks up the phone and dials Neal's Yard Dairy.

"Oh, hello, yes, I'd like to order a hard cheese . . . a sheep's cheese, preferably. What have you got that's special?" She has in mind a Beenleigh Blue, something that will crumble nicely.

Once she's placed her order and has hung up the telephone, she stares out her window at the catalpa, with its long brown pods hanging off the branches. It's an Indian Bean Tree she has watched grow outside this window for years. She wonders if all mothers feel this fragile duality of satisfaction and anxiety. The first day of walking Derek to school, leaving him there alone, and not knowing how he might fare, she watched him walk up the steps, looking at him as she would look upon an accident, and her heart lurched. Surely this is not how all mothers look at children? The mothers Victoria sees in the morning stride along with confidence, barely looking back to see if the child is keeping up. They appear ready for challenges, already preparing smooth transitions into the secure futures they've promised their offspring.

Victoria folds up Gwen's letter and puts it in her pocket as she walks out of her room. She pauses over the chest to consider wading into its other artefacts, but she senses the eddying futility that will swirl around her like river rubbish if she does. She has to keep in the flow. She walks to Derek's room and stands in his doorway. He's sitting on the bed, staring at the far corner of the ceiling.

"Would you like something to eat?"

He shakes his head. She stands waiting for something more to come to her, something to say or do or even feel that will reach him. He looks at her.

"Auntie Vic?"

"Yes?"

"The computer."

"What about it darlin'?" Speak son, speak . . . The poor little thing, his hair standing up and confused, part straight, part curly, makes her wonder what his father looks like. Must be handsome, anyway, his piano-key teeth included.

"Can it do surfing?"

She cocks her head.

"People say surfing on a computer," he adds.

"Blimey," she mutters—a word she picked up when she first moved to England, mistakenly thinking it would make her sound more like a British lady. "Here love, I'll show you."

Where on earth did he come from? When Gwen wrote to her after Derek was born, Victoria suddenly felt like her mother's daughter. Her mother had preferred secrets to facts. The secretive dust over their lives had been the very thing Victoria wished to escape by leaving her family. But when Gwen mentioned the baby's tiny fingers, his large feet, Victoria didn't want to know that the boy was possible. How could a mere collision of gametes be enough to thicken a bloodline and have it burst like an artery—a child from nowhere, no one's family, no one's sad copulation? She wanted to believe, as her mommy had, that just because a man and a woman lay together in a tomato field one night didn't mean that within a couple of years there'd be a boy running fatherless through the streets of Kitty. Then another boy, and another, all of them with Daddy's slanty Shanghai eyes. Victoria resembles neither of her parents, but looks more Chinese than black, and nothing like the wild boys running past the gate. But the women he took to that field, while his wife helped their young daughter with lessons inside the house, would later walk past their gate and glare at Victoria as she read her schoolbooks on the veranda. Some of them were young, sometimes only a few years older than Victoria, but most were women who'd moved to town from the country: Amerindian—"Buck"—women, fine-boned Indian women, and thick tar-skinned women. All the while, in the house, washing the dirt from the tomatoes, was Victoria's faded mahogany mom.

By the time Gwen came along, Victoria was a teenager. She didn't believe Gwen was Daddy's child, mostly because she'd never seen him lie down with their mother in the field. She never heard familiar sighs, only foreign squeals. It's no wonder Gwen was squeamish with tomatoes when she was a little girl. Tomatoes represented brothers she would never know.

"Here, you take this, it's the mouse. You drag it along the pad and follow where the arrow goes on the screen."

Derek sits beside her, captivated by the screen and the clicks of the mouse. Victoria is clumsy with computer commands, but she is learning, thanks to Lenny, who gave her the desktop PC after buying a new one for himself. She's been able to expand her hunt for recipes—with and without tomatoes.

When Victoria left, she wanted only the truth, or at least something bald-faced and blunt, not the amorphous deceit shrouding her family. The government was no better than her relations at truth, so Guyana was a place for leaving. Her father had refused to leave, even when it became evident that the country was going to ruin under a despot. He told his family he would not abandon the plot of land given to him by God. Politics created a society of two warring factions—Indian and black; her mixed family fell between the cracks. Public Guyana went on around them, while its more intimate dramas took place right in their garden. As soon as she was old enough, Victoria joined countless others in the slow haemorrhage of the once most prosperous British colony of the Caribbean. Canada would be fresh, untainted, she assured herself. But when truth disappeared in Toronto, she followed it to London.

"Give people good food—not just good, but joyous food—and they're bound to get well faster," she said at the job interview to be a cook at St. Mary's NHS Trust hospital. After an outbreak of food poisoning the previous year, her timing couldn't have been better. A few years later, when she was promoted to Assistant Chef, Victoria instructed her junior cooking staff to consider each and every tomato a potential phoney, and to make sure they knew to whom it was being served. Patients with renal problems can't handle the potassium in them. Although the nutritionists at the Royal Hospitals Trust keep them on the menu, Victoria has, as much as possible, omitted tomatoes from her recipes over the last few years, convinced that genetic modification will result in complications. While her aversion based on childhood associations continues, she thinks it might be time to cook with them again.

"This is a game, like the real card game, same one. You must know it. You deal a hand then click on the card. If there's a black nine, like this, you can put that on a red ten. And here's a king . . . wait for a space." Handing Derek the mouse, she watches him click then drag cards to complete the solitaire rows.

Victoria thinks of pissaladière. It's a recipe she's tried once, for a special hospital function. But, as with all hospital food, it was neutralized in bulk. Nine hundred patients, two hundred staff to feed twice a day. How could anything ever taste good? And if it doesn't taste good, how can it help a patient's recovery? Not to mention all those eggs. You can't be sure about eggs anymore. Every day she's forced to use hundreds of them at the hospital, and then dozens more in the early mornings at Lenny's.

The catering business is growing, and they are gaining a reputation for baked goods. The extra money has not yet balanced out the extra effort, but she hopes it will soon. They'll have to expand if they're to make anything of it, if Victoria is going to keep the boy clothed and fed. Last week they had new orders, one for a brunch party, where their bread and pastries were such a success that they've been asked to cater for a summer wedding.

"Here, that's a silly game. Let me show you something else." Victoria takes the mouse from Derek and clicks her way to the Net. She loves this technology, how one door leads to the next, and the next, like a funhouse ride, but without the associated queasiness.

Lenny teases her about her weak stomach, her squeamishness about meat and produce. He says a cook should be dispassionate, like a surgeon. She trusts her gut and humours him. Lenny Brown. Bless him. Great in the kitchen and persistent in the bedroom. All that passion for a round old bird like her. Five years now, since they met. At first she couldn't get used to the fact that anyone wanted her again, and that a nice-looking, finely aged English man such as Lenny would find pleasure in placing his hand on her rippling waist or running his tongue along her neck. On top of all of that, Lenny whispers endearments, holds her hand.

"What do you like then, what should we search for?" she asks Derek.

"Hmmm," he says, hesitating. "Stories . . ."

"What kind of stories?"

She watches him consider the question for longer than she thinks any other child might. She's still getting used to his curious nature.

"Any stories," he concludes.

She clicks through the server's entertainment pages, noticing the bodies of porn models and actresses. Should she hide these from him? Is that what parents do? It's what her mother would have done, but even Victoria knows that ideas about raising children have moved on considerably. She admires the sleek figure of one of the women.

Victoria hasn't always been this round, this stiff. Twenty years old when she left home, she was even beautiful. Fleeing to Toronto, she found herself on a BWIA flight that made a stopover in Barbados. Alone there, on a south coast beach for a whole day and night, she first felt the tug of that invisible thread that used to run, sometimes taut, sometimes loose, between her and a man. Men on the beach wanted her. One man in particular, a coral tradesman with reef-worn fingers and a long neck, took her to a club and danced with her through the night, never letting her out of his sight. Near dawn they went to the all-night stalls near the brothels in Baxter's Road, and he bought her a flying-fish cutter. She almost fell in love with him. He tried to convince her not to leave the next day, but Victoria had no intention of stopping; nor did she want to disappoint the Georgetown woman who was her sponsor in Toronto.

The woman owned a restaurant on Dufferin Avenue, in the mostly immigrant-populated west end of the city, and on Victoria's first day of work in the kitchen told Victoria she had the poise of a prancing deer. It was her figure that made Kola follow her through the Toronto streets and want to touch her back and run his hand down her spine. He said he'd noticed the fine line of her back in the market and felt he'd known her before, in Africa, where he'd come from a year previously. But Victoria had never met anyone like Kola.

Lenny doesn't like it when she mentions Kola, who started entering their conversation a few weeks ago. Sometimes she refers to him as though he's just touched her. This surprises even her, let alone Lenny, and she's been trying to catch herself before she says anything. But nothing could beat how Kola would touch her back.

She shouldn't be thinking these things around the boy, should she? Poor little mite. Look at his white knuckles.

"Don't grip so hard, Derek. It's not going anywhere. Just rest your hand on it and press gently, then click. Type the word in the search box there, and click here."

Victoria thinks she might pay a visit to Len tonight, when the boy's asleep. Perhaps it will do her hip good; it's been stiffening up these last few weeks.

---

http://www.Camelot.com

WELCOME TO CAMELOT
Come to meet Arthur? Or perhaps Launcelot? Be not dismayed, for they are here. . . .

Arthur
Guenevere
Launcelot
Merlin
Mordred
Sir Gawain

Arthur

click

"How After that King Arthur had Tidings,
He returned and came to Dover, where
Sir Mordred met him to let his landing;
and of the death of Sir Gawain."

Back

click

Mordred

click

"How Sir Mordred Presumed and Took on Him to be King of England, and
would have married the Queen, his father's wife."

A computer-animated hand holds Excalibur. The sword's handle is decorated with an ornate helix pattern. Hand and sword are rising out of dappled water. Derek wants the sword to sink and disappear into the lake once and for all. It's the sword he wielded in the yard in Georgetown, and through the house, though his mother had told him to stop that sort of play inside.

His mother and grandmother had been preparing a pepperpot to take to Granny's best friend in Berbice, whom she hadn't seen in months and who was ailing. Ailing, as they said, many times— "Mavis is ailin' badly"—with something not a single doctor could diagnose. Along with the pepperpot, Gwen and her mother had cooked some callaloo, and some peas and rice, and were packing them up even as Derek was hot in pursuit of the crystal dragon. The creature had been spotted in a flash moving across the driveway, then entering the house and swishing its tail at Granny. It breathed fire underneath the pepperpot and made it boil up and overflow. *Mark ye, ye crystal beast, thy moments are numbered . . .*

And slash, slash, slash went Excalibur at the tail of the beast hovering near the stove. *CHARRRRGGGGEEE!* His hands joined at the hilt, the blade held high above his head, Derek began his final assault. The magical sword carved into the crystal tail, lopping it off. The blade landed flat on the pepperpot, and in the crystal dragon's swooning, in its final life-lusting twitch, its jaws tipped over the pepperpot and sent it spattering onto the kitchen floor. The pig's foot catapulted to the far corner of the room and the beef, like black ice cubes spilled from a cocktail, shot across the white linoleum.

Derek's mouth fell open like a hoop. The crystal dragon vanished. Dead. *I slay thee.* . . . But suddenly the sounds about him were high-pitched and hollery and someone was yanking up his collar as though he'd been hung from a hook on a wall. When he turned his head, he saw his mother, the fair Guenevere, her eyes lit like the thin flame of a pilot light that would ignite the room. Then his granny rushed in and, "Oh my goodness, chile, oh God, three days of boilin' and makin' it jus right. What on earth possessed you boy."

His mom shoved him aside. "Derek, that's it, I've told you for the last time. You're a hard-ears boy—whoseva damn ears they from—who don't think of anybody but heself. I shoulda neva given you that damn thing. You are to neva, eva, eva to play those violent sword-swipin' games again, you hear me? Not just in the house, but anywhere. You're always killin' things and killin' me. Go to your room. Now!"

It was Granny who later came into his bedroom and took him next door so that Thomas's grandmother could watch him until Gwen and Granny got back from Berbice. But they never came back.

---

http://www.Camelot.com

Launcelot

click

"How when Sir Launcelot heard of the Death of King Arthur, and of Sir Gawain, and other matters, he came into England."

CHAPTER TWO

Eggs

ᏬᎲᏬ

PISSALADIÈRE

shortcrust pastry, made using 4 oz (100 g) organic, self-raising flour

filling:
1 lb (450 g) ripe, organic tomatoes
1 medium-sized red onion
1 clove garlic
1 oz (25 g) unsalted, organic butter
bouquet of parsley stalks and thyme
2 tablespoons concentrated tomato purée (made previous day and
refrigerated overnight)
2 eggs
4 oz (100 g) grated Beenleigh Blue sheep's milk cheese
1 tin (50 g) anchovy fillets
6 black olives or sweet pickled prunes
freshly milled pepper

Roll out prepared pastry to a circle on a lightly floured work surface
and use it to line an 8-inch (20 cm) round quiche tin or flan ring set on
a baking tray. Chill the pastry while preparing the filling.

Scald the tomatoes in boiling water and peel away the skin. Peel and finely chop the onion. Peel the garlic and crush to a purée with a little salt. Melt the butter in a saucepan over low heat. Add the onion and fry gently for 5 minutes to soften but not brown. Add the garlic, chopped tomatoes, herbs, and tomato purée. Draw off the heat and allow to cool until the hand can be comfortably held against the side of the pan.

Heat the oven to 375 degrees F (190C). Stir the eggs, grated Beenleigh Blue, and a seasoning of pepper into the tomato mixture. Pour mixture into the pastry case. Arrange a lattice of anchovy fillets on top and decorate with black olives or pickled prunes. Place in preheated oven and bake for 40 minutes. Serve warm or bake ahead and reheat for 10 minutes in an oven heated to 350F (180C).

"Delicious, Vic, absolutely delicious, as always," Lenny says.

Except for those eggs, she thinks. She touches his fingers and presses her thumb on the underside of his wrist. She gets up to clear the dishes.

She could taste it in them, something foreign, something shot through the eggs to make the yolks bigger. Huge bright yellow yolks. Or maybe it's the hens that have been shot through with growth hormones—rBGH, or its equivalent for chickens. Victoria has read that they place modified poultry genes into fermentation tanks containing bacteria, then inject the genes into ovulating hens to make the eggs multiply or just expand in size. She knows a little about chickens from back home; the ones in Kitty used to wander into their garden, scratch at the earth, and pick out the seeds her daddy had planted. Between them and the people who stole peppers and aubergine from the front row of the garden that ran along the pavement, her daddy had a time of it.

Hormone-treated chickens would need more and more protein,

Victoria guesses. And how would normal chicken feed supply that? No, it was clear, soon farmers would have to start grinding up chickens and putting them back into the chicken feed, just like they did with beef. Mad chickens. It'll be the salmon after that. Everything eating itself in a lunatic coyote dance. That madness has a taste. So, no more supermarket eggs.

"Come on and sit, Vic. I'll do the washing up later."

"There's enough left for tomorrow. Heat it at 140."

She sits beside Lenny on the sofa.

"How's the boy?" he asks, touching her shoulder.

"Comin' along. A bit stunned most of the time; it would be a shock, wouldn't it? He won't budge out of the house. Cold all the time, and it's warm for February. He wraps himself up in my coat and sits and stares at the telly, but now I've got him on the computer. We have to get him to school; I don't want him to fall too far behind."

"Oh, let him be. He'll be adjusting for the rest of his life."

She takes Lenny's hand again. "He's beautiful, isn't he? Handsome, skin the colour of a new pound piece," she says almost dreamily.

"Hope he has no trouble at school," Lenny returns casually.

Victoria's heart lurches again as she thinks of Derek walking up the school steps.

"Hmm," Len says, shaking his head, considering something she cannot guess. He is always one step ahead of her, with England in his bones the way she'll never have.

"Maybe you should consider public school."

"You must be joking." His extravagance always floors her. He's never had much money, but he'll spend his hard-earned profits from the business like a rich man. "That's what it's for," he will say to her when she objects to his small gifts.

She stands up again and walks back into the kitchen. Tomorrow's orders are pinned to the refrigerator door with a magnet: a dozen spelt flutes, a dozen sourdough rounds, a dozen pumpernickel, thirty-six mini quiches, twenty-four mini pavlovas.

"Three dozen quiches and two dozen pavlovas?" she calls towards the sitting room.

"Overflow from Pan and Co. A retirement party," he calls back.

She washes her hands, panic rising as she thinks of getting Derek to school in the morning. Lenny will need her help. She's always amazed by his composure. He used to have his own bakery, but lost interest after his wife died. When property values in the neighbourhood went up he couldn't afford the rent, so he retired. One day he saw Victoria in the Waitrose on Finchley Road looking over the paltry baguettes: "And *zey* call this *pain*," he said in a French accent. "They'd do better calling it as it's spelled: pain. Pain in the gut, if you ask me." She'd smiled, and they've been talking about the ways of the world ever since.

She pulls a metal container along the counter toward herself, opens it, and pours spelt flour out onto the scales.

Victoria used to tell Lenny about Guyana, how the country had been created, ruled, and then set free by the British, leaving behind an ethnic soup of people, trying to find common ground upon which to be governed. She told him about how the blacks and the Indians fought each other in politics, about the Chinese and the mulattos who'd mostly left, and about the Amerindians who had mostly died out. As she told these stories Victoria would see herself as a doll inside a doll inside a doll of all the people in her family and where they came from, where they went. One of the lives that contained her had been from China. Her great-uncle, the dentist, had been shot by the Japanese in Hong Kong. Shoved into his dentist's chair and faced with a pistol, he was asked to smile and show his teeth. Then bang! His teeth, hair, and brains in a *carpaccio* of genetic material over the headrest of the chair it had taken him two years to pay off. With that gun pointed into his mouth, what matryoshka was Vic's great-uncle opening up in his mind? In that

31

second, what was he thinking? She realizes now that she told Lenny that story as a way of avoiding telling him more about Kola.

Lenny joins her in the kitchen. "Vic, really, we have time. I can do it myself before lunch tomorrow, you know that."

She ignores him and continues to measure out the basic ingredients for each batch. He gives in and counts out eggs for the pavlova meringues.

"Len, I almost forgot to tell you. Remember that Asian man who was in the hospital a few months back, who had the boilin' oil splashed on his legs and his right eye stamped on?" She massages a packet of butter slowly.

"Oh, God, yes," Lenny answers.

"He was back in the hospital last week, in the psychiatric ward, 'cause he's suffering from fear of black people. What do you make of that, then? A judge told him he should move to the countryside: no blacks there. Isn't that ridiculous? Who could say such a thing? He should be stripped of robes and deported naked to the Midlands himself. You know Len—"

"But he's got a point, I mean if someone's health is endangered by—"

"You can't be serious!" She glares at him, but his gentle eyes subdue her. He shrugs and leaves her with her exclamation, daring her to think about it before she goes on.

She puts the butter aside. Kola didn't like butter. Her mood is more familiar in Kola territory than in Lenny's. Where is the anger coming from? Surely not Len, and not simply the story itself. Maybe the boy. The boy is fanning the single cinder of fire left in her.

Kola, Kola, Kola. She stamps her foot. How could it have ended like that? She quickly examines the heel of her shoe, pretending to check if it's on solidly, to cover up her fury—to make it appear to Lenny that it's about the shoe and not the mad stamp of a woman who thought her days of smouldering had ended but who now feels herself starting to ignite. She should start reading again. That might calm her. The last time she had any concentrated period of reading was in Toronto, with Kola's books—shelves and shelves of political theory, social science, philosophy, and literature, collected over the six years they spent together, back and forth between their separate apartments. Those volumes were responsible for the only book-learning Victoria ever undertook, and her education is skewed towards dialectics in anger. After Kola disappeared, she read each of the more than two hundred books he'd brought to her tiny flat, searching for some clue that would tell her where he had gone. The reading dropped off as she embraced the routine of restaurant work and then hospital kitchen duties at Toronto Western Hospital. When she started to see one of the hospital's financial clerks, the two of them watched movies and read only the occasional magazine.

The financial clerk was a man in his fifties who had a musty smell and uneven, yellow teeth. He smoked, and she wouldn't let him kiss her, but he provided her with a lifestyle she'd never known before—expensive dinners, movies, day trips to Niagara Falls and Lake Simcoe, and he bought her a television. As she watched game shows and television movies, she was unaware of the numbing trade she had engaged in. She gained the comfort of having someone she didn't have to talk to but who would look after her, and he fulfilled his need to be kind to a woman who seemed to have nothing, and yet everything he didn't. She lived just to the side of herself for years. As the hope of Kola returning waned and she approached forty, she watched with fascination as she allowed the financial clerk to come inside her with groans of pleasure that sounded almost like disgust. When she missed her period, she was horrified by herself and the man. She considered having the child, but it was then she received a single letter from Kola, revealing his whereabouts after thirteen years. Her decision was easy. In the open-backed gown on the trolley at the Morgentaler Clinic, she planned how she would get to London, how she would find Kola.

A Gikuyu from Kenya, Kola had fled his country to live in

Canada. He had things to say about everything Victoria had never given a thought to. He spoke of rebellion like most people speak of weather, praising it, damning it. Kola had rebellion in his touch. His family had been involved in the Mau Mau rebellion in the 1950s. He told her about Kenya's troubles, and its tribal battles for the physical possession of its people: the circumcision of the Gikuyus, the removal of the lower front teeth of the Luo children. And she listened and stored up his indignation inside her like coal in a scuttle. And it was Kola who had taught her how to really cook.

"Len, we need to find some better eggs. Cheaper, free-range eggs that don't make me gag to look at 'em, you know."

"OK, OK, Vic," Len says, feeling put in his place. "I'll look into it." He examines her face. She looks down, knowing he's about to get to her, always does when she drifts off like this.

"What's really bothering you, love?" he says, on cue.

"Nothing, just tense about the money, I guess, and making sure there'll be enough, for the boy, and when my birthday comes—"

"Your birthday?"

"Yes, Len, yes . . . don't you see?" she says, annoyed, and then wants to take it back. She doesn't want to hurt this dear, dear man who has helped her through her roughest times.

"Yes, I do," he says calmly and with a breeze in his voice that blows right through the room and carries her for a while. She relaxes. He knows she's talking about the early retirement from the hospital she'd agreed to take over a year ago.

"I'm afraid of not working. Afraid I'll become the Bluebird of Piccadilly."

"Who?"

"Nobody, nothing."

Len is not a roamer, a waiter, a watcher, just a man who had a wife and a shop where he loved the smell of bread. He is a simple man who loves to play the piano and talk about the cracked ebony keys on his keyboard like they are ingredients—one, the E above middle C, and another, the G two octaves below—which add a tangy sound to his playing of Bach. His lifelong dream is to bake, and his second is to play the grand piano he's saving up to buy.

The only lifelong dream Victoria ever had was to leave the glaring eyes of her father's mistresses and their bastards in Kitty. Everything after that has felt haphazard.

"You know how long I've been in England, Len?"

"How long, love?"

She pauses. Why does time seem to have started again all of a sudden? When Kola disappeared, she disappeared too, waiting like the Bluebird of Piccadilly, and everything she did felt as though it was through gauze. The recently dead, Kola had told her, are part of the living dead, intermediaries between earth and the spirit domain who are useful for luck and guardians against catastrophes.

"Over twenty years."

"Doesn't sound like it. Sometimes we lose you to something in your voice I can't figure out. Not much Guyana, a little bit of Canada, not quite England."

"My bush voice."

"Eh?"

"That's what Gwen used to call it. My bush voice. When I got mad or wanted to cry, I'd retreat into the bush and sound like an Amerindian."

"Suppose that's it then."

But sometimes it's not just her mouth that goes into the bush; it's her whole self. Her spirit drifts over the underbrush and winds through mahogany and rests by a creek where vines hang from heavenly trees. Snakes, indifferent to her, slither past. Then she feels it, that force, the secret force of the jungle that the Amerindians believe kills men. The Kanaima. The Amerindians would live forever if it weren't for the Kanaima. They know that being sociable and friendly can ward off the Kanaima, and yet the need for friendship only reinforces the Kanaima's power. Death always comes.

"Liqueur, Vic? A little Drambuie?"

"Sure, that would be nice. . . . I was thinking, Len, that we should go full-time, with the baking. Expand, and we could be earning more, and maybe we'd move out of those two rooms, so the boy could have more space, a garden maybe. We could have a real business."

"Victoria Layne, that's the most sensible thing I've heard come out of your mouth since you've been coming here. Cheers!" he offers as he hands her a glass.

"Cheers," she says, surprised by herself.

"Come here, darlin'."

She likes it when he calls her that. He's the only man she's ever let call her that. Kola was more intense in his affection, and the few after him never said much that was particularly endearing. With them she negotiated the ebb and flow of her weekly survival. Although still somewhat detached from Lenny, at least she's not doing that. She likes Len's face, crinkled in yesterday's smiles.

"Staying over tonight?"

"Can't. The boy. But I will come upstairs for a somewhat less-than-polite bedtime story . . ."

"Race you . . ."

It feels like April as Victoria strolls home along Hamilton Terrace. The weather is not right. All week the temperatures have been above normal, reaching sixteen degrees in mid-February. And except for the day before yesterday, mostly dry. Surrey and Kent suffered floods from overflowing rivers in November, but the winter rain has been erratic. That's good for Victoria's hip, but it's not good for the soil. England and its weather are out of joint.

Oh, to be in England
Now that April's there,
And whoever wakes in England
Sees, some morning, unaware . . .

Oh, to be . . . now that Feb's there? Just isn't right, something out of sync now.

Lots of rubbish in the street tonight.

Glad to be home, Victoria climbs the stairs towards their rooms at the top. She hears one of the other lodgers—the German musician—on the telephone, speaking accented, burly English, saying something about a concert at Wigmore Hall he's going to attend. When she reaches the top landing, she tries to still her heavy breathing and goes to look in on Derek. Poor golden squab, covered to his ears in the duvet. He'll be all right. She'll have to see to that. Who'd have thought that at sixty-one she would become a mom, and on her next birthday lose her job?

He sits on a horse draped in cloth bearing a heraldic coat of arms in red and gold. On his head he wears a metal helmet, its visor pulled down to his chin. His arms are covered in chain mail, his chest is protected by a breastplate of the finest lightweight metal. A lance is tucked loosely under his arm. The sun is rising. When a foe appears on the horizon, he readies his lance, bracing it. The approaching horse is darker, taller than his own, and its rider is sporting a brimmed riding bonnet, white breeches, and fine leather boots. Every few feet the rider swings a polo stick casually, slicing the empty air. The tall, dark horse gallops past and leaves the knight errant in his stunned panoply wondering what kind of vision has just befallen him. Derek stirs, sensing someone in the room. He burrows deeper into his quilt, returning to his horse. Derek is dreaming England, and no one will ever know.

CHAPTER THREE

The Holy Grail

The trees throughout Hampstead Heath are spray-painted with moss.

There, send that to the boys at St. Michael's elementary in Georgetown. To Nathan, Kirk, even to Thomas, and tell them these are important words from Inkland: dried ink from the hand of Derek Layne.

Derek sits proudly at his desk in the sixth row of his Year 3 classroom at George Eliot School on Marlborough Road near Swiss Cottage, having written the required composition. *Your best writing. One hour. Go.* The rain has finally stopped, after a surprising deluge this morning, but the single-pane windows next to Derek's desk still bear its mark like tear stains. It's his fourth day at school this week, and he feels momentum building with the subtle accomplishments of writing and maths. Mr. Darling has been particularly lenient with him, allowing him to take more time than the others, ignoring the motley flow of his letters. Darling has told Derek that he's sure to catch on, and that soon he'll be caught up with the others, even though they are already eight.

But Mr. Darling has noticed that in the forty-five minutes so far allotted to a major composition, Derek has written only one sentence. Passing by the boy's desk again, he notices an addition:

*The trees throughout Hampstead Heath are spray-painted
with moss. And huge birds with Concorde beaks are black
and cawing.*

Derek sees a seagull fly in the right field of his memory, the
Guyana field. In the left field there is Hampstead Heath, with its
dark birds that swoop like bad thoughts. Last Sunday, when the
morning's drizzle had let up, his aunt took him to the heath,
where they walked up and down muddy hills. Even under the
towering trees, whose bare grey branches were the size of entire
tree trunks in Georgetown, the world was looking green. Green
covered everything like a coat of algae growing in the damp. The
green was crawling, spreading itself over the park, devouring
things in its path. When Derek stopped to poke at some insects
near a rock in a clearing, he looked up to see his aunt through a
viridescent hue, as she padded over the grass, her gait resembling
that of the waddling ducks at the Highgate Ponds. Two dogs
whizzed past her, chasing the same stick. Startled, Auntie Vic
jumped slightly and looked around. Derek felt his own muscles
leap a fraction as he stood up straight, automatically protective.
He caught up to her, and they walked together towards Parlia-
ment Hill at the centre of the heath. There, the wind was high and
families raised reluctant kites into it. From the top of the hill,
Derek could see central London's buildings in the distance, varied
and staggered in height like a Lego city.

"OK. Time's up. Hand in your compositions now." As Mr.
Darling finishes his instructions, the recess bell rings. The shuffle
of books and feet replaces all other sounds as the boys and girls
stream out of the classroom, handing their notebooks to Darling
as they leave. Derek closes his book and gets up slowly. His hand
trembles slightly, yet proudly, as he places his notebook into Mr.
Darling's hand.

The schoolyard is paved in large cement squares. Behind the

school, the football field is cordoned off. The field is being readied for spring, when the gym teacher will force the children to run around it eight times for their two-mile trial. The grass is a deep green, just as it was on Hampstead Heath. England is green. Guyana is bronze. The blend of mud and red river silt make it so, he thinks, as he stares off beyond the football pitch.

"So, what are you about, then?"

Derek turns, stares, and blinks. Coming towards him is Richard Lorry, the boy who sits in the last row in his class. Richard the Lorry. Richard the Truck, all boxy with an air-brake huff as he grinds to a halt in front of Derek.

"I'm talking to you."

Blink.

"Cat got your tongue? Or maybe a lizard . . . or maybe it's a lizard's tongue . . . and maybe you are just a nuisance." Richard spits at Derek's feet but keeps his eyes on his face. Derek is sure Richard is examining his birthmark, but just to be sure, he keeps his mouth closed, his teeth concealed.

Three boys appear at Richard the Truck's side. They are all taller than Derek, with the exception of blond-haired Stephen, who reaches only to Richard the Truck's shoulder. Among them is the Mind-the-Gap boy. With straight, jet-black hair and a parrot nose, he reminds Derek of an Indian boy he knew in Guyana who used to want to be a dancer until he succumbed to teasing and joined the school's wood engraving club so he could have a knife. The third boy has muddy-coloured hair and bright green eyes. Derek feels a knot form in his chest; he resists the urge to tug on his collar and scratch the back of his neck.

Richard Lorry is older than the rest of the boys in the class; he's been held back due to failing grades. Derek has heard Stephen and the others speak of Richard as though he is some kind of king, a ruler among boys. He has feared this moment, sensing that, like all new knights, he would have to be tested.

"Leave 'im alone Richard," says the boy with sparkling green eyes. He tugs on Richard's arm to divert him from the trembling figure before the group.

"Come on, Richard."

"Don't you think we could 'ave a little fun with this yellow squeak?"

"What about it. He hasn't done you anything," the boy with English eyes says and walks away, followed closely by Stephen, who looks as terrified as Derek feels. Richard and the Mind-the-Gap boy stay, staring at Derek, who has started to sing, to distract himself from the pressure he feels in his groin, a tingly, achy sensation that warns he might lose control of his bladder. He hasn't felt this in many years, but since he moved to England he's not entirely sure whether he is ageing forwards or backwards. He sings slightly louder. "Jingle bells, jingle bells, jingle all the way, oh what fun it is to ride on a one-horse open sleigh."

Richard the Truck and his lackey leave, but not before Richard gives Derek a shove on the shoulder that sets the word *ride* off in a sliding-hoof pitch, off-beat, and at *a one-horse open sleigh* Derek feels a trickle escape into his pants.

After the boys have disappeared around the back of the school, Derek walks in the opposite direction, towards the Nursery. Near the windows of the school's kitchen, he looks up to see a tall, fleshy girl with thick, straight black hair to her shoulders staring at him, smiling. He lowers his eyes again. Once he's behind the Nursery, he presses his back against the building, willing himself to disappear into the chilly cement wall.

"What ya doing?" The girl has followed him. He looks up at her and is struck by how the shoulder-length hair frames her open face and generous mouth.

"Nothing. Go away," he says, but wishes she would just make everything better.

The girl disappears, and he's left alone. He slides down the wall to the ground. He holds back the tears. He can't cry now, not when he was just starting to believe he could survive at this school.

He hears footsteps and panting, and looks up to see Stephen's flushed face.

"Kendra said you were here. It's OK. You did just right. He backed down. He's impressed if you make him back down. But not by singing. You gotta try something better next time—bigger'n singing."

Derek has no idea what Stephen means, but he senses that he's safe, and pockets the name Kendra as the key to safety. He starts to relax, but in that instant his bladder gives way, and he can't stop it. Tears now follow.

Stephen offers a hand up.

"Auuch, you didn't. . . . ah, no . . . what'd you go and ruin it for? Peeuuww. Look," Stephen checks both directions, then looks back at Derek. "Come with me."

Derek stands up. The warm, wet trouser legs stick to his thighs. He's accosted by the smell of his urine. Like a cardboard boy, he follows Stephen, who has entered the Nursery and heads towards the lavatory.

"Strip, then. Off with 'em."

Derek is silent, frozen.

"I mean it. You can't go back to class like this. They'll murder you. Strip!"

Derek obeys. He stands shivering in his underpants, but Stephen motions for those too. Stephen takes the trousers and douses them under the hot-water faucet, spritzes them with hand soap, and rubs the cloth together to lather the soap. Derek wonders where Stephen learned to clean clothes, but all he knows about Stephen is that he lives with his mother on a Finchley Road estate. In a few minutes the soap is rinsed and the urine smell is weaker. Stephen repeats the process with Derek's underpants, then pushes the button on the hand-dryer. Hot air hums through the room.

When the garments are more or less dry, Stephen casually hands them back to Derek, who uncups his hands from around his crotch to put his clothes on. For the last few minutes he has been thanking Stephen over and over again in his mind, but still hasn't been able to say a word. Even so, something between them has been acknowledged.

"Just don't do it again," Stephen says. "I was like you last year."

"What do you mean, like me?"

"Just moved here."

"From where?"

"Cornwall."

"Where's Cornwall?"

"You really are daft. Don't let Richard know you don't know a bloody thing. Just pretend."

And *pretend* becomes another key to safety.

"And follow along behind him. He lets us watch videos at his house after school. His mom doesn't get home until six, and she lets him stay by himself. You can come with me. It's an over eighteen."

"My auntie's fetching me after school."

"Ask her," Stephen says. "It'd be a good idea." He turns and walks out of the lavatory. Derek follows him quickly out the back of the Nursery. The bell catches him halfway across the schoolyard, so he runs.

By the time the last-period bell rings throughout the pickle-smelling building of his school, Derek has learned the capitals of Tunisia, Egypt, and Morocco, and has read that the elephants of Meru Park in Kenya can drink up to three hundred litres of water a day. And in his mind he has circled and posed and rephrased the question he wants to ask his aunt when she picks him up. He has come up with several possible explanations as to why it would be better for him to go over to Richard Lorry's flat after school and not home with her. If he tells her the truth—that he's afraid of what will happen to him if he doesn't—he'll never get to go anywhere the other boys go.

Victoria walks briskly up Marlborough Hill towards the front steps of the school, noticing first Derek's back as he crouches down, staring into his satchel. The back is noble, she thinks, the shoulders defiant. They remind her of children she knew as a child: Mona, Jaylene, and Caroline. *Jaylene and Caroline always need to be seen . . .* the other children chanted. Girls who seemed to have life in their control. Victoria reaches out to touch Derek's tensed shoulder, but pulls her hand back just before contact. "Ready?" she asks, stepping up beside him.

He flaps shut the satchel and gets up quickly. His eyes dart toward the front of the school, where Stephen is shuffling back and forth, kicking the toes of his thick-soled boots into the concrete ledge of the pavement and flipping his long blond fringe away from his eyes to look up, irritated, at Derek.

"Auntie Vic . . ."

"Yes, child, come; we're going."

"Some boys are goin' to watch a movie at another boy's house . . . and they invited me. They're waiting. . . . Can I go with Stephen, Auntie Vic? Please?"

Victoria shifts her weight, surprised. She catches sight of the fidgeting Stephen and, farther along, a small pack of boys, one kicking a ball at the fence surrounding the school, another kicking stones, another pacing. Something is brewing inside these boys, and it reminds her of her own school days. That day, in the schoolyard, Mona, Jaylene, and Caroline had been taunting her with songs in their high, better-than-you voices: *Sen-Len Yuk, is the chinky-eyed buck, who did nothing but fuck, and fathered all the bastards in RoeBUCK street*, singing about Victoria's father. Mona, Jaylene, and Caroline sang at her until she reached into the tiny pocket of her uniform skirt, her fingers gripping the metal object inside the pouch intended for gentle-girl-things like tissues and hair ties, and pulled out her father's dirty-old-man toenail clippers.

"Who are these boys?" Victoria asks, wanting to know what it is that has them all incessantly moving.

"Classmates, Auntie Vic."

"Where do they live?"

"Over in those buildings, on Finchley Road."

"Hmmm. . . . and it's OK with their mothers?"

"Yes." It's the first lie he has told his aunt, and it feels like a sword hiked up over her head. A glimmer from Excalibur blinds him with guilt; he looks back into his satchel.

Victoria looks about again and sees Stephen staring at her, while the other three have started to walk away.

"Is that him?" she asks Derek.

"Yes, Auntie."

"Come here, lad," she calls.

Stephen plunges his hands into his trouser pockets, hikes up his shoulders, and approaches.

"Now, what movie will you be watching?"

"Dunno, it's my mate's—probably a western, or Disney, or one of those."

Victoria knows when she's being lied to, but Derek is her nephew, the last of her flesh and blood, and her flesh and blood has had enough humiliation to last it into the next two generations, should there be any more.

That day in the schoolyard she had walked over to the three girls quickly, and with her daddy's clippers gave one clip to Jaylene, *clip*, and two to Caroline, *clip clip*, drawing better-than-you blood, and too late for Mona, who ran away in horror and called Miss Clive Who-Was-Not-Alive, the gym teacher. Victoria ran and hid behind the school. But after recess, in the Health for Young Ladies class, when the girls were to learn about the way the female organ expels blood to make room for eggs, Miss Clive, who had heard the story of Victoria's reprisals, said: "Victoria Layne, you will stand holding these five-pound weights in your hands, your arms straight up over your head—in that corner—until I say you can put them down. And then we'll see who thinks she is so powerful that she can draw the blood of classmates."

So Victoria raised the barbell weights in her hands, gliding them up beside her ears over her head, and fully extending her arms toward the wooden ceiling of the classroom. She held them there, counting, not listening, catching only snippets of the class lecture on blood, eggs, and tubes. She counted until the numbers fell away and a crimson-violet light took over. Inside the light, Y shapes like insects swam before her eyes. The Ys joined in a line and slithered like a snake above her head. Y, Y, Y, like a question. She grew dizzy. Her knees buckled and she collapsed into the corner.

"Auntie Vic? Can I go or not?" Derek's voice asks urgently, snapping her out of her reverie.

"Who else is going to be at this boy's place?" she asks Stephen, looking at him severely.

"Just a few of us from our class," says Stephen brightly, "and Richard's mom," he adds. Derek feels a surge of excitement at the ease with which Stephen tells the lie. They're making progress.

"What's the address?" Victoria asks, and Derek senses victory.

"McRoy House, Flat 18."

"Right, well, I'll pick you up, in the front of the building. In two hours. Half-past five, on the nose. Right in front, Derek. Got that lad?"

"Yes, Auntie Vic."

He picks up his satchel and swings the strap over his head so that it crosses his chest like a fillet for a sword's sheath. Stephen is already walking, anxious to catch up to Richard and the others. Derek smiles nervously at his aunt, then follows Stephen in a gentle trot, leaving Victoria on the pavement checking her handbag for the money she will need for tonight's dinner, and remembering that she never made friends with Mona, Jaylene, or Caroline.

Derek has retreated inside himself. Way up, deep inside, like a turtle in its shell. Careful not to use his hands or to give himself away, he shifts his weight on the springy armchair and feels for a testicle in his pants, then for the other, but they seem to have disappeared, as though hiding from the bullets flying about on the video screen in front of him. A man with a handgun has just blown away three other men in a room. A few minutes earlier, bullets peppered the twitching torso of a man who had refused to hand over money he owed the gunman. And just before that, a man fed up with his chattering girlfriend shot her in the head . . . *shut the fuck up* . . .

The air in the room is stale with smoke and chip oil. He glances over at Richard Lorry slumped on the striped sofa, his greasy brown hair fanned up on his head like a cock's comb. Richard's eyes are fast with bullets—moving in little left-right twitches like an eye-tremor. Richard is turning into a bullet, Derek thinks, as he retreats further into himself. There's more gunfire from the video, and Derek's shoulders leap in excitement, while the part of him that hasn't left the kitchen in Georgetown is silently crying for help. This part of him wants to curl up inside someone: his mother, or, if he could, his father. Someone who could repair everything even as it shatters around him.

Finally, he eases his hand down the front of his trousers to readjust himself. His throat is dry. He feels he might choke. "I have to go now," he says in a barely audible whisper to Stephen, who is sitting on the floor beside the armchair.

"What? It's not over," Stephen whispers back.

"My aunt, she'll be waiting for me." He has no idea of the time but hopes his aunt is outside.

By the time he is downstairs at the front of the building, his testicles have settled back into place and he is breathing easily. But the air is damp and cold. He tenses his shoulders to brace for the chill. He shivers, pacing in the darkness. The images from the movie skitter by his mind's eye again, accompanied by a rush of pleasure. It's this thrill he tries to suppress. *You're always killin' things and killin' me* . . . he recalls, and tries to remember his mother's stories instead. The baddies in his mother's stories were mostly funny, telling jokes and tricking people. Derek folds himself back up into that little boy on her lap. Suddenly he feels sleepy. His mother told good stories. He makes a conscious decision to retrace them, to tell them back to her in his thoughts. Maybe he'll even write them into the computer.

"Blimey," she says under her breath, putting down the newspaper, realizing she'll barely make it on time. The poor squab'll be lost or snatched. Vic, how could you. . . . I thought you were getting better at this, she says to herself. Walk now, come on, faster.

Having intended to spend only a few minutes sitting in front of Waitrose with her shopping bags, she had picked up a *Daily Mirror* left on the bench. Flipping through it disinterestedly, she came upon an article about a potato farmer rushed to hospital suddenly after supper. The man grew the best Jersey Royals in Jersey. Called the Jersey Fluke, it's a potato that will not grow in England or France—nowhere but on Jersey itself. Victoria became absorbed in the story of the potato, reading that the Jersey Fluke was the result of a dinner party in 1880 at which a farmer revealed to his guests a sixteen-eyed tuber he had discovered in his garden. His neighbours passed around the huge, reniform potato, intrigued by the unusual quantity of eyes. The guests decided they should cut the potato open, and it was divided into sixteen pieces, each with an eye. The next day the farmer planted all the pieces, and the following spring he had a large and early crop of kidney-shaped potatoes. The Fluke. But the farmer in today's *Mirror* had been rushed to the hospital, where they cut him open to discover that his guts had been shredded as though he'd swallowed glass. The journalist described what the doctors might have seen as "slivered morsels of intestine floating about in bile." Victoria tssked, disbelievingly, but her imagination reeled as she considered the dividing and splicing of guts as an appropriate side-effect of tampering with food. The man's guts went mad, like a cow, she thinks. His stomach splayed itself out like a slipping, sliding, struggling bovine on the telly news. The doctors in the article couldn't tell what the man had died of, but Victoria suspected the potatoes; her mind was off on the trail to incriminate them.

And now she has to hurry. As she makes her way down Finchley Road as quickly as she can, she's glad the potatoes in her bag are not Jersey Royals. These are from Spain. "Why d'you suppose," she says to herself aloud, "I'm having to buy a spud that comes all the way from Spain?" The supermarket is filled with foreign produce. There are more and more organic vegetables—but from distant countries, not from a neighbour's garden. People are more food-conscious than at any time Victoria can remember, but she distrusts this new language of food—this new taste for new taste. In the supermarket she can buy fresh frozen pakoras, lychee fruit, and ingredients to make the Chinese dishes her daddy used to cook. The world of food is available in a single long aisle of cans and plastic wrap. Hundreds of years of gastronomy are packaged for take-away dining. Something about it does not sit right with her. She's always believed, just like her daddy, that it's best to know the person who grows what you eat.

She spots Derek standing on the pavement up ahead and her shoulders leap with relief. "Derek!"

RED PESTO POTATOES AUX ÉPINARDS

Prepare a purée of sundried tomatoes and chopped flat-leaf parsley. Roast a handful of pine nuts until they are brown, and fold them into the tomato and parsley mixture, covering them with a tablespoon of extra-virgin olive oil. Set the mixture aside. Boil new, baby potatoes in sea-salted water until tender.

In a saucepan, sauté one medium-sized, finely chopped white onion in olive oil and add a clove of crushed garlic. Next, add two large bowls of washed and dried baby spinach and cook until the spinach is just wilted.

Remove the cooked potatoes from the water and cut each in half. Set out a bed of the spinach mixture to cover a medium-sized serving plate. Arrange the potatoes over the bed of spinach. Spoon the sun-dried tomato, parsley, and pine nut mixture over the potatoes, not covering them but dappling them decoratively. Sprinkle with crumbled goat's cheese, some freshly ground pepper, and a sprig of basil. Serve immediately.

"You don't like it, do you, luv?"

Derek is suppressing heaves. As he chews the tomato-dotted spuds, he manages what could pass for a grin.

"Spuds are good for you: vitamin C and B . . . and from the earth . . ."

Derek swallows again, picks up his glass, and takes a swig of water. The gulp of spuds, the flow of spuds, the landing of spuds.

He still has not answered Victoria's question. His mother taught him that he should answer all questions put to him, never to be afraid of responding, no matter the subject. But he thinks Auntie Vic will feel the fear, not the thrill, of the bullets, and he dare not frighten her again. He is still wary of her, even after all these weeks in Inkland. The weeks that have passed like slow drips. Drips of rain, drips of the sound of the tap that needs fixing in the wash-room, drips of good moments these last five days at school, drips of touches from his aunt. He is learning not to recoil when she reaches out for him.

From downstairs, the sound of an infant's harmonica-like cry wafts up. Two days ago, Sonia and Martin, the couple who own the house, brought home twins. Derek has not seen the babies yet, but he hears them through the night and tries to make out which is the girl and which is the boy by the way each cries. Sonia's voice is tender, even as they wail, and he hears her erupt in giggles. These sounds make him sad, but he's afraid to be sad and be sent back to Guyana to live alone. So he swallows his next mouthful of potato, smiles again at his aunt, and will try to answer her question. He goes to speak, but he feels a leak in himself somewhere—the dripping of something fundamental to being Derek. He has been trying to stop it all day, to patch it the way his mom taught him to patch the tire of his bicycle, but it seems to trickle forth, nevertheless.

He loses his hold on the red and green purée and sprays the table and the sleeves of his cardigan with a gangrenous-looking mixture of spud and spinach.

"Oh Lord," Victoria chants, like a woman in church. Derek doesn't move.

His aunt brings a wet cloth to his face, to his chest, then pulls his school cardigan off with a long, evangelical sigh that Derek mistakes for annoyance.

"What have you been eating today, Derek?"

This question he can answer easily. "Some crisps."

Bad potatoes, Victoria thinks as she wipes up spinach from the table. She vows that the boy will be made to eat better, avoid the poisons in the junk-food diet of kids his age. She will make him dishes from home: curry, pudding and souse, peas and rice—dishes she hasn't made in thirty years.

"And what movie did you watch? You still haven't told me."

"I don't remember the title. . . . just an action film."

"And what happens in it?"

The creature between Derek's legs squirms at the thought of bullets.

"A man gets out of jail . . . and he tries to get his friends to help him . . . and they go to a bank . . . in a car . . . actually, I can't remember, but it was a funny movie, not really scary or anything . . ." He stumbles in the gap of lies.

"Doesn't sound like a movie for children to me," Victoria says to his lowered eyes. She rinses the cloth again and leaves it draped over the faucet. Her hand automatically reaches for the refrigerator door and pulls it open. Staring inside, she wonders what else she can feed him. She has no experience in growing boys. She knew how to grow his mother because all Gwen needed from her were games and a place to cry: the hollow between Vic's collarbone and breast, where she would rest her head when their daddy didn't come home.

By the time Gwen was born, Victoria was already used to fending for herself, because her mother had never been attentive. Mary Layne never truly recovered from the death of the infant son born two years before Victoria. It wasn't until the birth of Gwen that Victoria's mother really stopped grieving, the new child giving her one extra mark on the side of life in the ledger of births and deaths. With Gwen came laughter, and when Gwen was old enough to speak, her mother would often talk in rhyme, taking on roles as invented characters. Each week she took on a different name, inventing a new personality. She would become Josephine, Gilda, Rita, Marilyn, names she liked, for the women she could never be, and the lives she could only imagine. Victoria, with her baby sister, played along, grateful for the laughter, careful not to unbalance her mother's fragile levity.

But what about boys? What games do boys need? What will make them grow? She shifts a plate of cold carrots and leftover lamb, noticing the congealed fat beneath the meat and dismissing it outright as an option. Snakes and snails and puppy-dog tails, that's what little boys are made of. Because of what they eat? The boys probably watched something they weren't supposed to, and that's why Derek's stomach is upset. She turns to look at him: has he gotten thinner since he arrived in her care? She panics. The stories she knows are little-girl yarns, not for anything made of snails and puppy-dog tails. Pulling a tub of organic goat's-milk ice cream from the freezer, she searches her memory for a story worthy of a boy.

"Derek."

"Yes, Auntie Vic."

"Do you know what the Kanaima is?"

"No, Auntie Vic."

"Your mother never told you?"

"No, Auntie." He's relieved they have left the topic of the movie.

"You know the Barama River in Guyana?"

Derek looks at her and nods at the sound of a familiar name. Victoria searches for an ice-cream scoop.

"Well, the Amerindians there, Carib people, believe in a spirit—or a spirit person or animal—that is like an agent you hire if you want to take revenge against someone. They used to say 'a man has fished as deep as he can delve for vengeance if he resorts to visiting the Kanaima headman,' and the Kanaima will teach him the art of revenge. But he can never turn back. He joins with the Kanaima, and he gains the habit of evil, not just revenge."

She pauses, questioning her judgement, but when she looks over her shoulder she sees she has captured Derek's attention. She doesn't remember knowing this story before, but something is drawing it out. For a moment she fears the story might be coming from the bush ghosts themselves—their revenge upon her for deserting her mother, her sister, her father, for not looking back as her country went to the devil. But the rabbit-shaped birthmark around Derek's right eye seems to brighten as he looks at her, hungry for her next word.

"They eat no meat, except for Dukwaru birds—an almost invisible bird that also makes the Kanaima invisible. The Kanaima eat kosako because it causes their victims to feel choked and pricked. By eating rupe they can run fast, and by drinking only rainwater they can keep clear-headed. At night, instead of building fires to keep warm, they rub their skins with pepper.

"Kanaima roam the bush seeking to waylay a victim—doesn't matter who, but if a man has a weak character, that's likely the one they will choose. Those who are susceptible to the influence of others fall prey the easiest."

Victoria pauses to scoop some ice cream. She mistakes the flush on Derek's face for a sign that he's enjoying the story. She scoops another dollop and replaces the lid of the plastic tub. She places the bowl of vanilla ice cream on the table. Derek picks up his spoon intently, careful not to catch his aunt's eye.

"The Kanaima catches his victim in spider webs rubbed with the juice of the kuraru plant, so that when he touches the web he falls into a trance, and that's when the Kanaima leaps on him, twists his joints, and stretches his tendons.

"They put black powder into his mouth, which makes him cough and sneeze, and, if he swallows it, his guts decay. Then they pierce his tongue with a snake's fang so that he can't tell anyone what happened. Their victim is left to regain consciousness alone. When he does, he picks himself up and goes home. He develops a fever and aching joints, and then dies. The only way his family knows that it was the work of the Kanaima is by the blue finger marks—the bruises of manhandling—on the victim's neck and arms."

Derek gulps down his ice cream. A needle of cold shoots up the inside of his nose into his forehead. He winces and squints. The creature between his legs has retreated again. For the second time today, his heart is racing and his skin is tingling. He feels suddenly tired, and he never wants to go outside again.

"Excuse me, Auntie, I have to wee." He stands and pushes the chair back. He rushes from his aunt's room, down the hall, and into the washroom. He looks in the mirror at his tongue, searching for the piercing of a snake fang.

Always doing wrong. He doesn't mean to, he just finds himself there, on the road to wrong, with darkness all around, things lying in wait in the bushes. When he comes across wrong he doesn't know whether to scare it off by charging with a sword or to bow softly and walk away.

He brushes his teeth. In the mirror his birthmark eyes him suspiciously. From the adjoining house comes the muffled sound of the Slovakian woman in conversation with the German musician. He listens for the woman's accent and the deep, slippery way she speaks English, which reminds him of a trombone. Their voices are muffled, then go silent. Soon the sound of a strumming guitar rises softly from behind the door. If only he could go back to Kitty. If only he could see her again, then this feeling under his skin, as if his bones were being grated, would disappear. He puts down the toothbrush, rinses his mouth, and curls up on the cold tiles of the bathroom floor. The guitar strumming continues erratically on the other side of the door. Derek chokes back tears, but they break free—soft, quick, hopping sobs. When they slow down and he can breathe again, he stands up.

He doesn't return to the kitchen; he goes into his own room. He slips off his trousers and shirt, folds them carefully on the arm-chair, and retrieves the flannel pyjamas folded beneath his pillow. He shivers, slips them on, and sits on the edge of the bed. Search-ing the room, his gaze falls briefly on his desk and his schoolbooks; he ignores the flicker of obligation. His eyes scan the floor. He reaches for a book beside the bed and opens it randomly.

"And thus upon a night, there came a vision to Sir Launcelot, and charged him, in remission of his sins, to haste him unto Almesbury: "And by then thou come there, thou shalt find Queen Guenever dead. And therefore take thy fellows with thee, and purvey them of an horse bier, and fetch thou the corpse of her, and bury her by her husband, the noble King Arthur."

Crawling under his duvet with the book, he reads on. *So this vision came to Sir Launcelot thrice in one night.* His breathing calms. Sleep overtakes him before he turns the page.

CHAPTER FOUR

Kanaima

ᴓᵐᵐᴖ

COOKS UNLIMITED

An agency with a difference. We are the UK's premier personnel agency for food professionals, with exciting jobs in the UK and abroad.

HEAD CHEF—*Country Pub/Restaurant*

CHEF DE PARTIE—*Smart London Pub/Restaurant*

COMMIS CHEF—*Reputable London Restaurants*

LODGE COOK—*Scottish Shooting Lodges*

GRAND PRIX CIRCUIT—*Tour the circuit and cook for VIPs, Sponsors, and Officials*

COOK/HOUSEKEEPER—*Positions in London and the Counties*

YACHTING COOKS—*Cruise the Mediterranean this summer*

New opportunities daily. Register to find all the exciting possibilities.

Anything is possible. She puts the newspaper down and stands up from the table. She looks out into the dark street. In the distance, light is fluttering like a fresh sheet, and the day seems to have promise. Another summer day without structure. Victoria doesn't know how she will manage too many more. Her hands remember work. The long-promised restructuring of the hospital kitchen has finally been implemented, and her position has been eliminated. Early retirement landed her gently into her first summer since adolescence without regular work. The first few weeks of leisure were a delight. Freedom was unleashed like an animal in her. Hours and hours of baking and cooking, weekend walks and outings with Derek and Lenny, and visits to London sites and museums that, like Internet surfing, have clicked open pathways in her thinking that had been blocked for years.

But since school term ended, the days are endless. Orders have slowed for the summer. She stares at her cooker, as though waiting for instructions from it. If she doesn't find work soon, she'll expire with this feeling of uselessness, and the boy will become one of the Swiss Cottage urchins she sees hanging about at the housing estate near the school. What's she to do with him? She takes him to Lenny's in the morning, and he plays on Lenny's computer while she bakes: *ciabatta*, seven-seed loaf, raisin bread, peach danish, cheese straws. Much of it is made for Derek and Lenny. The catering jobs trickle in, but they are expected to grow in the autumn. While she's kneading dough, she makes plans for the money she dreams will come. She wants the best for Derek, a good education. He will be the first in her family to go to university, she has sworn to herself. Lenny thinks she should pay more attention to the material things that will help him fit in with the other boys, while she's determined to save everything she earns so that the boy will have a good future. But she has taken Lenny up on his offer of music lessons, and today Derek will go to the Royal Academy's summer school session, to learn to play the recorder. If Lenny had his way, Derek would also attend computer classes, but Victoria is not comfortable with debt, so she has turned that offer down, and she and Derek paddle along each rivery day to its eventual end at ten or eleven o'clock when she insists they both go to bed. Dawn comes quickly again.

Victoria imagines herself a chef in a smart London gastro-pub or a swish country restaurant. She positions herself in front of her full-length mirror and considers the apparition. This oval torso in a shooting lodge? Mistaken for a goose, riddled with buckshot, and stuffed for dinner, likely. No. They will have to advertise in order to expand the business. Corporations and government—that's where the money is. Then she'd be able to be extravagant with more than just food, perhaps buy a DVD player, and she and Derek could watch their own movies, proper ones, right here.

She believes that all the trouble with Mr. Darling started with the movies Derek and his friends watch.

It was after talking to Mr. Darling that she felt most like the Bluebird of Piccadilly. Derek's teacher had chastised her, implying with all his puckered politeness that she wasn't fit to raise a child. She was not doing her job; Derek wasn't doing his homework, and his compositions were pure fantasy. She left the meeting and padded through the rainy streets of Swiss Cottage in her best houndstooth coat, feeling like a tamed animal going feral. Perhaps that's how the Bluebird of Piccadilly started her circling of Eros, padding after her lost pride; perhaps she was circling the spot where she might have dropped it, retracing her steps, trying to remember the moment she became too old to be ogled, and yet too young to be treated with respect by pompous teachers. Perhaps Eros and the shaggy coat were the remnants of her vitality. Perhaps she even had a child she couldn't afford to feed. Victoria runs her hand through her hair and pushes it behind her ear.

She looks for Gwen in her reflection. Love's a car crash, she thinks suddenly, and walks quickly into the hall to rummage through the chest. The letters are arranged chronologically in delicate piles, the most recent at the top, like dented signs from an old road she can turn down if she wishes. She knows those near the bottom, where love is more like a bullet, are to be avoided; there's no question they're more than she can bear at the moment. But, here, this is the pile she's looking for.

Darling Vic:

Derek is five today. We had a party for him, and he wore a striped paper party hat. The elastic chinstrap engraved a trough in his chubby cheeks. But he sparkled, so happy. How did I manage to have a child with such peppery hazel eyes? What must his father look like? Derek's skin is not dark, but on days after a picnic at the seawall he looks like toffee, and I want to lick him all over.

There are days when I wish I could meet the donor. I fantasize that a family would fall into place. Derek never asks me where his father is. When he was three he used to call strangers in the street Daddy, but he's stopped that now. He looks less like me now than when he was born. His bush cheeks and wild buck hair mark him as Mummy's grandchild, no question, but his face is changing, and I can see Miami in him too. He is so sensitive. If I am unhappy or cross with him his face will blanch and his eyes go wide.

But what I really wanted to tell you, Vic, is that I've met someone. Love is a surprise. Robert is a maths teacher at Bishop's High School. I've never met anyone who talks like him, in abstractions and as though everything is a puzzle to solve. When I wake in the middle of the night and he's next to me I'm always surprised, and then I fall back into a deep sleep and feel lucky to have the shape of him in my bed, my life . . .

But Victoria knows that, more than a surprise, love can be a casualty. Robert didn't stay long, and then a year or so later another potential father for the boy moved to Grenada to run a hotel. Love ends up mangled like crumpled metal and dashboard scrap. In the seconds of a chain reaction that began with the twenty-fifth passenger stepping up into the minibus and ending with Gwen and Mary's heads rammed into the windshield of their car, all would-be fathers became irrelevant. And his real daddy? Roaming the streets of Miami probably shooting himself off in tube after tube, making half-brothers for the little squab. She digs deeper into the chest and removes an earlier letter.

I don't want Derek to know his father never cared whether he was in the world or not. It was his option, but . . . sometimes I don't understand what I've done . . .

And so Gwen invented stories. She told the boy his father was a revolutionary away fighting wrongdoers in Colombia, his identity a secret, his mission noble and worthy of a hero. She built a father for him the way a writer builds a character, borrowing fragments of fact from the lives of everyone she'd ever known, entwined with fancy and longing. As a result, Victoria knows that Derek's head is full of myth.

She must find her own discipline—some structure to her days, a grip on the future—and that will guide the boy and keep him in line. In her slow tack towards motherhood, perhaps this spare time will be a good wind. As she replaces the letters and closes the chest, she has a sudden craving for Chinese food. Food like her grandmother used to make: funsi, bean curd, chow mein . . . But without the mad, bird-flu chickens.

It's the blondest hair he's ever seen, and he can't take his eyes off it. Derek hurries toward the woman's car, which is parked on a side street off the busy Marylebone Road. He tries to keep up; she walks quickly, turning now and then to make sure he and Kendra are still following. Kendra is the slowest of the three, dawdling, almost lost behind a young family on the pavement, and ignoring this woman's anxiety about her illegally parked vehicle.

"Christine's coming to pick me up, do you want us to drive you home?" Kendra had asked him as they packed up at the end of their music lesson at the Royal Academy. Derek felt a warmth in his chest and nodded absently, the way he might have if someone had asked him, Do you breathe air, Derek? He didn't even think of his aunt, whom he was supposed to call when he was ready to be picked up; nor did he pay a moment's notice to Kendra's obvious contempt for the woman in the way she said her name. *Of course*, was all he was thinking. Of course, I'll go anywhere you tell me to go.

Derek and Kendra have spent the afternoon in a class of six students learning how to play the first few notes of "Greensleeves" on the recorder. He feels like a failure compared to Kendra, who produces the notes effortlessly. Kendra does most things smoothly and without effort. He knows this from his vigilant observation of everything she does.

It has already been months since she slipped over to him after his humiliation in class. "That was so cool," she said. He avoided looking at her, but she didn't budge. "People don't like it when you try something different. They don't believe you."

Derek sat still, staring at his papers, not following her meaning, still shocked by his own gumption in front of the entire class. With her dark eyes on him, he knew something was up, and that Darling's hasty exit from the classroom had something to do with him.

"Like inventors," Kendra continued, but when he looked up at her, she looked down at her shoes, and her words trailed off. She looked up quickly again. "Or artists. They die before anyone believes in them." She turned and walked back to her desk.

He stood staring at her shoulders and the way they glided forward and back with her stride. Glancing over to the door, he wondered where Darling had disappeared to.

Darling had asked them to write a composition for homework, and the next day he demanded results. "Now, class, you'll read them in front of your classmates today. It's quite a different thing to read your own work, owning up to it. Speaking the words makes them your own," he said, the sentences rising up from his belly with spitting, crisp consonants. His cardigan hung open and his tummy was gibbous-moon-like, poking out from behind it.

Two boys read. Then Darling was beside Derek's desk. Derek's shoulder twitched. He had completely forgotten about the assignment. After dinner the previous night, as he'd brushed his teeth and examined his tongue for the piercing of a snake fang, he'd wanted to be in bed more than anything in the world, and the sound of guitar music in the adjoining room lulled him to sleep. When Auntie Vic came looking for him, he was already tucked under his duvet. He was far away from any more words about the walking vengeance of the jungle. When his aunt whispered from the doorway—"You have studies for tonight, Derek?"—all he could do was shake his head with fatigue. But the next day Darling, his belly hovering above Derek, was asking him to read.

Derek rustled some paper at the end of his notebook, slid off his chair, his back straight with false bravado, and walked to the front of the class. Breath was like broken glass in his windpipe. But he cleared his throat and began, pretending to read from the blank page:

"The Kanaima is a spirit-person who roams the bush, punishing boys . . . or even sometimes girls . . ." He looked up anxiously at Darling, then quickly back down at his blank script. In the two previous compositions, the boys had included titles for their pieces, so Derek cleared his throat once more and began again:

"Part One: The Kanaima. They live on a river, in a place called Baraman, because it *bars* all *men*—who aren't spirit men—from entering." Feeling proud of his spontaneous parsing of a word, Derek relaxed and released himself into the story.

"If a man does enter Baraman, he has to face the wrath . . ."—he loved that word, and it came out forceful and intelligent, propelling him confidently into the story's reinvention— ". . . the wrath of the Kanaima, who really want to get revenge for all the things men have ever done since the beginning of history. Revenge is very important to the Kanaima, because they know how much evil has gone on in the past—things like killing . . . with swords . . . or dangerous games . . . So people who get trapped by the Kanaima when they're in the bush are usually people who deserve it." He looked up again towards the back of the room, where he saw the cream-puff grin on Richard Lorry's face. Derek continued, even more confidently.

"Part II: How the Kanaima catch their victims. They eat a bird that makes them invisible, and then they catch the man in a spider web they spin from their own body fluids."

He described the victim's trance with such vivid and fantastical detail that he was lost inside his own tale, experiencing the out-of-body ecstasy of a writer in his flow, and he didn't hear Darling clear his throat loudly, nor did he hear Richard burst out with "too right!" after a description of the smoke that rises from the victim's arse. By the time he reached the end of his virtual composition with "they put black powder in your mouth which makes your guts decay if you swallow it, and they pierce your tongue with a snake's fang so you can't tell anyone what happened," the girls and other boys in the class were exploding into giggles.

"Derek, please sit down. I'll speak to you after class," said Darling. Derek snapped back into the room at Darling's tone, and sat down at his desk with all eyes on him. "OK, class, we'll take a break now. I will be back in five minutes. Prepare your desks for geography." Darling disappeared like the moon at midday.

As soon as he was out the door, Richard Lorry was on his feet and at Derek's desk. "Damn good, that. Fucking good. Got any more like that one?"

Derek felt the creature between his legs curl up and hide. "Maybe," he said, in an unripe lie.

Richard fidgeted and looked about, hesitating to speak. Derek could feel his hands grow moist. He put his notebook down on the desk and concentrated on Richard's prominent chin. Derek wondered what Richard's parents looked like and what it would be like to do whatever you wanted the way Richard was allowed to.

"You comin' over, to my flat?" asked Richard, with a hint of friendly respect that Derek didn't know if he should trust. He nodded, and Richard strutted off to the back of the room.

Then Kendra came to him. Kendra like a curious, wild pony, her huge brown eyes staring at him with the power to see through him. She praised what he'd said as cool, rambled on about inventors and artists, but Derek understood only that she approved of him. When she turned and left, he broke into a smile.

After school he again begged his aunt for leave to join the other boys at Richard's. She consented, with the condition that he not eat anything there. To his delight, he found Kendra, slouched on the sofa, flipping through a magazine, and paying no attention to the movie the boys were watching. When Kendra saw him, she got up and pulled him aside. She showed him something her father had given her—a thin, metallic, battery-powered pen, whose tiny vibrations made calligraphic letters easy to achieve. They talked in the kitchen for the duration of the movie, while Richard and the other boys scoffed and swore at the video screen. Kendra told him that the blood in violent movies was really red acrylic resin, and that he needn't take it seriously. He told her, defensively, that he already knew that, but when she casually mentioned that computer animation was like puppetry and that animators could change the slightest movement of a head by clicking a series of numbers, he knew he was out of his depth.

Since the beginning of the summer holidays he has seen Kendra a few times—in the park, in the supermarket with her father, in the passenger seat of the Volvo—but now, thanks to divine good fortune, Kendra is in his music class.

Kendra's mother was an artist, Derek found out today. A painter and musician from Delhi, her mother moved to England as a student and stayed after meeting Alexander, Kendra's father. But she died three years ago. Derek doesn't know how, but he knows that Kendra thinks that anyone who does anything fun and beautiful will be taken away early in life.

"Hurry up, Kendra," shouts Christine, car keys ready in her hand as she turns towards the two children. The wind tunnels her blonde hair up against the sides of her face. Derek thinks she's beautiful. Christine is tall, slim, and wearing a dress that clings to her hips. Her shoes are high-heeled and strappy. Kendra's lucky, he thinks, if this woman is the substitute mother she has to present to the world. But as Christine turns towards her car, Derek catches the look on Kendra's face: a curled-lip, studied indifference that shows she doesn't share his feelings.

Christine's car speeds through the city towards Derek's house. He recognizes when they're close because there they are again: a line of people walking across the zebra crossing on Abbey Road. Sometimes in pairs, mostly four at a time, groups of tourists cross there and take photos of one another. They walk in long strides over the white lines, while patient drivers with indulgent looks stop to let them pass. And they do it again and again, taking turns as the photographer, as each gets his chance to walk the white lines. Derek has never questioned why so many people choose this crossing to take photos, because he's used to it now and it's a convenient marker on his way home.

When they arrive at the end of Blenheim Terrace in the Volvo, Derek sees his aunt's face in the window on the third floor. Suddenly he remembers that he hasn't phoned her, and he feels a pang of guilt, knowing she might have been worried. By the time he has collected his things, said goodbye to Kendra, and has been shepherded to the front door by Christine, Derek feels the itchy burning around his right eye again—the feeling he gets that something unpleasant is about to happen.

"He said you didn't have a car, so I thought, why not, why shouldn't we drive him, save you the trouble of going all the way out. He didn't say how you'd come—he's not very talkative is he?—but at least you didn't have to get in a taxi, let alone a bus, and it's just on our way. I didn't know that Kendra had a friend so close by. We'll have to get him over to ours." Christine has rattled through her first contact with Victoria with barely a breath between sentences. Her face has gone through a rack of expressions, trying them on as one might new glasses, to see what image they represent to the world, but in front of Victoria's blank stare none has fit the moment. This face never lies, thinks Victoria, sensing that beyond all the polite words, it is the eyebrows and lips that convey what the woman is really feeling—and she is asking for approval.

"Derek?" Victoria looks at her nephew. When he isn't quick to answer, Christine holds out her hand and grabs Victoria's in a vigorous shake.

"I'm sorry, I'm Christine, Kendra's . . . father's friend. How do you do? Derek should have called, it's my fault. I was in a hurry. Double yellow line. . . ."

"Thank you," Victoria says, nods, and gives the woman a fraction of a smile. Her eyes rest on the woman's still almost-youthful arm, which is confident the way her face only struggles to be. "Come along inside Derek. Thank you again," Victoria adds, and she looks down and catches sight of the blonde woman's strappy shoes just before closing the door.

Derek is pleased that nothing too strange happened downstairs. He goes into his aunt's room and switches on the television while she prepares supper. He watches bears in a nature program.

"I don't much like cars, anyway," his aunt says as though halfway through a conversation he's been part of without knowing it. "The bus is easier for most things . . ." and, as she continues, the tone of her voice changes and it sounds as though she's asking Derek to forgive her. He channel-hops with the remote, but nothing else interests him. Back at the nature show, an eagle is perched on the ledge of its eyrie, feeding an eaglet.

DRY-BRAISED YI NOODLES

2 yi noodle cakes
1 cup dried shrimp
1 tablespoon groundnut oil
1 clove garlic
grated ginger root
1 can crabmeat
1 cup fish stock
½ cup chopped spring onions
1 tablespoon soy sauce
1 tablespoon oyster sauce
salt to taste

Victoria pours two and a half litres of water into a large saucepan and places it over the high flame on the stove. Besides, it's healthier for the boy to do some walking and experience things, and not just watch the world from the back seat of a car, she thinks as she breaks each noodle cake into three pieces. She stares at the pot as the water begins to boil. As she submerges the noodles, she can't get the image of the woman out of her mind, especially the shining hair, confident hands, and firm arms like those of someone who's used to driving a busload of children all over town. Victoria tries to push back the family shame that seems to return as quickly as the water with the noodles returns to a boil. She checks her watch to make sure they boil for no more than a minute, until they are tender but not soggy. She drains them in a colander and puts them aside.

She pours boiling water from the kettle over the shrimp, just covering them in the liquid, then leaves them and goes to chop the spring onions. After paring the onions into white and green threads, she drains the shrimp, reserving the soaking liquid. She chops the shrimp into pieces the size of matchstick heads.

Very quickly the hollow feeling takes over—the one she had missed even a few months ago but which now feels like a cold slap. Hollow like rotted wood. Her actions feel empty. Anyone can boil a few noodles, she thinks. It takes more than that to raise a boy. She searches the shelf for groundnut oil. At the stove she heats the wok over high heat until a hint of smoke rises, then she adds the oil and swirls it around. She tosses in the shrimp. *Laud gimme strength . . . hollow, hollow hollow . . .* and stirs them for a couple of minutes until they brown. She removes them to a small dish.

Her movements are deliberate now. She rinses the wok, dries it, and reheats it over high heat. More oil, then garlic. Once the garlic is a nutty colour, she adds ginger and stirs. Maybe Lenny will help her get another driver's licence, she thinks, as she opens the can of crabmeat and empties it out into the wok. She stirs the mixture with the base of her wok scoop. Salt, she thinks, and searches the shelf. The box of Malden sea salt presents itself like a pinch of hope. She grinds some between her fingers and sprinkles it over the crabmeat.

Or if she just made more money they could afford to take taxis. The young blonde woman's triceps flash into her mind. They are smooth, trim, and perfectly one with the opposing biceps. She sees a hand on these arms, a man's strong hand guiding the woman along a high street. The man belonging to that hand knows things about the world and feels life pulsing in a single arm. He is a man in the midst of discovery. What does Kendra's father do for a living, she wonders. She pours in the stock from the measuring cup and stirs as it comes to a boil. She adds the noodles to the crabmeat mixture, and then the silken threads of spring onion. She searches the shelf again for a bottle, grabs it, then shakes out a few dashes of soy sauce. Oyster sauce next. Reaching into the hot pan to lift out a noodle, she brings it to her lips to taste. She adds another shot of oyster sauce. She removes the mixture to a warm serving dish, then sprinkles the shrimp on the top.

Perhaps food and stories are not enough.

"Derek! Come for supper!"

CHAPTER FIVE

The Bluebird of Piccadilly

She has always thought of Easter as a sunburn on the year. Good Friday scorches with its ritual recounting of death, but the next few days gently peel away its effects, revealing life beneath the hard skin of winter. Then everything is new. Spring unfolds as it must. Then May . . . May rushes like an open tap. Even in Guyana, she remembers, Easter arrived like a holler, while the rest of the year followed in whispers.

One Good Friday when she was a young girl, her father took her to visit a man who owned a rum shop open all year round. Without telling his wife where they were headed, Henry lifted Victoria onto the crossbar of his bicycle. With his daughter sitting side-saddle in front of him, he pedalled down the road, arriving at the rum shop before noon. Victoria saw the man's leg first. It was lying over the stoop, sticking out the front door of the shop, and a sandal was dangling from the big toe. Her father lifted her off the bicycle before dropping it to the ground and running into the shop. She tiptoed forward, terrified by the sight, as she got closer, of vomit sliding down the man's cheek. For a moment she was certain the man was dead and that death was still lingering in the sandal. But soon she heard coughing and cursing, then more coughs and growls from the man, as though he'd suddenly turned into a pig. Her father came out of the shop scowling, shaking his head, and mumbling that the man had drunk up all his own stock.

Placing Victoria back on the crossbar, Henry, in a serious voice he knew she would obey, said, "Don't you mention this to Mommy, you hear? Tell her we went for a ride to the seawall." Victoria clung to the handlebar as they made their way quickly down the road. Inside her, secrets were inflating like balloons.

A squeal comes from one of the twins downstairs. Martin's voice swoops down, and the squeal turns into a giggle. Victoria continues to tidy Derek's room, folding his clothes carefully into the drawer, and examining the condition of the boy's socks. Since last summer, she's kept track of his growth, noting the sudden spurts and then the weeks and weeks of nothing—long plateaus during which she worried that he might have stopped growing. But she is slowly understanding the formless rhythm of a child's development. Now she tries to cope with moods that seem to have a direct correlation to the amount of sleep Derek gets or the sugar he consumes. While she still hasn't told her nephew all the things she thought she would when he first came to live with her, she has learned how small things make a difference to him: the number 7 football jersey and the trainers with a checkmark logo.

Shopping for clothes is not something she's ever been adept at, and London prices have kept her in modest attire. In Toronto, with her financial clerk lover, she learned a thing or two about style and quality when he treated her to shopping sprees at Eaton's and Simpson's. But since then she's had neither the opportunity nor the desire to apply the things she feels instinctively about how a woman her age should look. She tries to remember Easters she spent in Toronto, the long, slow days after Kola left, the Polish shop on Ronscesvalles Avenue—open at 6 AM—where she'd buy her morning tea and a Polish doughnut before going to work at the hospital kitchen. She doesn't resist the nostalgia of early spring afternoons as she sipped more tea and nibbled on a slice of babka while the sloping light edged into her apartment with the promise that the snow and ice were over, and that after this weekend everything would be awake. Will Derek ever see Canada? She would like him to breathe the smell of May there, the wide-open, fly-buzzing smell of a summer about to explode.

Her first Easter in Toronto, Victoria was twenty-one—and thin. Her age has fooled people her whole life, but in Toronto it was particularly troublesome as she tried to make a life of her own and employers and landlords frequently mistook her for an adolescent. After sharing her sponsor's cold basement apartment through the winter, she finally met the fiery Polish woman who agreed to rent her a room above her shop.

It was that Easter she first tasted muthya and ugali sukuma wiki in the tiny studio apartment where Kola would visit and cook for her. Chopping the ginger and the onions, Kola told her of the Gikuyu proverb that said one who eats alone dies alone, *muria wiki akuaga wiki*, and he talked incessantly, about Kenya, about politics, about bloodlines and kinship. "It's the Chinese blood that makes you so young," he said as he stared at her. During the first year, they would take turns cooking, either at his place across town on Bloor Street or at hers. She would try to impress him by cooking Chinese food—recipes she'd learnt from her father's mother, Beatrice Layne. Beatrice Lena Yuk had become Beatrice Layne the way Yanchow rice becomes fried rice—by giving herself away in marriage to a man who had Chinese as well as English blood, and by adapting her Chinese heritage to South America. And in Toronto with a nightly portion of spicy ginger rice and yoghurt, Victoria was giving herself away to Africa.

Never mind that now.

She closes the top drawer of Derek's dresser, picks up the laundry on the floor and walks back to her room. She's been making plans all week for this Easter, for Derek's second Easter in London. She barely remembers last year's. It's taken her this long to get her stride with the boy. They have settled into a routine; he doesn't frighten her when he appears behind her, and although he has made little progress on the recorder, Derek has caught up at school. He has friends.

"Derek."

"Yes, Auntie Vic?"

"Come away from that screen. You'll go blind and I'll go broke with you surfing for hours on end . . . Come and help me roll this pastry."

"Coming, Auntie Vic."

As she takes out the eggs for the quail, sorrel, and parsley pie she's going to bake in the afternoon, she thinks about last week's meeting at the school. She taps an egg a bit too briskly on the corner of the bowl, irritated at the thought of what Kendra's father said. The shell shatters, the yolk and albumen splatter through her fingers. She throws all of it in the rubbish and takes another.

The meeting had been organized by parents concerned about the standards of school meals. A young woman in the front row had spoken of BSE, genetically modified foods, and the possible health consequences for their children. Victoria had sat in the back row, and nodded in agreement with the woman's fears. Then Alexander Hodge stood up and spoke: "This Dr. Ritman you cite is a lone ranger. Ostracized by his peers, as I understand. What's he claiming? That ingesting a gene resistant to insecticides will cause stunted growth in humans? Please, the leap is huge . . . irrational."

Victoria disliked Mr. Hodge instantly. The word irrational grated on her. Victoria's life has been predicated on the irrational. It's how she was made, and there's not much she can do about it. When he sat back down, Victoria sat up to see who was sitting next to him and spotted the flowing blonde hair of Christine. She imagined the woman's changeable face trying on its expressions, her eyebrows betraying embarrassment. Kendra sat unselfconsciously on her father's other side, playing with strands of her hair. Suddenly Victoria felt protective of Derek in the girl's company. The meeting continued as others made their points, which seemed to boil down to the fact that good food was expensive. Once again Victoria felt on the side of the irrational, as she railed silently at them for thinking of food as a privilege. She would scrimp and save for the best food rather than spend money on silly shoes like the ones Mr. Hodge's girlfriend seemed to like.

"Here, you know how to break eggs. I need three," she says, handing Derek the carton.

She watches out of the corner of her eye as he carefully taps the egg on the side of the mixing bowl. "Is Kendra good at her studies, then?"

Derek cracks open the egg and lets the yolk and albumen slip gently into the bowl. "I don't know," he says with a shrug. "She's not in my class this year."

"I bet her father helps her, he seems clever—a little too clever," and she pictures the back of his head, his curly brown hair, and the strong nose in profile. She grabs a quail breast and places it into the simmering stock.

No matter what the curly-headed Mr. Hodge said to the crowd of anxious parents at the school, Victoria still doesn't entirely trust eggs. But these should be fine. They come from a butcher in Borough Market who knows his farmers, who know their animals. "The only thing these eggs have coursing through them is the pauk, pauk song of the hungry chickens as they roamed for food," he almost sang as he held up one in each hand. Victoria bought them immediately. She is proud of her choice of Easter lunch. She shreds the sorrel and chops in the parsley. It will be a fine pie.

Over the last fifteen months Derek has learned to ask questions so that his voice goes down at the end instead of up. He is no longer hanging on to the last sound like a lost owl in the night: "Could I have some butter, please?" Now the inflection goes up on "butter" and comes back down on "please," the way Stephen has taught him, so that he doesn't stand out. Stephen says that how you sound makes all the difference in this country, so Derek is trying to sound like someone he wants to be; he is learning to keep his mouth puckered and to force sound delicately through his teeth.

His aunt passes him the soya spread, and he knifes a dollop onto his roll.

"Come on now, eat up and we'll go out for a walk after lunch—to the heath—there's a fair on."

Hampstead Heath (teeth) like me new 'ampsteads? Na, I'd prefer the custard and jelly (telly) or to go out with the other dustbin lids (kids). Derek is silently practising, trying to put the words together. He could say he'd like to stay home, *stay around the cat and mouse (house) and Bob squash (wash) me boat race (face) and me bushel and peck (neck) and bacon and eggs (legs) or walk down to the rub-a-dub-dub (pub).*

The sounds of Inkland. Derek is proud of his new songs. He looks into his plate at the breast of a little bird like a sparrow (*a bow and arrow*). The rest of the bird must have been smothered by all the pastry, he thinks. He looks for it, poking the crust with his knife.

"Now eat up," comes his aunt's voice from across the table. She has out her special plates, silver cutlery, and a white cloth with red flowers embroidered along the outside edge. Auntie Vic is wearing her glasses today and not squinting. She smiles the smile she uses to keep things steady, the embarrassed one that comes at awkward moments, like when she walks in on him and his hand is on his penis. Or the one she used to give him when he first arrived, when in the mornings she'd come into his room and find that in his night fright he had wet the bed. He doesn't do that anymore, and the fear has faded to a faint tremor from its once indiscreet pounding.

Auntie Vic still comes to walk him home from school at the end of the day, but now she waits at the corner and lets him take his leave of Stephen and the other boys without trying to listen or to pull him by the hand like a toddler. He's grateful for that, and, so instead of goodbye, he has a chance to say "bloody later," like Richard does.

Derek has been following the thieving, cajoling, and general thuggery of Richard the Truck. Everything that Richard says turns into a curse, and into the law of the schoolyard. Richard the Truck makes most boys in the school pay taxes. A tax for passing this square in the yard—50p. Pay up or I'll take your jacket. Tax for getting your jacket back. You want me to tell your folks you've been smokin'?—60p. By following closely behind Stephen and not being too obvious, and by virtue of something in the story of the Kanaima, Derek has been so far spared a taxed existence.

Do thou thy worst . . . wit thou well I shall defy thee . . . says Sir Mordred. Richard is like Sir Mordred, but Derek is not tempted to fight him. He must not wield another sword, slay another dragon or mortal, or surely the fright will return with a thunder crack.

He spears a slice of the dainty breast and brings it to his mouth, biting lightly, then voraciously, hunger reminding him of his tongue, his teeth, the nectarine flesh inside his mouth. He gobbles down the pie, then takes a swig of soya milk, which he's grown accustomed to these last few months. His aunt now refuses to let him eat anything related to a cow.

"Good," she says with gleeful eyes as she takes a small nibble from her own plate. He's noticed that his aunt is not as plump as she was when he first came here. Finishing all the food on his plate, he gulps back the milk, and wipes the back of his hand over his mouth, holding back a belch he knows would displease her.

"Now you run along and get your shoes and coat on while I clean up. We're going out today. It's chilly, but the sun is bright and it's an Easter fit for Jerusalem."

LONDON'S FAMOUS HAMPSTEAD HEATH
EASTER BANK HOLIDAY
FUN FAIR
Attractions, rides, food

The ground is still damp, the path muddy, but the air is fresh here on the heath. Families with prams and strollers make their way about the grassy area where chip vendors, gaming stalls, and toddlers' rides vie for custom. Farther on, there are more sophisticated rides: a zipper-like spinning carousel and some bumper cars.

"Oh, look at that," Derek says and sets out towards a stall at the far end. Victoria follows him over the grass, passing a woman in a striped, velour top hat selling jewellery.

The smell of manure is missing, but the other images flow back in from memory. Her father once took her to a fair like this one, but which had stilt dancers, pony rides, and a rickety Ferris wheel. She ate salt nuts, sweet nuts, and guava candies until she felt sick. The pony shite smell grew thick with ammonia, so she didn't want to ride one, but did so because it meant a lot to her daddy. When he called her his little filly, she knew he was in a family mood, and that he and her mother were sleeping in the same bed at night. Her daddy believed in her at those times. He wanted her to go to the best school, to be with the nuns at the St. Ursula College, where no dark children ever went, but where, before independence, the Portuguese, the English, and the occasional Chinese got the best schooling in Georgetown. After independence the college had to change its grounds for admission. Victoria attended the college for one year, but was not allowed to return the next term, for no explicit reason, but she knew in her skin it was because of her father's indiscretions and her mother's shame. She continued her studies at Bishop's High School, but at the convent school she had discovered nuns, and wanted to become one more than anything in the world. The nuns were from Ireland. They gave lessons in etiquette: how to eat a sandwich properly, how to fold a napkin, where to place the silverware at a table. Victoria loved them, but didn't feel loved in return. By the time she left, she had learned the secret of being a nun: hide your head to save your soul, eat as well as you can, and love an absent one until your heart turns hard and your blood runs cold.

Perhaps she learned the lessons too well. The final conversation with her father had been fuelled by the veiled righteousness of the nuns. Henry was tall for a Chinese man, and his patchy, long-bristled goatee was at her eye-level as Victoria marched up to him with truth clutched at her breast like a crucifix beneath a tunic.

"I won't stand for it any longer," she burst out.

"What're you talkin', Vic?"

"I won't. Won't stand for it. Not another outside woman, you hear? Not another one . . ." and then her trembling lip got in the way of more words.

Her father's wide grin was like a slap in the face.

"Eh eh! You little miss high and mighty! I bring me pigs to fine market!" And then the grin turned sour. "You eva talk to me like that again and I'll beat y'ass black and blue, ya hear?" He turned his back on her and continued to hoe. She watched as the dirt turned over and over, burying everything. That was it—the moment her life became ruled by volition. She left Georgetown a few months later to face the to and fro of her will and its consequences forever.

Victoria looks about for Derek. She spots him near a stall. A dark-haired man with a beard, shuffling cards at a table, calls out to the crowd to join him in a game. Victoria hurries past him and the toddlers' carousel.

Kola took her to the next fair, the Canadian National Exhibition. She rode a roller coaster that tossed her heart up into her throat. He bought candy floss, just like what's being whipped up in the stall here.

"Oh Derek, that will rot your teeth," she tells him.

"No it won't," he says firmly, as though he knows something she doesn't.

"Let's play one of those dart games," she says, trying to distract him, but it doesn't shift his attention from the pink cotton candy.

"Or look, there's a game where you spin a wheel and win a toy," she says, noticing a stuffed bear. But Derek stays firmly planted on the spot.

At the Canadian National Exhibition, Kola shot darts at balloons to win Victoria a stuffed giraffe. Giraffes, he said, are important animals, have special powers that humans once tried to harness. He told her of rock carvings of giraffes that had been engraved more than six thousand years ago. He spent four times the cost of the toy giraffe slapping his quarters down in order to break enough balloons to win the beast for her. By then they were seeing each other daily, and she was letting herself believe she'd finally escaped the distrust her parents fostered.

She takes a pound coin from her purse and hands it to the vendor. He swirls a cardboard stick back and forth in the revolving drum and pulls out a pink bonnet of sugar fleece, which he gives to Derek. Victoria reminds herself to make sure the boy brushes his teeth well tonight.

"What about that ride, Derek? Do you want to ride the bumper car, dear? Mmm? Go for a little drive?" Suddenly she needs to be alone. The combination of Kola and her father is too much. She absent-mindedly places more coins in Derek's free hand.

"No, Auntie Vic. No, thanks—"

"Look at the other boys. Looks like fun to me . . . now go on," she says as she takes the stick of candy floss from his other hand.

"But . . ." Derek stops, realizing she is not really paying attention.

"Go on, speck. It'll be fun," she says finally, now looking at him.

Derek wipes his right hand on his trousers to brush off the granules of pink sugar. He heads slowly to the entrance to the bumper car circuit. Victoria feels relieved for the space to think. Why is she remembering things from more than thirty-five years ago as though they happened last year? Why does she have difficulty remembering to tell Len they need to order lard, when the sound of Kola and the smell of pony shite in Georgetown are today as palpable as skin?

Kola was once asked by a man who was trying to obtain immigration papers for him: "How does it feel to be a problem?" Victoria now asks herself, "How does it feel to be an echo?" A long, lonely syllable. Like the puzzle of all the missing socks. Where do they go? Where do sounds fall when they are broken?

Asked by Kola early in their relationship when she'd felt most fully alive, she had to think before answering. She came up with a moment in Barbados, after she'd left home, when she climbed the cliff at Pico Tenerife and stood staring out over the Atlantic. The pounding of the waves on rock was persistent and almost measured, like a pulse. This was not silence, which implies absence; it was its opposite. The peace she felt came from the sense that nothing was missing. She told him so. She never got the opportunity to tell him that moment paled in comparison to meeting him. Some days she can't even picture Kola's face, but the feeling that knowing him had healed every gash in her childhood has returned from time to time. It's like the echo of something infinite, of a sound she thought she'd never hear again. She looks up at Derek driving his bumper car and senses that this slow course to motherhood comes with the possibility of that sound.

Derek looks over at his aunt, who throws him an "aren't-you-courageous" grin. The bumper car bangs into the barrier, crashes to a halt, and loses power. He climbs out and heads down the stairs of the exit. Victoria's eyes are wide, her straight white teeth gleaming in a smile.

"That's a boy, well done."

Well done, is it? Derek thinks. Well done to drive and crash and burn? All the crashing and burning all over the entire earth. He wants none of it. He would *rather a nanny goat (boat). Rather a ball of chalk (walk).*

"There now, what ya thinking?"

"Nothing, really."

"Nothing? Now that couldn't be true. When I was nearly nine years old I was always thinking of something," Victoria says, pressing him, always suspecting him of missing his mother.

"London's big; that's all," he says, as they climb a path through holly bushes, leading to a wooded area with imposing trees. The sun pokes through stark branches and spotlights Victoria as she reaches out to hold his hand.

"Big? Is that what's got you worried?"

"Not worried. Just thinking . . . that I—"

"Now, don't you worry about getting lost. I won't let that happen." She suppresses the rising panic at the thought. "You just make sure you always tell someone your name and address, phone number . . . and postal code. Postal code will always help; that's what I found out early on. People pay attention to codes."

"I'll never get lost. I always know where I am."

"Well, good for you, lad. Good for you," she says, and squeezes his hand with pleasure. "You should walk to school on your own, you know, but you'll really have to be watchful, and not talk to people. And, remember, the river's always south—it's good to live near water, with rivers especially, like home. It's good to have a tide," and her mind drifts off as they walk up the slippery incline of well-trod mud. Victoria squishes through a bicycle tire track, and the ache in her hip becomes pronounced. Derek digs his trainers deep into the ridges left by others, spoiling them, mashing down their outlines, and raising a new ridge of dark earth around his own foot. The heath is moss and mud, with blossoms that seem to have arrived suddenly with the fair. They pass a family with three children slightly younger than Derek, the eldest two chattering about the dog they want.

"Auntie Vic?"

"Yes, son."

"Does everyone here sound different?"

"You mean different from home?"

"No, that I know already," he says, shaking his head, annoyed by how she often takes him for such a baby. "I mean different from everyone else."

"You mean different from one another?"

"Yea, Stephen says there's no two people who have exactly the same accent."

"Is that right? Maybe he means . . . I don't know, people like to talk about what others sound like here. Do you hear the differences?"

Derek nods.

"They're always pointing out differences. Tiny island of difference, this. They don't make so much of differences in other places . . . Never you mind all that."

At the top of the hill they come to a gravel path. Victoria puts her hand on Derek's shoulder and rubs it, then takes his hand again. They walk along the path through the moss-sprayed trees. A cyclist whizzes past them and Victoria clutches Derek's hand tight until he gasps and tries to pull it free. She doesn't let go, but lets up on the grip.

"Do they also talk about colour at school, Derek?"

"Hmmm?"

"Colour, do the boys talk about colour?"

What colour was the shape of the hexagon he drew during his maths period before the Easter break? Red? Probably red. And colours of flags: Turkey, red with a white crescent and star; Germany, black, red, yellow; France, blue, white, and red. Mrs. Sydney pointed out that Mauritius had one of the most colourful flags in the world, with red, blue, yellow, and green stripes. Derek wanted to raise his hand to tell her of Guyana's red, yellow, and green flag with a black and a white stripe, but lost his courage. Guyana's didn't have any blue in it, so Mrs. Sydney was probably right.

"Did you hear me?"

"Yes, Auntie Vic?"

"Do they talk about, tease about it, you know, colour."

Tease about colour, he wonders? Stephen and Richard Lorry are always joking about the puke-green colour of Nathan Samuel's soup . . . "Yes, sometimes."

"Gosh, thought so, thought we'd have that sooner or later, like home all over again. And what do you say, what colour are you, then?"

He searches for an answer. His aunt has slowed down and is looking at him intently. She does this—tests him, asks questions about how he is, what he feels like, complicated questions like his mother used to ask. *Derek, what is it you think you're doing with that when I told you not to touch it?* He never knows what to say, but he tries hard to get the answer just right this time.

"Blue, I guess," he says with a shrug, feeling he's hit it just right.

Victoria almost trips, off-stride with delight. Her smile spreads wide, and she picks up her pace again in step with the wondrous being beside her. She squeezes his hand gently, and, for the first time in almost thirty years, gives in to a feeling like air billowing under her breast that might make her float.

On the first day after the holidays, Victoria lets Derek walk ahead of her, proud of his independence. She's relieved that school is starting again, having exhausted all the amusements she could think of over Easter, as she and Lenny had special orders that made them busier than ever. But even the few feet between them now make her anxious.

Derek speeds up, and is almost running by the time Victoria spots Kendra up ahead at the corner opposite the school. She walks faster to try to reach them, but when she notices the curly hair of Kendra's father ahead of the girl, she drops back. Derek catches up and says hello to Kendra, who smiles and gives him a little shove to the shoulders. Alexander Hodge, talking on his mobile, hasn't noticed the boy yet, and, irrationally, Victoria hates him for how he possesses the space around him, comfortably, confidently. Born to it. As the three of them step off the curb to cross the street, Derek turns and looks questioningly at his aunt. She smiles and nods her head, and he gives her a quick wave goodbye. Kendra, Derek, and Alexander walk together to the school.

Victoria turns and wanders back. There are tiny eruptions in her stride, and she takes note of how much energy she has these days, so different from the early days of having Derek in her care. This rush of potency feels something akin to the initial eruptions of infatuation, when nothing is difficult, nothing is dark. She doesn't want to lose this feeling just yet. What's she to do with herself? Her baking is finished for the day, a 4 AM start with the ovens ensuring that, and now the day spreads before her like a net. You won't catch me, she thinks, and walks quickly towards St. John's Wood High Street.

At the window of the expensive butcher shop, she considers the organic stuffed leg of lamb, which she can't afford, but, pretending she can, examines the rows of flesh in the window. She catches her reflection in the glass. Blimey, Vic, where did you get to? She touches her neck—not a neck she remembers. The skin a gently sagging bark. Her mouth looks like it has forgotten how to pronounce new words. She runs her fingers through her hair and continues to walk.

Her entrance into the salon farther down the high street seems almost automatic. The young woman who greets her and shows her to a chair where she can consider colours and styles has hair like Christine's, and for one absurd second Victoria considers going blonde; then she turns the pages of samples to darkest brown, ebony, and black. Black will make the pale skin stand out too much, she thinks. In a numb and bored mood in Toronto she had considered a henna, but had been convinced by her financial clerk that her natural black suited her best. But she can't remember her skin being this pale. This pallor is England's fault, and plagues everyone who lives here.

"Espresso—would that be good for me?" Victoria asks. The hairstylist says "perfect" with enthusiasm that seems out of proportion for hair colour, and Victoria follows her toward the sinks at the back of the salon.

IMPERIAL EASTERN/HYDE PARK
Exciting Hotel Employment Opportunities

At Imperial Eastern/Hyde Park, London, our mission is to completely sat-
isfy and delight our guests. We are committed to making a difference
every day.

On completion of our major refurbishment programme we will be the
grandest hotel in London.

To bring our high standards to the next level, we are looking to recruit the
following committed, reliable, and enthusiastic individuals:

Chefs—all levels

Waiting staff

Sommelier

Conference and Banqueting Co-ordinator

Reservationist

Room Attendants

We offer you a caring, motivating, and rewarding environment along
with an excellent salary and benefits package.

With the heat of the dryer swirling about her ears, Victoria puts
down the *Evening Standard* classified section, irritated. The adver-
tisement initially sparked hope in her. She imagined an audition
meal—a Buddhist dish with cloud ears, golden needles, hair algae,
Ginkou nuts, mushrooms—but what's the use, she thinks. No one
will hire a woman past her prime.

As the stylist runs her fingers through the now coffee-coloured
hair, Victoria stares at herself in the mirror and thinks that, of all
people, the Bluebird of Piccadilly might have known what Kola
meant when he wrote in his letter from London: . . . *here I've been
able to be lost among people who pay little attention to my past* . . .

". . . fuller, more textured," the stylist says as her fingers move through the hair around Victoria's ears. "There, how's that," she adds as she brushes the hair toward Victoria's cheeks.

"I can't remember what he looked like," Victoria whispers. "Do you think it's a bit drastic?" she asks the stylist.

"Not at all. Suits you."

"Thank you, then," Victoria concludes, and picks up her purse from the floor beside her.

What she remembers most is his elegant handwriting, and somewhere near the bottom of her chest are the letters Kola sent her from across town—a meagre distance he felt unable to negotiate in the depths of the Toronto winter. Bell Canada had refused him a telephone line because he was unable to provide the necessary documents to verify his address. Kola arrived illegally from Kenya, to escape circumstances that Victoria never fully understood. She could imagine the flow of neighbours he spoke about, of visiting without appointment and never being denied food or drink. She remembers Kola's insistence that no one must starve, we must all eat together. But she could not visualize what detention without trial would have meant for him, as it had for many of his family and friends. She did not consider that it was possible for a man to be detained merely because he knew people who didn't like the government.

In his final letter, postmarked from London, thirteen years after he disappeared, there was evidence of just how much Victoria had ignored in what he told her while they were together. He had littered their relationship with stories during which he'd suddenly howl like a beast as he described the brutal treatment of Gikuyu prisoners in both the British detention camps and the Kenyan government's. He cursed the British and Kenyans alike, and he told her things about the underside of Africa that she didn't want to acknowledge. This last letter set her off across the Atlantic, here to London, in search of a place where people *pay little attention to my past*. Perhaps the Bluebird of Piccadilly knew Kola then. Perhaps he noticed her, as he had Victoria, and perhaps one day Victoria will sit across from the old bird in a West End café and wait for the woman to unravel her stories. She wouldn't be surprised if the Bluebird talked endlessly about her life and casually recounted the year when she met a tall African man who taught her how to eat muthya and who rubbed her feet to the whisper of an African lullaby.

The sky is an unusually clear blue over Piccadilly when Victoria emerges from the Underground station. She has a slight ache in her wrists from the early-morning kneading of dough. Orders for their egg bread have doubled in the last two months, with a delicatessen in St. John's Wood taking fifteen loaves a day now. She turns her right wrist in steady circles as she waits for the walk signal to cross Haymarket. The sunshine is hopeful, and Victoria is feeling lucky.

Piccadilly and hope.

There she is.

The Bluebird, wearing her blue-shag coat, is standing against the railing, staring at passersby. Victoria walks past, deliberately not catching her eye, but then realizes that the Bluebird catches no one's eye. Her gaze is as blank as a rock's facing the sea. Victoria climbs onto a step under Eros and looks for a spot to sit down. The steps are crowded—tourists, teenagers, and lovers in rendezvous. Some watchers, just passing time. All of them waiters under Eros. From her handbag Victoria takes out a yellow handkerchief and places it on the cement step before lowering herself down. Favouring her right hip, she lands slightly off balance to the left, but smoothes her skirt and straightens up as she looks about. A young Japanese woman with bleached hair and wedge shoes nestles closer to her boyfriend. On her other side, a traveller in a bandanna pulls his knapsack closer to make room for Victoria and gives her a smile. She composes herself, thinking how lucky these young people are, how free. The world requires greater dignity of you when you're Victoria's age, but is mostly forgiving until then. She stretches out her legs and looks around at the crowd. The Bluebird of Piccadilly begins her circuit around the statue.

Had Kola seen the Bluebird, he'd have had some story about her, would've followed her and asked her what she thought: "Penny for your thoughts," he might have said, as he had to Victoria. He was the first person in Toronto to care about what she was thinking, to penetrate the fear in her face and get beyond it. Her scowl was inspired by Toronto's buildings, organized along such straight lines, and rising at such straight angles that in the winter light the towers appeared to fall skyward, as if from a force opposite to gravity. In the financial district she felt diminished and shadowed, so she kept to the west end, where the houses were small and brick, with painted wrought-iron railings. In the summer months, older European men in white singlets worked in their front gardens tying the branches of their tomato plants to stakes to keep them growing tall. Some houses had rows of snap beans and lettuce that felt familiar to her, yet she rarely exchanged a word with these Italian and Portuguese families.

Pulling on this thread from her memory, she sees the storefronts of Portuguese dress shops and bakeries, both displaying white chiffon, silk, and lace on their life-size and cake-size mannequins of brides. The cakes had silver icing bows, gold trim, and lace trellises leading to the top layer where the groom and tiaraed bride stood. The dresses were flanked by mannequin ring bearers in their tiny tuxedos and bridesmaids in flouncing pink gowns. Victoria remembers feeling as though something essential about Europe was displayed in those windows. As these images are drawn forth like a loose strand from a tightly woven garment within her, she's amazed at how accessible this vision remains after decades. So she continues the unravelling.

In Toronto she used to walk a lot. "Penny for your thoughts," Kola had said over her left shoulder as she made her way through the throng of shoppers in Kensington Market. She felt at home in the market. Jamaicans, Trinidadians, and Guyanese sold pepper sauce, plantain, and coconut. Kola spoke to her just as she was reaching for a soursop fruit. When she didn't answer him right away, he tried, "OK, a quarter then, that will make me a poor man, but richer for getting a word from you."

Her father had always warned Victoria not to talk to strangers. Though she was no longer on speaking terms with him when she left Georgetown, the last thing he said to her was, "Don' look dem in the eye or you're gone, over to dey power." This warning stayed with her those dark late-winter days. So she walked past the tall man with charcoal skin and yellow-tinged eyes for whom she felt no fear. She bought groceries—red bean paste, funsi, yi noodles, bird's nest, shark fin, dried shrimp—to cook herself a feast in her apartment, but the sight of food made her so hungry she decided to stop and eat. She wandered into a noisy noodle restaurant on Spadina with her heavy bags. She walked to the back, looking for space at the long tables of soup slurpers. Spotting a vacant seat, she was about to pull out the chair when a voice across the table addressed her.

"That's good thinking, you had." When she looked up she saw the man who had spoken to her in the market.

"Between soup and shopping, always choose soup." It was the first of a daily dose of Kola's aphorisms that would continue for six years. She couldn't help but smile at his directness. She pulled out the chair, sat down, and he held out his immense black hand.

"Kola," he said with a smile.

Kola wasn't his real name, but the nickname his friends had given him upon arrival in Toronto from Nairobi. His real name was Kuria.

"Why are you called Kola?" she asked.

"My brother's friends used to tease me that I was like a tree. I don't think they meant my branches," he said, holding out his arms, "as they are skinny and weak."

She later found out his nickname was an attempt to hide his

identity and kinship to Tairus wa Kamau, his older brother. Tairus had friends in Toronto who had escaped Kenya as political refugees, and Kola was living with them. Their uncle had been a friend of Dedan Kimathi wa Waciuri, the high priest of the Mau Mau movement, and from an early age Tairus had been involved with radicals. Far too young to join the men who fought in the Mau Mau rebellion, Kola's childhood games had been infused with revolutionary rhetoric and codes, but as soon as he was old enough, he left Mombasa for Nairobi, to join the last of the radical groups still fighting for political change. He performed minor tasks, relaying messages and cleaning the headquarters of the leaders, where he'd eavesdrop on their plans. He stayed there for two years, but his family needed him, so he returned to Mombasa and began a career as a cook. He became restless there, and cooking suited only the "rooted side of his tree," he joked. He returned to the radicals' camp, but got into some kind of trouble there. He and some of his brother's friends managed to find passage to Canada. Others, including Tairus, were not so lucky.

Victoria listened to his story, ignorant of the political context in Kenya. But when he spoke of injustice and suffering that she could see for herself in her Guyana mind's eye, she understood. While she slurped down her noodle soup, he told her about a child he'd met from a village that did not belong to the ruling party's tribe. The village got none of the advantages that the party's tribesmen received. "This is Kenya after all," he said emphatically. Victoria ordered rice with black bean sauce and picked at it slowly as he told her that the boy lived with his sister in an unused drain behind a railway track. Their mother had died of a terrible illness; their father perished when their hut was set on fire by a mob during an election. The boy and girl escaped, and set out walking, naked, their burns weeping, until they found the drain. They slept there on a discarded plastic tarpaulin and begged for food every day. Beset by intestinal worms and lice, the children could barely tell Kola their story when he found them.

As he spoke, it was as if a thread was being drawn out between them, like something woven by a fastidious insect. The thread connected the vowels in both of them that screamed against injustice. While Kola's concerns were for a nation, his rantings stirred in Victoria the sense of more intimate injustices among relations, between her mother and father and between her neighbours and her family.

Even that first day, Kola was telling her the truth about himself, about what his life involved, but she preferred the gentler, mythical side of Africa and asked him to tell her about the landscape.

"The planet Earth has six continents rising from restless oceans," he said, as they stood outside the restaurant in the nippy March wind. His hand slid from the back of her neck, along her spine to her waist. She held her breath. "Of these Africa is most prominent; it separates two oceans, spreads north and south, through two hemispheres . . ." It was as though he was reciting a poem. He guided her along Spadina, both of them full on soup, rice, barbecued duck, stir-fried watercress, and abalone with cashews. He insisted upon walking her home and, on the way, at her entreaty, he told stories that gave in to her fantasies of Africa's beauty.

She found herself staring at his chin as he spoke, and when he caught her eye, she would look away, still mindful of her father's warnings about strangers. Kola smiled and stared straight ahead, each of them wilfully not looking at the other, allowing the recognition to thicken and knowing that they had already begun to trust one another like they had trusted no one else before.

When they reached her front door, he prolonged their conversation, telling her about being in the bush.

"A medicine man in my ancestors' times met David Livingstone. The medicine man had been impressed at first with the English doctor and told my ancestor about a conversation the two of them had. Although both Livingstone and the medicine man believed it was God who made the rain, the difference was that the medicine man prayed to him through medicines.

" 'We can pray to God in His name alone, and not by means of medicines,' Livingstone said.

" 'God told my people differently,' replied the medicine man. 'He made black men first, and He did not love us as He did the white man. He made you beautiful, and He gave you clothing, and guns and gunpowder, but God has given us one little thing, which you know nothing of. He has given us the knowledge of certain medicines by which we can make rain. We do not dispute those things you possess, though we are ignorant of them. You ought not to despise our little knowledge, of which you are ignorant.'

"Livingstone said he did not despise what he was ignorant of, but that he thought the medicine man was mistaken in his belief that medicines could influence the rain at all.

" 'That's just the way people speak when they talk on a subject of which they have no knowledge,' the medicine man said.

" 'God alone can command the clouds. Only try and wait patiently: God will give us rain without your medicines,' countered Livingstone.

"The medicine man became irritated with Livingstone, and waved him off. 'Until this morning, I thought white men were wise. Whoever thought of making a trial of starvation? Is death pleasant, then?' And he left Livingstone to answer the wind."

When Kola finished his story, he looked slightly embarrassed, then made light of it by telling her that when he was a boy he had prayed for rain, but it had never come in response to his prayers. He inherited a lust for rain, crops, and glistening leaves. "But they don't always come. It's not safe to believe too much in anything," he said.

In that moment the only thing Victoria believed in was him.

He kissed her hand, slid her key through the lock, and opened the door for her, guiding her through, but remaining outside. He asked her to meet him the next day, at the same restaurant, and she agreed. She climbed up the stairs to her sparse room and crawled under the covers, shivering from the long walk home, but tingling from the touch of Kola. She knew then that she had come to Toronto for a reason, not just to freeze in the icy air and stares of strangers. She'd found the truth she'd never been able to find in Kitty.

Kola met her the next day, and that evening after supper he walked her home again, but on the way there he stopped near a park and began a call that sounded like a wounded animal. She stood staring at him as the noise grew into a howl in the night. When he stopped, he said: "My friends taught me that. They used it in the detention camps to talk to one another." Victoria could not respond, but it was a sound that stayed with her.

He continued to meet her, night after night, and she eventually took a job washing dishes in his friend's restaurant. She learned the food of Kenya, the spices of Ethiopia, and the palm wine of Nigeria, which loosened her like a rattling pane in a large window. The window looked out onto a vast continent that was neither hers nor his anymore, merely a promise in and of itself.

For six years, she and Kola ate the finest foods of many cultures. They read, talked, and fantasized about a life with more money. Victoria told him she'd take him to Barbados when she got rich. He promised to build them a house of their own, somewhere warm. And for six years she felt protected. His hands would roam over her with a fiery touch, and she would feel like revolution itself. On the nights she stayed at his apartment on Bloor Street, she would wake in the morning to the smell of stew: strange mixtures of beef and banana; chili, fish, and coconut; spinach with groundnut sauce. And more bananas, which Kola made into matoke and would eat as though it were chocolate. A simple dish of steamed plantain, mashed, then drowned in salt, it aroused immense pleasure in this tall, elegant man who looked like he'd been fed on the finest food in all civilization. Something from his boyhood lived in that banana. Then one morning he was not there. Nothing missing, nothing moved. Just the absence of Kola.

God, the day has gone! How long has she been sitting here?

Victoria looks around. She can make out a speck of blue coat disappearing along Shaftesbury Avenue. Where does the Bluebird go when the sun sinks? A new crop of waiters now surrounds Eros. She stands up quickly, shaken by the freshness of the past. It takes her a few moments to readjust to London.

What time is it! Shite, the boy!

Derek has counted to 2,421. He paces back and forth in front of the school, his thoughts blurred with castles and cliffs and the ringing bells of a medieval war. He has returned to his castle, and quickly dismounted from his horse. This is the fortress where it all began. Derek is inside the moment when he slew the crystal dragon in the name of Guenevere and ruined everything. The dragon is dead, the pepperpot is spilled and soiling the floor, and his mother is scolding him about killing everything. Then she never returns.

The sun is much lower in the sky than when school was first let out. The other children have either been collected or walked the short distance to their homes. Derek has tried that. When he didn't see his aunt waiting for him, he assumed—though she hadn't formally announced it—that today was meant to be the beginning of his independence. He walked towards the street he thought would lead him to Blenheim Terrace, but the houses were unfamiliar, the cross street completely different from the one he'd expected. He tried the opposite direction but, there too, could find no road called Blenheim. Always moving in the wrong direction, it seemed, he made his way into the surrounding neighbourhood and circled the school, staying on this side of Finchley Road, but not finding his path home. Panicked, he thought it best to find the school again and start over. Now he's given up. He is pacing in front of the school trying not to believe that his aunt too has left him. He's sure he hasn't done anything wrong recently. He can't think of anything that would make her decide not to pick him up anymore. Perhaps he only has to think bad thoughts for there to be killing.

Or perhaps a lie is enough to kill.

"You comin' over tomorrow, Kanaima boy?" asked Richard Lorry at recess.

"Don't know," Derek said, shuffling his feet, trying to take the timidity out of his voice before saying anything else.

"We're watchin' *The Butcher Boy*—a kid who hacks up a whole family."

"Don't know," said Derek.

"What, you scared?" Richard asked, narrowing his eyes and stepping closer.

Derek wondered why it was that Richard the Truck was always going on about being scared. He wasn't sure if Richard liked being scared or if he was so afraid of being scared that he had become obsessed with the idea.

"No," Derek answered casually. He was trying a new tactic. He had seen Richard trying to tax a ten-year-old, who laughed at him and walked away. Richard had looked humiliated. "Of course not," Derek added.

That had been the lie. Derek *was* scared. Scared of having to tell his Auntie Vic another fib that would summon the Kanaima. Trouble, trouble, trouble. That's what life would be like from now on.

As he stands in the dark counting, two thousand, four hundred, and forty-two . . . his head hurts. He places his satchel on the ground and bends to open it, hoping to find something there to absorb him.

"Derek, darlin', I'm so sorry . . ."

He lifts his head up from the satchel to see the sweat-beaded face of his aunt—her eyes like a sad Siamese cat's as she holds out her hand. She grabs his shoulders with her fingers and pulls him up toward her, wrapping her arms around him and pushing his head into the soft fleshy space just below her breasts. Stroking his hair from his crown to his neck, she lets out breath that sounds like a sob, but Derek is revelling in the baked-bread smell of his auntie's clothing. Tears come, and he wants to say her name, wants to say Hi Auntie Vic, oh Auntie Vic, but all that his choked throat allows is,

"Mum . . ."

CHAPTER SIX

Bread

She punches hard. Smack, with her knuckles, then smack again. Victoria folds the dough, forcing it to take shape, commanding it, yet her fingers are full of respect. *Bread is devotion . . .*

Devotion takes needing and kneading, and it takes hands—hands like hers that are thick and enabling. Not long, piano-playing fingers like Lenny's—which are much better with fine pastry—but thick palms that take hold of stubborn bread dough.

She thinks Derek should know about the bread she makes every day. He spent the summer mostly in front of the computer, growing like a good idea. Some mornings he'd meet his classmate, Rory, who also lives on the Terrace, to kick a football about in the street with Rory's older brother and his friends. But Derek would start to feel ignored by the older boys, return home before noon, climb the stairs in a surly mood, and talk to her differently, mimicking Rory's brother's street-cred accent. For the duration of the afternoon and evening he'd be aggressive and uncommunicative, but by morning the Derek she knew would return, thanks to forgetful sleep.

She punches the dough again. *Bread is daily . . .*

Lenny is a saint. In July he took them on holiday to Wales, and he's insisted on sending Derek back to the Royal Academy summer music school. But this year Derek was not as keen, since Kendra has moved on to the flute and is attending classes every

Saturday throughout the school year, while he is still struggling with the recorder.

Victoria checks her list: she needs to make six more egg bread and ten organic spelt loaves before seven. She checks her watch and looks at her accomplishments: the shapes, sizes, the dizzying knots, braids, and ovals. Who eats all this bread? Who needs all this bread? Victoria Layne kneads bread. This evening she'll come back to prepare for tomorrow's orders. She'll bring Derek. She doesn't like him staying at home in the evenings, or going to Stephen's house, where she knows there's no adult at home until late.

She pats the belly of dough on the counter, sprinkles flour on the board, then picks up the risen mound and places it on the flour. Her final punch releases the yeasted air, the smell she loves. *Bread is love. . . .* A warm wind rattles the windowpane over the sink. October tomorrow. October's a puffy, ready month. Full of change. She pulls at the dough, drawing out strands, crossing them over one another. The summer was full of orders for special events, music festivals, the Henley Regatta; now orders are streaming in from grocers and corner shops throughout North London. Victoria's daily act of devotion is triumphant. She has more money than ever before, and life is backing her up like a chorus.

"Lenny, pass me that pan, love."

"Right, Vic," and he scurries across the kitchen towards her with the pan. He doesn't look her in the eye.

"You OK?"

"Why d'ya ask?"

"You seem a little distant," she ventures, knowing she's about to step onto emotional ground, sacred territory in the kingdom of Lenny. Englishmen know their territory, she thinks. She remembers asking her Asian friend, Carrie, at the hospital, what it was about English men that made them so guarded. Carrie—the same woman who had told her about Prince Albert's substantive member—responded with a dismissive wave, and "Football."

"Football?"

"You see football? Don't knock football. I feel for them. Football? That's how they love."

Lenny is not a football fan, but Victoria knows there is something strategic about getting into this territory that she has still not mastered. She risks it: "I mean, like there's something bothering you."

"Funny you should notice," he says coldly.

Here we go, she thinks, and tucks the skirt of dough around the dough belly to make a tidy knot. She thumps the loaf into the floured pan before they really get on with it.

"Of course I noticed, Len. Not that bad, am I?"

Len is silent as he unwraps the third pound of butter, which he spills into the mixing vat.

"You don't come by much anymore."

This is what she's been expecting. She wipes her hands on her apron.

"And when you do, you're not really very . . . present . . . except that one time on holiday this summer . . . not like we used to . . . I feel . . ." And those two words, *I feel*—like an Englishman's kryptonite—start to weaken him.

"Len—"

"I feel . . . like you're not interested, really."

"But I am interested, Len. I've just had a lot to do, with the boy. Everyday—"

"The boy gets you everyday, yes, I'm not asking for that . . ."

"What then?"

"Just a bit of loving, like we used to have, I guess."

The skin along her neck prickles and the tiny hairs stand rigid. She feels as if she's been split in two, with one half progressively shrinking over the past twenty months. The half that used to rise to Lenny's touches, the slow and gentle loving that arrived as effortlessly as sleep at the end of the day—that half of her is now distinctly diminished.

She pulls another portion of dough onto the flour-sprinkled counter. She kneads the dough. *Our bodies knead; our bodies need . . .*

"I've not much room for that since the boy came, that's all." She can't lie to him. Too much of her brain has been filled with images of Derek absent-mindedly walking out into the street, not seeing a bus, or Derek falling, cutting himself, or Derek being kidnapped in a crowd.

Lenny looks blankly at the bowl of butter he will cut into the sifted flour in the vat. Victoria knows what she should do, knows all the cooing words that would make him feel better, but she can't say them. Even her lips have the fatigue of Derek on them, the strain of questions posed so delicately as to not make the boy's face erupt in fear. Each month is a step forward, but she's still disappointed in herself for not as yet imparting anything like knowledge to the boy. She wants to tell him things she's learned in all her years—the key to getting by, the importance of principles—but talking to him has not been easy. He is less and less like the delicate newt who arrived almost two years ago, but still some days she sees in him a scared, fragile creature trapped in sand that doesn't match its skin.

Every day there's something new to worry about. Yesterday she read that plastics in the environment are acting like hormones, creating lower sperm counts for boys—some males not dropping testicles at all, or not until they're thirteen or fourteen. Girls are becoming women before they're ten. Imagine: because of that Tesco's bag and this tub of lard we are losing our men. She sets the loaf aside to rise.

"Len, on the tube on the way here, a ghoulish-looking toxic bloke, middle-aged and bloated, was sitting across from me, holding his overcoat over his lap. A young woman sits down beside him—maybe twenty-five and unaware of anything but her own life. And here is this bloke with his coat over his lap and his hand under his coat and all the while he's looking sideways at her and I see movement under his coat and he's rubbing himself thinking no one can notice, but I notice. I watch for a while to see how long he'll go on, and he does, slipping her a glance or a sniff from time to time and still rubbing. I look about the carriage to see if anyone else has seen this, but they haven't, or they're ignoring it, because, Christ, I'm thinking, if we let sex out in the open then we'd really have to deal with one another, wouldn't we, but we keep it in our heads because it's too powerful. Anyway, no one else in the car was paying attention. So I get up and go over to the girl and say, 'Miss, look, I hate to ask you to get up, but this man here is getting his jollies sitting beside you, and I figure if I sit beside him it might just be too much of a challenge for his pathetic imagination.' The girl looks stunned, at me, then at the man, and she doesn't know what to think. I nudge her leg and say, 'You move along now,' and she does. I sit down next to the ghoul, who won't look at me, just pretends he didn't hear what was going on. And I say to him, 'Look, I think you'd better save that for home.' And still he doesn't look at me, but he gets off at the next stop." She wipes her hands on her apron. "It took the life out of me, that did." She looks at Lenny, hoping he has understood.

And he has. He looks at her with the same look he did that first day in Waitrose years ago. It's full of the kind of love she recognizes. Otherworldly love. In this world, Lenny and Victoria share truly little. Not history, not family, not culture, not likes and dislikes, just this small corner of understanding, where they both feel safe. She wishes she could give him more of her other parts.

Henry VIII changed matrimony. He petitioned for a divorce from Catherine of Aragon on the basis that the marriage was incestuous. Catherine had been married to his elder brother. This changed all of England.

Derek knows better than to call it Inkland anymore.

They have been studying English history, and Mr. Straw, his new teacher, explained the story of Henry VIII and then asked the class to write a composition. Derek had to search the dictionary for the meaning of incestuous, and now he is smug with the power of the word and his ability to use it well. He loves compositions. Sometimes he likes what happens in his compositions a lot more than what happens in real life. Mr. Straw talked about English kings and where they come from. He told the class that Prince Charles can trace three thousand distinct lines of descent from Edward III, who lived between 1312 and 1377. From the way Mr. Straw talked about bloodlines, though, Derek also understood that Prince Charles has a direct link to Muhammad, through Edward III's son, the Black Prince, Edward of Wales, whose mother had Moorish blood. Trace one's lineage back far enough and it will, inevitably, merge with all the others.

Derek is fascinated by this fact, imagining that everyone in his class is on a branch of the same huge tree—did Mr. Straw call it a *peditree?*—which links all ancestors: William the Conqueror, Tutankhamen, Confucius. The whole western world is somehow linked to the Emperor Nero, and couldn't it be possible then that if King Arthur did exist—even though Stephen says he didn't—that Derek is his heir?

Derek wants to write and write and to tell everyone who reads his composition about the fact that Henry's divorce changed England. Before it, people married their close cousins. If Derek had a cousin, he would not marry her because then all the branches in the *peditree* would take a longer time to cross and he would not have children who were related to Arthur or William the Conqueror.

And his father? Which tree did he belong to? The one with William the Conqueror and Henry VIII or the one with Confucius? His mother never did tell him the secret. *One day I'll tell you the secret your father wanted me to tell you, but not until you're old enough.* Derek is sure he is old enough, but now he will never know. The secret is floating somewhere, untold.

He is happy to be back at school. His aunt says he has strained his eyes playing at the computer. But he sees everything.

For their summer holiday, Lenny took him and Auntie Vic to Wales. When Derek heard where they were going, he didn't want to admit that he was hoping its main attraction would be just that: whales. But just in time, before he said anything to sound foolish, they crossed over the bridge from England and Lenny declared they were now in the land of foreigners, and that the word Wales came from an Anglo-Saxon word meaning "outsiders." Derek caught sight of the Welsh flag of the Red Dragon flapping in the breeze and felt a rush of apprehension, but Lenny seemed so happy to be out of London that Derek pushed aside his doubts. Lenny announced that they were on holiday from too much bread, too many pastries, and too many tarts, and that they were here to eat the fruits of the sea. They drove through Pembrokeshire and arrived in a town called Fishguard. Derek was not so daft as to ask if it was lined with fish in helmets, armour, and holding muskets, but he did wonder whether perhaps the name meant that the town was actually guarded *from* fish.

"It's good to live where there's a tide," his aunt said, as he'd heard her say before. As their car pulled into the public parking lot, her eyes searched the coastline. Lenny led them to a restaurant he called the Best in Town. He walked so quickly Derek had to push himself to keep up, because he wanted to ask Len about the road signs in Wales and why they were impossible to read.

"Is it true that a woman with a pitchfork stopped the French from taking over Wales, and that was the last invasion Britain ever had?"

"What?" asked Lenny, at least slowing down so that Derek could catch up.

"A boy in my class said so, and the teacher said he was wrong, that it wasn't exactly like that, and that history books tell all sorts of different stories and he should make sure what was a story and what was history . . ." and then Derek ran out of breath from walking too quickly.

Lenny stopped, drawing Derek to his side, while Auntie Vic kept walking towards town. "It's a good thing to read a lot of books, you know, but there's a saying, History is written by the winners, and that's also a good thing to keep in mind," said Lenny, gently, with the little smile Derek likes.

When they sat down for lunch, Lenny and Derek ordered lobster, while Auntie Vic ordered halibut, because she doesn't trust lobster.

"Len, that thing's like a scavenger, feeds on waste at the bottom of the sea," Auntie Vic said just as he was about to suck flesh out of a pincer.

"Vicky, I don't care. Tastes good to me, and with this little bit of help"—he dipped the white, pink-rimmed flesh into the garlic butter beside his plate— "it's all the more tasty . . . like the inside of a certain arm I know," he said mischievously, and then cringed as if he was expecting a smack. He got one, on his shoulder, then Auntie Vic flaked a morsel of halibut with her fork and ate it delicately. Derek happily sucked the flesh from the spidery legs and the large pincers of his lobster.

That night his tummy erupted. Lying in the fold-out single bed in the hotel room, with Auntie Vic and Lenny in the double bed near the window, he tried not to moan. Doubled over, he tossed about on the tiny bed, breathing heavily. But when he heard rustling in the bed beside him, and sharp intakes of breath, he held his own. Raising his head, he saw the silhouette of his aunt, her jiggling flesh and her bosom floating above Lenny like a balloon over a basket. Lenny put his mouth on the breast and began to suck. Derek lowered his head and burrowed it under the pillow, trying to release the vision from his mind. Eventually he fell asleep again.

During the rest of their holiday, the three of them explored beaches, and Derek collected flotsam along the rocks and hunted for adders along the coastal path. At night, he made sure to get to bed first, long before Vic and Lenny, and he refused to eat lobster again, even though Lenny ordered it at almost every meal.

School is a relief.

Kendra is not in his class again this year, but each day he waits until the final bell rings at the start of classes to see her rushing in from the street. She is always late. He likes to watch her black hair fly as she takes the stairs three at a time. Stephen spends his recesses with Kendra, and Derek tags along behind. But he is still shy in her company, and the only thing he can think of to talk to her about is music classes. Even there he isn't in her league.

Kendra knows everything, and she has everything even a boy might need. She gets so many things, Derek thinks, on account of Christine. Kendra told Stephen that her father is always trying to keep up with Christine because she's ten years younger than him. She works at Shell as an accountant, but somehow she seems to know everything about the latest things to eat, buy, and do. Christine is on the pulse of things, Kendra says, then rolls her eyes. Kendra is rarely picked up after school by her father, but when he does meet her he always has a gift for her, a computer game or electronic gadget that is at the cutting edge of technology. Kendra is the best-wired girl in the school.

Derek envies her, but he has all the books he can borrow from school and the Swiss Cottage library, in addition to his favourite Camelot websites and the comics he gets from Lenny. And he has Stephen to talk to, and Richard Lorry to consult on all things evil.

"Poke the eye out of an owl and you get the strength of a giant," Richard told the boys casually one afternoon as they made their

way from school to the corner shop where they regularly buy
Coke and crisps, and where Richard always tries, but never suc-
ceeds, to buy cigarettes.

"You've done that?" Rory asked as they loitered outside the
shop until they had to go home.

"Sure, course, what d'ya think?" Richard answered.

He was putting one over on them, but Rory was new to the
group and frightened of putting a foot wrong. As for the others, it
was their habit to go along with things, just as they went along with
Derek's exemption from harassment over his aunt. They were
used to the fact that she still came to fetch him most afternoons,
while they would walk home together along Finchley Road.

Derek never feels wholly a member of the group except when
they want him to tell them stories about the Kanaima. He knows
nothing more about the Kanaima than his aunt told him that night
more than a year ago, but now he invents things: stories about
Kanaima who have taken friends of his at a young age, or narratives
of Kanaima coming to London. He writes them into the computer,
prints them out, memorizes them, and recites them to the boys at
recess and lunchtime, if they ask him. So, yes, at the end of this first
school week, Derek is happy. This afternoon he is working on his
multiplication tables and has come across an interesting problem:

> *Twenty-nine Navajo volunteers during World War II turned their*
> *native language into a secret code that allowed Marine commanders to*
> *issue reports and orders and to co-ordinate complex operations.*
> *Although the best Japanese code crackers broke U.S. Army, Navy, and*
> *Air Corps codes, they were never able to break the Marine Navajo code.*
> *Devise your own code, using multiples of nine as representations. E.g.,*
> *1=A, 9=B, 18=C, 27=D. Write an urgent message to a classmate.*

He has never been particularly good at maths, but he likes the
problems with words in them. He's tempted to make the story
longer, to write about a Navajo warrior who crosses the Atlantic

to bring the secrets of his language to the British code makers, but he knows he doesn't have enough time.

As he devises multiples of nine for words with T and W in them, perspiration starts to bead along his hairline and the outline of his birthmark. It's hot in the classroom, with the last day of September clinging to the breast of summer.

Other people's choices. What are we to do with them? Victoria flicks a knob on the radio by the sink and the news that a farmer in Norfolk shot and killed an intruder is trapped abruptly in silence. The man believed he was being burgled, but the intruder turned out to be the man's cousin, paying a surprise visit after many years. Sometimes she can't bear to listen to the news. As much as she tries to hear it out to the end, the actions of people frustrate her. Other people's choices must be God, she thinks. No better evidence. I am God, he is God, we are God. And action is our evidence. That's why it always hurts to believe in something. Someone else's belief inevitably gets in the way.

She washes up the last of the breakfast dishes, then wanders into her room.

"Derek, love, can't you think of anything better to do with your Saturday than stare at that screen? We're going to have your eyes checked."

What does a boy need to be doing?

"But, I'm doing work, Auntie Vic."

"What kind of work?"

"For a composition."

She is suspicious of the tone in his voice. Glancing over at the screen she sees pictures of ghouls, weapons, and castles. "And what kind of composition would that be, Derek?" He doesn't answer immediately. "What kind of composition could you be writing about beasts that don't exist, knights who fight all day and never eat, and wizards who live alone with their magic?" She teases him, knowing it's the boy's favourite site. But he still does not answer her. "Derek?"

"Auntie Vic, you wouldn't understand."

Now she's vexed. "Answer my question, young man." He blubbers suddenly and it's true, she doesn't understand. "Boy, what's in you?" Her heart sinks as once again she feels this isn't the right way to speak to him. She holds his shoulders and turns him towards her.

"But Auntie Vic . . . you . . ."

"I do understand. I do, tell me. What is the composition about?"

"Gwen," he spits out with a ring of defiance.

She is chastened. She looks for Gwen's features in his face, but they appear only in his nose and lips. What holds the boy's features together is the genetic glue of a stranger. Maybe he too has a rabbit blemish, and maybe one day on the street he and Derek will recognize one another for being marked with the same trapped wildness.

"Come on, Derek." She pulls the chair back and grabs his hand. "Let's go. We could both use a bit of airing out."

The sun is bright as they emerge from the station at Dalston Kingsland and walk towards the Dalston Market. The boy needs a taste of home. She plans to buy black-eyed peas, weerie peppers, cassava bread, and casareep, in order to make some spiced chicken, peas and rice, perhaps even a pepperpot.

Victoria and Derek inch along, zig-zagging through shoppers whose bags press against Derek's ribs. She reaches for his hand and grips it tightly as she takes in the smells, along with the sounds that tinkle like bangles. The array of faces is so different from those in St. John's Wood. Here humanity seems as mixed up as stew. The stalls of fruit, grains, and vegetables are rickety yet imposing, as each vies for shoppers' attention. Swashes of colourful silk and cotton are pinned to posts, and the fabrics can-can in the breeze. Victoria feels a rush of celebration.

Markets comfort her. The bustle, the smells, the chatter, the red, green, and brown layers of offerings. But London doesn't make much of its markets, in that English way of hiding the good things. Don't flaunt the food, because there's pleasure there. Hide the lettuce that unfolds like lips between a woman's legs. Hide the bulging, ripe tomatoes filled with seed. Hide all reminders of desire in plastic packaging, neutralizing it. This market is slightly better, with its blend of pleasure and utility. She picks up a thick plantain and holds it, weighing it, feeling its firmness and breadth in her fist, rubbing her palm along it. She hands it to the vendor and takes out her change purse. Farmers need to have a good sense of humour, she thinks.

As they walk along, she notices the contrast between stalls, each with its own character, displaying specialties from various islands, Africa, and India. England's an odd place, she thinks, with all its potential for bounty and yet an adherence to restraint and inequality that holds it back. With all the rain, all the promise in the long days of June, why shouldn't this imported produce grow here? Not only cows and sheep can survive this climate. And not only residents of South Kensington or Hampstead with their posh-nosh delis and delicacies from Spain, Italy, or New York should be able to sample the sensations on the lip and tongue that blaze with the glory of the earth. It would take just a little imagination, she's sure, for the food in these British Isles to be celebrated in every neighbourhood of London. Destroy the supermarkets. A farmer's market on every high street would do. In markets you can touch and smell from one season to the next. You can look a farmer in the eye as he hands you what he first touched as a seed. She stops in front of a vegetable stall and examines the lettuce.

"Is this price because it's grown here or far away?" she asks the vendor as she holds up a head of romaine lettuce she knows is more expensive than at her local Waitrose. Asking the question she's aware of her tone, the subtle irritation beneath her words.

"What do you mean?" the stocky black man asks defensively.

"I'm not complaining, really, I'm not. Just a question. Where's it from? England? Israel?"

The bald vendor takes her in with his eyes. His raised eyebrows and slow grin are almost an insult. He can't be from the Caribbean, Victoria thinks, because his mockery would have been more immediate, more obvious at this point, while this man has the slow defiance of Kola. He doesn't answer her, just holds the grin there for her to absorb.

"It's not that I want it to be cheap," she continues. The man looks confused. She isn't able to put into words her theory on distribution or explain to him that she'd be willing to pay more to the person who grew this if she knew him. Children need the best—

"What do you want then? Lettuce, or caviar. I have no caviar," he says, now annoyed at her.

"I'm sorry. I just thought you'd know. I'll take this one," and she pays him. He slips the romaine into a bag and hands it to her. She passes the bag to Derek and puts her temper back into its compartment for the time being. But the dissatisfaction remains. She can hear Kola now: "Organic? Everything is organic in Africa, we can't afford pesticides." Food is personal. In many African traditions, he told her, the cook herself places it in your mouth. It's an offering of communion. Of trust.

She turns, sensing trouble. *Dear Victoria: It's me,* was how the letter started, and on it went, but after years of silence from him as her life numbly trundled on, these four words sparked and brought her to London. The rest of the letter she brushed aside, firm in her belief that if she just had him again everything would be all right. *They said I was guilty* . . . But the only one who was guilty was Victoria, for believing that one person could fulfill another person's life. She's suddenly fatigued by the thought of Kola. She should know better. She doesn't need his words to confirm for her that life contains death the way a mango contains a pit. What's the point of all the theories, all the tiny futile acts that are meant to make life more equitable?

Mangoes. Rows and rows in a stall up ahead. She will make a pie.

Victoria guides Derek by the shoulders through the press of bodies in the aisle. The singsong of language comes from all directions. "How much nuisance ya tink a man can handle . . . I put she out!" The man laughs. Another voice jumps in, "But she neva wanted to come in, Joseph, that's where ya missed ya mark." Does the boy feel better now? She looks down at his stunned face. Must be the crowd. He's not one for a lot of people around him. He likes to be by himself most of the time.

"Derek, you fancy some cook-up rice or something different tonight?"

"Curry, Auntie. Curry," and his eyes brighten. She holds his collar and gently tugs him towards an Indian spice shop.

"We'll make one like Granny's," she says as they enter.

The shop is lined with open bins of cumin, turmeric, curry powder, masala, barrels of channa, and rows of pepper. A woman behind the counter is wrapping samosas for a man wearing a long butcher's apron. In the far corner of the shop two young men in leather jackets stand idly, looking out of place. They make a show of shopping for spices but look like lads who've never cooked a meal in their lives. A few words are exchanged, then the man with the chains looping along the breast panel of his jacket leaves the shop. The better-groomed of the two stands looking awkwardly at cans of lentils. Derek saunters down the aisle and the man nods casually in his direction. Victoria tries to keep an eye on her nephew as she ladles turmeric into a plastic bag, twist-ties it, then moves on to the cumin. When she looks up again, Derek is holding out a can towards the man. She catches only a few words of the conversation; Derek is saying something about lychees.

"Good, good, that's a good reason," replies the man.

"Derek," she calls. He turns around, puts the can back on the shelf, and joins her at the cash.

"Can I have one of those?" he asks, pointing to the samosas.

"Hmm," Victoria hesitates, thinking of the batter, but then

remembers the mysterious composition he was writing at the computer before they left. "Of course," she says, and nods at the cashier, who puts one in a bag for him.

As they leave the shop, Victoria notices the leather-jacketed man with the looping chains waiting on the street corner. She reaches for Derek's hand, but he pulls it back. The man has black hair, shaved short with a tuft of cowlick at the front like a salute. His eyes dart down the street. Victoria wonders if the jackets make the men feel protected from the warmth everyone else is basking in. The other man comes out of the shop. Both of them appear to check their watches. Victoria takes the samosa out of the bag and gives it to Derek, who bites into it as if into knowledge. She keeps her eyes on the men in leather, who have reconvened across the road and are looking about like anxious birds. A thought flashes across her mind—They believe in something—then it disappears, as she turns her attention to Derek.

"Had enough shopping now?" she asks, feeling a slow churning in her belly.

A third man, tall, with a trimmed beard and wearing a suit, joins the two on the corner. Very quickly the three of them turn and sprint off.

"What about some tamarind candies, or plantain chips, Auntie— or, better make that tamarind candies AND plantain chips," Derek says, full of pleasure as he moves off quickly ahead of her.

"Well . . ." The churn in her belly becomes more pronounced as the air cradles them in something unavoidable. Kola. . . . Suddenly the air has become dense with the souls of lions and snakes and monkeys—all the animals in the space in between life and death, the arena of transformation where some souls get caught. She can feel it approaching. And then, as only her gut knows to expect—

Ripping glass, exploding brick, metal and wood crashing onto concrete, and she is face down on the pavement staring into a quivering fleck of aluminium so silver she thinks at first it is mercury. Her eyes slither over it. Then another blast, farther off, or maybe it seems so only because her ears feel as though they have filled with blood and sounds are not penetrating. She tries to push herself up. The boy! But her arm doesn't accept her weight. The sounds blur and become like the weak buzz on an electric alarm clock. She has to find the boy. When she musters the strength to roll over on her back, all she can see is smoke and someone's bleeding leg beside her. A grown-up leg, not the boy's, thank God. The billowy smoke above her looks like puffy clouds, a cliché of heaven. She feels a sharp pain along her leg, and when she touches the sticky flow of blood around the shard of metal lodged above her knee, she's relieved she has feeling. Death isn't with her yet.

She sits up and looks about. The first thing she sees is mangled metal that was once a car. Then shattered glass, strewn paper, and dishevelled cloth. Yellow. Everything is covered in yellow powder. Exploded heads of yellow lettuce and yellow-powdered beans, yellow-powdered tomatoes oozing their seedy flesh. Turmeric. The spices from the Indian shop have fallen over the market like morning dew, covering the pavement, the stalls, matting the hair of coughing, sputtering figures trying to stand up through the smoke. Someone comes towards her. Through a gurgling that feels as if blood is being pushed through her ears, she hears, "You're fine, you're fine, come, get up." She turns to find a tall dark man, his black hair streaked with red and yellow powder, holding her under the arm and pulling her up.

"Derek," she gasps, and then begins to weep because someone is there to hear her.

"Let's go this way," says the man, and he guides her slowly through the wreckage, as other people along the road pull themselves up to standing. A woman is screaming; a man is moaning loudly. Victoria and her companion walk around them. Victoria searches through the yellow dust on the faces of two children across the street, then just to their right she sees him.

Derek is trembling and apparently unhurt, looking about in amazement. Victoria's chest unclenches, but then she can feel the pain in her leg rush to her hip. She looks to the blood dripping from her knee to her shoe. Her dress is shredded along the side, and for a moment she is ashamed of her spotty, loose skin bared to the man who is holding her as they walk towards Derek. But now she knows just how much she wants this life, how awake she finally is again.

Sirens begin to wail.

The ring of the explosion is still in her ears and the two sounds together are almost unbearable. She limps over to Derek. Huddled up against the wall of the pub with their mother are the two children she spotted first. All of them are covered in powder.

"Derek!" she says loudly so that she can hear herself over the sirens and the gurgling. He looks up at her distrustfully, as though she's responsible for all this. And she is. She is responsible. She and the men in black leather and her daddy and the Bluebird of Piccadilly. All of them guilty of believing in something that has let them down and then turning it in on themselves.

I'm sorry, she says silently.

She pulls Derek to her by the hand and they limp toward an ambulance that has just arrived. "I don't need help," Victoria says, seeing others around her in far worse shape. The paramedics don't protest. One of them kneels beside a man whose arm appears to be missing. The young mother in white and her two children approach the paramedic, and she demands that they be taken out of the area. "Good God," she says, then grabs the paramedic's arm, begging him to take her home. The young Asian man drops Victoria's arm and takes the woman's, guiding her and the children towards a police constable.

Derek is shocked silent.

As the dust and smoke begin to settle, people in the street seem to slowly become aware of what has happened. A middle-aged Caribbean man starts to curse, but *fuck* turns shorter and more clipped each time he says it, until he's spitting *ks* as he cries over them. A shopkeeper in an apron stands over a young woman, helping her to her feet. A few people remain sitting on the ground, although they seem unhurt. Those who do stand do not move far from the spot where the blast left them. Everyone waits.

"I was flung, Auntie Vic, I went flying, but it didn't hurt. I'm not hurt," says Derek with a sudden frenzy.

A second constable approaches the people around Derek and Victoria.

"Did anyone see what happened? Anything that might help us?" the officer asks.

Victoria weighs her answer with the image of the two men in her head, and decides she has to say something. She leans to step forward, but her wound hinders her, so she stands still and raises her voice.

"I think I saw something," she says hesitantly. The constable approaches her. "The men I saw looked like they had things in them that had been stored up, for a long, long time," she says to the constable.

"Can you be more specific," he says dryly, writing something on his notepad.

"No, I can't," she says. The constable looks annoyed. As he's about to move off, she throws out the more concrete details of what she saw, the men's faces, their leather jackets, their discussion with the man in the suit and their flight a few seconds before the explosion. Then from the burst-open compartment of Kola's lessons, she adds, breathlessly: "People will always react to feeling wronged."

The constable doesn't look up, merely continues writing on his notepad. Derek watches her speak, and his shoulders relax, his chest lifts slightly as he steps forward to pre-empt anything more from his aunt and to tell the constable that one of the men talked to him. Questioned by the officer about what the man said, Derek has to tell the truth and not the exaggerated story he is already writing in his mind.

"Well, he asked me . . . well, it was only about the cans."

Victoria and the constable wait for his next words, hoping for a revelation.

"The cans?" the constable asks.

"Yes, he asked me what I would pick if I could have any of the cans on the shelf in front of us, and I chose a can of lychees."

"Why?" asks the constable.

Derek hesitates, wishing his answer had motive and intrigue, but he has to admit it was because it was the only thing among the rows of cans that looked sweet. The constable calmly takes notes, then considers them as he releases his fingers from around the pen and folds it into his fist. He tells Victoria and Derek that another officer will drive them where they need to go, but that they'll make a stop at the station, and be asked to provide a statement.

A policewoman holds Victoria's arm and guides her toward a car, where she and Derek get in the back seat beside the woman in white, her two children on her lap. Squeezed in with the others in the back seat of the police car, Victoria feels safer. "I can't believe it, I can't believe it, I can't believe it," the woman says, over and over and over. Nor can Victoria, but she keeps quiet for Derek's sake.

"Derek," she says simply, as she hugs him. He nods and keeps his eyes fixed on the other two children in the car—a black boy about five and his sister, who is slightly older. They cry quietly. Victoria wonders what Derek is seeing. Are they familiar, like a family he used to play with in Kitty?

The policewoman gets in the driver's seat, and a few moments later a male officer gets in on the passenger side. The car pulls away and inches around debris, heading away from the market. Victoria doesn't mention that her blood is soaking the upholstery of the back seat.

"We're taking you to the station, just around the corner. You'll be fine now," the male officer says. The young mother leans forward, around her little boy. Victoria notices that she has unusually green eyes for her dark skin.

"But what the hell happened? Who did this? Was it really a bomb?" she asks angrily.

"Can't say that for sure, yet," the officer answers.

"But you can, I know you can. You know, damn it. Don't you think you should be telling us?"

The two officers exchange an uneasy look.

"We're doing all we can to find out what happened, but we don't know anything more at the moment," the man says, turning around to look at his frightened passengers.

"You always say that. That's always the line, but you do know and you're just not saying . . . this bomb—"

"Now, dear," Victoria interrupts. She reaches across Derek to touch the young woman's leg. "I think with the young ones in the car we should be careful what we say, and we'll just have to see what happens when we can. Calm yourself now, for the sake of those two." The woman's eyes go narrow with spite, but she bites her lip as she's about to say something to Victoria.

When they reach the station they are helped out of the car, and Victoria notices that the woman is trembling. Victoria puts her hand on the woman's back, but she jumps and flashes shocked, hunted eyes at her.

"Shsssh, shssh . . ." Victoria tells her.

The woman clutches the children to her thigh. Inside, there are others, all in various states of ripped clothing, with yellow- and orange-powdered hair and faces. Victoria doesn't know why they're all there, but she sits down with Derek on a bench, amidst sobs and curses from a group of men who speculate on the explosion.

A short, fair-haired man spits on the floor, then continues his conversation with a black man in a striped shirt. The fair-haired man says a many-syllabled family name, which sounds South Asian, but Victoria can't make it out. The black man sucks his teeth. "We should have seen it comin'."

"You think it's them?" asks the fair-haired man.

"Every day it's comin', just like this. They'll never reconcile."

"The grandfather wouldn't be too pleased. Even back then he wanted it to stop, to change, you know?"

She wants Kola. Kola would know about the hope of change; he would know that bread and colours and scents are the only things that we can count on, and that change is often as slow as food to a hungry belly. But change can be fast, too, if it comes violently. Like it did for him.

"For the love of God, for the love of God," repeats the woman in white on the bench beside her.

"The police'll never get 'em," says the fair man. "And even if they do, won't matter. There's a whole brood—brothers, cousins—waiting to grow up and explode something else."

"For the love of God," the woman repeats.

Victoria looks at Derek, who is staring at the woman. She puts her arm around him and pulls him to her, but he resists and sits up straight. His birthmark is dusted with turmeric; it looks like fine rabbit fur. His eyes scan the room. There are things she wants to tell him now but still cannot. She sees his mind working at a hundred thoughts a second, all parallel and darting in that way he has, filing this scene into his brain, where the fear will act like yeast in bread, puffing itself out as sustenance.

But fear is empty. Kola is gone. Your mom is gone. You are alone. I am alone. Perhaps we have to believe in something to continue living at all. But God does not engage with you in belief, Derek. God is a syllable, a sound repeated over and over and over until there is meaning. And if there is no meaning then there is sound—a shrieking, glass-breaking sound that echoes in the universe like a howl, the lonely howl of a syllable without a word to attach itself to.

CHAPTER SEVEN

Blood

ᚱᚱᚱ

Dearest Victoria:

No, I didn't tell you. Yes, I am ashamed—not of the fact itself, but certainly of the fact that I withheld it from you. And that was only because I thought it would upset you. And now I ask you to forgive me, as I write this to explain.

Finally the noise on Bloor Street has been muffled by the snow. I am dressed in all the clothes I own, with a blanket over my shoulders, trying to get warm after my shift at the restaurant. (The draught through my window has not been reduced as much as I would have hoped by lining the glass with tape and cling-wrap.) I think the cold could kill me faster than any jail term.

In Nairobi I had a room half the size of this one, but I was never in it. Even when it was not safe in the street, I felt safer than I do outside now in this deep freeze. In Nairobi I would roam the streets and talk late into the night at the restaurant with my friends.

And my wife.

Yes, I had a wife for three years in Nairobi. Her name is Akinyi, and she was—still is—from the Luo people, but I am a Gikuyu. This means nothing to you, but for us it meant everything. Kenya was not a modern place when I left. We have dwelt on old tribal rivalries. (But is this any different from the rest of the world? Perhaps we are more modern than I know.) Akinyi and I married for love, but we came from long-warring tribes. Years ago, after a Luo government minister was assassinated in Nairobi by a Gikuyu man, things got worse, and the hatred between the two peoples escalated to the point that the ruling party forced every Gikuyu to take an oath swearing an allegiance to Kenyatta, his government, and Gikuyu rule. Those who resisted were threatened, beaten, and sometimes killed. I feared for my life—and now feel a coward for it—so I too took the oath, in which I pledged allegiance to Kenyatta and swore that I would not let the government leave the house of his people. This period was a shameful time for me, as I watched the Gikuyu rulers change, and many Luo arrested and detained without trial. Perhaps our marriage was our way of defying my oath and everything we thought was going wrong in Kenya.

For three years, our life was never peaceful. Our families made it difficult for us. The situation became impossible, as the Ogutu family and mine agreed on nothing. Akinyi and I did not divorce, but we agreed to go separate ways and be open to others. She moved to Miami, with an American lover. I had never loved anyone else, until I met you.

Akinyi and I met once again in Miami, as I was on my way here to Toronto, and she told me she wanted to have a child with me. I refused at first, then agreed, but then we quarrelled and did not meet again. We have not spoken since. I don't know if I made the right decision, but it was made.

I'm sorry. I was not lying. I was trying to spare you the unpleasantness. I have been guilty of this economical use of the truth before. I have a lot to learn about how to meet my past. Victoria, you walk in the street as though time is neither behind you nor ahead of you. The day I met you, time was suspended, and there was only the present. I have been looking for that in myself ever since.

I have no direction now that I'm here in Canada, and when the future arrives it will catch me off guard. Since I left Nairobi all I've done is restaurant work and listen to the sound of cars down in the street. I need to find something that's mine again. I'm restless to feel useful.

My friends and family have done brave things. I am not so brave or *sure of anything, but I need to discover what is in me. Perhaps that's what I have hidden. I'm sorry if I hurt you. I will tell you everything. Can I come home, to yours, tomorrow?*

All love,
Kola

Derek folds the letter up carefully, puts it back in its envelope, and slides it deep under the pile of others in his aunt's chest.

Kola had been in Miami. Derek knew there was something more to this man who writes like the passage of a slow and quiet train. Miami, he knows, is the key to his father. Derek has been reading letters from Victoria's chest for the last few months, sneaking a look while his aunt is in the loo or downstairs doing laundry. The ones on the bottom are from this man named Kola. Initially looking for letters from his mother, he came across Kola and has been slowly making his way through them at every chance he gets. But his aunt's eyes are seldom off him. Some days he feels he might splinter under her piercing stare.

Since last October, the bomb, their few hours at the police station, and the afternoon in the hospital to treat Auntie Vic's leg, Derek has felt smothered by his aunt's fears. That week, she kept him home from school for the entire five days, claiming to his teachers that he was in shock from witnessing the explosion. She, on the other hand, began to disappear in the middle of the day for hours at a time, leaving him alone. She'd return from Lenny's before he woke, make breakfast for him, leave it on the table, then call to him from his door, "I'll be back soon. You stay put today." She'd return late in the afternoon. When he asked her where she was going, she mumbled, "Just down the road, to deliver some food." He found out she had begun to make a daily pot of stew for the Kilburn Salvation Army Shelter, where she'd dish it out through the lunch hour to hungry men and women.

"Why are you doing that?" he asked her that weekend.

"Because I have to, Derek. To do something. It's all I can do."
She left it at that.

Throughout the autumn and winter terms, she's delivered him
to school every day, even though he knows his way around their
neighbourhood very well now. He rebelled against this over-
protectiveness, complaining to Sonia, Martin, and everyone who
would listen how unfair it was that he was the only boy in his year
who still wasn't allowed to walk to school with his friends. Lenny
came to dinner one evening, bearing a treat of real vanilla ice
cream, and Derek made a point of complaining just as his aunt
served their dessert. Derek stated his case to Lenny, then spooned
ice cream into his bowl, took another scoop, forgoing the black-
currant compote his aunt had prepared, and tried to hold back a
grin that she might have found smug. He handed her the scoop.

"Vic, that has to stop," Lenny said and put his hand on hers
before she could dollop the ice cream onto the compote. In a long-
held look, something between them acknowledged the common
sense in his words. Auntie Vic nodded, put the ice cream on the
blackcurrants, then gave the scoop back to Derek. She turned to
the counter to make tea.

The next day he walked to school by himself, but she still
insisted on meeting him at the end of the day, whether he walked
home with her or not. For Christmas she gave him a pager.

The bomb had the opposite effect on Derek. Nothing frightens
him now. And his contact with the alleged bomber, who has still
eluded the police, is the source of something private and nascent
in him, providing him with an unconscious awareness that one
day he is going to become a man.

Derek loved the bomb.

That night he watched television news reports that displayed
images of the shambolic yellow market. He looked for himself
among the faces of victims caught on camera, but was unable to
spot his form or that of his aunt. When the news reader declared
that there were many injuries but no deaths, his heart leapt at the

memory of the exploding glory he had felt beneath his feet. No deaths. Just the thought brings a rush to his chest; the coexistence of destruction and life provides a thrill he would not be able to articulate.

The addition into his life of the pager has also suited him well, in part because it impresses Richard the Truck. While most upper-year students have mobile phones—some from the harvests of swarming or taxing—only a few ten-year-olds in the school have them, and not another, as far as Derek knows, has a pager.

"The bomb's saved ya," said Kendra to him one day. It was a day of ballistic rain. Hard on the face, and close, like an insult. It was late January, and Kendra had run from the far end of the playground to where Derek sheltered from the rain under the large oak. The lunch bell had yet to call them back to class. "Richard thinks it's cool you were in that explosion, so do the other boys. The older boys don't give a toss about us, anyway," she said as she hugged her arms and jiggled up and down to offset the damp. Kendra was now quite a bit taller than Derek, and he had noticed earlier that week in the hallway that she was growing nubs at her chest.

Everyone knew about what happened to Victoria and Derek in the market, because Sonia had seen them being dropped off at the house and had noticed Victoria's limp. She asked Victoria for the complete story. Sonia told Rory's mother that her two lodgers had been caught up in the explosion. The newspapers reported that the police couldn't make sense of the attack: no political or terrorist group came forward to take responsibility, so speculation turned to the long-standing family and gang-related feuds in the area that might have incited the bomb. One of the tabloids even mentioned that one of the suspected bombers had talked to a child at the scene. The news spread through Derek's school and neighbourhood.

One morning the week following the incident, as Victoria and Derek neared the school, they heard the sound of clicking heels hurrying after them. Derek turned to find Kendra walking behind him, but the clicking came from Christine's pumps as she made her way enthusiastically towards Victoria.

"I heard . . . how horrid for you . . . you both seem fine . . . but is there anything I can do?"

His aunt stared, speechless, at the woman, and Derek was embarrassed for them both. Why wasn't Auntie Vic saying anything? What was the matter with her? Finally it was Kendra, mouth twisted in a sneer, who said to Christine: "Like what?"

"Alexander goes on about these crises . . . on and on . . . we don't witness them enough, he says . . ." and with that Christine noticed Kendra's icy stare and Victoria's blank face. A shadow seemed to pass across her own. Her cheeks drooped, and Derek felt sorry for her, although he couldn't have said why. "Whatever we could do . . ." she said, more quietly now, and Derek wondered why the woman was trying so hard.

His aunt muttered "Thank you," and Christine gave them all a quick wave and headed for the idling Volvo a little further up on the other side of the road. Derek followed his aunt's eyes to the car, where a muscular forearm and a rugged hand rested loosely on the top of the steering wheel.

Kendra stood silently by his side as they watched Christine and her father drive off, and from that moment Derek felt something new between them. When she turned up, months later, under the tree, he was no longer nervous in her presence. He wanted to tell her about Kola and the fact that his aunt had letters from a man who used to carry guns in Kenya.

Derek thinks that if Kola were here, he would be free, and his aunt would laugh more. Most of Kola's letters are not as serious as the one he has just finished reading; they are about everyday things, short notes with jokes and stories about his Kenyan friends in Toronto. Derek hasn't deciphered everything in the letters, but he wants to meet this man with coal skin who speaks of plots, assemblies of men with guns and explosives, and finally about escape. Perhaps there is a link to his father. Perhaps they have fought the same wrongdoers. Perhaps even Kola . . . What Derek needs to know is if Kola has ever been to Colombia. And, of course, there's the secret his mother promised. The slow-train man might know more. But Derek is afraid to mention him to his Auntie Vic; she'd know he had been snooping.

He bends down and peers into the chest again and pulls out a photograph of a tree weeping with the weight of snow. The person in the photo is barely recognizable in a bulky coat, scarf, and hat, but it must be his aunt. She looks young; her face, between the hat's brim and the scarf's striped panel, is radiant. Kola must be behind the camera, because his aunt looks happy.

He's startled by the sound of a voice coming through the fire door to the adjoining house. He gently closes the lid of the chest. Straining his ear to hear through the wall, he listens to the beautician talking on the telephone, in Slovakian. He likes the sound of the language, the consonants that cough into vowels as she describes something, then laughs. He listens for a moment longer, then returns to his room to wait for his aunt to come up from doing the laundry. He is waiting for her permission to play in the park with Stephen and Rory, who has just returned from his summer holiday. Before they left, Rory's mother regularly drove some of the boys to Regent's Park to play football or to take turns on Rory's skateboard. Yesterday Rory invited him to a cricket match, and Derek lit up at the thought of being included. Later, when he thought of Rory's tone of voice, he wondered if inviting him for cricket and not the other events was an attempt to tease him about his Caribbean background, but he didn't care, he wanted to be in the park.

"Can I go to the park to play cricket?" he asked Auntie Vic as she collected the sheets and towels to toss into the washing machine. She gave him a squinting, considering look. He tried to stare her down, feeling the light magic of the day. There was a tingling in his knees, like the need to run.

"I'm putting the laundry in. Give me a moment," she said, and went downstairs.

He hears her coming back up.

"Well?" he asks, hurrying to the door before she returns to her room.

"Well, what?" she asks, absent-mindedly.

"The park?"

"Oh, well, no. I want you to come with me to the shops, and maybe they could use an extra hand at the shelter."

"But why? I never get to!" he dares.

"You know I don't trust those boys—"

"But Auntie Vic, it's just a cricket game. Stephen and Rory from down the road and some other boys . . . not Richard," he adds for effect as he moves toward the kitchen. His voice carries through the house, down the stairs, like an unconscious cry for help, toward Martin and Sonia's flat. He knows they are sensitive to small cries. The twins, Max and Monica, are walking, almost talking, but mostly pointing and knocking things over. They cry for help when they spill something, and Sonia always comes to their rescue.

"The sun is shining," Derek adds in the direction of the stairs. Who could argue with the sun?

"The last time you played cricket, you came back from school with a cut knee and blood soaked into your trousers. I can't have that," says Victoria, putting the washing powder back in the hall cupboard.

He has been expecting this. "That was not proper cricket, on grass, that was at school and I grazed my knee on the pavement!"

"Still, I don't think so." She carries the laundry basket into her room.

Derek's throat feels itchy with the things he wants to say. So what if there was blood on his trousers? He learned in science class that every adult body contains about five litres of blood—half of it red cells, which, uniquely, have no DNA. Their genetic instructions are jettisoned as they develop. This is why, Stephen told him, if you get a blood transfusion you don't turn into the person whose blood has been injected into your veins. The red cells of a single person spread out flat would cover the area of a football pitch, two thousand times the surface area of the skin. Blood is the body's main defence. How is this possible, Derek wonders, when blood is the first thing to leave the body in an accident? And if his blood is not unique, why are people always making a fuss about blood ties and where their bloodlines run?

"My daddy played cricket, Auntie Vic," he lies, hoping the bluff will win him the advantage. He holds blood and kinship up like a sword.

"What? How would you know such a thing?"

"Because Mom told me," he says, but dragging the name of Guenevere into his lie does not seem right. "Do you know anyone who plays cricket?" he adds, hoping she will get distracted and say, Yes, a man I knew once, a man named Kola, who talked of having a son. . . . He was very good at cricket.

He sees his aunt's face tremble slightly, and then a decision floats darkly over it. He has no way of knowing that she's near the end of her tether. "Derek, boy, come and sit down in the comfy chair. I'll make you a treat," she says, trying to shake the dark mood that has gripped her for days now.

"I don't want a treat. I want to play cricket."

"No, you don't," she returns sternly.

How could she know? There she goes again, treating him like a baby, like a crawling, dribbling infant. "I'll do what I want," he says as he turns on his heels and heads down the stairs.

"You get your backside up here, young man," Victoria calls out, her Guyanese accent as thick as cassava. Her tone and the words "young man" stop his lanky form in its tracks. He's not yet skilled in defiance. As he turns to head back up the stairs, he spots Martin in his study. Martin gives him a wink and a nod, looking up from sorting the post on his desk. Martin's calm confidence gives Derek strength as he returns to his aunt's room.

"Now sit down and listen to me," Victoria says forcefully, the mood tugging again. He throws himself into the armchair by the window and, despite a slight trembling, tries to give his aunt attitude.

"This isn't fair," he mumbles into his shoulder.

From the door of her room, she can reach the kettle on the counter in the kitchen. Victoria pushes the button on. She tries to collect her thoughts, unable to shake the growing sense that some reckoning must take place. Derek is sure she's counting on the hot drink to subdue him. Something hot to scald his disobedient tongue, rush his throat to compliance. She stands near the door. He can sense her anxiety. It spurs him further into attitude. The kettle boils.

"What did your mom tell you about your daddy?" she asks, just as the kettle clicks off.

The truth, Derek thinks. She told him the truth, of course. He runs through the list of words, the flash of faces, the whiff of scents that are his father. In Guyana he would see a man lurking surreptitiously on the street and be sure it was his father looking for him. Masculine smells in the crowded market would make him think of someone he'd never known: the father that came with so little, just a story he'd ask his mother to repeat time and again. *Pursued by wrongdoers.* Tell me again, Mommy, how my daddy had to go away and hide in the bush. For years he didn't understand what pursued by wrongdoers had meant. His mother had told him the story in bed, late at night when he couldn't sleep. His father had been like a knight, had fought for the rights of poor people in Guyana, and had provoked the government to the point of endangering his own life. He had to go into hiding, leave his wife and baby, and go first into the bush to live with the Amerindians, and then to Brazil, and even farther still, to Colombia. He had to live in seclusion. Years later, just months before she died, his mother told Derek that his father would never come out of seclusion, that he would never see Derek again, but that the secret he had for his son could be revealed to him as soon as he was old enough to understand.

He was old enough now.

"Did she tell you who he was?" Victoria's voice hums like a bee over a delicate blossom.

"He is an important man," Derek answers, with certainty.

"Yes, I'm sure he is," she responds. She looks at him and waits for more.

"A revolutionary," he adds.

Victoria pauses. Things click into place. She suspected but never confirmed her suspicions. The lies—the stories—her sister told the boy about his father had come from Kola's life, adapted from the snippets of information in Victoria's letters from Toronto. "Of course," she says.

Derek reacts to the doubt in her voice. He turns to look out the window. She pulls out a chair from the table and turns it towards him, sits down.

"Did your mother tell you how you came to be, luv?"

The reckoning. Is this it? Now? She knows only that she can't hold back life much longer.

"What do you mean, came to be?" His tone is snarky now.

"How you came to be in this world, darling."

"You mean about babies?"

"No, I mean about you, about how she got you—"

"She got me from my daddy."

"Yes, she did, luv, but she never met your daddy." Her eyes go glimmery, as though she's about to cry.

This isn't fair, he thinks.

"Listen, Derek, there are many ways of having a baby these days. One of those ways is for a woman to go to a doctor and to ask that doctor to put the seed of a man inside her using a tube, not the man. The man gives his seed beforehand, and it's stored for women who don't want husbands."

Derek hates her. He hates everything she is and everything she's saying.

"What I'm saying is that your mom didn't know who your dad

was, but got advice from a doctor who told her the seed was good, and it is, we all can see that. You're a lovely boy, Derek, a lovely boy who will grow up to be a lovely man, if I can help it."

She stops as they both wonder where this is going. There is something more precise than fear between them now. Fear has metastasized into the pain making its way along its route to their hearts. Something is changing and neither Derek nor his aunt knows how to control it, let alone stop it.

Derek watches his Auntie Victoria the way a cow watches a man in a passing field. Alert but uncomprehending. He blinks.

"The point is, Derek, you don't have a daddy who has the stories your mommy told you. Your daddy doesn't know about you—"

Derek snaps to attention. "I'm going to talk to Martin," he says quietly. He doesn't look up at her for permission.

"Yes, child, of course. You talk to Martin, and when you come back we'll have some tea and later you can watch the telly if you want."

What in God's name possessed me, she thinks.

He arrives at the study door and quietly watches Martin writing at his desk. Martin senses his presence, looks up, and takes off his reading glasses. They exchange a nod, both underplaying what they know.

Silence.

"What do you think you'd like to do then, Derek?" Martin asks gently.

"Nothing."

"I'm sure we could do better than nothing. I heard you quarrelling. What's it about, son?"

"My dad."

Martin nods again, but asks no more questions.

Derek waits, confused. All he wanted was to get leave to play cricket in Regent's Park with Stephen. All he wanted was to be outside on a warm August day before school starts again and he has to sit and not squirm through the long school day. He's been squirming a lot these days. His teacher mentioned it before term ended, his aunt has mentioned it, and even he has noticed it. He squirms and jiggles his knees up and down and taps his foot anytime he has to sit for long. He wants to go out today because in just over a week he'll be back in school confined, holding his bouncing tight inside himself.

"Look, Derek, why don't I ask your aunt if I can take you out? Just for a break," says Martin after an awkward minute.

Derek's face tingles. He smiles. Martin has never shown him much attention except to rub his head or pat his shoulders when encountering him on the stairs or at the front door. Martin is the editor of a Sunday magazine. He's not often home on the weekend. Derek steps into the study and examines the photographs on the wall beside Martin's desk.

"Let's see . . . it's carnival weekend," Martin says cheerily. "You must like Carnival, don't you? Did they have it in your country?"

Derek looks from the photographs to Martin's kind face and considers the question. His country. Where is that but in the long difficult tunnel of *before*? He has recently had trouble placing everything in time. England these last two years has soaked him up like a blotter soaks up ink. He speaks with a London accent now. He has almost forgotten the scent of the sea.

"Don't tell her we're going to the carnival. Tell her something else," he instructs Martin.

"Well—"

"She doesn't need to know; she'll just spin off into something, and I'll never get to go."

"I'll see what I can come up with, but I'm not going to stretch it too far," Martin says as he pushes his chair back from his desk and gets up. He tells Derek to sit in his chair and wait for him, then heads upstairs. Derek can hear his polite tones as he speaks to Auntie Vic, and then something that makes her laugh. Martin is all right.

The photograph on Martin's desk is of Max and Monica, both sitting, knees up, in a cardboard box with pots on their heads. Their straight blond hair sticks out from under the pots and their eyes are laughing, even though they're trying to look serious. Derek finds something sad about the photograph but would never be able to explain what he means. On the wall to the side of Martin's desk is another photograph that looks as though it came from a magazine. It's of Stonehenge, taken from a very peculiar angle: the pair of pillars resemble two figures offering their shared burden of the lintel stone to the viewer. Yellow wildflowers dot the field, and the figures appear poised to lie down after their offering has been accepted. This photograph is not sad, Derek thinks, but there's something about it that makes the hair on his arms stand up. Using his feet he rolls the chair closer to the wall, trying to get a closer look at the photograph and the text beneath it, which is an excerpt from an article about the Iron Age Celtic people. A few phrases jump out at him.

As part of the Druid caste, the Bards were supported by their communities. While the Druid held power, performing ceremonies and rites as judge, priest, and magician, the role of the Bard was quite different. It was his task to know by heart the histories of the people of the land, and to recite these . . .

Derek's breath quickens. He looks down towards the floor and examines his trainers, noticing the loose laces. He bends over to retie them, making a double knot. His heart is fluttery and light. He has no idea what a carnival in London will be like, but he can't imagine it's anything like the madness in Georgetown at the yearly Crop Over festival. And people say that's nothing compared to Trinidad.

MATOKE AND LAMB STEW

2 pounds lamb, cut into cubes

4 medium matoke (plantain) or small green bananas, peeled and cut
into 1-inch-thick slices

4 tomatoes, peeled and sliced

4 onions, sliced

3 tablespoons oil

2 cups coconut milk

salt and pepper to taste

Kola taught Victoria how to make this East African stew. It's filling, and easy enough to finish in the time she had for cooking this
morning. But as the meat simmered and she sliced the bananas
and onions, she felt it needed something green—an injection of
antioxidants, and vitamins A and C. In the last ten minutes of simmering she added a package of mange-tout, which gives the dish a
European touch, more appropriate for these diners, she thinks.

She looks along the queue of those waiting to be served. It's not a
busy day at the shelter, a dozen or so people, and she wonders if
perhaps she wasn't needed, since three others are also serving,
while the uniformed director greets people as they enter. The
Salvation Army building is small, but its high ceilings give it a certain grandeur, and it's surprisingly airy for all its dowdiness. Cheap
cotton curtains with a pattern of blue flowers and corn husks divide
the open reception area from the dining hall with its pale-yellow
walls. Hanging on the far wall near the washrooms is a print of a
mountain in Japan. On the wall behind the long wooden tables is a
modest portrait of Jesus. Victoria feels comfortable here, despite
the Lord's gaze. This morning's conversation with Derek was evidence that her conviction towards disbelief is hardening. She
doesn't want the boy to invest in things that don't exist. Delusion is

laid like a delicate egg when belief is seeded. She's had her share and wants none of that for her Derek. She'll do what she can to give him the opposite. But it didn't have to be like that . . .

She ladles a serving of lamb, matoke, and mange-tout over a mound of rice on a plate, then dips into the pot again for some coconut sauce to cover it. She hands the plate to a man in a black toque and wonders if he's not too hot in this weather. The man stares at the dish unhappily, but Victoria looks to the next person in the queue, a plump, middle-aged woman with matted grey-streaked hair. She's wearing a trench coat. Victoria notes that all the diners have cardigans, jackets, or coats on, even in this heat. Coats, she knows, provide protection from far more than just the elements. She takes the woman's plate of rice and dips the ladle back into the pot, delivering a generous helping of stew.

"Cheers," the woman says as she takes the plate from Victoria. After examining the food the woman looks up at her. "Gorgeous. On the days you're not here we miss you, darling."

A flush spreads up from Victoria's neck and along her cheeks at the thought of someone missing her for a change. "Is that so?" she asks innocently.

"Of course it is, you're the best cook we've ever had." The woman grins, exposing a row of blackened teeth. Victoria dips the ladle in again and puts more stew on the woman's plate. The woman nods and moves on.

When the director of the Salvation Army first asked her how much time she could give to volunteering at the shelter, Victoria wanted to say, "as much as I should have given my sister," but she couldn't bring herself to those words. "I had a friend who would have been ashamed of me for having done nothing for so long," she said instead, watching how the director's fingers proudly played with the cuff of her black uniform.

"We're grateful, whatever your reasons," the woman said, holding out her hand to Victoria.

"My friend died," she said and paused for effect, not intending to shock, simply hoping to rip through the ban on talking about Kola she had unwittingly imposed upon herself. "I think he'd like it if I cooked here," she told the director, who withdrew her hand and led Victoria to the kitchen. Since the incident at the market, Victoria has felt more conscious of the consequences of her actions, but this is treacherous territory, and she is still reeling from the morning's confrontation with Derek. And, still, the tether of reckoning is tugging at her. She needs to break it. A thought comes to her. She drags a name out from her memory. The name of the woman who had telephoned her: Akinyi.

She puts down the ladle, wipes her hands on a cloth, then gathers her things and asks the server beside her to take over her pot. She's out the door very quickly and walking north on Kilburn High Street, past shoppers, their buggies and bags grazing her as she marches briskly along the pavement to the top of the street. There's a pound store selling cheap baskets and dishes, an Asian grocer, then one bar after another. Not these, it must be further on. Akinyi didn't know the name of the bar, but said it was near the theatre. Victoria has pictured it in her head all these years. She imagined it not far from the Salvation Army and now acknowledges why she chose to volunteer at that particular charity. Whether it's the place where events actually took place, she has no idea, but it will have to do. She must look at it. This is the reckoning that has been tugging at her for months, not anything to do with Derek.

She arrives at the corner. The entrance to a bar called Also is a black, grimy door, its white lettering greyed with soot and inattention. She stands and stares at the door. Images come to her, with Akinyi's voice relaying them, the long-distance connection making them reverberate. Victoria goes around to the back of the bar, down a small alleyway. The back door is locked and chained. The uncollected rubbish from the night before smells of stale garlic and burnt rice. Looking down, she stares at a cracked square of pavement. Her legs feel weak. Is this how he felt? She bends down, then drops to one knee on a slab of gritty concrete. As she tries to balance herself, placing the other knee down, she hears Akinyi's voice again . . . *he knelt* . . . and although the concrete hurts her bare knees, she stays there, like that, feeling it on her bones, and noticing how it cools her skin. She lowers her head and tries to release Kola. He is not larger than this moment, merely as small as life itself. This thought comes as a surprise. Perhaps all she's needed to do all along was say goodbye. She focuses on the woman's voice: *He knelt, and the man—*

"You OK there?" a voice comes from down the alleyway.

Victoria is startled, frightened. Coming towards her quickly is a young, tall, skinny man with ebony skin. He arrives at her side. She hurries to stand up.

"Oh, I just dropped something," she says, brushing the dust from her knees and picking up her purse. The man nods as he watches her, then takes out keys and begins to unlock the chain on the door, all the while keeping a wary eye on her. Victoria nods, clears her throat, and hurries off.

He couldn't have been more wrong about a tame carnival. All Saints Road in Notting Hill has turned into Port-of-Spain. Pans. Mas. Weed. And more black faces than white—happy, dancing, you-can't-do-me-nothing faces. Biting-of-both-lips-smirks. Bodies feeling the grind. Hips, hips, hips. Derek is astounded. These are the expressions of his mother when she was dancing. Holding her arms up above her head, looking down at her feet, her lips folded together, her whole being would be focused on her pelvis.

And here is a sea. A sea of people like at home. Derek becomes disoriented. He looks down at people's feet, then at his own to put them into context, but he bumps into a woman in front of him. He reaches out for Martin's hand.

"What d'you say?" Martin asks as he takes Derek's hand.

"Strange."

"How do you mean, strange?"

"I don't know." He can't think of the words he needs right now. Wasn't his dad in hiding? Won't he see him one day? A face in a crowd always had the potential to be his father's. A set of hazel eyes in an unfamiliar man were eyes that might recognize him. What is going on?

"Martin?"

"Yea?"

"Can we go play cricket?"

"Cricket?"

"Just to the park, so I can see my mates, play a few innings."

"Isn't that exactly what your aunt didn't want you to do?"

"But she probably didn't want this either, so no matter what you told her, that isn't what we're doing anyway."

"You're right." Martin pauses and looks at his watch. In the Underground he told Derek he had only a couple of free hours before he had to pick up Sonia and the twins in Hampstead. Martin's time is measured out precisely to balance work and his home life. Lenny doesn't like Martin, calls him a poser, but Derek thinks Martin is being exceptionally cool today.

They head back towards the tube station, pushing through the hordes of people in the streets, down Westbourne Park Road, Kensington Park Road. Whistles, horns, music from the loud-speakers.

"Do you think Auntie Vic has ever been here?" Derek asks Martin as they turn towards the stairs when they reach the Underground.

"She must have been. She's lived in London a long time."

Then why hasn't she brought me here, he wonders. "We mustn't tell her we came, Martin."

The stream of people coming up the stairs blocks their way. "Blast, I forgot, you can't go in at this station today, only out." Martin looks around for a solution, checks his watch again. He holds Derek's shoulders and guides him to the intersection where they cross and head east toward Kensington Gardens.

"You hungry?" he asks Derek.

"Always," Derek says, but it's not true. It's what he is used to telling Auntie Vic, because he knows it's what she wants to hear. Most of the time he's *not* hungry, but he eats, or pretends to eat, nibbling the inside of sandwiches. He's learned that if you spread the food over the whole plate and come at it from the middle, the plate can seem emptier faster than if you eat from the outside in.

"You know what I'd really like?"

"What's that?"

"A hot dog." He looks up guiltily into the brown eyes of this man he's barely spoken to in two years, feeling comfortable with him and not knowing that what he's feeling is freedom. He has forgotten anything his aunt said about him not having a father, and he smiles.

"I think we can manage that," says Martin with a wink. They continue to walk down Bayswater alongside the congested traffic, then turn into Kensington Park. At the concession stand near the Diana, Princess of Wales Memorial Playground Martin buys them two fried hot dogs, one with loads of fried onions for himself, the other plain for his young companion. Derek smears his hot dog with ketchup, takes a greedy first bite, and the red sauce drips down his chin and onto his light-blue T-shirt. He doesn't notice, and Martin doesn't say anything.

Flesh sizzles like something from an oven, she thinks, as she walks more slowly now, along the footpath among the large oaks of Kensington Gardens. She watches two young women sunning themselves on the grass. One of the women checks herself under her bathing suit to see if there's a difference in colour. Why is flesh all we've got, when it can be burned so easily? You'd think we'd have something more resistant to protect us, wouldn't you? Something that is more than food.

Victoria feels better, here in the park. The coolness of concrete on her knees, the cold chain on the bar's back door. She shivered as she waited for the bus to bring her here. This heat is good. She settles down on a bench behind Kensington Palace. Two boys on rollerblades whiz past and then retrace their path, skating backwards, zig-zagging through fluorescent-coloured cones set up in a straight line, each a foot apart. One of the boys does the course on one foot. Now that's a miracle, she thinks. That's physical, something you can believe in. If you can't touch it, she assures herself, it can't be real.

She almost touched the moment just then, at the back of the Also bar. Almost felt the thing that has haunted her for years. Flesh and blood. Of all the feelings that have stayed with her since the explosion in Dalston Market, it has been this one, of the simultaneous fragility and certainty of flesh and blood. She understood it as a child, but when she left Guyana with too much knowledge of it, she found Kola and believed in him. When he disappeared she believed in his return. When he didn't, she believed in nothing. Now flesh and blood is important again. But this morning, watching the boy tremble at her words—that was too much. She saw his mind flood with his mother's words, desperate for them to hold him up. God, what has she done? The only comfort comes in the thought of the truth. "The truth, my darling, will set you free," Kola would say, mocking the neighbourhood preacher. But where is free? Where has she sent the boy? She has promised herself time and again to find a way to talk to him about what she knows and the things she's learned, but this morning's whipping of truth did not arise from anything inside her that is wise, merely from that tug to face what's real. She has to repair the damage.

The sun is strong; the park is crowded. She has chosen it over Regent's Park so that she won't run into Martin and Derek on their outing. Sweet of Martin to take the boy, but she is trying not to resent it. She watches more rollerbladers whiz through the obstacle course. She'd like to try that, in another life. On the other side of the footpath, a diminutive white statue of Queen Victoria catches her eye. The queen is drained of life and lust like a blanched almond, so unlike her consort. Victoria stands up, sucks her teeth, and walks in the opposite direction, towards Bayswater.

As she walks briskly her chest begins to feel tight. She coughs, first from the back of her throat and then from deeper down, feeling it in her stomach. Tighter still, the pain rises like a belch that won't move quickly enough for relief. She stops and stands, holding her right hand over her chest. Her left arm is stretched out beside her as she tries to balance herself in the coughing fit that has taken hold.

"All right there?" asks a voice beside her. This time the voice doesn't frighten her. She looks up to see a young man in khaki trousers and a black shirt holding a skateboard to his chest with one arm, his other arm stretched out toward her. Her shoulder comes level with his chest, and he lets his arm fall to touch her. Victoria coughs a few more times and feels the pain along her chest move from her bosom to her throat. In a final fit of coughing she feels the pressure release.

"Should you sit down, m'um?" the young man asks. Victoria smells lime coming from him, or is it urine? It's a combination of sweat and smoke, an unusual perfume. He must have been skateboarding at quite a speed to smell like that.

"Thank you, I'm fine," she tells him.

"Come and sit," he says, and she follows him obediently to a bench along the footpath. The coughing starts again, and she has to hold her chest. With her left hand she reaches for the young man's hand as he offers it. Coughing and hacking, she sees purple shapes before her eyes, feels fluid rise up from impossible places. Finally, when the fit subsides, she composes herself and wipes her mouth with her hand. She looks into the young man's face. She's surprised at the gentleness there—beneath the stubble. The same look as Derek—probably about twelve years older. Derek's questioning hazel eyes. But every time she'd catch them looking at her she'd deliberately try to obscure what they might perceive. *Not*

*me, boy, don't look for her here. I'm not your mother. I'm just looking
after you. Don't look to me to be her* . . . And she'd squat down at the
shrine in her dead heart so that it would not be opened up by the
boy's questions.

"Would this help?" asks the young man. He holds up two sticks
of chewing gum. He unwraps one, puts it in his mouth, and then
holds out the other for her. She takes the gum from his fingers,
unwraps it, and slides the stick into her mouth. As she bites down,
the saliva spreads through her mouth and brings relief. The young
man smiles.

"Thank you," she says, so sorry for having couched what she
said to Derek this morning in the simple truth. "Thank you," she
says again and gets up from the bench.

Derek is almost finished his hot dog. Even the sleeves of his T-shirt
are splattered with ketchup.

"No cricket, but lots of rollerbladers. Besides, cricket's out-
moded, done, done, done. Even the West Indies are losing to
England these days and that's a sure sign of the game's demise. A
reversal of a reversal. It'll be the death of it," Martin muses, talking
almost to himself.

Derek watches a rollerblader swerve through the crowd behind
Kensington Palace, on a path that heads to the Serpentine Gallery
and Hyde Park. The woman is too old to be doing that, he
thinks—she's almost as old as his mother—but she dances and
glides effortlessly, looking like a schoolgirl. She is wearing headphones, listening to music that makes her sway. Inside she is probably flying, Derek thinks. More than anything, he wants to fly.

"If we make our way over to Hyde Park we can take the bus up
Edgware Road and get back home before your aunt does," Martin
says. "She'll still be in Kilburn now," he adds.

Derek feels full but doesn't want to give up on his hot dog. He sips from his Coke and watches the bladers. The path with the coloured cones resembles a runway, and he imagines them taking off at the end of it, going up, above the pond, above the buildings, above the gold statue of Prince Albert, flying like clumsy birds. He's with them, flying easily. He's the fastest among them, and then he twirls—

"Eh, eh? What are you two doing here?"

The voice of his aunt is chilling. His flying self hurtles toward the paved path and thuds in front of her.

"Victoria, hi . . . we were just heading back," Martin offers.

"From where, then?" Victoria asks suspiciously, staring at the remnants of bun and sausage in Derek's hand and the stains on his shirt.

"Just a walk. We wanted to see the pirate ship sandbox . . . Max would love it . . . And there's water . . ." he answers, pointing awkwardly in the direction of the playground. Derek hasn't been interested in playgrounds for some time now. He hadn't even considered the one with the pirate ship, and assumes neither had Martin until that very moment. Brilliant, he thinks.

"You've come a long way—did you take the tube?" she asks, now feeling very anxious. "And what have you been eating?"

Derek pauses and takes a deep breath. In that breath, he thinks, of course, his daddy knows about him. Of course he will come back for him and take him away from this old woman with her cod-liver smell, her choking food, her stare that is always, always, always there.

"A hot dog . . ."

"Those things are made with the worst—"

"Auntie Vic, it's just a hot dog. People eat them all the time. It's not a big deal."

"I bought it for him, Victoria," Martin interjects.

Victoria glares at Martin. She has to remind herself that Martin is the father of twins. Then again, she doesn't know what the twins eat or what damage is being done. She thinks about acrylamide, the poison she read about that forms in food. The carcinogen that arrives into the system just from eating something cooked.

"I just thought he needed—"

"I think I know what he needs, don't you? I'm the one looking after him day in, day out, and you just come along and . . ." Victoria stops herself. She's being unreasonable. The hot dog is not the issue. Today everything has been drawing her towards that moment on her knees. She bites down on the gum in her mouth and chews harder. She relaxes. The three of them stand silently for a few seconds.

Inside, Derek is thrumming. The wave of the unnamed man inside him, the one he came from, the one he will become, is cresting towards recognition.

"It's like a hospital," he says loudly with a tone that surprises even him—a tone he sometimes used with his mother and Granny before . . .

"What is?" Victoria asks, trying to suppress her indignation. "What is?"

"At home, living with you. It feels like I'm a patient you have to feed at the hospital. I'm not sick, you know!" And now he does feel wretched, and his stomach starts to rumble, making a fool of his words.

Victoria's heart starts to race. The boy is right. She knows this already. "Derek, let's go home. Martin, thank you. I'll take over now," she says as she guides Derek's shoulder toward the path heading to Bayswater.

"Look, I'm sorry if I've done something wrong," says Martin behind her.

Wrong? No, it's she who has been wrong, thinks Victoria. She has forgotten the important things about being a child, and has been so far from life that no one wants her when she's like this. She relives the feeling of concrete on her knees and says silently, Goodbye, darling, to something in her heart.

"No, Martin, I'm sorry. It's fine. We'll see you back at the house." She continues to walk. Derek is a few paces ahead of her. She catches up to him. He looks up at her, worried. Resisting the impulse to take the boy's hand in hers, she keeps her eyes fixed on the fringe of his hair.

"Derek, we'll try to find your dad."

PART II

CHAPTER EIGHT

Kendra

❦

"No, the chicken saw the deer crossing the road," insisted Max, making Derek laugh and snort his juice up into his nose. He had been trying to get the twins to tell two jokes. One was a basic Why did the chicken cross the road? The other, What do you call a deer with no eyes? *No idea.* But Max's version made about as much sense as the others. Derek rubbed the boy's blond head. Monica ran toward them and offered Derek a painting she had just completed. "It's a tractor. I am Bob the Builder."

"And who's Max?" Derek asked Monica.

"Umm . . . he's just Max."

"No, I am Thomas the Tank. Call me Thomas," clarified Max.

When their mother called for them, Max refused to leave, picking up Derek's recorder and blowing on it indiscriminately, so that Derek had to hold his ears, then gently peel the instrument out of the boy's hand. He ushered the twins down the stairs, closed the door behind them, and went back to the computer, hoping to get some time on the Net before school. He checks his watch as he logs on.

The twins are now almost four years old, and their adoration of Derek has grown with each of their morning trips to the top floor, where Victoria and Derek have taken over more space. With the help of Victoria's expanded income from the catering business, Derek's former bedroom is now their sitting room. He sleeps in a smaller room, which overlooks the luscious back garden, on the other side of the house, where the Slovakian woman used to live.

The beautician and the German musician had fallen in love. Early one morning, when he'd risen to go to the washroom, Derek heard them beyond the bathroom wall. The Slovakian woman's coos were like the sound of her language—broad and coarse, with fluttering breath in the lapses between syllables. She screamed, held it back, and cooed again, but then the sound of the German musician took over in a huff until his pounding grunts ended in a groan. A few months later the couple moved out, having found a flat together on Belsize Road. Derek enjoys the fact that his bedroom once belonged to the Slovakian beautician, whose scent, he believes, he can still smell just near the dresser.

With the door between the two sections of the house now propped open, the flat is more spacious, and the rooms feel much more like a home. In the sitting room he can watch television. In his bedroom he can surf the Net or write his stories away from the watchful eyes of his aunt. And, if he needs to—and more and more these days it seems he does—he can pull on himself and relieve the irritation of the erections that arrive like gusts of evening wind. This wind feels dangerous; it has a power he can't yet control, so he tries to ignore it, or service it as quickly and cleanly as possible, to lull it. He is thinking of asking Richard Lorry for one of the magazines he circulates in the playground. He wonders how it might help this irritating feeling, but for now, since he has important things to do with his mornings and evenings, the gusts will have to be quelled with a tug.

He stopped surfing for Camelot sites last year; the myths had grown stale for him, the quests too naïve, the battles too ordinary—nothing that contained explosions. His quest has become more vital and immediate. Eighteen months ago, his aunt's explanation of how he was fathered confused him. Surely a father was a father, no matter where he was. But since exploring his own aching organ, he has a better idea what the fact about his father means. Derek knows about babies. He knows about sperm.

WWW.SPERMBANKDIRECTORY.COM

What is an anonymous sperm donor?

An anonymous sperm donor is a man who chooses, for any number of reasons, to donate his sperm anonymously to a couple who cannot have a child due to male factor infertility.

The donor will generally not meet the couple, nor will he receive information about the whereabouts of the child conceived with his sperm. Sperm banks differ on the amount of information they will provide the donor about resulting pregnancies. You will need to speak to the sperm bank with which you choose to work about their specific policies and conditions.

What is involved in being a sperm donor?

You may approach a sperm bank directly or fill out our on-line application. We will forward it to the laboratory and they will contact you. You may be asked additional questions over the phone and, at that time, you will be asked to come in to the laboratory for a meeting. During this first meeting, the laboratory will spend significant time with you, have you fill out a questionnaire about your medical and family history. At that time they will go through their rules and procedures. Often labs will ask you to produce an initial semen sample in the collection room. This initial sample is tested by the lab to see how much sperm is in the ejaculate, its quality, and how well it freezes. Most labs have private collection rooms with videos or magazines to help with production.

So, not Camelot. Derek has a simpler quest. As simple as seed.

He has been searching the Web for fathers. He found a football star who was born in Guyana; a policeman who won a medal for bravely rescuing a woman from a burning car; the writer of the young adult novel he was reading after school; and even comedians he has watched on television. Time and place aside, any one of these men could have sired him.

The idea came to him not long after his discovery of Kola. After all, this man had been involved in the things his mother had described his father doing, and there had been a long gap in the regular correspondence with his aunt, until one final letter from London. And Kola had disappeared just like Derek's father. Kola, Kola, Kola, Derek would repeat as his head hit the pillow each night. The man's name was like a password to sleep. When he eventually confronted his aunt—one of Kola's letters in his hand— and asked her if this slow-train-talking man could be his father, Victoria showed him pictures of the man himself. He was tall, with a burnt-toast face, and bore no resemblance to anyone Derek had ever imagined. No matter how he tried, Derek could not put Guenevere's face and Kola's together to make his own.

And besides, this man was gone forever, so there was little use in pursuing that path. "Even now it amazes me that men can do that to one another," his aunt said when he asked her what happened to Kola. He waited for her to continue the story, to spread it out before him like a fan to his imagination, but she brushed the topic aside, telling him he wouldn't understand. When he pressed her, she pronounced crisply: "Cain against Abel, simply put," then turned away. He understood only that Kola was not alive.

His fascination with Kola's life has not ended, and he continues to mine the letters for nuggets of guidance, but as far as fathers are concerned, he has to believe in seed now.

Genius Sperm Bank Information

Genius sperm banks select sperm donors based on achievements and genetic quality rather than on the donor's physical characteristics, race, or sperm quality.

http://www.geniusspermbank.com

click

A delicate knock at his door is followed by giggles and, "It's Bob and Thomas. We are here." Derek clicks off the website and disconnects from the server. "Derek, Derek!" Max yells from behind the door, as though Derek has been lost.

Derek opens the door to see Monica and Max dressed in matching OshKosh overalls; Monica's fringe stands in an electrostatic salute. "Why you not dressed?" Monica asks him.

"Why *are* you not dressed?" Derek corrects. The two push their way into the room and sit on the floor waiting for him to entertain them. He considers trying to tell the chicken-crossing-the-road joke again and to disentangle it from the deer joke, but he decides that would be too much effort. How do children ever learn anything if they start out like this, he wonders.

Slow as dough, he is, Victoria says to herself, turning back to catch sight of Derek as she walks just ahead of him up Blenheim Terrace. There is the smell of damp soil in the air, but the sun will be strong today.

"You're just coming to the corner, right?" Derek calls out, staring down at his feet, carefully dodging cracks on the pavement.

"Yes, love, just getting some air this morning," she assures him. Dough rises faster than he walks, she thinks. Even I can outstride him. Especially now, since she's recently given up bacon, salami, and white flour. The fat of pigs, and all that dough. She is a stone and a half lighter and looks almost youthful. Her face is no longer a puffy pouch. Barely wrinkled by luck of Asian ancestry, her cheeks now have contour, and her lips seem fuller. She also wears contact lenses, so she sees clearly all the time, rather than just on the days she remembers to bring her glasses.

And somehow she listens better, although she's not sure how that's linked to fat. She answers all of Derek's questions if she can, and he has so many more. His twelfth birthday is in November, and his mind works faster by the month. But this sperm bank business is still a problem.

Victoria's exhaustive attempts last year to trace Derek's father through fertility clinics in Miami were fruitless, the clinics informing her they could give background information on donors only to clients. Derek could request information once he was eighteen years old, but he'd receive it only if the donor had agreed in advance to its release. They were on a dead-end road to his father, but she didn't want to destroy the boy's hopes, so she enthusiastically told him they should wait a few more years and try again.

She stops and waits for him to catch up. She can't help it, she wants to touch his face, feel the smooth cheek, but as she reaches out, he bends down and opens his satchel to look for something.

"What?" she asks, staring at his hair, which he has convinced her should be left a little longer than she would like.

"My library book on archaeology. Have you seen it?" He rifles through his books and papers.

"No, didn't we decide that was your responsibility?"

"I know, I know . . . oh, here." He's relieved.

She's relieved too, proud of the way he has taken to books and the search for information. She turns and keeps walking, full of energy, feeling like she could bake for England. She has to admit that the energy is like that of someone in the full-blown stride of love. There's a place where all love becomes physical. She needs to channel these feelings, to put her hands on them. It's the deeper things she needs to learn to say to him. She's fine with the everyday chat and issues, and their relationship is more solid now. But Derek still appears to harbour many secrets. This tendency must have been inherited, she thinks, and so relies on the instincts of flesh and blood to help her understand.

This course of thinking is working in other areas as well, and if she focuses on concrete, material things, then not even the slightest breath of Kola remains there, below her ribs. She has no time for that now. She's had to reduce her Salvation Army shifts to once a week. The catering work has tripled, and she and Lenny have taken on a part-timer, Matthew, a student who does the canapés, their special: wrapped medallions of venison.

They stay away from beef on principle. And chickens. God help the chickens. She's read that featherless chickens are ready for selling to the market. A cross of a bare-skin bird and a regular broiler, the chicken doesn't need plucking, can grow bigger, and is somehow even lower in calories. Sterile, you can bet on that, she thinks.

If only she could get Derek to keep away from Mars bars and hard candy. Most days he would prefer chips and burgers with his friends to the organic produce and meat she brings home from the farmer's markets or, if she feels she can afford it, Planet Organic or Fresh & Wild. He is weak in the face of Coke and crisps.

"You have your lunch in the knapsack, Derek?"

"Yes."

"Don't you throw it out, now, you hear?"

"No."

"Who're you eating with today, then?"

"Probably Stephen . . . and Kendra," he says, her name bringing a sense of adventure to his day.

Kendra's a girl of too many gadgets, Victoria thinks, and gadgets disconnect you from real effort. Last year, when Derek's pager got wet in the rain and stopped working, she considered buying him a mobile phone, but Lenny convinced her that discussing things with Derek was the only way to keep him safe. "He has to know what's right, wrong, safe, and dangerous, and then you have to let go, so that he finds out," he told her. She's working on letting go, but she's worried about Kendra's influence on the boy. Kendra is more grown up than any twelve-year-old Victoria has ever known, what with her TV-gained opinions developing unchecked.

When they reach the corner, Victoria sees her waiting for him. The girl looks lost and nailed, she thinks. Nailed in, nailed to, nailed out from, but as though the loss of her mother connects her to something much more important in the world than Victoria will ever grasp.

"Derek!" Kendra calls, with excitement.

Derek smiles, then frowns, self-consciously, looking at his aunt. Victoria knows to turn and leave without saying a word. She would have liked to go as far as the school, perhaps just to catch a glimpse of the janitor again. "I'm never wrong," the man said the last time she visited the school to deliver a letter of permission Derek needed for an outing. He'd grinned at her, his crooked teeth putting her off slightly. But his teeth were the only marks of imperfection she could detect on the young Italian janitor, who couldn't have been much more than thirty. He had spotted her several times in the neighbourhood, he told her. "You're a beautiful woman, the way you look straight ahead."

"What do you mean?"

"Your face . . . there's something. I'm never wrong."

She didn't believe him, but she would have liked to have had a look at him again.

Derek walks quickly to the corner. He and Kendra share a non-touching moment of affection. Victoria turns and heads to Lenny's, where for hours she will knead and bake and get so covered in flour and butter by the end of the day that need will rise like something set aside. Each day she exhausts herself, but that is what she has now.

Derek unfolds the wax-paper wrapping of his sandwich, just to see: organic dark rye bread, roasted peppers, roasted aubergine, a sprinkling of goat's cheese.

"Spectacular," Kendra exclaims, straining her slender neck over his arm. She grabs a piece of aubergine, tastes it, and licks her fingers. "Mmmm, juicy. Perfect as usual."

Derek hands her the sandwich. Kendra is the only one who doesn't tease him over the delicate gourmet meals his aunt packs for him. Stephen and the other boys roll their eyes or jeer outright. Since his suspension, Richard Lorry has not been about enough to make a deal of it one way or the other.

Richard entered the adjoining Quentin Kynaston School last year, but his playground activities got him suspended twice. Richard will sell you anything you might need to buy. He's an excellent source for batteries, comic books, magazines, bicycles, if you arrange to meet him on a Sunday in the back square of the school—and ganja if you are old enough. He refuses to sell it to anyone under twelve. Kanaima-protected still, Derek doesn't have much contact with Richard, but Stephen remains under his control, and Richard calls upon him to carry out "errands" or collect "taxes." As a result, Stephen stays away from school as often as he can manage to persuade his mother that he's ill. Derek visits him some days after school to bring him the important homework. But today Stephen has come to school, and Derek is delighted.

"Right, let's go you lot," Stephen says to Kendra and Derek. Kendra finishes off the last of Derek's sandwich and the three head off toward Finchley Road. When they reach McDonald's, Kendra disappears quickly inside, looking agitated, scanning the restaurant, searching for someone. Derek comes up behind her but before he can ask her if she'd like to share some chips, she bolts to a table with Richard Lorry and a group of older boys at the back of the restaurant.

"Give us a fag, will you, Lorry?" says Kendra to Richard in a voice Derek has not heard from her before—a voice that flutters between syllables, like the accent of the Slovakian beautician. When Richard takes a cigarette from his pack and hands it to her, Kendra lightly touches his belt, right near the buckle. Derek searches for Stephen, and for a few awkward moments can't locate his friend. Finally, he sees him at the counter.

"Order me a shake, will you?" he asks as he steps up beside Stephen in the queue. Kendra and Richard appear to be smoking for one another: inhaling simultaneously, then exhaling at the exact same moment, their chins raised, gazing along their noses, watching the two separate streams of smoke caress in the air.

Derek looks away, towards the group of kids from the high school who gather each lunch hour. Girls in uniform talk, laugh, and jeer at the boys at a nearby table. The boys look uncomfortable. One of them throws a cup down on the floor and stomps on it—bang, like a gun. Boys need to smash things when girls make fun of them. As he sits down at the table across from Stephen, Derek thinks it's his birthmark that keeps him immune from the girls' taunting. He wonders if they feel sorry for him. But it could be his friendship with Kendra that keeps them quiet. Kendra keeps everyone quiet with her equipment. The other day she brought to McDonald's the latest in music storage, all in a mobile phone: a digital device onto which music can be downloaded or voices and live instruments recorded on the spot. The data can be amplified or sent to another phone. When one of the other girls joked about Kendra texting love songs to senior boys, the party went silent. No one laughed, knowing how useless it was to attempt to undermine Kendra's capabilities. Luckily Derek has been included inside Kendra's circle of power. At least up until recently, but now she seems to have found more time for Richard than anyone else. Derek glances back in their direction in time to see Richard grab hold of the top of Kendra's back pocket and pull her closer to him. Kendra succumbs, but notices Derek watching her. He turns away, quickly grabbing one of Stephen's chips. He devours it and licks his finger.

"You know how many brothers and sisters you could have?" The voice surprises him. He turns to see Kendra above him holding out her portion of chips.

"How many?" Derek asks as he takes one.

Kendra sits down on the hard, plastic, yellow chair beside him. "Well, do the math," she continues, her tone as firm as muscle. "If each bloke is allowed to wank into a vial ten times at each bank, that's ten kids out of one place. And who knows how many banks he's made deposits in. Maybe two? Three?—"

"Fuckin' hell," Stephen says under his breath. "Maybe twenty!" He bites into his cheeseburger.

Where does she get all of this, Derek wonders. How does she know the words? And the spaces between the words and the inflections that rise to slap him?

"You could have twenty, thirty, maybe forty half-brothers and sisters. Think on that. It sends chills." She shakes her head and then falls silent. But the thought sends more than chills through Derek. He feels as if he could collapse.

"That's impossible," he says quietly in a way that Stephen and Kendra know means that he no longer wants to discuss the topic.

Somewhere in the world are people others would call brother and sister—boys or girls who might put into context his face, his hands, his desire to take everything apart then put it back together again, to sculpt something to belong to. What difference does it make to him now, here? No amount of fake brothers and sisters could mean much in a McDonald's. The restaurant is becoming more crowded as queues of older boys and girls laugh and push each other impatiently. Derek pretends he's leaning over to see something at the far end of the restaurant so that he can brush against Kendra's shoulder and smell her staleness. He loves that smell. A boy waiting for his mates at the side of the queue places an empty soft-drink cup upside down on the floor, raises his foot slowly, and pauses, calling on his audience's attention. He brings his foot down on the cup, but there's no bang. Just a dull papery crunch and the roaring mockery of his friends. The boy shrugs and kicks the accordionned cup aside, blaming it.

*

To Teutons and Romans the bean was a stimulant and its flower symbolized sexual pleasure. Bean soup had such a high reputation for being erotic that in the seventeenth century beans were banned from the convent of Saint Jerome in order to prevent inopportune excitation.

Blimey, a soup unfit for a nun, this is, Victoria thinks as she stirs the black bean soup that has been simmering since morning. She closes the chapter on beans in the book given to her by Lenny. With a little veg, the soup should be filling enough for the boy, who is growing with the resolute pace of a stalk. "The love of food and the food of love," reads the book's jacket title. It's a book about the aphrodisiac qualities of food, its pages full of the sex she and Lenny have not shared in months. She places it carefully in the shelf over the stove.

As Derek shuffles into her room—all knees and elbows, not much flesh to speak of, and looking grumpy after an hour of homework—Victoria feels a moment of excitement. Morning and evening, she feels the same twinge, seeing him in her room, having survived the day or the long night in which he might have otherwise mysteriously expired. Over the years, the feeling has transformed from dread to anticipation, and now to excitement that something she has undertaken is working.

"Don't forget about tonight, Auntie Vic," Derek says as he pulls out the chair at the table.

"I haven't forgotten, Derek, but really, I don't want to make a fool of myself."

"Why would you?"

"I'm thirty years older than the other mothers and fathers."

"So?"

"So, they'll think I'm not . . . modern enough . . . too doltish to know about books. . . ."

Derek doesn't disagree with his aunt, but gets up from the chair and takes down a bowl from the shelf above the sink. If he eats she'll feel better, which makes them both happier. His friends do make fun of his aunt because she sneaks down the street to watch out for him, thinking that she isn't noticed, but tonight will be different. Tonight she'll meet his teachers and the other parents. His friends will see him beside her as they walk through the corridors. It's the first parent visit Victoria has agreed to attend.

Derek has become a fine student, not working so hard as to be singled out from among his classmates, but receiving steady seconds and a first in English composition. His compositions stand out among the class; his literary world is full of ghosts.

"And besides, what's the benefit in meeting teachers? They change every year. Not like at the convent where the same old crows, year after year, scorch your soul inside out," Victoria says, then goes silent, remembering how it felt to be at school and so alone. "I'll get ready. Come, or we'll be late," she concedes.

A few parents are drinking coffee by the reception table in the lobby. Hanging on the walls are students' bristol-board history and geography displays; carefully set up on tables are this year's three winning science projects. The first-prize winner is a miniature wave machine that demonstrates with undulating water just how the amount of water affects the size of the wave. Derek looks about anxiously and keeps Victoria in sight as he wanders over to the bulletin board and pretends to read the postings of appointment times for parents and teachers. Out of the corner of his eye he searches for Kendra down the long cream-coloured corridor.

Victoria passes her hand through her hair and pats the lapels of the suit jacket she carefully chose before leaving the house. Navy, with silver buttons. It looks smart with the flared grey trousers, she thinks. The navy pumps she bought in Camden last year add a touch of youthfulness.

She looks about nervously, feeling hot in the jacket. Of course, janitors don't work in the evening, silly bird, she tells herself. She examines the biscuits on one of the tables—store-bought and sugary—and takes one as something to hold in her hand, since she doesn't drink coffee. In her peripheral vision she sees a forearm reach for a biscuit. She doesn't look up to follow the arm to its shoulder, but the sight of it makes the hairs on her own arm rise. When she does look up, the man, who is wearing a white T-shirt, is standing with his back to her, searching the lobby, the fingers of his left hand tucked into the front pocket of his jeans. He has a trim, boyish figure. Parents gather in the lobby, many nodding and chatting familiarly, in a way Victoria knows she'll never manage. Only the man in the T-shirt and Victoria seem to be unacquainted with this type of social intimacy. She looks for Derek and spots him at the door to one of the classrooms, talking to Kendra, who gives Victoria a cool, mature nod. She turns again towards the front door. Perhaps the janitor is sweeping, the way he was the first time she saw him. Her eyes scan the lobby. No. She hikes her handbag under her arm and reaches for a cup of coffee.

"I think you must be Mrs. Layne," a voice beside her says. Victoria swings around, spilling hot coffee onto her hand, and tries not to react to the scalding. She faces the voice, wanting to correct the Mrs. with a Ms. or even a Miss, but no *M* words arrive when she looks up from her hand to face the T-shirted man, whom she now recognizes. His curly chestnut hair sets off the blue eyes, which appear like a clearing in the bush.

K arrives. Ko . . . but it doesn't feel right. It's the only sound that comes to her, but she doesn't say it. A moment later, a word—"yes"—does form.

"I'm Kendra's father, Alexander."

"Yes," she says again, looking for her fingers, something to shake the man's hands with, but her props are in the way. She places the cup and biscuit on the table, quickly wipes the spilled coffee from her right hand with a napkin, and reaches for his.

"I'm Victoria, very pleased to meet you," she says as they shake hands. Alexander looks her in the eyes, forcefully. "Have you seen the teachers, then?" she asks.

"Not yet, Kendra's going to take me through in a few minutes." He breaks his gaze to look anxiously at his watch. "I hated school," he says, looking back at her. He doesn't smile, and she's taken aback by such unusual directness. "It left me fearful, which wasn't quite fair, I think," he adds softly. He peers again at his watch, and she notes the flow of hair on his arm toward the wrist with only some grey ones going against the grain. His hand is broad, ridged, and crusted like a loaf. She scratches her neck. He looks at her again, then away, toward the hallway. The only other school meeting she's ever attended suddenly becomes vivid. This man's use of the word irrational had felt like a personal insult. Now she's confused, feeling herself pulled and pushed by his eyes. She looks at the curve of his head. Lenny says you can tell a person's breeding by examining the spot where the neck meets the skull. Alexander's is gently rounded, proportional. Well-schooled by the sound of him, not Cambridge or Oxford, something less rigid. Perhaps northern. Something, in any case, that will put her to shame. She picks up her cup of coffee again and actually sips it. The taste is foul. She regrets it, as she now regrets this whole outing.

"Kendra tells me that Derek is very bright, a good writer," says Alexander.

A writer? She flashes to Derek at the computer. "I . . . yes . . . well," she says hesitantly. "And Kendra," she offers, "she's a lovely girl—very grown up."

"Grown up too fast, that's for sure, but she's been like that since she was a baby." He smiles for the first time. Victoria likes the smile; it's like his voice. She wants to ask him why his daughter needs all those gadgets. She wants to say at least a dozen things that will defuse her irritation and alleviate this confusion; she wants him to go away and yet also never to leave.

"Girls are much more well-equipped these days than in mine," she says, then feels foolish for referring to herself as a thing of the past.

"I admire you," he says, and in those words she can hear he's definitely Yorkshire. Sharp and direct. The way he is looking at her is likely how he regards everyone, she thinks, and decides to relax.

"And why's that?" she shoots back, more brusquely than she'd intended.

"Raising Derek, the way you are . . . to stand up for himself, the way he does."

The way he does? What's he getting at? Giving in to the comfort to be found in his eyes, she feels like a child being told a story. Tell me . . .

"Kendra's mentioned you," he says, the mystery partly lifted.

"Oh?" she says, surprised the girl has even noticed her.

She wants to ask him what was said, but he continues. "You know, they never prosecuted the members of that gang for the bomb in the market."

Her raised eyebrows pose questions that include, Why is he telling her this and how does he know it's relevant?

"Christine told me first, then Kendra explained," he clarifies.

The mention of the blonde woman's name and the image of the car keys in her hand cause Victoria to withdraw.

"It's something that'll happen more and more, I think. American-style gang wars." He shakes his head.

"It's hardly limited to America." She's about to mention Guyana or Kenya, or the many other places where brother kills brother, when Derek comes up beside her.

"Auntie Vic? We can go in now."

"Of course, let's go in. I was just speaking to Alex."

"Alexander," he corrects softly.

"Alexander," she repeats, and nods as she follows Derek down the corridor to his classroom.

It's a bad mirror, is all, she thinks. She turns away from it quickly and puts on her nightgown, which falls over her like a drape, hiding the skin that no longer seems to fit its frame. Life is like a slow roasting, she thinks, as she examines the roughness of her elbows. It's like the skin on an overcooked fowl.

She hears one of the twins—probably Max—roar with tears from the room below her. She can remember them at one week old, when she brought Sonia steamed broccoli and brown rice to help restore her strength, and held one infant and then the other in her hands as if they were fragile dolls. Now they tell stories and share imaginary worlds with Derek. Is she losing track? Derek a writer? Blimey. Is that what he does at the computer at night? Why has it taken a stranger to tell her this? She glances quickly back into the mirror. Her cheeks have a spot of colour. "As I blush, I die," she sings from an old Venezuelan song that comes to her with a rush of heat that feels almost tropical.

She takes cream from a jar on top of her dresser and smothers her face with it. "I'm never wrong," the Italian janitor claimed, but Victoria is not convinced. She rubs the cream in vigorously, massaging upwards, pushing back the effects of gravity. There were rivers behind Alexander's eyes, strong currents to take you someplace you've never dared contemplate. She turns the bedding down and crawls into her bed. Under the duvet she feels protected. Her hand smoothes her nightgown over her belly, and then along her waist, where the skin that was once filled out by fat now sags toward the mattress. She turns on her side and presses her finger into her right buttock. There's no firmness to speak of. She rolls over on her back, feels her thigh, where there is still a faint muscle. All the walking has helped. She's slimmer but saggy. She flips to her left side and places her palms together, firmly under her cheek. Perhaps she'll start visiting Lenny at night again. That would do her some good, tighten things up, keep the juices flowing. She pulls the duvet up to her ears, then gently places her palm back against its mate near her temple. She sleeps fitfully.

"Vic, darlin', step up. Step up, you're holdin' up the queue luv."

Victoria takes a couple of steps to close the gap with Lenny and Derek, who are eagerly advancing in the lineup for the capsules. She is not keen. Victoria and heights have never been particularly suited. When she and her financial clerk in Toronto went out on one of their first dates, it was to the top of the tallest building in the city, from which they looked out over the expanse of concrete, the grid of streets and their ordered lights. Her indifference to the man himself was challenged by her sudden vertigo, and she gripped his arm tightly. She felt certain she'd hurl herself from the height, just to see what it felt like. She gets these impulses when she's up high; she wants to hurl something, someone, or herself out into the wind to watch it glide and fall. Strangely enough, in Barbados, at the top of the cliff at Pico Tenerife, she'd felt an unprecedented peace as she sat staring out to sea and relishing her new freedom. Soon enough, she began to wonder how it was that rock piled so high upon itself could balance just so, for eons, without toppling. Heights demand falls. This has become a private philosophy of which she is barely conscious.

"Pigs have been implanted with jellyfish genes. It gives them fluorescent yellow snouts," she says, out of nowhere. It's just a bid to shock them and stall their entrance into the capsule that will take them up and up.

"What on earth are you talking about, luv?" Lenny says as he walks back toward her in the queue. He looks at her as if he knows it's all a bluff and takes her arm. "Believe me, it's perfectly safe. Nothing better engineered since the Eiffel Tower," he says and pulls her forward.

The London Eye is a millennial monument. Victoria looks up. The advertising says it stands 450 feet high above the Thames, and is constructed of 1,700 tonnes of steel and glass. Innovation. She must not be closed down to discovery, she thinks. She looks at Lenny's hand on her arm and feels safer. She tries to rouse other feelings from his touch—excitement? Confusion? Even irritation? Nothing else comes.

"I've wanted to show you this, a spectacular view," he says as they draw nearer to Derek, who steps along aggressively in the steadily moving queue. He wants it to move faster. Kendra has been on the Eye several times: once with her father and a couple of times at birthday parties to which Derek had not been invited. Stephen's mother thinks the Eye is a waste of money, so Stephen hasn't been on it either. Football's her thing, on account of her new boyfriend's passion for Chelsea. But now Derek finally has his chance.

The whole weekend has been filled with outings, thanks to Lenny Brown. Lenny and his giddy laugh, his way of fussing over Auntie Vic and teasing her when she gets too nervous. And they've certainly eaten well these last two days. Pizza, cod and chips, chocolate. Not Auntie Vic's food. Derek has been to his first proper London restaurant this week: a Greek restaurant in Mayfair. He's seen an action sequel in Leicester Square, been to the Tate Modern, and now is waiting his turn to see the city from the sky. He steps forward, coming up close behind a young man who keeps kissing his girlfriend.

"You excited, son?" Lenny asks him.

Victoria shoots Lenny a look, protective of the use of that word in relation to Derek.

"Na, not really," Derek fibs, but he smiles widely.

Victoria touches the boy's head and sweeps the hair back from his forehead. Derek intentionally sweeps it back in place. "Enjoying yourself, aren't you?" she asks tenderly.

"Yes, Auntie Vic," he says, still smiling. She takes Lenny by the hand and smiles at him too. In that moment they are a family. She blushes.

CHAPTER NINE

As I Blush . . .

ᕤᙏᙢᕬ

The wind was strong as he made his way across the moor, and the sprinkling of rain quickly became a pelting. His horse slowed, but he dug in his heels to spur it faster. The boy knew he had to make it home before the sun fell. He knew that there at home his father was waiting for him to tell him of his adventures at sea, and how his ship had sailed from Portsmouth to Lisbon and had traded in food and gold. His father was a very successful sailing merchant . . .

"Derek!" His aunt's voice cuts into his writing. He has gone off topic again. His composition on the history of sailing ports has shifted to fiction. He writes pages and pages of it and often has to do homework twice in one night: once for himself, once for his teachers.

"Derek! Come a minute, please."

He gets up from his desk and goes into Victoria's room. "Yes?"

"What's this?" His aunt is holding up a state-of-the-art mobile phone, which she has just taken out of his jacket pocket. He doesn't answer right away, running through the phone's chronology in that split second. First it was "tax" collected by Richard Lorry from a boy in Derek's year because Richard said the wealthy should be forced to pay more; then it was payment from Richard to Stephen for delivering a package to a man waiting at the bus shelter near Boundary and Finchley roads. Stephen begged Derek to hide the phone for him, for a few days, until he could get to the McDonald's next to sell it. He knew his mother would never let him keep it, would punish him for even having it. Derek gave in, thinking he could hide it in one of Max's Lego boxes. But he forgot that it was in his pocket in his rush to sit down at the computer and write the story about a boy who stows away on a cargo ship bound for Africa. But now the phone is awaiting its next scene.

"A phone," he says, stalling.

"I know that," his aunt says, impatiently. "My question really is, where did it come from? Is this another of Kendra's little trophies?"

The name gives him an idea. He decides that Stephen has had enough grief lately and if he gets into more trouble Derek will never get to see him. "Her dad gave it to me. It's an old one of his, doesn't need it anymore." The lie comes easily, and, for a second, pride at his invention pushes aside any guilt. But the new look on his aunt's face worries him.

"Charity?" But it's not a question for him. "Derek, you shouldn't have accepted it. You don't need a phone . . . I could have bought you one if you did," she mutters.

He's less sure about this new chapter and wants the phone to disappear. "I'll give it back to him," he suggests.

"That's impolite."

"Or I could give it to Stephen, he needs—"

"We'll have to thank Mr. Hodge properly." She pauses, looking down at the phone, turning it over, pressing the call button and putting it to her ear. "You could ask Kendra to visit one evening after school. You could do homework together, and she could stay for supper. I could cook something she'd like."

"Um . . ." Derek is put off by the thought of Kendra and his aunt seated at the tiny table in their sitting room eating an elaborately organic meal and drinking carrot juice or wheatgrass, or whatever is Victoria's latest concoction that is "just right" for children.

"Umm . . ." he repeats.

"We could invite her out, if you prefer. I think it would be nice to get to know her; you're always over at her place and she's never been here." Victoria's pride is rising to the task. She thinks about the high price of wild salmon, but she could manage it. Or sea bass, with saffron. Yes. "We could invite her father too," she offers, thinking about the ambiguous feeling she remembers getting in his presence. He hadn't liked school either.

Derek tries to control his panic. He doubts Alexander would cover for him, and besides, how would he even broach the topic?

"You think about it. Ask Kendra what she thinks," she says finally and hands him the phone, distractedly, and goes out to the kitchen.

The bell rang at least five minutes ago. He's waiting for her at their designated spot on the corner in front of the school, but Kendra is nowhere in sight. This is unusual. Derek shuffles his feet and jiggles his knee. He paces, picks up a stone, and tosses it onto the road. He kicks another. Children pass him as they head home. Still no Kendra. Picking up his satchel, he decides to head back to school to see if he can find her. They are meant to be doing homework together at her house before Auntie Vic gets home from Lenny's.

At the side entrance to the school he spots her, but she's running toward the back of the schoolyard, her arms raised gently from her sides, her fingers spread, hands undulating in an Indian dance, her black hair bobbing like the mane of a shelty. She disappears round the back of the school, and he follows, up past the Nursery to the cluster of trees near Finchley Road, where the tough kids hang out to smoke and trade. Derek loses sight of her but keeps going, sure that when he catches up with her she'll remember their plans and turn around, and this creepy feeling in his legs will disappear.

When he reaches the ridge where the bower of juniper and oak trees begins, he walks more stealthily, secret-agent-style, over grass and around bramble. His knees feel wobbly. Suddenly there is a muffled squeal. He ducks down beside a hawthorn bush, then raises his head just high enough to scan for the source of the squealing and rumbling. Obscured by the long branches of the large oak are two bodies rolling on the ground as though in battle. Or not. He ducks his head again and stares at his satchel. Listening. The sounds are not unlike those of an animal sucking on a bone. But the weakness in his knees knows better, and he waits for the squeal again, wanting to be sure it's really Kendra's.

"No!" comes her voice, and he lifts his head again and sees her sit up, pushing back the hair that has fallen over her face. "Stop it, you arse," she continues, and gives the figure on the ground a slight shove with the heel of her palm. "Look," she says, and takes something out of her pocket. Derek knows what it is she is show-ing the figure beneath her, because he saw it already this morning. It's her latest gadget. A pocket-sized navigator. Or, to be precise, a Global Positioning System, a GPS locator, she called it.

"It's the latest. My dad says maps are a thing of the past thanks to this, and he doesn't want me to ever get lost, poor sod." Derek gulps. The tremor in his knees picks up tempo.

"Come here, I won't lose ya," says the voice from the ground, and as Derek pokes his head up over the bush again Kendra is swept beneath the form and her squeals resume. Derek sits on the ground, hugs his knees, and tries to keep his breathing even and inaudible.

"No . . . Noooo!" Her voice is high and light at first, with a hint of a giggle, but then it deepens and takes on a more insistent tone. Derek's heart leaps. The noises have changed and they're faster, scratchier, and Kendra's No punctuates them. All of a sudden the NO lengthens into a scream and Derek shoots up from his spot and rushes out from behind the bush. He marches in the direction of the soft grass where the two bodies are struggling. When he's close, he freezes at the sight of Richard Lorry holding his penis in one hand and pulling at Kendra's underpants with the other. Kendra is trying to draw her trousers up from around her ankles.

"Kendra," he says softly, but they hear him.

"Get the fuck out of here!" Richard hollers, still holding his penis, but dropping the hand that was tearing at Kendra's pants. Kendra scrambles onto her knees, but trips as she pulls up on her trousers.

"I said get the fuck out of here, you bloody bastard!" Richard screams.

Derek doesn't move. He can't. His knees are locked.

"Kendra," he says again softly, though he'd meant to be louder. Kendra grunts and moans as she pulls herself up and tucks in her shirt. She turns and starts to run. In a flash she is galloping through the wood into the clearing toward the school. Derek watches her, then turns to face Richard, who is now on his feet, zipping up his fly.

"You're dead, Layne," says Richard breathlessly, with less conviction than Derek expects. Derek stares at Richard the Truck and really wishes he was already twelve.

Two brawny, glistening sea bass. She picks one up, rinses it, puts it on the foil, then rinses the other. The knives are sharp. One to filet them, but first this barong. Perhaps the choice of seafood is inappropriate. According to Lenny's book, in some cultures fish can be seen as an aphrodisiac. She's nervous. All she wants is to hold her own, not to feel beholden. Of course, that's all. She raises the barong and slashes off the head of the first fish.

"*Al, sonrojarme, muero,*" she sings to herself. The barong strikes again on the second bass. She strains her memory to remember more words, but they don't come. It's been a long time since she's sung that tune. A Venezuelan woman at the hospital reminded her of the words several years ago, but she knew it long before that. The sea bass recipe is courtesy of a Venezuelan chef, but the song comes from the Venezuelan dancer her daddy had befriended and brought to the garden to shame his wife. When it was done, the woman strolled away from the tomato patch, singing, "*Al, sonrojarme muero . . . As I blush, I die . . .*" The tune seems so innocent now.

Victoria tears off a dorsal fin with her hands.

The rest of the meal is already prepared: the nuts and figs set out in suitable bowls; the ceviche chilling in the refrigerator; the rice steamed; the saffron sauce for the sea bass sitting at room temperature on the counter; the water for the asparagus ready to be set to boil; the pears Roquefort cooling before being set to chill in the chocolate mousse.

"Have you set the table, Derek?" There is no answer from the next room. Victoria calls him again. She listens at the stairs and can hear Derek playing with Max and Monica. He's spending a lot of time with them these days. When she came home after work four days previously, expecting him to be still at Kendra's, she was surprised to find him downstairs at Sonia's tossing Max about and playing sweets shopkeeper with Monica. At supper, when she asked him why he hadn't been at Kendra's, he merely shrugged. When she pressed him on whether or not he'd extended her dinner invitation to Kendra and her father, he asked to be excused from the table, went into his room, and turned on the computer. It was Victoria who had to call Alexander to invite them for this evening. Derek remained in his room in a sulk and fell asleep early that night. He's not been himself since.

"What's bothering you, lad," she attempted this morning at breakfast.

"Nothing," he said without looking up from his muesli.

"School?" she ventured. He shook his head. "Friends?" she asked, not wanting to specifically mention Stephen, knowing that Stephen often doesn't turn up at school and that Derek misses him. Then she wanted to ask if his sulking had anything to do with Kendra, but anyone who knows Derek knows she is sacred territory, and Victoria didn't want to trespass. He remained silent.

171

Victoria worries that the opportunity for shared confidences between the two of them passed her by a couple of years ago, when she wasn't capable of hearing them. Now that she is, Derek is a boy with a man's steel countenance growing beneath his delicate skin like the dark shading that will dawn over his lip in a few years' time. She scoops out the fish's innards, takes the sharp filet knife, and cuts gently along the dorsal bone. She produces two perfect filets and sets them aside.

She opens the cupboard. Her heart sinks at the sight of the dinnerware, all odds and ends, chipped and out of fashion. The flower pattern is disappearing from the edges of most of the plates. She wipes them and lays them out on the small dining table, along with glasses, cutlery, and napkins that she bought today. She checks her watch. Turning back to the counter, she catches a glimpse of herself in the shining toaster. She looks at the image and pinches her cheeks.

Almost a decade ago, over a period of eight months, her cheeks were constantly flushed, her head dizzy, her mind sputtering like an old engine. She'd walk to work at the hospital in confusion about what was taking place inside her, and some days she'd stand and cry as she stirred the soup, her tears sliding into the pot, salting the dishes further. When menstruation stopped, her red cheeks disappeared, as though blood had divorced her, packed up, and moved on for someone younger.

"Derek, will you go downstairs and meet them at the door?" she calls down the stairs to the twins' bedroom. "Derek?"

There's giggling, then Max yells up: "He's been eaten."

"Derek, you heard me, please go down and show them up," she says firmly. Eventually she hears his footsteps descend.

When Alexander, Kendra, and Derek appear at the top of the stairs, Victoria is wiping clean the kitchen counter of the last drips of the chocolate mousse. Only the sea bass is left to be broiled and drizzled with sauce.

"Oh, hello, hello, welcome, come in, come in," she begs them, instantly conscious of the shabbiness of the room, the mustiness, and the dust. She wipes her hand on her apron and notices the lined skin on her knuckles.

"Very sweet of you to invite us," Alexander says as he takes the hand and shakes it, looking into her face. Victoria has never liked being scrutinized; she quickly drops her hand, wipes it again, and then removes the apron.

"My pleasure," she says while the apron is still over her face. She ushers them to the table, explaining that the first courses are ready and they must sit—and besides, it's not really a sitting room per se, the room is multi-functioning, and she hopes they don't mind the chairs; they are a little wobbly, but the table is solid and . . . well . . . please take a seat.

Alexander takes the wine he's brought out of its bag and hands it to her. She thanks him, "You needn't have," and takes it to the counter beside the bass. He takes both his seat and a cashew in one graceful sweep. Kendra pulls out a chair and slumps into it, not looking at anyone. Victoria looks anxiously at Derek, whose face is clenched as he reaches for a handful of cashews. He throws them, one by one, into his mouth. She clears her throat.

"Do you cook much for yourself, then?" she asks Alexander, hoping it's the right question, really wanting to say, I hope you'll like what I've prepared.

"No, we don't," says Alexander. "I'm no good at it, I'm afraid." He picks up a bottle from the table and pours some chilled organic Pinot Grigio into Victoria's glass. "This looks fantastic," he says.

She watches his eyes examine the table and realizes how foreign he is to her—his smooth skin, his colouring, his jawline. He has full, confident lips. His boyishness is offset by the freshly pressed white shirt, and his chestnut curls hide the impinging grey well. His nose is aquiline, and, second to the rain-blue eyes specked with yellow, it is the defining feature in this man who seems both as fragile and determined as a majestic bird. A part of her misses the comfort of Lenny and the hair that pushes through the open collar of his shirt, but the rest of her is ringing with something new. Alexander looks up from the feast before him and gives her a grateful smile.

Victoria offers the ceviche around in silence. Kendra twirls her hair in two fingers, her elbows on the table. Victoria can't understand why the girl hasn't said anything, not even to Derek. Her irritation rises again. Is this how to raise a child? Alexander examines the flesh of the ceviche as though it is still living.

"It's not cooked, I hope that's OK . . ." Victoria offers, calming herself.

"I love it," he says and pops some in his mouth.

"Dad, you're disgusting," Kendra moans from beneath the hair that has fallen over her face.

Victoria looks from one to the other and back again. Alexander smiles to himself as he chews.

"He loves dead, uncooked things," Kendra says, looking up at Victoria. It comes out as an accusation.

"It's a joke between the two of us," says Alexander. "Please excuse my daughter's bad manners." He raises his glass to the chef. "This is special."

Victoria clinks glasses with him, then sips her wine quickly. The duelling begins inside her again, the push-pull of his first gaze. Perhaps she should just thank him for the phone and end the evening. He's an accomplished, professional English man. He doesn't belong in her little room. Why has she gone to such trouble for this odd pair? She takes some ceviche.

Alexander looks about the room, taking it in for the first time. Is he judging? Assessing the clutter of the tiny space she has to make her life in?

"Have you lived here long?" he asks.

"Yes, quite a long time," she answers, thinking he's probably the kind of man who is into minimalism, leather, and stainless steel. "We don't have much room, and things seem to collect," she adds.

"The English love to hang on to things," he comments, absent-mindedly.

"They're not English, Dad," Kendra says acidly as she picks at the ceviche on her plate.

"I didn't mean them," he says, then turns to Victoria and continues. "No, sorry, I didn't mean that at all. What I meant to say was: Kendra's always accusing me of being ruthless. I like to get rid of things."

"And why's that? Because they don't matter in the long run?" Victoria feels an odd connection to this man, and she wants him to confirm her own sense of the absurdity of having things when you could lose everything in a single moment.

"Perhaps. Or maybe letting go allows you to let go of life, in the end . . . Kendra, help me out, I'm babbling."

"You're in this alone," Kendra says, smirking. The girl still hasn't looked at Derek.

Victoria turns to Alexander to interpret what's going on between him and his daughter. Focused on his glass of wine, he lifts it to his lips, sips.

The frank pursuit of meaning is something Victoria hasn't engaged in since Toronto, but here in this room where she's accumulated scraps of a London history, she feels the need to defend her life and to tell Alexander that some things are important to hold on to.

"I've left everything I own twice in my life," she says, but it comes across aggressively.

"You have?" He says it in a way that doesn't feel like a question.

"It's not glamorous," she replies, trying to soften her tone, but realizing she hasn't.

"Brave."

"Necessary." Victoria takes a sip of wine and reminds herself that this is the man who said the word irrational as though it was a disease. She's nothing if not irrational, because now she's drawn by the way his directness feels like intimacy.

"All I meant about things was . . . think about technology and where it will take us. We think it's into the future, but maybe it just makes the present more bearable, more important. In the present all we have is ourselves to deal with. There's a wonderful freedom and privilege then," he says.

"As long as everyone can have it," Victoria adds.

"Agreed." He nods at being put in his place. "Your home is lovely and comfortable, Victoria."

Kendra puts both elbows on the table and rests her chin in her hands. Derek looks straight at his plate. Victoria is confused by the tension between them, but her focus is on Alexander.

"So, you work with technology," she asks.

"I do, yes . . . video imaging, mostly in the medical field, as well as some graphic art."

"And how do dead, uncooked things fit in?"

"They don't, really," he says through a smile and takes another sip of wine.

Another man with secrets. But this one's not going to trap her. She's prone to secrets, but she's not going to believe in him. Death is not coy. The present must take that into account. "Please help yourself to more," she says, pushing the dish towards him.

She guides the conversation towards small talk: school issues and the best shopping in the neighbourhood. Alexander's mood loosens with the wine, and he teases Kendra about being surly. He describes a project he's doing for an engineering firm reconstructing a bridge in the south of France. Victoria watches him speak, enjoying the comfort her small room has created for them. Then, suddenly, upon mention of a similar project he did in Italy, it's as though the bridge itself collapses into the river and his playfulness disappears.

"That was when Smita died." All the comfort in the room congeals, and Victoria stiffly clears her throat. She holds up the bottle of wine to offer him more. He nods.

They eat in silence for unendurable seconds. Victoria gets up to grill the sea bass.

"Dad doesn't like the past," Kendra says finally, a little more relaxed, even though the chill between her and Derek hasn't yielded for a moment.

"That's distorting the facts, Ken," he defends. Her comment puts Alexander back at ease. He raises his voice so that Victoria can hear him at the counter. "It's not that. We had a row last night, at a dinner with some office friends. They were saying how much better the monarchy is now because they've begun to show affection in public. It's a ridiculous case in support of an outdated institution. They said this country likes its past, and I said it should be ashamed of it. And I had my reasons, but Kendra doesn't like it when I go on."

"I think this country likes to be at odds with itself," Victoria says over her shoulder, realizing now that this may be exactly why she likes it here.

After a few minutes of grilling, Victoria returns to the table with the main course. She serves each of them in turn, beginning with Alexander, pleased with the way the saffron sauce dribbles off the flesh of the bass onto the shabby plates.

"I remember you at a school meeting," Victoria ventures, not tasting her food yet. "You said the fear of GM foods was irrational." She's trying to draw out the resentment the word pricked in her then, to remind her of her distaste for him, which is rapidly disappearing. Anything he says now might only make her feel more free, able to say whatever is in her mind. She's burning to ask him why he hated school and to tell him how much she did too.

"Did I?" is his only response as he bites into the sea bass. "My God, this is spectacular." He chews and swallows, takes another sip of wine. "I suppose it's not that I'm for it or against it, I just think we need to keep our fears in check. It would be horrible if we stopped everything we were afraid of."

"Have you never been afraid, then?" she asks. Gloves on, fists up, now. Distance is more comfortable territory. "There are people all over the world who have lots to be afraid of. What would you say to a pointed gun?" she challenges, feeling she's ventured farther than she'd intended. But for years now she's thought this TV-talk-show way of discussing fear as the only enemy arises from privilege and indulgence. Only children could possibly say that.

At first Alexander thinks she's joking, but quickly sees she isn't. "No, you're right, that's true. That's very different. I didn't mean that kind of fear," he says.

"It's the same as the other kind, just more immediate, I think," she adds, finally slicing into her filet of bass and tasting it, proudly.

Alexander reaches over and touches Kendra's hair gently, his hand resting on her shoulder. Victoria suddenly feels like an ungracious host. She drops her sparring stance.

"Would you care for more rice?" she asks.

Alexander declines, raising his hand and shaking his head with a smile. Kendra finally looks up at Derek. Their eyes lock. Alexander watches them. His hand moves down Kendra's back and gives it a gentle rub.

"You're lucky to have Derek to work on your project, or I'm not sure how you'd get anything done." He turns to Victoria. "She's stopped practising the flute, what with the two of them meeting every day after school, but she'll have to get back to it over the holidays."

Kendra's eyes shrink to slits as she challenges Derek's discretion. Right here, right now, come on, if you dare, she seems to be saying. Derek takes a drink of water, replaying the image of Kendra's trousers at her ankles, the sound of her long nooooo.

"The project's almost finished," he says, concentrating on his food. There it is again, the electric bolt that comes with controlling a moment. The power of a lie or an electric blast. Both bring this feeling to his chest. Besides, it's Richard who should pay for what he did.

"Yep, shouldn't be much longer," Kendra adds, puts her knife and fork together and pushes her plate away, satisfied.

Victoria notices the firm planes of Kendra's face. Her shoulders and the dip along her collarbone are almost womanly. She can't remember ever being as young and yet as composed as Kendra seems.

"Delicious food, Victoria. You are a master, that's clear," Alexander says, wiping up some saffron sauce with his last forkful of rice. "You must find it like work to cook for guests."

"No, work is baking, mostly. This is playing," she says, and there's a crack of pleasure in her voice that Alexander picks up on. He looks at her again. What is he seeing? Nothing to be discovered, surely. She adjusts her face and tries to look serious. "You shouldn't have, really . . . with the phone. He doesn't need one, and if he did . . . I could have . . ." As she speaks Derek goes rigid. "But thank you just the same."

Derek drags up a fake cough.

"Sorry? What are you thanking me for?" Alexander asks.

"The phone," Victoria says.

Derek's lip starts to tremble. The lightning bolt feeling is best left for more heroic moments. He didn't mean for this to happen. He stares at his plate.

"What phone?"

"The one—"

"I gave it to him, Dad," breaks in Kendra. She pulls her plate towards herself. Derek looks up and watches her as she runs her index finger along the edge of the plate, collecting the last dribbles of saffron sauce on it. She puts her finger to her mouth, sucking it with relish. "The food was so delicious. Derek's bloody lucky," she says without looking up and with a smile to no one in particular.

"Kendra, please," Alexander says, bristling at her language and manners. He hands her his napkin. "You gave him a phone?"

"An old one, Christine gave me an old one of hers, and—"

"I've lost it anyhow," Derek interjects, trying to stop the domino of lies.

"Oh, Derek!" Victoria is trying to keep up with the shifting ground of this conversation.

"May we be excused?" Derek asks. Victoria is both proud of his manners and confused by what has just transpired.

"Of course," she says.

Derek and Kendra get up quickly from the table and skitter into Derek's room. They leave the door ajar and head straight for the computer.

Victoria clears the plates. Did Derek know the phone was Christine's? Has she been a fool to stage this encounter? She runs hot water over the plates and composes herself, trying to hold on to her sense of the evening's purpose. There's a buzzing silence in the room. Turning off the tap, she rubs her forearm briskly and sits back down at the table to serve the dessert.

"She's quite something," she says, indicating in the general direction of Derek's room. Alexander nods and stares off into the distance. Victoria knows there are only a few avenues their conversation can take. Her senses are alert, humming. She braces herself and ventures out: "The missing can be unbearable, can't it." Alexander looks at her squarely. They both know she is referring to Kendra's mother, but Victoria is surprised at the effortless leap into intimacy with this stranger. He doesn't miss a beat, and casually begins to tell her about Smita—Smita the musician, Smita the painter, Smita the woman who could talk and read into the night long after he was exhausted and had tuned out the world and its concerns. A well-educated Brahmin, Smita's perspective on life and death was eagle-like and unwavering. "She left nothing unopened or unturned," Alexander says, and Victoria feels herself shrinking down into her chair, moving to the far corner of the table with her elbow, unable to take up any space in this room now filled with the song of Smita.

"I recognize myself less and less every day," Alexander says, and she realizes that what she might have thought was arrogance is actually a cover for deep feeling. She was wrong about him. Not arrogant, not naïve, this is simply a man coping with the gaps life leaves. She wants to tell him everything, but she restrains herself.

"What do you mean?" she asks.

"I get lost between work and Kendra. I have a study at home. I sit and play, really, and when I come out I don't know what's real."

Why is he looking to her as though she has an answer? Victoria shifts her weight, feeling her lower back against the chair as she sits up straight. Does he think she's a wise older woman? Is she that much older than he is? He mentioned that he had Kendra at forty-three. She is twelve—he's fifty-five? Victoria has only nine years on him, and much of those, she thinks, are years of waiting. How much could waiting count in the bearing out of age?

When only streaks of chocolate mousse remain on the bottom of the indelicate parfait glasses, Victoria is relieved supper is over. Expecting Alexander to leave as quickly as is polite, she starts to pile up plates at the sink. She realizes it might be rude to leave the room so she sits down again. As though picking up a thread from a previous conversation he begins on the subject of Guyana. He asks her about her family, where her relations are. When she stops feeling trespassed upon—so many years of not expecting any Englishman except Lenny Brown to ask her anything about herself—she tells him that there are no more relatives. Except for Derek.

"I like your accent; it's very confused. Refreshing," says Alexander, and then he is exploring her face again. What's he finding? The Guyana jungle? She rubs her arm again, near the recently stiff elbow joint. She picks at tiny crumbs on the tablecloth.

"Well, I suppose I should fetch my daughter and get home. She has a music lesson in the morning, and I have work. Victoria, thank you so much for the evening. The food was some of the best I've ever had." He gets up from the table.

"Kendra!" he calls towards Derek's room.

"Yep," comes her reply from Derek's desk.

"It was my pleasure," says Victoria, thinking that Kendra's mother must have made splendid Indian food. Victoria tries to picture her, the envelope of beauty that Kendra came from. Kendra doesn't have much in her from this man with the speckled eyes. She is dark and round, yet refined like a sculpture.

And there she is in the doorway, with Derek. Victoria can't take her eyes off the girl.

"OK, let's go," Kendra says, giving Derek a nudge on the shoulder for him to show them out. Victoria stands up. Alexander reaches out his hand.

"Thanks again."

"Thank you for coming, Alexander," she says, drawing out his full name. Her broad smile encourages him to step closer. They stand close for a moment before he turns to leave.

When Derek returns upstairs, he finds his aunt motionless, staring out the window at the Indian Bean Tree. Kendra touched him. "You're all right," she said when they reached his room, commending his silence at the table, covering for her absences after school. She said nothing more about the phone, having given it her own chapter in front of the adults, then leaving it to him. She put her fingers on his neck, near his hairline, and rubbed it gently. His hair has been standing on end ever since. He tiptoes past Victoria to his room, to the desk where he and Kendra were adding her illustrations to his latest story. He picks up Kendra's drawing of a merchant ship and slips it into his journal, underneath the letter from Kola he has not yet replaced in his aunt's hall chest.

She steps quickly along the last one hundred metres of the pavement before Lenny's flat, pumping her arms to get more oxygen flowing. The sun is warm on her shoulders, shining for the first time, it seems, in months. May has arrived like an answer. A calming yes to the shivering questions of winter.

She can feel the strain in her triceps as she thrusts her elbows forward in her march. She skips up the step to Lenny's door. Taking out her key, she notices her laboured breath. Shameful, that. Like an old machine. At the click of the key turning in the lock she makes a decision to walk faster all the way next time.

"Morning, luv," Lenny welcomes.

"Morning Len. What do we have on today?"

"A few new ones, I'm afraid."

"You're afraid?"

"There's too much for us. You'd like to work Sundays, too?"

"No," she says abruptly, as though it would be his fault. She is afraid she's offended, but he hasn't noticed.

"Nor do I, but . . ." He hands her the orders that represent extra hours of baking that week.

The thought of the increased income calms her. Derek wants to continue music lessons, but he wants to play the trumpet—Lord help us. She is thinking of buying him a guitar for his twelfth birthday. Deep down she's balking at the thought of the extra hours. A voice in her says that's enough, for a little while, a bit for me now.

"We could get Matthew to come in full-time, he needs the dosh," suggests Lenny.

"We can't really afford to, can we?"

"If we got more work, we could expand, invite someone with their own clients, make it a joint venture."

"I can't think about it now, Len. Can it wait a day or so?"

"That can, but these orders can't. You OK?"

"Yes, very OK," she says, smiling, her face radiant.

He gets up from his stool and stands in front of her, his own smile growing. "Good to see you like this, sweetheart," he coos, as he puts his arms around her. "Shall we start work a little later, maybe?" He pushes his chest and belly close to her, hugging her tightly.

All Victoria's cells react; she freezes in his arms, a chill immediately detected by Lenny. He releases her.

"Hmm, suppose not." He places the purchase orders on the table and picks up his apron, slipping it over his head. After a few choked seconds he looks at her: "Is it me?"

She flinches. "No, no, Lenny, not you, not you at all. Just me. Just not quite there, is all."

"You've been saying that for a year."

"And that's how long I've been feeling it . . ."

Lenny ties the apron around his waist, preparing to work on the ten-pound batter already in the mixer. Victoria watches him, her chest tight with guilt. Why not Lenny? Why can't I love Lenny? She walks to the back door of the flat to open it and let the May breeze blow through the already hot kitchen.

It's after seven when she arrives back at Blenheim Terrace, having stopped at the Salvation Army on her way home. Beth, the woman with the matted hair Victoria serves regularly, took the plate of less-than-perfect *petits fours*—omitted from an order Lenny delivered to South Kensington—and gave Victoria a loose-teeth grin. She held one of the small pastries in her palm and nodded over and over.

"Shouldn't be having these at my age, but what the hell, eh luv? We seem to be doing pretty well, you and me," she said through a bit of spittle. Victoria nodded, but the idea that Beth thought they were the same age struck her with mild terror. How old does she look? She's knows for a fact that the woman is younger than she is, probably in her fifties, nearer to Alexander's age, but Beth looks almost a decade older than Victoria. Victoria wonders how old Christine is.

When she clicks shut the front door to the house, she hears noises from the sitting room. Derek is there with Max and Monica. Occupied, not needing her. It's a relief.

"Derek, let's go up and have some supper, dear," she calls out at the door to the sitting room.

"Already had it," he calls from the sofa amidst a high-pitched "Look! Look!" from Max wanting him to notice his latest tractor.

"What? Where did you do that?"

Sonia comes from her kitchen. "We had some pasta together," she says, wiping her hands on a dishtowel.

"Oh." Pasta! White flour and egg, little else. Victoria bristles slightly.

"Hope that was OK. Derek said he was hungry," Sonia adds.

"He doesn't usually eat pasta," Victoria can't help but say.

"Well, he did a fine job of it this evening," Sonia returns, with an innocent smile that Victoria cannot argue with. This woman is a real mother.

"Well, thank you," Victoria says, trying not to sound territorial. "Come up, Derek. You have homework, don't you?"

"Finished it," he says.

"Let him stay and play for a bit, won't you?" Sonia asks.

"Yes, of course," she concedes. "Thanks. Send him up when he's a bother." She makes her way up the stairs, scolding herself for her resentment.

As she reaches her room, slightly out of breath from the stairs, the telephone is ringing.

"Hello . . ." she breathes into the receiver.

"Victoria?" The voice has the same resonance as her own.

"Yes, speaking," she says, not letting on she knows who's calling. It's Alexander, calling to thank her for the lovely meal and company the previous night.

"Pleasure was mine," she says, finding herself sounding formal.

"You're a natural," he offers.

"With the dead and uncooked." She can't resist, and hears his breath quicken, a smile forming on the other end of the line. A long pause. The disorienting image of her father's hands and the soil underneath his fingernails flashes into her mind.

"I'm envious," he says. She imagines him alone at his computer, the glow from the screen lighting his face. Kendra is probably in front of the television being educated by all of life's excesses.

"You must be very good at what you do," she says, thinking

about all the girl's gadgets and how casually wealthy he seems in comparison to anyone she knows.

"I suppose so, but it certainly doesn't feel natural. The ceviche was perfect."

"Very easy."

"I've never been to the Caribbean," he adds out of nowhere.

"It didn't have much to do with me. I learned it from a Venezuelan," she says. He's a well-travelled man, dabbles in exotica, she thinks. She's nervous again; there's nothing exotic about her.

"I just cook," she says flatly. After a pause she adds: "You create things."

"In a way. Maybe I could show you. There's a design show next week. My work is represented in it . . . informal . . . are you free Wednesday?"

"Yes," she says quickly. How's that for irrational?

"Terrific."

"Thank you, very much."

"Don't thank me yet. Pick you up at six—it's open until seven-thirty, and we can grab a bite after?"

"Thank you. Yes."

"I look forward to it."

"Yes." She looks into the receiver before replacing it.

Turning to the hall mirror is the most automatic gesture. She moves her hair away from her face. All she can see is her seven-year-old self—a small girl, terrified by sounds from the garden late at night.

Someone knocks at the door.

"Come in."

Sonia enters with the twins' pyjamas draped over her arm, their toothbrushes in her hand. "I came up to get them ready for bed and thought I should have a quick word, if I may."

"Yes?" Victoria asks, panicked. Will this be the eviction notice? Where will she afford the space she has here for Derek? Will he have to change schools?

"Has Derek spoken to you about this fellow at his school—or used to be at school—this Richard fellow?"

"No, why?"

"Um, he hasn't?" Sonia hesitates.

"Not recently, anyway."

"Well, seems he was expelled, but now he's back. With a vengeance, bullying, pushing drugs." She stops and waits for the effect.

Drugs? Victoria's hipbone starts to feel vacuum-sucked. "What did Derek say?"

"That Richard used to leave him alone, but he's now taken to picking on him. He wants Derek to help him sell drugs. Or at least that's what it sounds like to me. He's asked him to deliver packages."

Good God.

"I thought you should know," concludes Sonia. "He asked me not to tell you, but I had to. Don't tell him I did, please, but do ask him how he got the cut on his face . . ."

The cut? Damn it. Why hasn't she looked at him? Victoria bolts out of the room and heads downstairs to fetch Derek.

"I told you, it's nothing," he says later, as he stands in his pyjamas, bathed and ready for bed, with Victoria still fussing with the scrape and bruise near his eye.

"Nothing does not look like this, boy," she says severely.

Derek holds his breath as she dabs the cut again with something that stings. He wants to tell her to leave him alone, but that would be rude. Besides, alone is the last thing he really wants. Alone is what he almost is anyway, and he's sure he doesn't want any more of it. What he really wants to be is twelve. Things will be easier then. He hates having such a late birthday, behind everyone in his class. He'd be able to handle Richard the Truck if he were twelve. Obviously his Kanaima shield has lost its power. He'll have to find another source.

"You must know why he'd do something like this, Derek, but you're not telling me," Auntie Vic says as she twists the cap back on the stinging liquid.

"I have no *idea!*" he says, overemphasizing the last word, acting now. There's no way he'd tell her about Richard and Kendra in the bushes. Richard showed up at the front of the school at three-thirty, dragged Derek by the arm down the road, stopped at the corner, and in front of anyone who cared to watch, kicked him in the groin and punched his face with his right knuckle, silver skull ring and all. "Eyes to yourself, Kanaima boy," he said, then walked off. Derek crumpled into a heap of eleven-year-oldness until Stephen rushed to his side and hauled him to his feet. "I've told Kendra, mate. She won't let him get away with this," said Stephen as consolation. But Derek knew that Kendra was dealing with more than Richard's bullying now, and, for the first time ever, he questioned her capabilities.

His aunt's eyes are bright with concern. He'd like to be able to tell her things, the way he did with his mom, but he still finds this difficult. They have spoken intensely whenever he has brought up the sperm bank, but he hasn't mentioned that in quite some time. He wants to tell her that he and Kendra have devised a plan to trace his father. Kendra thinks that through securing lists of donors' characteristics from different sperm banks in the Miami area, they will be able to piece together the trail of identical traits, factoring in the area radius the donations were made in, identifying the frequency and timing of his visits, and eventually put together a picture of the man's activities and whereabouts. Surely he can be found.

"Now get to bed, and remember what I told you: that boy comes back and you go to the head teacher immediately, you hear?" Victoria's face is flushed. "I wish you'd told me this boy was a problem sooner, Derek. Why didn't you?" she asks as she folds his clothes into his dresser drawer.

He doesn't know how to answer. He has learned many things

well since moving to London, and one of them is the firm boundary between these rooms and the outside world. He shrugs his shoulders.

"I'm going to call the school to make sure they know this nonsense is going on," she insists.

"No," he says quickly, forcefully.

"Of course, I must, they'll stop him coming on the property."

"No, Auntie Vic, please . . . please . . ." and his voice gets so near to shrieking that his aunt stops her tidying to look at him. They take each other in for a few long seconds.

"Tell me if he comes back, will you?" she asks gently.

"Yes, Auntie Vic. Night." He walks to her and kisses her on the cheek as he has done only a handful of times.

CHAPTER TEN

Sashimi

⤬

Wood. That's it. Wood makes life possible. Look at the way it begs to cradle you, wrap you in its grain when you sit. It holds your food up to you, offers it like its own fruit right there in your hands. Wood is graceful in time, without denying it. Wood is our last protection from the earth before we become a part of it.

Gazing at the arm of the chair and the laminated chopsticks in her hand, Victoria thinks wood might just be a woman's perfect partner. She caresses the chopsticks, looks at Alexander, and smiles. He offers her a ceramic dish filled with curled carrot and a purée of radish. She dips her chopsticks into the purée and brings some to her lips. The taste is sublime, and her mouth lingers longer than necessary on the tip of the sticks. Alexander watches her. She feels herself blush. *As I blush, I die . . .* and wood will accompany her.

"The mahogany would be brought in from the interior, the Amazon rainforest—we call it the bush—and then carved, some of it going abroad first and then coming back as beautiful chairs, one I used to love called a Berbice chair, a curved recliner with long planks of mahogany that fold out from the armrests for your legs and feet." The Berbice chair, the chest and tables from her childhood—how proud her mother had been about the wood in their small house. "Wood was something my mother could count on," she says absent-mindedly, then catches herself and laughs. "Wood was certainly more reliable than my father."

Alexander joins in her laughter. After several outings, she is now used to the way he looks at her. He seems to light up when she laughs. She's telling him things, talking is easy, and she can hardly believe how much she has stored up. When she reveals things about herself, the yellow fleck in his eyes become more pronounced. This man is complicated, but kind.

Their first date had been to an exhibit of the latest technology in medical imaging, where she watched schematic videos of bodies, inert except for internal functions, as doctors described the illnesses, the excellent detection powers of the machinery, and the hope that early detection would delay life's passing. Then they attended a British Museum exhibit on mummification and funerary art. And last week they visited an exhibition of Francis Bacon's meat paintings. Alexander's passions puzzle yet intrigue her, and even in the face of rotting flesh she feels more alive than in the last thirty years. When they are surrounded by food, she is confident and in her element. After the Bacon exhibit, they drove to Le Mignon, a Lebanese restaurant on Delancey Street, and Victoria studied the ingredients of the hummus with minced lamb, which she wanted to make for Lenny, probably, she concedes, to assuage her guilt around Alexander's presence in her life now.

But one gallery visit had been contentious. At the Prehistory gallery of the British Museum, they attended an exhibition called "Objects of Power." It was filled with mundane and exceptional scraps of prehistorical society—mostly flint tools. Flint was fire, flint was power. Victoria enjoyed watching Alexander; the way his eyes fixed on objects, and how he moved about the gallery with his arms crossed, his fingers touching his lips.

"These people would have seen death as a release. We saw more clearly then," he said soberly as he stood in front of a portrait of a Neanderthal bearing a spark of fire. Fire that would lead to food, food that would lead to another day on the wretched earth; for one brief moment, fire would allow them to forget that this state of thirst and hunger was one to be vacated as quickly as possible. He seemed to imply that death in modern society was like a genius overlooked in its own time. Victoria felt her hackles rise as she remembered the interrupted moment on her knees behind the Also bar in Kilburn. Had Kola pleaded? No, she couldn't go along with Alexander's quixotic fancy, so in the café of the Great Court where the dome spread above them like a denial of the sky, she challenged him.

"That would mean that those who plunged headlong into death—warriors, sacrificial victims, suicides, even—could be the wisest, as though they know something about life we don't, as though life itself is not important, only the afterlife . . ."

"I don't mean it on that level—"

"You're always talking about 'that' level—as if mine is a simplistic one, perhaps." She could feel Kola rising in her, insisting on justice.

"No, no," Alexander said, aghast at the implication. "No, Victoria," he said and touched her hand. "It's just me, I'm talking metaphysically, that's all—it's what I'm interested in. It helps . . ."

She gave in to his gentleness, holding back the source of her indignation.

"I don't belong in my container," he said, slapped his chest with both hands, and laughed. She made a surprised face. "I've never felt inside what I look like on the outside. And one thing's for sure: I don't feel English."

"You are very English, in a way."

"What way is that?"

"You go out and discover things."

He squinted and considered what she was saying. As did she. The very notion of discovery challenged her. He was not only younger, he was young. Ageless.

"I do, yes, I guess I do," he concluded.

They changed the subject. He talked about his work, and she could feel him drift into what seemed an almost childlike state of wonder from which he watched the world in awe. Perhaps his obsession with bodies kept him in this world. When the subject changed back to his home life, Victoria was subdued, once again, by the sound of Smita.

"We went to Delhi every year, at Christmas, because Smita hated Christmas—all the hype and falseness. She'd get depressed as soon as December hit, and from that point she'd be making plans to leave for the holidays. Kendra loves Delhi. She's very different when she's there. Here, she confuses me," he said, with the yellow flecks in his eyes dancing. "In Delhi you see little girls on the street who were sold by their families to pay landlords when the crops failed. Or sold to repay other debts. Kendra stares at them and gives them money. You see malnourished children in some areas; emaciated, sunken-eyed, damaged hair, a dehydrated look that becomes a numb daze. You can tell they're beginning to close down: no smiles, no reflexes. Unbearable in a child."

And during the telling of that story Victoria gave herself to him, as she had to Kola the day he told her about the boy and girl who lived in a drain. Alexander drifted off somewhere, far away. Finally, looking at her again, he said, simply, "I miss being a family."

The declaration frightened her. She doesn't know if she's any good at family. He keeps mentioning how comforting it is that Kendra and Derek are so close. After each outing, when dropping her off at Blenheim Terrace, he would say nearly the same thing: "Thank you, I enjoyed that immensely. It's hard to do this alone, isn't it?" referring to the two children. "You're so easy to talk to." Then he would kiss her on both cheeks, squeeze her hand warmly, and beam at her while she fumbled with something comparable to say. By the third week and the fourth outing, she felt she knew quite a lot about Alexander, though she doubted he could say the same about her. She's been talkative—telling him about Derek, the shock of his arrival, the stress of caring for him—but she hasn't mentioned how difficult she found it at first, the oddness and the resentment she experienced at being thrust into motherhood. She didn't want him to think of her as unnatural.

Tonight she started by telling him about her first days in London, how difficult it had been to find lodgings, but how fortunate she'd been to meet Sonia's mother through someone at the hospital. Sonia's mother, whose family had fled from Romania, knew what it meant to search, what it meant to lose, and the importance of a warm room. She offered Victoria a room in the house on Blenheim Terrace in exchange for cleaning. Those early days in the house were marked by wood. Dusting and rearranging it, and trying not to panic about how she'd survive here.

Then the topic shifted to Guyana, and the fact that she'd never seen the bush or the great Kaieteur Falls, but both seemed to infiltrate her consciousness of life in Kitty. Wood and water. Alexander was particularly interested in the fact that some areas of Georgetown are below sea level and the houses are raised up on wooden stilts.

"I've been jabbering on and on, haven't I?" she says, suddenly self-conscious. She puts her chopsticks down across her plate. She has been talking more freely than she can remember since she was a girl and used to sit by the seawall with her mother, one day telling her that she wanted to paint a picture of the sea at night. The sea at night? But that would just be blackness ... and that had shut Victoria up. But she alone had known what she wanted to paint. The sound of water lapping. The steady magenta pulse of the dark ripples. These are the things she feels Alexander might understand.

"I like listening to your stories. I had no idea Guyana used to be so prosperous," he says, also putting his chopsticks down, waiting for her to tell him more. In the tiny Toronto apartment, as the cold wind howled outside, it was Kola who used to do all the talking, while Victoria listened. And she never made Kola laugh. Did anyone ever make Kola laugh?

"More than prosperous, a garden," Victoria says, taking a sip of sake.

"You do talk in metaphors."

She shifts in her chair slightly, wondering if he means that's a bad thing.

"It's beautiful."

She doesn't remember talking in metaphors before.

"What do you think of that one?" he asks, pointing to a dish of sashimi yellowtail with jalapeno peppers and lime juice.

"Melts in the mouth," she says quickly, hoping it's not too worn a metaphor, picking up her chopsticks again and adroitly clipping a slice of yellowtail between them. She's loved using chopsticks ever since she was a little girl. Her father insisted she learn how to use them because she was part Chinese, and it was an embarrassment to him if she didn't. She is confident and adept at their use even in this restaurant that is classes beyond her. The Nobu waiters are more sophisticated than she could ever learn to be, the clientele chic and commanding. She has never learned how to be commanding. Alexander doesn't belong either, with his almost studied, rumpled casualness, but he doesn't seem to notice or care. He is a connoisseur of the odd and unusual, and yet looks ordinary. Victoria has tried not to look at his lips as he sucks on the raw fish. In mid-chew of some black cod, he smiles at her. It sends a flutter through her belly. What is happening to her?

"These places can seem excessive to me," she says, deflecting again. "I feel guilty. At the shelter, you should see how they eat, especially if I haven't made something special. Not unnutritious, just bland. The things you put inside shouldn't be so bland. Blandness is an insult. You're spoiling me for them—each visit I try to outdo the last. Last week I made them duck with lemon and grapefruit, and mounds of saffron rice. Beth, a woman who eats there every day, told me she couldn't eat duck because she found it too chewy. I felt I'd failed, but, then again, her teeth aren't that good. I have to remember that. 'Vicky, we ladies have to take care of our teeth at this age,' she said, and that threw me."

"Surely at our age we don't have to panic yet," he says nonchalantly.

She swallows, and her eyes plunge to her plate, suddenly feeling caught out. She doesn't look at him. "Our age? And what's that?" she asks, fixed on the chopsticks.

"Well, middle age. In our fifties. I'm assuming you and I are roughly the same age," he says simply.

There's a pause as she draws courage. "I'm sixty-four," she says, looking up just in time to see the flicker of incredulity pass over his face. After a few long seconds, he says, "I had no idea. You look much younger."

"So I've been told most of my life," she says, but now she wants to drop the subject. She hands him the plate with the last slice of sashimi. She can see the slow reordering of history that goes on in a mind processing unexpected information. She gulps down the rest of her sake.

At the end of the evening, after dessert of lychee sorbet and a platter of fruit: star fruit, passionfruit, guavas—tastes of Guyana—she is confused. A certain tentativeness has restrained the casual warmth between them, although they valiantly continue the conversation.

"And so . . . would you care if anything in that meal had been modified by a scientist?" Alexander asks, after she's wiped her mouth with her napkin.

If the question is a test, she is not daunted. "Yes," she says simply.

"But why? It couldn't have done you any more harm than eating a banana could, and we've been manipulating bananas for decades."

"It's just an instinct. I want to know what I'm eating."

"OK, I grant you that, but say you know, then what?"

"Then it's my decision." She can hear her voice rise in pitch.

"Do you want me to say you are what you eat, our bodies are our temples, ecology starts on the tongue? . . . I eat better than I dress!" and then she laughs, so does he. She smoothes her blouse.

"OK. OK," he says, not with defeat but with respect. "But advancement is as important as food. We want it so we'll be immortal, but according to some we're only immortal when we die. That's the contradiction . . ."

She watches him carefully, knowing there's more to what he's saying than he's letting on. When he looks around for the waiter she panics, wanting a way to retrieve the warmth, but she realizes the main feature of this new territory is its blunt shape.

"Why do you bother with me?" Immediately, she wants to retract her words.

He looks insulted. "What are you saying?"

"I mean, we're from such different places, in more ways than one. You and your designs, your technology. Me and, well, me and Derek."

"You must have no idea how important that is," he says and examines his napkin. "And you're wrong if you think we're that different. I may look so, but I'm not . . ." he hesitates.

"Not what?"

"White," he says matter-of-factly.

She's horrified. What cards have they been playing? She leans back in her chair. "I can't believe you said that . . ."

"It didn't come out as I meant it. Colour is a position you adopt. What I mean is that if you think our differences have anything to do with how I was raised, you're wrong. I've fought against it my entire life . . . my family was very odd . . ."

She thinks about Kendra, Smita. "I see," she says, and she does. At least for now. An unclear silence follows. Alexander shifts in his chair.

"I feel like I can tell you anything," he concludes as he touches the spot where his ribs come together.

She looks at her plate. He reaches across and touches her hand resting on the table. She looks up. "And how do the dead and the uncooked figure into this?" she teases.

He's relieved. "That's Kendra's way of making fun. She knows I think that if you really trust death, there's no reason to be religious. Or to make any fuss whatsoever. We trusted being born, so why not trust dying . . ."

But he doesn't sound wholly convinced by his own words, and Victoria is afraid of being classified as more decaying flesh for his hypothesis. She pulls her hand away. He's wounded, but he struggles to continue.

"I used to talk to Smita, tell her everything . . . problems, thoughts, but I stopped when she became ill. I stopped because I started praying instead. But that was a secret." He looks at her, tearing into her eyes as though into an urgently needed package. She doesn't avoid his gaze. "I prayed she'd die," he says finally. "I prayed when I saw the pain. They say pain is in the eyes—they always use that expression in television and books—but it wasn't in her eyes; it was in her lips, and in her hands. Her lips and hands could barely stand the touch of air, let alone of me . . ."

He trusts me, is all Victoria can think, as he continues to speak of Smita's suffering, of watching her wither and drift out of life.

"Her head seemed to get bigger," he says, gazing off. "Everything else was getting smaller, her chest, arms, hips. The hair on her face kept growing: she had a few long strands on her chin—it was a strange sight. She didn't want us to do anything for her. She wanted to die naturally, so for two weeks she had no intravenous, no water. It was horrible. We were starving her to death. I couldn't understand how her heart could keep going, but it did. It was strong and just kept beating even though absolutely nothing was going into her." He stops to sip some water. Victoria notices how steady his hand remains as he holds the glass to his lips. His lips are glistening. He stops drinking but keeps the glass close to his mouth as he continues. "I wanted to be there for the last moment, to see it happen, but I fell asleep." He shakes his head in a way he must have done, exactly like that, repeatedly over the years. He puts the glass down. "I fell asleep and when I woke she had gone." He holds his napkin. "People always say that a dead person looks peaceful . . . it's not true. Not at all true. Smita's jaw had dropped open and her eyes had rolled back into her head, and she looked as if something'd been ripped from her. I knew the real Smita had gone, but the leaving hadn't been easy, I could see that on her corpse. But I'd missed it. I'd slept. It didn't seem fair . . ."

By the time the waiter brings them the bill, Alexander is apologizing for the gloomy topic. He tells her that he wants life more than ever, but for it to be real, connected deeply to someone with whom he can just be himself. "Smita wasn't religious, not at all. She just lived. For her death wasn't all this beating of wings, it was merely something she did," he concludes.

Only once before has Victoria felt love growing like a pelt over her, and one day it was torn from her. This man, too, could turn a corner and disappear, as had the other.

"Thank you, Alexander, that was the best meal I've ever eaten," she says, perhaps a bit too formally. She picks up her purse from the chair next to her and brushes the hair back from her face.

"My pleasure," he says, with a sudden grin that could be construed as mischievous.

When they leave the restaurant he guides her down the stairs with his hand on the small of her back. The hairs on her back and neck scream, but she hushes them. It is just a helping hand for a new friend. At the bottom of the stairs, she puts her jacket on without his help.

---

www.familysearch.com

Search registers for birth parents and children
Search registers for ex-cons
Search registers for friends and family
Genealogy software
Discover your ancestors

click

Contact us

"People do those searches so that they can find out if they are related to somebody famous," Kendra declares. "There's nothing about sperm donors on this site. Go back to the one in California. They have astronauts. Maybe he's an astronaut, or a nuclear physicist, or a prize fighter—nah, prize fighter's too dull—you do have a bit o' spark, if you ignore the moron stare," she says as she taps Derek on the head. He clicks to the next page of family-finder offerings.

"But my mom did it in Miami."

"Hmm . . . California would have been more interesting." Her hand falls to his shoulder and stays there. He can feel every finger outlined like small pebbles pressed into sand. His senses are alert. This new bond between them demands some sort of recognition, he thinks, but he's not yet come up with the right gesture. Should he touch the hand? He wants to make something for her, perhaps to write a poem with her name in it. He thinks he might like to follow her through the entire school day, just to make sure she's safe. But he can't even bring himself to touch her hand.

"My dad doesn't like California," she says as her hand slips off his shoulder. She pauses to consider something even more important, then throws herself on the rug in the middle of her room. She stares up at the ceiling. Derek turns from the computer to Kendra's long fleshy figure splayed out on the floor of her bedroom. He catches sight of the skin along her hips, exposed from beneath her T-shirt, as her arms stretch up above her head.

"My dad asked me what I thought of your aunt the other night. Suspicious, that. He asks that about women he dates. But, I'll tell ya, they're not usually grannies."

Derek flinches, then stands up abruptly out of the chair. Kendra sits up and crawls on her knees towards the chair. She tugs on Derek's trouser leg.

"Shit, sorry. I was just winding you up, really, just teasing—don't get upset." She grabs his ankle and pretends she's being dragged along in his wake. Derek stands perfectly still, taking in the sensation of her hands on his leg.

"Let's have a look at something in Miami," she says, letting go of his ankle and getting up. "But I'm not sure it'll do much good. There was no law that said he had to be traced. He could have been a med student, or someone just wanting a wank. Oh, sorry, really, but you have to be prepared for that possibility . . . What's the fuss? There are worse things. You could have been cloned."

That does it. Derek turns away from the desk and heads to the door.

"What?" Kendra asks nervously.

"I'm going now."

"Really, Derek, I was joking . . . can't you take a little joke?"

Not from you, he thinks, and heads through the door and out of Kendra and Alexander's house.

He walks down Blenheim to the smell of lilacs, to the sound of blue inside him like a bell. Not the same sound as the sky, he thinks. At least not the sky in the afternoon. Perhaps the sky at dusk, the blue that's like a clanging ladder to the person he will be beyond this pavement, beyond those clouds, beyond the sky itself.

When he arrives home Victoria is cleaning. He passes her on the way to his room. His aunt is different, he thinks. She asks him a lot of questions: about Kendra, and about what happens at school. Every day last week he was quizzed as to whether Richard had tried to contact him again. But thankfully Richard has not been by the school all week. Had he come, Derek is sure he would have won this time. Because Derek is going to modify his tactics. Sure, a sword, a gun, an explosion, they're good, he likes them—especially the feeling in his chest or even in his groin when they strike—but if Richard had been back this week he would have used words against him. Words can do things a punch in the nose can't. Because a punch or a kick, or even a bomb—they last just a moment. Whereas he has lots of words that have been around forever. *In prison you have only words, and you have to use your own powers just to get beyond the physical torture*, Kola wrote in his final letter.

Kola says important things, Derek knows. This last letter in the pile has inspired him to return to the Camelot sites he once frequented, but because of Kola's words he now sees them differently. He no longer seeks to be like a knight; he looks for details on Merlin and his magic. Merlin raised Arthur in the forest. Merlin kept the wizard's way. Wizards live backwards in time. For a wizard, nothing is separate; everyone is everywhere at one time. Seeing from the future can show you what is pointless and what is worthy. Derek is more and more convinced of the power of the invisible.

"Come a moment," Victoria calls from her room. He gets up and, repeating Merlin's words to himself . . . *The wind can leave you hanging* . . . he goes to her room and waits by the door. But she stands and stares at him in silence. What now? Her face looks open and happy. Why did she call him? . . . *The stars can make you hungry* . . .

"I haven't been very good at talking with you, Derek."

Derek is silent, staring at her curiously. *Until you let them fall into your cup* . . .

"I mean, I wanted to tell you, if there's anything you want to say, to tell me, I hope you will . . .

And you drink . . . Derek nods. He turns and heads back to his room. What is she on about now? . . . *to become air and light* . . . He has more important things to think about. *And see how time is a droplet of both* . . .

On the lookout for yellowtail, Victoria walks quickly, pumping her arms, concentrating on the word *lithe*—a word for which she'd like to become the metaphor—as she moves through Borough Market like an eel through coral. She's decided to grill yellowtail tuna for Beth and the others at the shelter. She concentrates on her shopping, trying not to count the days since she's heard from Alexander. Don't fret, it's been only a week, she tells herself. Ten days, in fact. She spots a fishmonger's stall. Swordfish, John Dory, scallops. "Any yellowtail?" she asks. The fishmonger shakes his head and gestures towards the other selections. She'd like to spoil Beth, give her something special. With Beth's bad teeth, a succulent sashimi of yellowtail might just be the perfect thing, but would she eat raw fish?

"Many fools have the best intentions, darling," Beth said to her last week as they watched a Salvation Army officer struggling to keep a very drunk man from pissing in the lobby. The man cursed the officer and told him to stick Jesus up his arse. Beth giggled, then burped, not bothering to cover her mouth, and Victoria could smell the rot taking hold of her the way moss eventually swallows a rock. Perhaps Beth would do better on vegetables, she thinks.

Victoria looks at the food again, the way Alexander would describe it, like painting. In the pink flesh of salmon she pictures a tongue. As a vendor pours rice from a burlap bag onto the weight scales, she sees sheets thrown open again and again as bodies toss beneath them. She tugs at her dress as she turns down the next market aisle. The stalls here are paler. Bread. Bread gives her the desert. Sand and wind. A long time without rain. A long time without love. She stamps the ground and throws her basket down in the market aisle, huffing in frustration. A woman nearby bends to pick it up for her.

"No, please, leave it. I can get it myself," Victoria says rudely. The woman straightens up and walks away. Victoria picks up the basket and heads towards the vegetable stalls.

Alexander waits for her in his car on Blenheim Terrace. She peeks out from behind the curtains of her top-floor window and can see him sitting behind the wheel, occasionally checking the mirror, looking at his watch, probably wondering what is taking her so long. She is dizzy. She has eaten almost nothing all day. Looking at her hair once again in the mirror, she checks the roots. There was no time to go to the salon today, so she used a bottle of water-based colour picked up at the health food store. Her trousers are new, as is the red cotton top that falls flatteringly just to her hips. Smoothing down the sides and front of the top, she lets her hands run over her belly and hips, then she holds the flesh at her sides, gripping it, to hold on to something; otherwise, she may not make it down the stairs. Her striped mariner's cardigan is from Selfridges, her biggest splurge in years. She slings it over her shoulders. Picking up her keys and bag, she calls out towards Derek's room: "I'm off. You be good, now, you hear? Sonia said to go down in a few minutes. The twins want you to play with them before they go to bed. And don't watch telly with them, play a nice game, OK?" She waits for his answer but it doesn't come. She hears the keyboard clicking and knows he's fast at something on the computer. She heads down the stairs.

"I was worried you'd changed your mind," Alexander says as she shuts the car door.

"I'm sorry, I was running behind."

As he starts the engine and releases the handbrake, Alexander glances over at her, and she guesses he is seeing something different now that he knows her age. She feels self-conscious, runs her hands through her hair, which is damp with perspiration. As she brings her hand down, she notices a blotch of colour on her palm. Wiping it quickly into the upholstery of the seat, she is mortified. What a batty old fraud.

"You look lovely," he says.

"Thank you," she says, casually, as she runs her hand once more over the cotton shirt at her stomach.

"The restaurant's unusual. Not many people know about it. It's run by a friend of a colleague—a sculptor who gave up art and got the backing for his restaurant from one of his collectors. He's an amazing cook. Mother is Italian, father is Scottish . . ."

Victoria nods and looks straight ahead, willing her glands not to perspire and the colour on her hair not to run down her cheek. She knows that talking will help. If she tells stories and talks, they won't have to return to that shapeless, blunt territory that seemed so cold. But they drive in silence towards Marylebone Road.

"I wasn't sure whether tonight would be a good idea," he says cautiously after several minutes.

Oh, OK, here it comes . . . this is where she'll know.

"I thought maybe I'd offended you last time."

"Offended me?" she asks, and is relieved he's referring to his statement on colour. He hasn't said: *I hadn't realized your age . . . nothing more than friendship is possible between us.* She can't find any more words. The car hums, making a song of their silence.

Fig, grapefruit, and goat's cheese
Truffle soup sprinkled with crumbled pancetta
Duck à la piece
Curried monkfish (served with artichoke sauté and fragrant rice)
Passionfruit fritters with mango ice cream

"Nothing else, thank you," she says to the waiter, who has been very attentive the entire evening. Victoria rubs her hand over her tummy. Rarely has she felt so sated.

"Well, that was something," she says to Alexander as he holds an invisible pen in the direction of the waiter and signs a signature in the air, requesting the bill.

"Glad you enjoyed it; I hope you understand what I mean about progress. Ordinary people in the past never ate like that," he says after the waiter nods and leaves.

They have been discussing an imaging project Alexander is working on, which tracks the movement of nanoparticles, the most basic atomic-level particles that can be manipulated by scientists. When Victoria asked him why we'd want to manipulate them, he answered that he thought she underestimated the good intentions of most scientists. She finished off the last passionfruit fritter and didn't challenge him because she was so pleasantly full. But she wants to defend her own good intentions. She sits up straight to tell him about the Turkana.

"The Turkana are nomads, who herd cattle, in Kenya, on Lake Turkana. Many years ago some Norwegians were trying to help their starvation problems, after years of drought. They decided to build a fish plant on the shores of the lake so that they could process the Nile perch that could grow to four feet and longer," she says and holds her arms up and palms wide apart.

Alexander watches her. "That big?" he teases.

She scowls and continues. "They thought they could feed the nomads, if only the people would learn to eat fish and not meat." Her voice becomes urgent. "The fish plant failed, many millions of dollars later, because every few years a part of Lake Turkana disappears. The river feeding it dries up in the drought." She sips the last of the wine from her glass, shaking her head, but the wine doesn't lull the urgency in her tone: "How could the Norwegians not have understood that drought affects water? The Turkana knew that. Someone told me the fish plant still stands, empty. The

Turkana call it 'the new mountain,'" she concludes, exasperated.

When she raises her eyes, she sees his face coming towards her. He kisses her on the lips, quickly, then sits back. She's stirred, looks at him, then down at the table, to her left, to her right, then back at him.

"Are you trying to shut me up?" she asks, smiling.

"Something like that," he says, smiling back.

They wait in silence for the bill. When it arrives, Alexander fondles it for a moment, searching for words. "I think most of the time I'm confused," he confesses. She understands. They share something fundamental. As fundamental as sleep. She knows he is a man who has been slightly out of this world for most of his life. Like her. Perhaps like Derek. Why do bodies house such discomfort?

"Sometimes I lose my bearings. I think living in a big family must be a better way to go about life, and I've never had that. I'd like to."

Victoria shifts her weight in the seat, uncomfortable with this line of conversation. "Did you know that in Kenya after a Luo husband is buried the elders of the husband's family can sit down and nominate a new man as the wife's new husband?" For some reason she needs to undermine the topic of family.

"Why do you know so much about Kenya?" he asks.

"No reason, just from reading, a long time ago," she answers, boldly. She looks him in the eye to feign the truth in her answer.

In the car they are quiet again. As it pulls up to Victoria's house, the silence goes even deeper, like an ache to bone. With the engine idling, Alexander takes her hand and holds it in both of his. He leans towards her. She dips her head to the side. A light shock of static passes between their lips; they pull back slightly. She lets out the breath she's been holding. He leans in, and his mouth clasps her bottom lip, her top, then rests on both, which part to make way for just a touch of his tongue. She tastes, but pulls back.

"Thank you," she says as she sits up straight. "I had a wonderful evening."

"As did I," he says.

Too formal? Has she run away again? Opening the car door, she slips out of the passenger seat and bends down to smile at him and wave. Silly goose. A wave like a schoolgirl. Really, she thinks, as she shuts the door. Really.

Inside the house she is trembling, feeling ridiculous. She heads upstairs.

When she's undressed and in bed, sleep is far off, like a friend from the past, and she feels abandoned to her mind, while her skin tingles with clichés of arousal. Over and over she hears the aching silence between them and feels his lips grasp her bottom lip. Again and again, as in a childhood rhyme, she hears him say, *As did I*. But then she stops the replay and for an absurd moment feels guilty of betraying not Lenny, but Kola. She laughs to herself, finally, and turns over on her other side, putting the pillow over her ears.

Kendra and Derek sit on the sofa in Sonia and Martin's living room watching *The Wizard of Oz*. On the floor in front of the sofa, Max is lying on his stomach, elbows on the floor, his chin in his hands. "This is the witch part, don't look," says Max with an authority that causes Kendra to double take, then stare at the boy's blond head.

"I'll protect you," says Monica, snuggling up to her on the sofa. Kendra pretends to be frightened for the twins' sake. She hugs Monica and squeals. Derek watches her superb play-acting, but slowly her pout returns. This is not her idea of a fun evening, stuck with Derek and the twins while her father takes out his aunt for the second night in a row.

"All right, we're off then. Thanks Sonia," says Victoria in the kitchen. Kendra nudges Derek and rolls her eyes. Victoria and Alexander go out into the late May evening.

The street smells of lilacs and Victoria files the smell for memory. They walk together towards Alexander's flat, where they've decided Victoria will teach him how to cook Brazilian fish stew.

She hasn't cooked it herself in years, but when she mentioned it to him on the telephone he was hooked on the idea: "Is Brazilian cooking like Guyanese?"

"No, not really," she said, but realized she had no real idea if that was true. Her knowledge of Guyana is schoolbookish now, bound between a front and back cover of family life. Her Brazilian stew is an experiment she tried out on Lenny many years ago.

In his kitchen she instructs him in a method of peeling and cutting onions that is designed to minimize tears. She runs the cold water tap at the sink, which works to absorb the onion fumes.

"Neither of us need cry this evening," she says playfully as she turns to Alexander, who seems adept with a chef's knife.

"I think I need a hat, like a cordon bleu chef, a tall white cylinder on my head, that would do it," he jokes. She looks at him, wondering if Smita excused him from kitchen duties or if he's just playing the novice for her sake. In either case, she doesn't care. He looks beautiful.

"I think the French have the most sophisticated approach to food—the delicacies, the fussing that goes on . . . I have a client with a home—"

"What? You think so?" she challenges, as she breaks off a crab leg and places it in the broth that has begun to simmer on the stove. She starts to scrub the mussel shells. "That's a narrow viewpoint," and she pauses, deciding what she thinks, which region's cuisine to mention. China? The peppers, the fungi, the roots, where everything in nature is potentially food. India? No, he'd know more than she would on that. She thinks of Ethiopia—the fine, varied spices ground into lamb and aubergine she tasted so long ago in Toronto.

"Italian food has a simplicity that is far more sophisticated if you look at it," she says, limiting herself to Europe.

"Oh no. Have you been to France?"

"No, I haven't, that's true."

He stops chopping and looks at her. She ignores him, chopping the monkfish into cubes, placing them into the broth. When she finally looks up he's back at work on the onions. He raises his hand to his eyes.

"Don't rub!" she cries. Too late. He's squinting and sniffing. She laughs at him.

"You know what?" he asks with his eyes still shut, tears rolling down his cheeks.

"What?"

He sniffs and tries to open his eyes but can manage only one. "We should take a trip to France. You'd see what I mean. I have a client with a home in Provence, and nearby is a restaurant where every dish they serve, from the hors d'oeuvres to the desserts, has truffles in it . . . imagine."

"No, I can't."

"You can't what? Imagine, or go?"

"Both."

"Yes, you can."

"What, imagine or go?"

"Both."

"A lot of pigs sniffing logs," she says, smiling, as she tosses the shrimp into the broth.

"Seriously, Chez Bruno's famous, what do you say?" He sniffs, then laughs.

This is too fast, she thinks, trying not to let it show. This is unreal. She goes to where he's standing at the counter and scoops up the onions with the blade of her knife. She places them in the steaming pot on the stove. As she watches the tomato broth return to a boil, and the crab legs, mussels, shrimp, and cubes of bream and monkfish are steamed gently, she has a twinge of impending disaster. Europe. She doesn't belong in Europe. Not bred for it like he is. But if there's one thing she's more and more sure of it's that breeding is accidental.

She smiles, shrugs, wipes her hands on the dishtowel, and walks out of the kitchen into the next room.

"It's not a big place, but I wanted to move after Smita died," he says as he follows her into the open sitting room. The room is sparsely furnished, but warm: a comfortable white sofa with silk cushions of many colours scattered across it, Indian wall hangings and Persian rugs, light fixtures of white muslin, and photographs of Kendra at many ages placed thoughtfully throughout the room. Smita smiles from the mantel. Victoria unconsciously smiles back.

"I have photos, of India, some of Uganda and Mauritius, if you'd like to see them . . . but also I'd like to show you my work. Not the medical stuff, I do photography for myself. Would you like to see?"

She nods.

As they walk upstairs to the study and bedrooms, she remembers that she left the gas burner on high, but as Alexander takes her hand she gets a thrill and hears a sound like a waterfall, then realizes it's from inside her. She can barely see straight as they walk towards the study.

She's disoriented by his study. A desk lined with computers is framed by shelves of disks, photographic files, and boxes of slides. Cameras and two printers take up another desk, and in the corner is a makeshift darkroom. Hanging on the walls is a series of metre-length Cibachrome photographs. In one graphic red-and-black print, the jaws of a beetle gape wide and menacing. The next print displays more insects, scrambling on top of one another. In the next, the radiant white paw of a lion lies still, while the beast's other paw is raised in the air above a blurred carcass. Smaller prints of more carcasses—antelope, moles, one of an elephant— line the adjacent wall.

Alexander sits in front of his computer and presses a button. The rhythmic sound of chirping fills the room and the lights go off as small spotlights fade in and the room is starlit. They are on the savannah. Victoria giggles. Alexander looks up proudly. He stands up, sniffs the air.

"It's smelling wonderful down there. Should we check on it?"

He leaves the equipment running and heads out of the room. Victoria follows him down the hall, but it is she who pinches his T-shirt and pulls him back to stop in front of the bedroom.

Their breathing is slow and taut. She is aware of every second as it passes. He faces her and touches her back. As his fingers move over her spine, her bones feel wobbly. He takes her hand and leads her to the bed. They both sit. Breathing in tandem. He takes her hand again and puts it to his face. She feels him kissing the lines on her palm, and she pulls back at first, but then relents, hoping he won't notice the dry, worried skin. She holds his face as his kiss moves up her arm and then to her neck, and there again she hopes he will not find it ringed and rippled. She clenches for a moment, then releases herself into him. His tongue reaches for hers. She gives him all of it.

The smells from the kitchen are rising up strongly, the tomato, bay leaf, and onion smells, with a hint of salty brine. Suddenly she has to pee, but she tenses the muscles at her sex. The movement increases her excitement. She's shocked at the wetness and gasps slightly, which widens Alexander's command of her mouth. He unbuttons his shirt slowly; she tries to help, but can't co-ordinate her fingers. He releases the kiss and takes off his shirt, then his trousers. He sits in his boxers, and she can't help but look him over, staring at the ripple of skin below his chest and the fleshy fold at the side of his waist, normally hidden by a T-shirt. She wonders if this moment might have been less possible for them thirty years ago. He takes her fingers and pulls her gently towards him, but she resists. She is acutely conscious of her tummy, the skin around her buttocks, the skin under her arm, the skin around her collarbone. Too much skin for this room. And suddenly she remembers the colour of her hair, the contrast between her head and below her waist, and she's embarrassed. But he tugs her hand gently, and she falls into his arms. He starts to kiss her again. He unbuttons her shirt and removes it, then slips her trousers and panties off with ease. She unclasps her bra for him. She can smell herself. She runs her hand over her stomach, then around her hips, and comes across the deflated raft of her buttock. He takes the hand, kisses it again, and slowly she feels his lips make their way along her side, to her breasts sagging apart from one another. He cups one in his hand, and lowers his mouth to the nipple. She grabs his head, drifting now, back into that achy silence. Her thoughts disappear. Time tiptoes out and leaves her alone with him.

They roll over and back, kissing. She can feel his erection along her leg. She takes it, boldly, and lets out a slight confession of delight. Guiding him into her she looks down at him in her hands and can't hold back a grin. She looks up to make sure he hasn't noticed. But he too is staring down at their bodies. When he's in deep, she closes her eyes. His rhythm is slow yet determined, and he continues the gentle caressing with his tongue. He stops suddenly, and pushes up on his arms to raise his torso above her. Looking at her as though examining a hand he'd forgotten he possessed, he stays in the thrust for a few seconds. She gasps quietly. He lowers his chest again, and resumes with more and more intensity. "It's hard to believe," he whispers. Then he rises up again, looks at her. She faces the wall, intent on oblivion. He moves more quickly. On the edge of her own release, Victoria opens her eyes to witness his eyes roll back, his face shiver.

Time returns into the room. Thought comes, and she wonders how we ever really know a place at all.

"Shit," she says and raises her head. The smell throughout the house is metallic and chalky. The broth has boiled down to nothing, and the fish has started to burn.

CHAPTER ELEVEN

Merlin

Brown wavy hair to her shoulders. The smell of toast. It's the smell of toast about her that he remembers most now. Toast, and sometimes a sour smell of grapefruit. Guenevere.

Derek lies on his bed staring at the ceiling. He is doing something he rarely has the courage to do. Usually if a memory of his mother flashes up, he pushes it away until it fades, but today he's coaxing it, trying to feel her around him, needing her, now, as he prepares to do something important. This flash of her, its sensations, its smells, bring him the morning Guenevere. In the mornings she was ruffled and groggy, finding it difficult to crawl into consciousness. She would be present, yet dreamy like a child—the way Monica is in the morning—catching herself in the place between sleep and waking.

The breeze from the window is refreshing, and he remains still. He has to focus, to concentrate on getting on the right Underground line, and getting off at the right station. His finger traces the route on the tube map to Dalston Kingsland. He gets up. He opens his closet door, stands looking into it. He has nothing in leather, so he chooses a black T-shirt and wears it hanging out over his jeans, which he tugs down low on his hips. The trainers go on last, the laces intentionally left untied. Kola's letter and Kendra's note are stuffed into his back pockets.

When Gwen was finally fully awake, she would take him on her lap, run her finger over his birthmark, and tell him a story of how it got there. Some mornings it was the same story; on others she invented a completely new tale that kept him clinging to her every word. Recently Derek has been telling himself the story with the wizard in it:

One day when you were a little baby, you crawled off after breakfast and disappeared into the bush without either me or Granny noticing. You wanted to see some of the animals and to find some new friends in the bush. As you were making your way over a fallen mahogany log, you heard a noise behind you and you turned around to see a wizard. He was tiny and had a pointy hat and a wand. "What are you doing here little one?" he asked you, quite surprised to see a baby in the jungle.

"I'm looking for some friends in the bush," you told him.

"Eh, eh, I neva. How do you suppose a baby like you could make friends in de bush? You'll have to go quicker than that if you want to catch up with any animals, unless ya care to make friends only with snakes and snails and sloths . . ."

"What can I do?" you asked him.

"Well, fa starters we have to make you unique so that you don't just blend in with the colours of the bush. I know, what about rabbits? They're very fast, and there aren't any rabbits in this bush, so if we turn you into a rabbit we'll be able to find you easily when your mommy comes looking for you, because she's bound to . . ." Then he raised his wand and said magic words, "Agwasa, gorri agwasa," and he turned you into a rabbit. You spent the day bounding through the bush meetin' all kind of animals, but by the time night fell you were getting hungry and tired. I was gettin' worried about you. I was callin' and callin', and callin' for you. When the wizard appeared again, you asked him to turn you back into a baby boy. Now the wizard was a bit sleepy himself, so when he said his magic words he said them with a bit of a slur and even though you were returned to your human state you were left with this red outline of a rabbit over this eye.

And as she outlined his eye with her finger, he would breathe in her perfume of toast and grapefruit and nestle into the curve of her shoulder.

Auntie Vic has been hugging him more in the last three months, since she's become friendly with Alexander. But she can't match Gwen. And as far as wizards are concerned, his aunt has bought him books—the latest Harry Potter—which she says Lenny thinks are the best things going for kids. But Derek knows better. Harry is a poser.

He checks the clock on his bedside table. Nine-thirty-six. He is supposed to meet Richard at the school at noon, so if he gets a move on now, he'll have time to look for the man and make it back to the school in time. He picks up the tube map and tiptoes down the stairs. He hopes he won't run into Martin or Sonia on the way out. He hears them in the room below:

"We could start her in football, she'd like that. She needs something physical," Martin says, but Derek isn't sure who he's talking about. Monica? Playing football? He's not sure he approves of that, but he has no time to think about it now.

Sonia tells Martin about the washing that has to be taken out of the machine and hung up, the groceries he should pick up for supper, and that she and the twins will be back from visiting their friends near five o'clock. Derek listens as she hurries down the stairs to the sitting room, alerts the twins with a rousing, "All aboard Flight 222 to Queen's Park," and they head noisily out of the house. He listens for the door to Martin's study to click shut. For a moment, he wonders if he should ask Martin for help, but knows this is one thing he has to do for himself. And for Kendra.

He walks down the Terrace and turns along Abbey Road. When he reaches the crosswalk by the music studio, he spots a Japanese man with a camera, so he dips his chin into the neckline of his T-shirt, covering his nose and mouth so as not to be caught on film. He arrives at the tube station, buys a ticket from the machine, and goes down the escalator. The signs are confusing, but he has memorized the names he has to follow. The tube carriage is full of people. Derek moves past a couple and their two young children, all wearing baseball caps. The father is reading a map of London. A short woman with red hair, in a hospital uniform, stands in front of them, holding on to the pole. Her eyes are closed. A dark-skinned man sits next to the family. He is staring at and fingering his mobile phone. Derek sidles up against the door.

"Move down, will you?" says an older man in a grey suit, his stringy hair pressed across his forehead. Derek does as he's told, and the man follows him, his waist close to Derek's chest. The suit is pinstriped and proper looking, and Derek thinks the man must be a businessman or politician. He studies him, the firm grip on the newspaper, the polished shoes. Shoved further to the wall with the next wave of passengers, Derek notices that the man's trousers are wet just below the fly. Around it are other stains; urine spots. He turns his face away.

A few stops later he hears the announcement for his station and gets off the train to make his first transfer. He boards a north-bound train. As he enters, the recorded message is played: *Mind the Gap. . . . Mind the Gap.* Self-consciously, Derek presses his lips together as he keeps his spot near the door and looks down at his trainers.

Dalston Market doesn't feel the same. Today it seems smaller, drab, and run-down, whereas he remembers it bubbling with excitement. The crowd seems less dense than the last time. He looks about, noting landmarks on his route so he'll remember his way back to the station. He walks along rows of hardware traders, with batteries, bulbs, and plugs for sale. One of the vendors is a boy not much older than him, and Derek watches him make a transaction with bills and coins. Everything he has been expecting to see isn't here. Of course, he thinks, they didn't rebuild the samosa shop exactly the way it was before the explosion. Of course they changed it, but he can't find a single shop that looks familiar.

Then he sees the pub. He walks towards it and stops by the wall in the spot where he observed the aftermath of the explosion. Men stand at an outdoor table, holding pints of beer, exchanging only the occasional word with one another, more grunts than speech. Dare he ask them? How would he phrase it? I'm looking for the bomber . . . I need his help . . . He knows me . . . He senses how stupid he's been. Of course the man isn't here. Perhaps he's in jail or hiding. And what would Derek have asked him, anyway? When do you stop using words? . . . How do you set a bomb? Stupid git, what were you thinking? But he still needs something from this place, that much is certain. A man whistles and calls to another to help him with a trolley filled with bags of potatoes. Derek watches the market go about its business. The bomb seems like a dream. He has to find something he can take with him to meet Richard. Something that will reignite his power, because Richard has not succumbed to any of Derek's words recently.

He walks away from the pub, checks the money in his pocket— £5.47—and heads across the market, pushing his way past two women dragging carts full of vegetables. There they are: spices piled high in burlap sacks lined up in terraced rows of three. Black, brown, and green seeds. And rows of powder: red, golden, and, there, the yellow one. He watches how it's done, how the merchant scoops some seeds into a plastic bag for a woman wearing a sari and a ruby stud in her nose. The bushy-eyebrowed man hands the woman the bag; she gives him coins. Derek walks cautiously to the stall, eyeing the yellow powder. He looks at the vendor but can't bring himself to ask. When the man isn't looking he grabs a bag and scoops a handful of turmeric, turns quickly, and pushes his way back through the crowd. There is no shouting after him; he's in the clear. He starts to run. At the train station, he empties the powder out of his fist into the bag, folds the plastic into his pocket, and wipes the remaining powder on his jeans, staining them bright yellow.

Arriving back in St. John's Wood, he knows that what's in his pocket won't help him much, won't explode anything. It is not the gut-destroying black powder of the Kanaima. But the trip was not a waste; he didn't come back empty-handed. The fact of the powder in his pocket gives him an energy he can't explain. He heads to the school.

Richard the Truck has arranged this meeting through Stephen, who says that if he doesn't go Richard will pummel him. He's seen Richard only once since their fight, and not at all since school let out over a month ago, but words have passed between them, delivered through Stephen and Rory, each exchange more charged, so that this last command feels inflamed. Richard is about to burst, and Derek has run out of words.

Kendra stopped disappearing after school. One afternoon, as she and Derek walked to her house to do homework, she was playful with him. With a bump of her hip she shoved him off the pavement and then giggled. He stepped back onto the pavement and walked closer to her. After a few moments of silence, she said: "He didn't get anywhere with me, you know . . ." and then her voice became shaky and more serious. He wanted to take her hand then, but she suddenly skipped off, turning and running backwards as she shouted to him: "Come on, get your arse in gear." Stephen later told Derek that Kendra had said Richard needed to be put in his place.

After Richard hit Derek on the nose with his skull ring, he said, "She won't talk to me, you bastard." At McDonald's, Kendra sits with Derek and Stephen and ignores Richard with a force Derek feels could eventually obliterate him if it weren't for how desperate Richard is to be noticed. He takes Kendra's note from his back pocket.

"You could have been cloned," it reads, with two identical happy faces side by side to illustrate. The note is scribbled on a printout from the Internet that details the cloning process, followed by a description of the discovery of the gene sequence by the Human Genome Project. Highlighted in yellow halfway down the page is a paragraph that reads: "Humans carry little more genetic information than mice, and barely twice as much as tiny fruit flies . . ."

Derek collects whatever Kendra gives him. He has stacks of her illustrations of his stories, her notes to him, and her school photograph. He keeps these in the small drawer in his bedside table, along with Kola's letters, which he has never returned to his aunt's hall chest.

He has been piecing Kola together. Using his letters and the Internet, Derek has been building a picture of Kola in Kenya. He turns to Kola for help, and has gone back to earlier letters in which he speaks of fighting. Kola seems to have become convinced of words only in prison. In his earlier letters, he talks of times for guns, attacks, and bombs. Perhaps Derek has to try fighting first.

Kola didn't like his older brother, Tairus, who, it seems, had disappointed him and then betrayed him. A revolutionary fighting against the British, Tairus had left home when Kola was a young boy. A symbol of freedom for his baby brother, Tairus joined a group of men who called themselves Anake a Forty, who had for years been trying to win back land that had been taken by the British. But things went wrong for Tairus, and Kola stopped believing in his brother after Tairus was released from two years of imprisonment on the island of Lamu. At night when he can't sleep, Derek wonders what kept Kola so tied to his brother that trouble later found him as well. The letter in his other back pocket is one he hasn't read before.

Toronto

Dear Victoria:

The snow has finally stopped. I thought I was becoming some sort of fossil, but the thaw has come. I can hardly stand another day of this. What will I do with the rest of February? But I will make it downstairs to post this letter after I've finished it.

You ask me why Tairus did not approve of my marriage, and I have been thinking about the answer, but it's not a simple story. If I were to say it's all the fault of the Berlin Conference in 1884 it would sound facetious, but perhaps not inaccurate. When the Europeans carved up Africa in 1884 the Gikuyu and Luo people were trapped in the same colony, an unhappy union. Although Tairus always said he was fighting to liberate Kenya from the British, I think he was fighting for the Gikuyu and no one else. His mind is very closed. I would have thought that two years of hard labour on Lamu would have changed that, but somehow it served to reinforce his narrow perspective. Tribalism will take a long time to disappear. . . .

Derek looks up from the letter. Through the window of the school kitchen, he can see the clock on the wall. Eleven-fifty-eight. He takes his time as he walks toward the yard, finishing Kola's letter, then returning it to his pocket.

At the school's back wall, perched on his bicycle, Richard the Truck is smoking a cigarette.

"You're almost late, you arse," he says as he throws down the stub, slides off the seat, and mashes the cigarette out with the front wheel of his bicycle.

"What do you want?" Derek asks, calmly fingering the powder in his front pocket.

"You're to deliver somethin' for me."

"What?"

"A package, is all."

"What's in it?"

"Nothing that's your business."

Derek considers its possible contents. "Why me?"

"'Cause you owe me. What's more, you'd better try to get good with me or both you and that cunt are gonna get it."

Derek thinks Richard sounds like a character in one of the videos he watches.

"You think she'll screw you, don't you? She'll never screw you. You're a useless git . . . and she's a tease," Richard taunts.

Derek tries not to erupt, but he can feel something crawling along his shoulders and up into his throat. He knows how good eruptions can feel, and how they change things. There's a battle going on in him between his new interest in the way of the wizard and his desire to attack. *Tairus*, writes Kola, *would attack police stations run by British police . . . he's lucky he wasn't killed . . . his reports of attacks meant everything to me . . .* Kola's brother knew when to attack. Derek touches the plastic bag in his front pocket again.

"And besides, you have that Kanaima shit to protect you," Richard adds.

So he hasn't forgotten. Richard still attaches something dangerous to Derek, a power he can't understand that will keep Derek safe from harm. Derek's shoulders relax.

"Where am I supposed to deliver it?"

"To St. Joseph's, other side of Swiss Cottage."

"Why?"

"'Cause that's the job, is all, shut your gob. You give him the package and he gives you some money and you bring the money back to me. Simple. Moron could do it."

"Get a moron," Derek says boldly.

"Look, you going to do it or not?"

Derek feels Richard's desperation. "I'll think about it."

"Think about it? For shite's sake!" He looks about, nervously. "OK, think about it and meet me here tomorrow, same time. You'd better say yes. The package has to be delivered tomorrow afternoon."

"Why can't you do it?"

"You're a dumb arse . . ." Richard gets back on his bicycle and pedals out of the schoolyard.

---

www.merlin.com

It was the Bard's task, through stories, poetry, and songs, to sing the praises of the way of the Druids. The Bard's songs also included tales of the way of the wizard: mortals and wizards, although alike, he sang, differ in their depth of thinking. Wizards do not limit themselves at all; every thought is crystal clear; all intentions are pursued; and, unlike mortals, wizards do not run into obstacles or conflicts that are inherent in the human heart...

Derek clicks on the next page to join the mailing list.

"How was your morning? I've finished early."

His aunt's voice floats in from the kitchen. Why should you care, he says to himself, silently, as yet unconscious of his resentment of her attention to Alexander. His aunt and Alexander have been seeing one another almost every night for the last two months. Alexander has been everywhere: at Kendra's when they're playing her SEGA computer game, here when Derek is writing his stories. Everywhere he looks, he sees Alexander's hand on his aunt's waist. He wouldn't mind, really, if it weren't for the fact that he seems to be drawn in and included in their small acts of uncertainty. Adults try very hard to be liked, he thinks. Just when he was feeling that he'd had enough of their efforts to outdo one another in the low-stake contest of food—his aunt's ingredients becoming more refined (raspberry vinegar, truffle oil, squid ink), Alexander's choice of restaurants becoming more obscure (North East London Turkish, South London Balti, Kensington Persian)— Alexander arrived at Blenheim Terrace with a gift:

"Here, chief, thought you might get use out of one of these," he said and handed Derek a black canvas case that fit comfortably in his palm like a chunky KitKat bar. The case was heavy for its size.

Derek thought he knew what it might be. His heart raced. His aunt stood behind him, watching over his shoulder.

"What is it?" she asked, and he could tell there were ropes all over her question.

Alexander stood beside her and put his hand on her waist. "I had one when I was his age; it'll be good to get him used to these kinds of things."

Derek opened the flap of the case and slid the Leatherman tool into his palm.

"A knife?" Auntie Vic asked, the ropes in her voice drawing tighter.

"Not just a knife. Look." Alexander took the tool and pulled out its pliers, scissors, screwdriver heads, and jigsaws, which opened out like blades on a metallic fan. "Much better than the Swiss Army—and look!" He slid out the tool's small corkscrew.

"For wine . . ." his aunt's voice frayed.

Derek turned and looked at her. Suddenly he felt sorry for her and wanted to put his arms around her and tell her that it was all right, he wouldn't go recklessly uncorking wine throughout Swiss Cottage, but she smiled at him, and he could see she was doing her best to please everyone. The ropes seemed to restrain panic. She didn't seem in pain. No, she looked quite happy. But her voice had a tight rein.

She insisted that Derek go with her to Lenny's one morning because Lenny had complained he never got to see him anymore. Just as Derek was about to show Lenny his present, his aunt had whispered to him to put it away. But it was too late, and Lenny said: "Knives? Where did you get that?" When Derek told him, Lenny's face went red. "Not right, not right, Vic," he said to her, then scurried out of the room.

Victoria followed him, "Lenny, really, it was a gift, what could I have done . . ."

Derek felt bad. Lenny was the first man he had known in London.

"Derek, you didn't answer me, how was your morning?" his aunt asks as she enters his room.

"Fine," he mumbles, and turns to block the screen with his shoulder so she can't read what's there.

"Good. I've got good news. We're going on a holiday!" She's as excited as Max is about a walk in the park, he thinks. Almost instantly, he's ashamed of his uncharitable thoughts. His aunt is much happier now. He turns around to look at her.

"Oh?" he says, remembering the only other holiday they took together, to Fishguard, along with the sight of Victoria's breasts in the next bed. "Where to?"

"To France. The south of France. With Alexander and Kendra."

A part of him stirs at the casual mention of Kendra's name, but he's wary. "What will we do?"

"Lots of things—we're going to the sea—we'll cross the Channel and drive south to a house in Provence. A friend of Alexander owns it. We'll stay over a week, maybe ten days." She leaves the room and continues to put away the groceries.

Derek lets himself feel excited. He'll have uninterrupted time with Kendra, and maybe Alexander will buy him something electronic this time. For a moment, he wonders how Lenny's going to react to this news. But he can't think about any of that now. He has to take care of something. Richard will already be waiting for him.

He picks up the Leatherman tool from his desk, unfolds its pliers, then slides out one of the knives. He examines the blade, then snaps the tool shut, deciding to leave it at home. Instead, he changes into the trousers he wore yesterday.

Just before reaching the schoolyard he stops and counts: one, two, three, and then breathes in deeply. *Spend your time pondering not what you see but why you see* . . . Wizards see and feel, immediately. The wizard simply is. Derek tries to put himself in the state of not knowing if he is dreaming or if he is in Richard's dream. He takes the plastic bag out of his pocket and clutches it in his hand. He breathes . . . four, five, six . . .

When he arrives at the spot where Richard is waiting for him, he feels light.

"You're almost late, wanker."

"I'm not."

"Just take this and get on with it then," says Richard. He hands him an opaque plastic bag, wrapped up in tape. "You give it to the bloke waiting at the back of St. Joseph's School and he gives you something and you bring it back to me. You clear?"

Derek nods. He stares at Richard, then opens his other hand, the small bag unfolding in it. He spills out the yellow powder in a straight line at Richard's feet. He turns and walks out of the yard, leaving Richard with a "What the fu—" dribbling from his lips.

Maps are useless where you are going, because the territory ahead is constantly shifting. You might as well try to map flowing water. In alchemy, the four elements—earth, air, water, fire—are mysteriously combined to arrive at life, and understanding the combinations and the powers of each can lead to transformations beyond the everyday imagination of mortals.

Derek holds Richard's package tightly and feels the crunchy texture of its contents as he makes his way across Finchley Road. When he reaches the back of the school and spots a boy standing by himself against the wall, he holds up the package calmly and openly. The boy panics, looks around, then runs up to Derek and snatches the package out of his hand.

"Don't be daft," the boy says, tucking the package into his jacket pocket. He glances around again and shoots Derek an annoyed look. Derek waits, not knowing if he's to ask for something or if it will just appear. *You must first be chaos before you can be a dancing star* . . . the Bard sings. The boy hands Derek fifty pounds and walks away. Derek folds the bill into his hand and watches the boy's back a moment before saying aloud: "You must first be chaos before you can be a dancing star," in a calm and powerful voice.

The drive through the south of France feels like a video. Vineyards, olive trees, and dry, red hillsides. Up in the hills are castles like those of d'Artagnan and the three Musketeers. Swashbucklers fence in those castles, Derek thinks.

As Alexander's car makes its way down the *autoroute du sud* toward Avignon, Derek is struck by the orangeness of things. The orange dirt, the orange tinge to the air, the orange glow of farm houses and chateaux. And in the back seat beside him, Kendra is wearing an orange shirt he hasn't seen before. It's been a long drive; he wishes it were over. He and Kendra have played all the car games they could think of, and for the last two or three hours have not talked at all. Kendra can read in the car, but Derek gets sick, so he gazes out of the window and concentrates on castles and hills as if they were answers to a test he will have later.

Auntie Vic has been mostly quiet in the passenger seat, changing the music—alternating between French songs with their spitting *R*s on the radio and classical recordings she and Alexander bought before they left. Alexander hums and smiles at his aunt as she changes the CDs. At the end of each, she flicks on the radio, looking for the French news. She asks Alexander to translate. Using a few French words of her own, she erupts into self-conscious giggles. The giggle is attached to those ropes, he thinks.

But there are advantages to the current situation. In this lighter frame of mind, Auntie Vic no longer pays much attention to when he sleeps or wakes. She doesn't stand over him at the computer. And in the last week of planning for this trip, she and Alexander went out alone, leaving Derek to eat downstairs with Sonia, Martin, and the twins. Derek takes the lax scrutiny as an opportunity to eat as the twins do—fish fingers, beans, and chips, not a green thing in sight. He has also spent many evenings with Kendra, at her house, eating pizza or Chinese take-away depending on Kendra's preference. And they drink Coke. All of these developments are good. It's just the giggle now. And the fact that when she does pay attention to him it's with full force. She probes his thoughts and feelings to the point where he wonders if he's abnormal for not having enough of them. But maybe she's just so filled with her own feelings that she can't help herself. "It's not too soon to go away together, all of us, not too soon at all," she said to him one evening, but he could hear the doubt in her voice. The ropes were there again, and he has been trying to understand what ropes have to do with love.

Derek knows adult love when he sees it. He knows that when Alexander and Victoria are together in the same room—or in this car—there is a current running through them that sends a charge out to everyone else around them. The current is like wind in a tree or ripples in a pond: evidence of a force he can feel. He felt it with his mother and Robert. Alexander touches Victoria constantly, and there is less and less of her to touch every day. She has shrunk. No longer the waddling granny he met four years ago, she has grown slim and seems shorter, and not just because he himself has sprouted up like a marsh weed. When his mother fell in love with Robert, Derek was five years old, but he knew the difference in her because of how she smelled. Even when she was bathed and lavender-smelling he could detect a tanginess coming from her that made him happy. The same strong scent comes from his aunt. He can smell it even now, wafting through the car, adding more citrus to the already pervasive orange tinge.

Alexander doesn't have the smell. Maybe only women get it. Alexander smells of aftershave and perspiration, a blend that smells like spiced skin. When he talks to Derek, he looks him deeply in the eyes. His eyes sparkle, and Derek likes that, but there's something about him that Derek doesn't understand. When he first met him, Derek thought Alexander was the coolest dad anyone could have—someone who had longer-than-proper, wild hair and unusual clothes, who let his daughter stay up as long as she wanted. But his outward appearance doesn't match his inner self, which seems weighted down by something awful. That's awful in both the senses that Derek has come to understand the word: full of awe for something inspiring, and, at the same time, the state of something dreadful and ugly.

Derek has been trying to piece together how this fits in with Alexander's love for Auntie Vic. Based on appearance alone, it would make more sense for Alexander to give Christine and not his aunt those long looks and kisses on the neck when he thinks Derek and Kendra aren't watching. Auntie Vic is not ugly, it's not that. It's more that she is like a locked-up laugh. Something that can't get through. Maybe that's why she giggles now. She's escaping through herself and onto her skin. Alexander's stare goes to her skin. He kisses it. Both of them seem lighter in each other's company, and that's another good thing. But Auntie Vic doesn't have Christine's flowing hair or long, slim legs. His aunt doesn't have anything long, really, except for the looks she gives Alexander. Many things have changed. Auntie Vic seems more fixed on moments, not as much on food. She is always telling Derek to take in moments, as though a moment is good for him, as though a moment has replaced a vegetable.

Kendra is more openly annoyed with both adults. Some days she seems to be growing out of her bones, things on the surface of her getting too small for the person inside. She doesn't want to be a musician anymore, she told him. She wants to be a doctor, or maybe even a psychiatrist, to help people figure themselves out. But, she added, she'd only want to do it for people with a lot of money. During a dinner at her house, as Alexander described for Victoria the practice of dharma, the code of life, and his belief that everything is part of a family, Kendra whispered to Derek: "My father never had to explain so much to my mother; they had an understanding," and then left the table. Derek later commiserated with her by telling her that his mother had never forced moments on him. She told stories, played make-believe and games with him. Her giggle had been there from the start. This was his chance to reveal to Kendra the most important things he knew, which at the time came from wizardry but also from Kola, whose words he still counted on. He took that moment to share some with her: *For all the moments my brother spent in prison, I don't think he understood much of anything,* Kola wrote. "I don't think he was all that revved up about moments," Derek told her. He is more and more convinced that moments are not as important as understanding.

"We're nearly there," Alexander says as they pull off the autoroute towards a secondary road, following signs to Les Arcs and Lorgues. They are going to a house in Lorgues, a Provençal town in the foothills of the Massif des Maures, half an hour north of St. Tropez. The mountainous district, Alexander told them as they drove along the autoroute, is known as Les Maures after the Moors who used to rule here.

"Greeks, Celts, Romans, and Moors, all had their turn here," he said. As they drive along the flat road with a hilltop town in the distance, he continues his guided tour. "People lived in the hills . . ." He points. "See the red roofs . . . and those shutters painted the colour of the olive groves . . . look," he says as they pull into the centre of Lorgues.

The car rattles over the cobbled lanes, and Derek notices the main square, its fountain, and, thank goodness, a video store. The church steeple casts a shadow across the centre of town, but the tourists sitting around the café tables all wear sunglasses. The wine they sip is pink. Derek watches an elderly man with an accordion slung over his chest stop on the pavement by a café and begin to play and sing. The people assembled around the tables do not look at him, but continue their chatter as he stretches and presses the bellows of his accordion. Derek imagines that in France he might become a troubadour.

They drive beyond the town, up into the hills. As they pass the pale yet splendid columns of the Château de Berne on their right, Derek spots something in the bushes across from it. He gasps at the same moment that Alexander shouts, *"Sanglier!"* excitedly, pointing towards the bushes. "Wild boar!" Derek's heart leaps.

Further on from the Château, they are surrounded by vineyards on the right and woods on the left. Turning down a rough dirt road, the car totters and bounces over rocks and ruts towards a magnificent garden, a pool, and a renovated farmhouse. The orange tint gives way to purples and browns. Traces of lavender. Dry earth. The vineyard in the field beyond the garden is leafy and pregnant with grapes.

The rambling farmhouse has tiny circular windows, with walls as thick as Derek's arm is long. They will stay on the top floor, which has an open sitting room, a kitchen, and a huge stone fireplace. In the far corner is a loft with a bed, above two bedrooms with views out over the vineyard and the hills in the distance. Derek claims the loft while Kendra sulks off into the small bedroom.

Unpacked and hungry, Alexander suggests that he and Victoria drive back down to Lorgues to fetch groceries, water, and other supplies.

"What are we meant to do then?" asks Kendra, her voice scratchy with the resentment that has been building since this trip's inception.

"Why don't you go and explore? There are trails, you could take a bicycle—did you see them out front?" Alexander asks.

"Not me, on any bicycle going uphill, thank you very much," she shoots back.

"Suit yourself, my dear," he says, refusing to be affected by her mood.

When the adults leave, Derek opens the doors to the terrace and the sirocco blows in. Not a sea breeze, this wind is parched, and forked. He gasps at the heat that comes in with it. Gazing out over the vineyard, he wants to sing. He turns back towards Kendra, catches sight of her profile lowered in a pout, and almost gasps again from something he isn't able to articulate as beauty.

"Why're you in such a foul one, then?" he asks.

"Who says I am? And, besides, stuck here for ten days with no telly, no computer, no cinema to go to, who wouldn't be?"

"Hmmm, maybe," he says, but doesn't share her feelings. The hills are clicking like a tongue. He has the urge to dance. "Let's go out."

Kendra frowns as she throws herself on the sofa. He pulls her up by the arm and drags her to the door and out of the house.

They march along the dirt path beside the vineyards and up into the hills. The sun is high and strong. The grass hisses like it knows a secret.

The next day, the four of them are settled in, accustomed to the surroundings and the heat. They rise early, breakfast on hot drinks and tartine with jam and butter, then swim in the pool. Derek and Kendra cavort and splash, toss a ball. They fiddle with a hose that leads from the pool shed, trying to spray one another, but when Alexander and Victoria throw them looks of disapproval from where they sit in the shade—Alexander reading a French newspaper and Victoria perusing a French food magazine—they stop. Derek crosses his arms on the edge of the pool and rests his chin on them. Kendra copies him. They spend a few minutes looking bored, before Derek slaps her forearm gently and motions for her to get out of the pool.

"We're off to explore, then," Derek tells Victoria and Alexander after he's dried off and put on his shoes. He and Kendra run towards the hills, the sun hammering down on their necks and shoulders.

As they make their way along the path, a lizard scuttles off into the brittle lavender bushes. Derek starts to run. As he speeds up, a large hare bounds down the path ahead of them. Kendra squeals and runs after him. They tear down the stone-strewn dirt path and head into the valley. Derek stops suddenly, panting. "Shhhh," he says. Kendra stops behind him. He listens like a hunter. The sound of a rushing stream emerges like applause. He starts to run again.

When they reach the stream, they are out of breath. The sound of tripping water drowns out everything else. Derek sits down, watching the stream as it tries to press rocks out of its way. Kendra picks up stones and pelts them into the stream.

"You know, I wonder if my dad still misses my mom," she says not quite loudly enough as she sits down beside him. Derek hears only "I wonder if my dad ever misses . . ." and is confused, thinking Kendra is either talking about throwing stones into streams or about something sexual. He doesn't respond.

"You like it here?" he asks.

"Not bad. Hot . . . It reminds me of a place in Italy we went to with my mom when I was young. My dad always took us away on holiday. Italy was Mum's favourite. Mine too. If she couldn't go to India she wanted to go to Italy. She never much liked London." She pauses, throws more stones into the stream, and continues.

"When I go to university, I want to go away, far away—to Canada or California. Australia even. I bet Australia has good medical schools."

Derek's spirits sink. "Is that because of Richard?" he asks.

She stops throwing stones and looks at him. A smile creeps onto her face. "What? You're joking. That thing with Richard was nothing. Don't go reading more into it and making up one of your stories about us. Sex is just sex. It's not a big deal. Everybody does it."

His throat is tight; he can't swallow. Her cavalier response floors him. He wants to kill Richard now. She sits down beside him; he can feel the skin on her arm against his. She digs up more pebbles and throws them into the stream from her seated position.

"Did you know that Stephen has been puttin' it into a girl? He told me the other day. Had his first shag. The girl's seventeen for

Christ's sake. I didn't think he'd even know how to do it. Not many boys do, you know. That's what she was doin' . . . teaching him. I don't mind kissing, but na, not anything else . . . and the kissing I've done has been—"

Derek's lips cut her off. He pushes his mouth tightly onto hers and accidentally bites her lip.

"Ah, bloody hell," she hollers, pulling away and wiping her mouth with her hand. "What the fuck you up to? What was that for?"

Derek sits silent, stunned by his own actions, feeling the blood rush into his face. He watches in a state of startled detachment as Kendra stands up and flails about, stamping her feet and yukking. His heart races with rage. What a stupid git. And what a bitch she is. He hates her.

"You lost your mind in this heat, or what?" she continues, standing over him, her shadow colossus-like above him. It stretches out to the stream where the silhouette of her hair in the sirocco looks like dry moths fluttering.

"Sorry," he says as he gets to his feet. He walks steadily toward the path and then up, inhaling the smells of pine and thyme that remind him of the old Berbice chair his grandfather owned. But he doesn't look up. He keeps his head down and, as fast as he can, runs up the path. Kendra doesn't follow him. He hears large rocks being thrown into the stream.

When he arrives at the farmhouse, Alexander and Victoria are locked in their bedroom. He hears giggles. Turning quickly, he goes back outside, but leaves the door ajar and sits on the steps, picking at the weeds that are sprouting up between the cracked tiles. A few minutes later he hears noises from inside and goes back in. His aunt is in the kitchen, but there is no sign of Alexander and the bedroom door is still closed.

"I'm making a special lunch, darling," Victoria says as she takes a headless carcass with legs from the fridge and holds it out for him to look at. *"Lapin aux olives,"* she says in what he thinks is a very bad French accent.

"What's that, then?"

"Rabbit with olives. You bake the olives right in the pan with the rabbit, with some wine, thyme and rosemary from right out of those hills, and on the top, you put a dash of sugar, so the flesh gets seared. It's delicious."

"Auuch!" he shouts, disgusted. He can't find anywhere to go where he doesn't feel annoyed and disgusted. He opens a cupboard and takes out a package of chocolate biscuits, not caring if his aunt notices or not. He throws himself down on the sofa and wolfs them down, one after the other.

The bedroom door opens and Alexander emerges, but Derek doesn't look up.

"Where's Kendra?"

"Still out."

"What are you eating? What's the matter?" Victoria asks, coming closer.

Alexander nods at Victoria, signalling that he'd like to deal with this himself. Derek gobbles down another biscuit. "Move over a bit, I'd like to talk to you," Alexander says as he moves towards the sofa.

Oh no. Could he know, Derek wonders? Did he see him pounce on her? He slouches down.

Victoria watches them. She steps back into the kitchen, pretending to be busy with the rabbit.

"Do you like it here chief?" Alexander asks, sitting down on the edge of the coffee table in front of him.

"Sure," he answers. What, we moving here now, he wonders? He's raging inside. He wants to go back to London. And never to see Kendra again. She'll have to fight her own battles.

"Good. It's good to get out of London, see something different. And maybe you'd like to learn French," Alexander says, which seems like a segue into more conversation, but Derek isn't in the mood to talk. What would Kola do now, he wonders?

"Yep," he says curtly.

Victoria wipes her hands on the dishtowel and steps back toward the sitting room, where she focuses on Alexander.

Derek looks at her, then back at Alexander's happy face.

"They have French at your school, don't they?" Victoria asks. There are the ropes again. She doesn't have the ropes when she talks to Lenny. He wonders how she sounded with Kola. Alexander's eyes are locked on his, and he's not able to look away again. Alexander shifts his weight. As though sensing Victoria's laser gaze, he rubs the back of his neck with his hand. The air is like a dry cough, with all of them caught in things they can't say. Alexander clears his throat and rubs his hands together.

"You know, it's just that . . . It's been some time now, months, and the four of us have been getting along quite well, don't you think?"

Victoria goes rigid, guessing what's coming. It's much too early for this. She has only begun to trust that he might really care for her. Trust is slippery. She opens her mouth, but he continues.

"Wouldn't it be grand if we were like a unit now, a team? If you have difficulties you can come to me . . . you might even, well, just for the sake of things, what if you thought of me as a dad, that might be a start. . . ."

What? Derek is stone still. He can't be hearing right. He shakes his head automatically and releases himself from the blue eyes. He looks up at his aunt for help, but she is still staring at the back of Alexander's neck.

Victoria's lip trembles. His words have set off a scuttering confusion that reminds her of her final conversation with her own father. She doesn't understand why Alexander's gesture offends her; perhaps it's simply her distrust of the word dad.

"You have no right . . ." she says, softly, stepping closer.

Alexander turns, shocked, with a flush moving up from his neck.

"Why didn't you discuss this with me first?" she continues in the same contradictory soft tone, watching Alexander as his face runs through the gamut of expressions of humiliation. Suddenly she regrets her words and feels like the foolish, indignant little girl she used to be. She wants to cry; she can't take it back now. She's gone too far. "Alexander, I'm sorry, but I just . . ."

But his back is to her again. Derek is sitting as still as the couch itself, watching her. She wants to run outside to think. What's wrong with her?

Alexander stands and turns towards her. "I didn't think—"

"You should have . . ." she says quickly, but it's really to herself. She needs to think.

He frowns, trying to understand. "I mean, I thought it was something that would please you. I guess I was wrong," he says, folding his arms and looking at the floor. "You don't want that," he adds.

She doesn't answer right away and the silence adds to the humiliation they are all feeling. "I do," she says, finally. It sounds like a false answer to a wedding vow. She walks towards Alexander and touches his shoulder.

"I should have talked to you about it," he says, looking at her, and she feels his defences lift him up and take him away from her.

"It's just that . . ." What is it just, she wonders? She wants to talk to him about her fears, the way he talked to her about Smita's death, but it's too late. Alexander takes her hand and rubs it non-committally.

"It's fine, fine," he says, full of grace and an easy forgiveness that makes her ashamed of herself.

"Derek," she says, turning to him with an almost hysterical desperation to repair things, "wouldn't it be lovely to think of Kendra as a sister?"

Derek's eyes light up with fury, his heart in a battle with itself.

"And Alexander, as . . ." she hesitates further.

Derek still hasn't moved. Something is rumbling forward inside him. Then it erupts: "Not another one! How many am I supposed to have anyway? Robert, Lenny, then Kola, and now you?" He stands up and storms past Alexander. When he reaches the hill path, he runs up and up into the woods.

CHAPTER TWELVE

Figs

༽ᨆᨆᨆᨆ

Bamboo Eco-coffins from China. The phrase plays itself at random moments in her mind. As she climbs the hill behind Kendra, towards the top of the fort, Victoria spots the Mediterranean over the crest, and the words carry her again. The sea. Burial seems suddenly absurd. Wouldn't dissolving into salt water be more seamless? St. Tropez is spectacular from this perspective. She stops along the path, perches her right foot on a rock, and inhales the brined air.

Bamboo Eco-coffins from China. Perhaps death is coy after all. Or at least the demonstration workshop had made it seem so. Entitled Creative DIY Funerals, the workshop was held at a centre devoted to the teaching and writings of Rudolf Steiner, whose philosophy included the importance of an organic transition to the other side. When Victoria saw the title of the workshop in the programme, she froze, standing at the door to Rudolf Steiner House, and she didn't want to enter. Alexander strolled in nonchalantly ahead of her. His broad back looked so confident, in the way she had come to know by touching it, that she followed him. They had spent evenings and weekends of the previous weeks together. During the love they made, he was poised, inviting her to lie beside him with merely a look and a slight movement of his head that was neither commanding nor entreating. He kissed her the way he looked at her, not really asking anything, but seeming to find something there he already knew. It always took her a few minutes to lose her self-consciousness, to stop feeling like a sagging-hem version of her self, but each time they made love they were outside of time. And they learned to share silence.

But his tastes still puzzled her, so at Steiner House she took a moment to watch him wander through the exhibit looking as though he was constructing his own version of the coffins, perhaps one wired for sound and image. His stance across the room looked firm, youthful, yet there was a touch of the old man—a dry grittiness—that couldn't be covered up. They listened to a seminar by a woman who described the UK laws that restricted natural desires for a natural death, and how the laws might be circumvented. With tips on improving the quality of dying, as well as creating individualized memorial services, the woman talked with a softness that allowed Victoria to float on her voice, so that when the words Bamboo Eco-coffins from China arrived, she was carried on them as though on a falling leaf.

But here is the sea to carry her. The sea, but it's cold. The sea, but it's not muddy. The sea, but not her dad. The sea, but not her mom. It's the sea and Alexander, and he is becoming everything. Her shoulders relax, then tense again at the thought of their confrontation, with Derek as witness and object. She's been trying to understand her reaction to Alexander's proposal to Derek. Was she protecting Derek, or trying to keep Alexander for herself? She hasn't had a moment alone to think it through, because she's been trying to make it up to Alexander ever since.

He reaches her on the path and stands behind her, his hands on his hips, his elbow up against her back. Still and unquestioning, it rests there firmly. Yet something remains unresolved. Derek races ahead, towards the cannon at the top of the citadel. When he reaches the weapon, he kicks it, testing its solidity. He sits on top of the gun barrel, and his shoulders bear defiance. Kendra climbs the hill lazily behind him. Derek doesn't look at her; he frowns as he looks down at Victoria.

Everything she's doing for him is wrong, Victoria thinks, and wonders if the boy hates her now. He's withdrawn like a snail into its shell. There's too much for her to think about all at once.

When Kendra reaches the cannon, she too looks at Victoria.

"You can hear peacocks calling from here in the night," Alexander calls up towards his daughter, "as though they're the new guards of the town."

But nothing is getting through to Kendra, who has been in a sulk for five days. Alexander has done his best to be cheerful.

At the top of the hill, the four of them gaze out towards the light-hearted Mediterranean. To their left, the terracotta roofs of St. Tropez are like a raised pebbled shore. To their right is a cemetery, and, further along the shore, the elegant seafront villas and the gardens of the rich.

"The town's name comes from a man—Torpés—who was beheaded, his corpse thrown into a boat and shoved out to sea, but it drifted back into this bay," Alexander tells them, looking at Derek.

Derek nods, his face expressionless.

"Or maybe you'd just prefer ice cream," Alexander concedes. Derek nods again, still without emotion. Victoria opens her purse to give him money, grateful that Alexander has suggested the diversion, despite the sugar content. Alexander puts his hand on hers as she takes out her wallet. There's something in his touch. Electricity, yes, but a negative charge. He reaches into his pocket, takes out a bill, and hands it to Derek, who heads back down the hill.

"We'll be right behind you. Wait at the bottom," he says to Kendra as she follows Derek.

"You're far too generous," Victoria says.

"I don't understand."

"I mean—"

"You're not just my guest . . . or are you? Is there something else I don't know?"

"Something else?"

He looks at his watch. "We should make a move. The boat leaves in twenty minutes."

Victoria blushes. The shame of punishment, just like at school. Something has changed; the invisible thread between them is broken. She leans up against the wall of the fort.

In St. Tropez he thinks he is more like James Bond—discreetly dangerous. Perhaps it is the gene of his real father expressing itself. He thinks of his mother and father embedded in his makeup like computer codes. He swings in binary opposition between them— magic and danger.

As the four of them stroll along the avenue of shops, killing time before the next ferry—Kendra had wandered off into the crowd with her ice cream and caused them to miss the last one—Derek is trying to move objects with his thoughts, intent on summoning his wizard. If he starts with small things, the big ones will come, he's sure. He'd like to propel Alexander and Kendra out of sight, but as his aunt stops to examine the scarves in a shop, he focuses on a basket with plastic fridge magnet souvenirs in the shape of baguettes, bottles of wine, cheese, and bunches of lavender. He stares at a baguette. Kendra walks casually in front of him and blocks his view. Nothing is working. He nonchalantly picks the baguette magnet out of the basket and slips it into his pocket. No one notices. There's some satisfaction in that.

In the car, when they finally turn off the autoroute towards Lorgues, Victoria is calmer, returning to a place that has become almost home after only a week. The drive up the hill to Fontcougourde is dotted with a week's worth of familiar corners, edges of road, wafts of rosemary. That's the bush behind which they spotted the snorting wild boar as large as a deer. Over there, the vineyards with grapes like clusters of bursting larvae. And there, the cedar smell that reminds her of Canada.

Inside the apartment, the air is cool.

Victoria sees Derek with his towel in hand. "You're not to go swimming alone. Wait for one of us."

"No," he says, and walks out the door.

Alexander and Victoria catch each other's eye, then both look at Kendra, who can't hide her satisfaction.

"You go with him, Kendra," Alexander says as he grabs a towel from one of the chairs and hands it to her.

"Yes sir," she says with a military salute, and heads out the door.

The breeze stops abruptly and a lizardy silence creeps in. Victoria finds herself in the middle of the open room, standing and staring, conscious of every flicker of movement.

"Who's Kola?" Alexander asks, sitting down on the sofa, removing his shoes.

"He's dead," she says quickly, at first not understanding what Kola has to do with anything.

"How does Derek know him?"

Victoria twigs and has to acknowledge to herself the gap around Kola that she's left in conversations, even those inspired by him. "He found a letter from him that I have, from a long time ago. He searches for trails to his father . . . he never met Kola."

Alexander tucks his right foot under his left leg, and she watches his calf muscle bulge in contraction. "I'm confused."

"He was my . . . lover . . . my partner, in Toronto. So long ago," she says, and doesn't want to continue. She's said her goodbyes. The monument to him that grew inside her for all those years has toppled. She sits beside Alexander on the sofa and also removes her shoes, but keeps both feet on the floor, which she needs to touch just now.

"You were in love," Alexander states.

Victoria scratches her right instep with the toes of the left foot.

"I don't think I ever totally understood him. He was the most unusual person I had ever met."

"How so?"

"He had so much experience, in many ways. I had lived a very sheltered life. And then I moved to Toronto and met him. He became everything to me, yet I really didn't know who he was." She scratches her instep again, then turns to face Alexander briefly. "How do we let ourselves do that?"

"How did you meet him?"

"A breath over my shoulder."

Alexander shifts his weight and leans farther back into the sofa.

"He surprised me. Always did. I think that's how I barely noticed six years passing. Every day was a surprise. But he was involved in things I didn't really know about, not only because they were kept from me. I could have known if I'd asked him. But I didn't. That's who I . . . was. Then he disappeared. I looked for him for many, many years. Finally in London. But you're—"

"No, don't. Don't do that," he says, cutting her off. "Continue. What happened?"

She doesn't look at his face. "I kept thinking if he came back everything would be OK. But my life was passing me by. I even started to be with someone else, got pregnant . . . but one day I received a letter from him. I dropped everything in Toronto and moved to London. He didn't give me any contact information, so I roamed the city, looking for him. When I wasn't working, that's pretty much all I did."

She curls her feet up under her and leans back on the sofa. "Now that I think about it, I think I depended on not finding him after a while; somehow searching was keeping me alive." She stops to consider what she's just put into words.

"But you know he's dead," Alexander puts forth.

"I finally called his brother in Kenya, and someone there told me they hadn't been in contact with him, not in some time. I left my name and number and asked them to let me know if they heard from him. More than two years went by . . ." She can't remember those two years, but gets the feeling that was when the hardness started to take root. "One day I received a phone call from a woman." She can hear the voice now, growly, and fired up, as if from its own furnace. " 'This is Akinyi,' she said, as though we'd spoken regularly. I didn't realize who she was until she continued. His wife. She was calling me from America, because she'd been sent Kola's things, found my letters, and traced me through a friend of his brother's. She told me Kola was dead. I could barely listen as she told me the story, because I realized that we'd both lost Kola, but she sounded almost untouched by it all.

"He had been deported from Canada, back to Kenya, where he spent time in prison for things he didn't do, because the government was afraid of who he knew, really, that must have been it. His brother had been kidnapped by government thugs and tied to a tree for three days before he was properly arrested, so perhaps it all had something to do with Tairus, I really don't know. She told me Kola had been in detention, confined to a dirty six-foot cell. Think of the torture. Like a caged animal. But he was a man. A man who thought too deeply about everything."

In all the years after the phone call, Victoria focused on the mental torture Kola would have undergone in Kenya. She couldn't bring herself to imagine the physical truth of his death in London—not until that day two years ago as she knelt on the pavement behind the Also bar.

"When he was released, he wanted to escape all of it, all of them, and went to London, and that's when I heard from him and went too, but I never found him. Akinyi told me she'd heard from Tairus's friends, and that it might have even been some of them who were responsible for his death." Victoria pauses to the echo of Akinyi's growly tone and all the accusations entwined in it.

"She said that outside, at the back of a bar in North London, a Kenyan man who was settling old scores between Tairus and his enemies held up a gun and told Kola to kneel on the pavement. Kola knelt—it's something that surprised me; he wouldn't have automatically done as someone told him. He was defiant, but the fear must have been too much . . ." She can feel the cold gritty pavement on her knees and loses track of the story for a moment. "He knelt, and the man put a gun to his head. Shot him. Dead. Right there. 'A bullet to the head,' Akinyi said, so casually, like you'd say 'a ring on his finger.' "

She listens for Alexander's breathing, unable to look up. She wonders if it is this fact, Kola's body lying on the cold pavement, that was the final ingredient acting in her during the years before Derek arrived, like aggregate in sand turns it to concrete.

There's a long silence, then Alexander stands up and touches her cheek, cups her chin in his hand, and lets his fingers slide down her neck.

"I'm sorry," he says gently, then drops his hand. He says nothing more. They are both embarrassed. He picks up his shoes and walks to the other side of the room. He looks out the window, over the vineyard, then turns to pick up a towel from the back of a chair. He heads to the door.

"I'm going for a swim," he says as neutrally as he can. Victoria releases herself into the sofa, suddenly exhausted. She lies down and looks up at the wooden beams across the ceiling.

Since their climb to the citadel the days have grown hotter. The landscape has become ever more tinted in orange. Victoria kneads her hip; it aches from the swimming and walking. Alexander has not made love to her in three days.

She wakes early on the last morning of their stay. Alexander is sleeping beside her, one arm around his head, his chin tucked into his shoulder. She watches him sleep. Come back, she mouths silently, but doesn't dare push through his reserve. She would have to answer for her own. She's ashamed of herself. He was being so generous to Derek. At home, things will be better again, the ground solid once more.

She gets out of bed in order to gather up laundry and pack their belongings into the Volvo.

A clanking sound comes from inside the dryer. A coin she would leave in with the clothes, but this sounds more substantial, and the noise is bound to wake the others. She stops the machine. Rummaging through the wet pockets of a pair of Derek's trousers she pulls out the baguette fridge magnet. She doesn't understand why, but she wants to cry. She breathes deeply, thinking, retracing, doing her best not to jump to conclusions.

She marches up the stairs to the loft. "Where did you get this?" Her voice is exhausted, but sharp. Derek stirs, but drifts off again.

"Derek," she says loudly. She holds up the baguette. "Derek, Derek."

He is finally roused and looks at her. As soon as he sees what's in her hand he is wide awake. He sits up.

"What?" he asks, stalling.

"Where did you get this?"

"I bought it."

"You didn't have any euros."

"I borrowed some from Kendra."

"You've barely spoken to her."

"I found it."

"No, you didn't."

"I did, I found it when we were walking in town." He rubs his eye as though he's sleepy, but tears are welling in them. The wizard is letting him down. He's got to work harder.

Victoria stares at him. They know each other now. Truth resides in every gesture.

"I can't believe this. I really can't. What's got into you?"

He continues to rub his eyes: "Nothing, nothing, I swear. It was a mistake. I didn't mean to."

Victoria turns and makes her way back down the stairs. God, let us go home, she thinks. She is desperate for London.

Once they have finally left Lorgues, driven up the *autoroute du sud*, and are on the Channel Tunnel train, she is calm. The sound of English is everywhere. Ten days have suddenly seemed unnaturally long. She gets out of the Volvo to walk to the toilets. Inside the tiny cubicle she stares at herself in the mirror. Her crow's feet are more pronounced. She looks like her mother, but even her mother never had this saggy, tree-bark neck, or at least Victoria never saw her mother this old. In her memory, her mother's face is smooth. What is it mothers know?

She misses Lenny. His kindness, his forgiveness. Lenny and the blind eye he turns on her negligence. She puts the toilet seat down and sits on it. This cubicle is enough to contain her.

Back on Blenheim Terrace, Alexander helps carry the luggage upstairs. All their movements are stiff with misunderstanding. Sonia and the twins come running up the stairs to welcome them home, and Victoria is relieved by the gentle intrusion.

"We made a boat," says Max as he holds up a piece of straight wood that Victoria assumes is a paddle.

"And a fort. But Max smashed it," says Monica as she stares up at Derek, thrilled that he's home.

"How was it?" asks Sonia, looking at Victoria, then Alexander. She looks about for Kendra. Only then does Victoria realize that Kendra has stayed in the car. She's not surprised, given that somewhere along the motorway in Kent, Derek turned to her and spoke for the first time since they'd left Lorgues: "Stephen and I'll be going to lunch on our own when term starts again."

Victoria didn't see the look Kendra must have given him, but she heard the little *hurrumph* before Kendra put her headphones on. Things were unravelling at an alarming rate. Alexander looked at Victoria. "Let's give it a few days," he said, and then concentrated on getting them home as quickly as possible.

He places the last of Victoria's luggage in her room and turns to her. "You all right, then?" he asks.

"Yes, thanks. I don't know how to th—"

He raises his hand and takes hers, brings it to his lips, and holds it there for a moment. "We'll talk soon. You get settled back in." He walks down the stairs. Victoria hears a dripping sound coming from somewhere, like the slow leak of a faucet. She turns towards the kitchen tap, but it's dry. She goes into her room and closes the door.

Two days go by before she hears from Alexander, and when he calls his tone is formal. "Just checking in to see how you're doing. Things have been mad at work since we got back. Sorry I haven't rung before."

She tries to keep her voice neutral, to stop it from sliding into need. "We've been busy too—Lenny is relieved I'm back; we have contracts for the autumn." Each word is like a little seed of loneliness that she's sowing. A few more pleasantries are exchanged and the conversation is finished. She hangs up. She stares at the wall.

London

Dear Victoria:

It's me.

I know it must be a shock, and I can't be sure this will reach you after all these years, but I'm writing now, while I have the chance, and there is a post office near to the rooming house where I'm staying. I will have to leave this place tomorrow, and am not sure where I'll go, but I've been given a few names of men from Mombasa who live in Kilburn. I arrived here a week ago, and don't know what faces me, or if I'll be able to stay. Again, I am a refugee.

At least here I've been able to be lost among people who pay little attention to my past.

I'm sitting in a restaurant near Piccadilly, drinking some very good coffee. The morning I left your flat, you were still sleeping. I wanted to buy you some good coffee and breakfast that would make you happy to wake up to. I met someone I knew, from Nairobi, who had been involved with Tairus, who, at the time, was running for local office in the general elections. He thought he could infiltrate the government in order to change it. The man asked me to help him, by driving him to pick up things that were coming from Kenya. He said he could count on me because I was Tairus's brother. But we were arrested. I found out later that this man had nothing to do with Tairus. He had betrayed many of Tairus's men in Nairobi and was involved in smuggling. I tried to clear myself, but they found out I had no visa. They said I was guilty, but I had done nothing wrong. They let me collect a few things—I've kept your letters all this time—then deported me very quickly. I never meant to leave you.

Back in Nairobi I was detained immediately. When Tairus came to visit me, he told me Akinyi was still living in America. I had no one. Tairus did his best to get me released, but now that he had entered politics, he was even more dangerous to the ruling party than previously. Two days before he presented his nomination papers to the District Commissioner, he was kidnapped and tied to a tree for three days. After the election he was arrested and detained at Kamiti prison, where I was being held, but I never saw him. They released me two years ago, with the help of a group who fights for political prisoners. Someone helped me come to London. I wanted to be away from all of that, to be free. Is that possible?

Prison is not a place for any man, particularly a man like me. In prison you wake up in the morning, there's no water to wash your face, no breakfast. You rely on your memories to keep you going. But just as you're getting some pleasure from them, you may get a beating, or whipping. Or when your pleasure is food, and you face the small portion of stale yam and beans set before you, the memories become too painful to indulge. Many men in our block died of disease. A few were beaten to death. Their deaths have been covered up. I wished that instead of cooking I had practised to become a diviner, or a wizard who knew how to heal misery, and I might have been a more useful man. I had to invent something in my imagination to block out what was going on around me, so I spent my time creating new words. I developed a secret Gikuyu vocabulary that could be mastered only if I provided the key. In prison you have only words, and you have to use your own powers just to get beyond the physical torture.

Tairus was tortured so badly in prison that something in him snapped. When he was finally released, he became associated with the Mungiki, a group that started after Mau Mau—people who believe dogmatically that Gikuyus were the first people on earth. They dress only in black, they wear their hair in dreadlocks. Now Tairus lives exclusively with Gikuyus and will not talk to anyone outside the sect. I think it is his way of giving up. He once believed there could be justice, but in fighting for it, he now believes in fear. So, I ask myself now, does it mean that the so-called first people on earth will die among themselves, alone, without the world taking notice?

I have come here to try to make a life, but it may not be possible. London is a difficult place. I will contact you again when I'm settled. If I can't stay here I will go back to Kenya, to face more uncertainty, but possibly to be more useful than I have been in the past, away from Tairus's closed world. His is the only number I have for contact ([254] 401287), the only place I would go if I leave here, but I'm hoping to find a way to stay. I'm sorry I haven't had the courage to contact you before this. Too much has happened, too much seems lost.

Love,
Kola
P.S. I wonder, did you ever get to holiday in Barbados?

Derek folds up the letter and puts it at the bottom of the bundle and back into the drawer. He has read it before, but the idea of prison has taken on a new reality for him. If he keeps making deliveries for Richard, will he go to prison as the other boys have said? The day after his punishment for the theft of the magnet was over he was summoned to the schoolyard to make another delivery, this time to the playground on Abbey Gardens. He felt prison like a promise in the gritty plastic bag he handed over to a young man wearing fluorescent trainers. In prison a man would have to be very strong, in control. In prison a man would have to know how not to be lonely, how not to miss anyone, especially a girl.

His aunt's punishment for his theft had consisted not only of a week's full-time work with Lenny on orders and deliveries, but also helping to serve food at the Salvation Army. "Derek, don't you see? Even people who need more than you don't steal it," his aunt said anxiously the first day. Any spare time he had was spent confined to the house. The punishment had seemed severe at first, but he slowly became grateful for the time to think and read. Studying his books and the available lectures on the Web, he has been practising being bigger than the things around him. When his curfew was lifted, he almost missed it. His moments alone have become his most important, because has been honing his perceptions and will.

After delivering Richard's package yesterday, he met up with Stephen at the back of the school.

"Here, hold this," said Stephen, and thrust a small frog into Derek's hand. The mouth of the creature opened and closed slowly. Stephen pulled out matches and a firecracker from his back pocket. "This should be a laugh."

Derek held the frog around its tiny neck, trying not to squeeze too tightly, his eyes fixed on the stiff movement of the animal's lower jaw. The frog looked barely alive, but squirmed valiantly when Stephen took it by its back legs. Stephen squatted on the pavement; Derek dutifully copied his stance.

"Hold it down," instructed Stephen. Derek put one finger on the frog's twitching belly while Stephen readied the firecracker and matches.

"Stick this up its arse," Stephen instructed.

"Why?" Derek knew it sounded like the wrong question, but he wanted to know if Stephen knew how stupid he looked.

"Watch," Stephen said, as he stuck the firecracker into the frog, struck the match and lit the fuse. Derek willed the fuse to sputter and die out, but it didn't. He and Stephen stood back and watched the frog do one final hop before its guts splattered across the pavement. Derek turned and walked away. What was the best way to control something? To destroy it, or to dance with it?

He walks into the kitchen and sees his aunt at the stove, preparing their dinner. He wants to ask her if they can go away again before school term starts in a month. Not to France, but to Ireland, to see the ancient forests of the Druids. He would like to encounter the magic spark that lurks in rock and wood and leaf, in all the things that fly, crawl, slither, or bound throughout the forests. He wants to learn to be in sync with them, to focus his will more powerfully. But Auntie Vic, he realizes, has been in a mood for some time now.

"Wish I didn't have to start school again," he blurts as he sits down to supper. Victoria places his meal on the table: a plastic container with a prepackaged dinner of chicken korma and rice. Last night it was lamb with rice. The night before, prawns with rice. He picks up his fork and pokes at the hard grains. Victoria attempts a smile as she pulls out her chair to sit opposite.

"Maybe Alexander wants to take another holiday," he ventures.

"I doubt that very much," she says casually.

"Then he's a liar."

Suddenly the air in the room is thick and heavy.

"You're not to talk like that, ever."

"He said things were different now—"

"Eat your supper."

"That's all you ever say—"

"Derek . . ." she breaks off and her voice cracks.

"And that." Derek eats up quickly, holding his ground.

He can't help it, he misses her. But every time he thinks of calling Kendra it's as if a giant hand is pulling him back by the spine. He doesn't yet recognize the hand of shame and humility, but he feels it. But things are getting desperate. Kendra is the only person who understands him, and only in her absence has he realized that he assumed the two of them would be together forever. If she has forgotten about the moment at the brook, he will be able to tell her about magic—real magic. In Ireland they could participate in the festival of Lughnasadh he has been reading about. *The season of growth has come to an end*, say the Druids. *Harvest, dance, drink and eat—these things celebrate what we have sown and nurtured. Their dying gives us what we need. Come, dance, eat* . . . The Druids had spirits like the Kanaima, but not as evil. He wonders whether acknowledging evil might keep it at bay.

"OK if I visit Kendra?"

"You've called her? How do you know she's home?" Her voice is a tiny lasso.

"I'll call her, then go, OK?"

She nods and pushes away her plastic tray.

The evening is a curse of sounds. Supper pots clang and television news blares from windows in the street. There's the sound of coming home and the sound of impatience. Food. Give us food. Mothers rush about to keep up to demands. Victoria finds these evenings difficult. She has seen Alexander just once in the past week, when she picked up the shoes she'd left in his car. He greeted her with one of his hugs that comes from deep in his chest. She felt almost shored up again, but once he let go he didn't look at her directly.

Victoria is finished cleaning up the kitchen. After almost an hour on the telephone with Kendra, Derek has gone over to her house. The sounds of the evening curse on. In the hallway she bends down to lift the lid of the wooden chest and a tired sigh escapes from the wood. She crouches to examine the letters and photo-graphs lying in careless piles. She rummages near the bottom, looking for his handwriting. The string-tied bundles of letters from Gwen, her mother, her friends in Toronto are all there, but not the packet of letters from Kola. After a moment she realizes, of course, Derek.

By the bed is a small table with a drawer, where Derek keeps his treasures. Although she respects his growing need for privacy, what she's looking for belongs to her. She's too fatigued to feel angry or to wonder what he's doing with her letters. She finds the bundle and removes the final letter. *Dear Victoria: It's me.* But a quick glance at it tells her that's not it, not what she needs now. She folds up the letter and returns the bundle to the chest in the hallway. She sits down on the floor beside the chest. Dipping into it, she pulls out a bundle from home and begins to read.

The night air is inviting. In the shadow of a skip outside a house under renovation, she spots the pointed face of a creature. Then its sleek torso and tail emerge from the shadows, and the fox breezes across the street in front of her. She squeezes the letter in her hand as she walks.

At the Kilburn Salvation Army, the queue is relatively short. Victoria has nothing to give them tonight, so she stands to the side and waits.

The letter in her hand is from her mother, sent to her in those early days in London. The handwriting is smudged, the hand shaky and frail, even though, at the time, her mother would have been much younger than Victoria is now.

Victoria:

Daddy's not well, but we doing our best for the time being. I get the shakes in my hand from time to time, and when I pour out his medicine it spills, sometimes on his chest. I don't think it's the right medicine anyway, so maybe it's not such a horror to lose it, but Gwen looks at me as if I do it on purpose. She trying hard to have a baby, and I keep telling her it's unnatural without a husband, but she fighting me, fighting all of us. I think she wants nothing more than a baba now. You know what? I think it must be because I lost my first baby before you. Maybe we all been trying to replace him. The girl is full of the stars, and I don't understand what she's going on about most of the time, but there's fire in she eyes as she talks about babies. But you were never so. I was grieving the baby the whole time you were in my belly. You came out and I could barely look at you because I thought it would be him come back to me, not as the three-year-old he died, but as a new model of heself. Maybe that is why you are always off running here and there, maybe I grieved too much and put you off. And Daddy didn't help. You know, Vic, some days I stare at him as he breathes heavy and I watch his mouth and I want to know when it going to stop breathing. I only telling you this because I know how you feel about him too, but, darling, we can't blame him, he has done his best for all of we, and you know I think he was brukup bad by Peter dying. We were never the same after that. You can't blame him for making babies everywhere, Victoria. It's a natural thing for a man to do.

As for me, I am glad I have my Gwen close by, because she helps me a lot with Daddy. I don't think he's staying on this earth much longer, to tell you the truth. And I keep wishing you could come home and make your peace with him, but you have a new life now. There was a time I wanted to run away with you. But I am not suffering, child. I am a strong woman and I take what the Lord gives. One day we'll share a good laugh again, I promise you. One day you'll sit on the porch with us and we'll remember when we were all together. For now, my dear daughter, I'm praying you are well and that you are keeping out of troubles there in the cold.

All my love,
Mom.

Victoria spots Beth coming out of the shelter in her brown woollen coat that is buttoned up to the chin. Her hair has been combed. Victoria smiles at her. Beth looks at her but doesn't return the smile.

"What, not you too, now?" Beth says, looking Victoria up and down.

Victoria hesitates, unclear as to Beth's meaning. "Oh, no, not me!" she says, perhaps too quickly, in panic at the implication that she too might one day need the Sally Ann's services. "No," she says, more calmly, adjusting the belt on her cotton dress. "Just out for a walk."

"Then walk," Beth says flatly, and she heads along the pavement towards the traffic lights. Her mood is clipped. Victoria doesn't feel welcomed but decides to follow her. She catches up with her and they walk with matching strides.

"You come from far?" Victoria asks her.

"Here, most of my life."

They walk in silence. Victoria wants to tell Beth how she's thinking of changing her name—to Marilyn, Gilda, Josephine, or Rita, for example. She's tired of her feelings.

That's enough, she says to the letter, and dashes it into the rubbish bin on the corner near the overpass. She has inherited loss as someone else might inherit a nose or the length of a forearm. That's enough, she wants to tell Beth. A new name would disinherit her. She's not queen of anything. But Beth is looking straight ahead and her bearing does not invite conversation.

Beth turns right along the wall that supports the overpass and through an alleyway leading to a sheltered, cubby-like corner.

"Well, this is me, then," she says as she turns towards a cardboard screen that balances a second panel of cardboard on its top edge as a canopy. Victoria notices bedding and two pairs of laced shoes lined up along the wall. Beth follows her gaze, arriving at the shoes, then turns towards Victoria.

"There's a woman, works at the Sally Ann," Beth begins. "She has something, you know, she burns with it, like it's the best shag she's ever had and keeps having. She does what she does with us, giving and caring for us, because she has someone she talks to in the night." She points up to the heavens. "He loves her and she doesn't even have to raise her arse in the air for him." She pauses and locks eyes with Victoria. "You think I'd be here if I was getting that?" Beth laughs. With a nod, she turns and walks towards the cardboard, not looking back, but with certainty in her shoulders that Victoria will now leave her alone.

Victoria turns quickly and continues towards Maida Vale. The houses are smart and bay-windowed. She wonders if it was wrong to have thrown away the letter. By the time her mother next wrote, Victoria's father had passed away and her mother's tone had become anxious. What would the world be like now? She would be the object of neighbourhood talk, all alone now, and that didn't seem at all fair. Victoria stops, shakes her leg to ease a cramp. She spots a phone box. Reaching into her handbag, she fingers some coins and retrieves a 50p piece. Inside the phone box, she reaches for the receiver, but hesitates. She leans against the door; minutes pass as she reconsiders the call. She examines the graffiti inside the booth. *Asma Rehman loves me 100%* is scrawled in black marker across the glass. Victoria's heart goes out to Asma Rehman and her friend for whom one hundred percent means always and enough.

She picks up the receiver. Dials. The phone is picked up on the other end.

"Lenny, have I become ridiculous?" she asks the receiver breathlessly.

*

Lenny fills her wine glass to the top and slides it over the tabletop towards her. She knows what he's thinking: that he was right all along; that he's the right man for her. That younger man with all his fancy talk and eye for design, with his fancy computers, lights, and audio system—none of that was right for Victoria. Alexander was wrong about food; what does he know about what we eat and where it should come from? Alexander has proven himself wrong about many things. Lenny has triumphed, and so he tops up her glass because he thinks that, as before, a few sips of good Pomerol will tip Victoria into his arms. And he will be vindicated.

But Victoria sips very delicately from her glass. "Delicious," she says, then puts it down on the table. She stares at Lenny's arms, stubby and spotted with age, and hairier than she remembered. The hair on his head is fair, with very little grey, but the strands are sinewy. She's ashamed of the repulsion rising in her. Lenny is in good nick for a man his age; and how dare she judge how he has handled time? She takes another taste of wine.

"You're looking good," she tells him.

"You haven't eaten anything, Vic," he says, skipping over the comment.

"Lost my appetite recently, I'm afraid, but you've gone to so much trouble."

"No trouble," he mumbles, and reaches for an oyster from the oval, floral-pattered plate that displays the raw, dead bivalves in their shells like pearls in finely set rings. He takes one and slurps it down loudly.

The food is exquisite. A gentlemanly meal is laid out before her like a jacket over a puddle of mud for a queen. Lenny has presented her with the most erotic dishes: oysters, widower's figs, coq au vin, accompanied by a fine bottle of Pomerol. Victoria wonders how he put the meal together so quickly. Its ingredients are so unlike Lenny. His eroticism has never been so formal. But he is competing and, at this moment, has a firm advantage. The widower's figs make the greatest impression. The large, ripe fruit are like delicate sexual sacks, ready to burst open with seed.

"Alexander would be amazed," she says, desperately wanting to talk about him with Lenny.

"Alex should get himself a cook," he declares flatly.

Lenny has never liked Alexander. He has called him Alex purposely since the day Victoria corrected him. When Victoria appeared at Lenny's door complaining about Kendra's father at the school meeting, he knew her voice belied her words, and he felt her start slipping away from him. She fondles her napkin. Lenny sips his wine.

"He has stopped loving me."

"Don't be silly." Lenny grabs a fig and splits it open. There's another long silence. He chews and swallows, takes another bite of the fig. "Maybe he has trouble fitting in with you and Derek." Victoria sees what's happening now. Lenny is stifling his natural response—words that would rage with a reminder that he, Lenny, had only ever wanted to care for her and the boy, provide for them, love them. She sees the words in his jaw as he chews the fig. He swallows and gets up to bring the coq au vin to the table. He serves her a thigh and some sauce, a breast for himself, then places the pot back on the stove and sits down.

"Chicken's corn-fed, from a new farm in Devon: they raise only a few at a time." He picks up his knife and fork. "You were right, chickens need the same attention as large farm animals. You'd approve of the place—pristine, just like you've always said they should be." He catches her eye. He puts his knife down, raises his glass, sips, picks up the knife again.

"That kind of man . . ." he says, shaking his head.

"What kind is that?" she asks, defensively.

"That kind, you know." He looks up, flustered.

"What are you accusing him of now?"

Lenny focuses back on his plate, his knife working along the chicken breast, cutting it into smaller and smaller pieces, not yet raising one to his lips.

"Lenny, answer, please, what kind of man?"

He looks up at her and puts his knife and fork down abruptly. "The kind that isn't *me*, Victoria," he says, in the loudest voice she has ever heard him use, drawing out her full name with pain.

Victoria's stomach flips, her chest tightens. Oh God, what has she done. She's lost him now too. Her throat feels choked. She stares at her plate. The love feast before her is slowly congealing; the remaining fig looks wizened and lost. Her mind shifts from the present to the past, and back and forth again. She wants it all to be simple.

Long ago she read about an Ethiopian vulture that flies over mountains in search of antelope carcasses. It swoops down to pick up a bone in its beak, and then rises to a great height, only to drop the bone to the rock far below. When the bone is shattered, the bird swoops down once more to eat the exposed, succulent marrow. Then it swallows the bone whole. Nourishment can be so complicated, she thinks.

Lenny rubs his forehead and then rests it in his hands. He shakes his head and drags his hands through his hair.

"I've been a fool," she says, holding back tears. "I'm so sorr—"

"OK. OK," he says, finally looking up. "Don't cry." She holds her breath. A long minute passes. "Don't cry, it was never going to be me, was it?" he says quietly. It's not a question but a statement of fact. She looks at him. "I did what I could," he continues, almost to himself. She exhales in puffs. She can barely stand the echoing need between them.

"There, there. We do all right, the two of us," he says with a wry smile, and reaches for her hand. "You have to talk to him. It's the only way. Stop torturing yourself. You're a good woman, Vic, darling. A great woman, and he knows it. But you have to tell him what's on your mind—and what's in your heart."

She takes a deep breath to hold back a sob. Lenny rubs her hand, and it's this gesture of the hopeless affection he feels for her that causes a tear to slide down her cheek. He rubs her hand again.

"Try to eat something," he says, gently.

CHAPTER THIRTEEN

Ravens Dreaming

⌒⌒⌒

"You're daft. You just like to be difficult and different," Kendra says bitterly as she swings her finger up from her keypad and points it at his face, at the birthmark in particular. She's chiding him for his dismissal of a certain wizard, but he knows the real reason for her outburst is that her men are being mercilessly slaughtered.

Kendra and Derek are in his room playing Age of Empires II, in which the Japanese battle the Mongols. Derek, as Ghengis Khan, has captured most of Kendra's samurai. The two are at ease in a way akin to the first precious moments of their friendship, yet now there is an undercurrent of taboo between them, dragging them away from the bank of certain topics: Richard the Truck, the brook in Provence, Victoria's mood. Sticking to their shared thirst for understanding, they are safe.

At the end of their holiday in Provence, Derek could not have imagined that he would ever speak to her again, but during the time he was grounded, relegated to his room in the evenings and to the company of solely Lenny and his aunt during the days, he couldn't bear their separation. He was forced to reinvent what it meant to be close to Kendra. Close but not touching. Since married people had to touch, by definition, that meant he would not marry her.

"Hi, what are you up to?" he asked when she answered the phone that evening.

"Not much, you?"

"Not grounded anymore."

"Grounded? What for?"

"Long story." He considered telling her but in that moment understood the nature of intimacy. It was dangerous to share everything with someone you were not going to marry. He thought he might have to ask her anyway.

"Will you . . . ?" he asked, then paused, allowing the words to just fill themselves in.

"Will I what?"

"Um . . ." he waited. Then he mouthed, exaggeratedly, the silent articulation of the words . . . *marry me* . . . and went on to say, "let me come over?"

"Yea, why not, just don't be a git."

So he accepted her acceptance, as well as her advice, and went over, vowing to himself that when he was finally ready, his power fully honed, and when it was obvious that he was no longer a git— then she might marry him. In the meantime, he'd have to be happy with what she chose to share with him.

"Here!" she said the moment he arrived at her house, presenting him with a book on sperm. "It's meaningless anyway, just a lot of swimming creatures who bang into eggs—a crazy blip that happens to make a person. So what. He's not special, not for wanking into a jar in any case. Stop fretting it!"

And so he created a secret compartment in himself where he is hoarding his love for her.

He captures her last samurai warrior, and she tosses aside her keypad. "How would you know it's not what real wizards do?" she asks, diverting attention from her defeat.

"Look," he says, moves the mouse and cursor, and clicks online. It takes a few long seconds for the bookmarked site to appear; the computer is old and barely handles a modem, at any speed. They arrive at www.druids.com.

"Harry Potter's for knobs," he risks, without looking to see his remark's effect. He is in his own territory now, confident and self-assured.

"You're one odd git," sighs Kendra, but her eyes are drawn to the screen. "A wizard's a wizard's a wizard, is all I say. And Richard isn't going to be afraid of any of it. He's one rotten, tough bastard. He only knows how to bash," and she crosses her arms. He looks at her. Avenge, protect, redeem. And then it hits him: Richard needs him. Like the dark needs the light, Richard needs Derek to organize an opposition. That's what he'll do. He wonders if Rory and Stephen will join him.

"That other wizardry's fake. Real people don't do those things," he says, as he moves the cursor on the screen to a signpost that reads: Tap into the Invisible.

"You see," he says confidently.

"See what? It's about the invisible," she laughs, and taps him on the shoulder. He reminds himself that he's still a git. He doesn't laugh.

She looks at him suspiciously. "You're going funny, everyone around me is going funny . . . Dad especially . . . he has—" Kendra breaks off, stands up, and starts to take off her clothes. She throws off her shoes and socks, and starts to unbutton her shirt.

Derek doesn't ask her what she was about to say. He doesn't want to hear about Alexander. Right now he is only concerned with keeping his eyes diverted from her waist, which he catches sight of in his peripheral vision, as she gives up on the buttons and hikes her shirt over her head, drawing her camisole up towards her ribs. He stares at the screen. The Druids had a similar perspective on magic to the Amerindians. The power of the circle might be not too far off from the power the Kanaima must have harnessed.

He clicks on a new page of the site:

> www.druids.com/ravensdreaming
>
> The hereditary Druid claims to be of a family line through which the ancient wisdom was never lost.
>
> The work of being a Druid is a constant process of becoming, of reaching the archetype of strength, wisdom, clarity, invulnerability and gentle humanity, together with an understanding of nature at its rawest edges. We stretch through our souls to the essence of life, to the spirit that vitalizes us, to the God that empowers us, in search of inspiration.

"OK, OK!" Kendra says. She has assembled a circle in the middle of the floor, made with shoes, socks, her shirt, a book on Druids, and Derek's pyjamas, outlining a space in which the two of them can sit. She places the Harry Potter book outside the circle, respecting Derek's demands on that issue. She sits down in the middle of the circle, wearing her camisole and trousers. Derek gets up from the desk and joins her. They sit, facing each other, staring.

"You two be OK here while—" Victoria cuts her question abruptly as she stands in the doorway, surprised by the sight of Kendra and Derek seated cross-legged on the floor and encircled by discarded clothes. They look up at her as though she should apologize.

"What's going on?" Victoria asks.

"Just a game," replies Kendra curtly, then picks up the Druidry book, opens it, and ignores Victoria. Victoria hesitates, but she is too preoccupied to linger or to sort out this odd sight for herself.

"You two be OK here for an hour or so while I visit Alexander?" They nod at her. Their blank faces tell her to get going, so she does. She returns to her room to glance in the mirror. Touching her hair, she wonders if it's thinner than a few months ago. Will that be how it goes? A balding old lady in the supermarket whose wisps of dry hair can't hide the frightened-looking scalp? She dabs on some blush, picks up her umbrella and a small package, and heads out.

"Brought you some olive bread," she says, as she shakes out the umbrella before entering Alexander's hallway. The rain has been falling for the last hour, and August has turned into November. She stamps her feet, shaking off droplets of water, and wipes her shoes on the hall mat.

The bread is wrapped in wax paper and tucked under her arm. She hands it to him. "It's not as good as what we bought at the market in Lorgues, but it's my second batch, not too bad."

"Thank you, really . . . very sweet." He kisses her straight on the lips. She tries to underplay any significance to the gesture. "Come in. It's wretched out there. I was just watching the news."

"Don't let me interrupt." The formality between them makes her flinch.

"No, I'd rather watch you," he says, and the yellow flecks in his eyes do their can-can dance. Her heart bucks. She holds the reins in tight. She wants him to explain himself.

They move into the spacious sitting room. Victoria glides onto the sofa. She recalls the smell of lilacs from their first night here. She breathes deeply and lets out the reins just slightly.

"Sorry I've been out of touch," he says as he sits down beside her.

"Me too." He is close to her. She can hear him breathe. Outside, a gust of wind tosses rain at the half-open window. He fingers the hem of his T-shirt. She smiles at him when he looks up, but the atmosphere between them stiffens.

He stands up. "You don't even know why, do you?" he asks as he closes the window to stop the rain from spraying the wooden sill.

"Something changed that day in France," she offers. She doesn't like this feeling of being small. She looks at him. His shoulders are tensed in that old-man way he has at times. She could hate him if she tried right now, just because of those shoulders. And yet she can picture him as a boy of ten, standing in a draughty room in the same way, waiting for the rain to stop so that he can run and run across a moor.

"I thought I knew you, but I don't think I do," he says, pacing and then turning back to the rain at the window. Victoria wants to scream at him to face her, to turn around and scold her, not to block her out with his shoulders. When he does turn, he has more to say. "There's something very tough about you, more than you let on. I thought I understood it."

He runs his hand through his hair and back. His fingers touch his nose and rest there, waiting for him to think of the right words, so that they can form the accompanying gestures. He's a man of gestures, she thinks, and wonders why she's never thought of this before. Everything in his life is full of movement and shape, not sound and syllables like hers. I haven't made enough gestures, she thinks.

"I was very naïve when I married Smita. She challenged me. My family was big on manners, not so big on integrity. I don't think my father ever said a real thing in his life . . . You were so convinced about things, your conviction about what was right and what was wrong. I was convinced by you."

And now? She swallows. She wants to tell him that maybe we just go backwards. Maybe we poison each other and destroy everything . . .

"I feel like a fool," he concludes, and the Yorkshire curve on his vowels is like a swinging scythe.

Victoria stands. She walks towards the fireplace, and now they're both pacing at opposite ends of the room. She thinks she can hear the sound of a baby crying, but this must be another internal sound.

"Either you don't love me or you don't trust me. Or both. I thought we were heading along the same path; that's why I spoke to Derek the way I did. I was wrong. For days it was my pride—I thought I must have been deluded. But a few days later everything else dawned on me. I didn't, I don't understand . . . Why hadn't you told me about Kola before?"

The crying stops. "I did tell you," she says, protecting herself now.

He turns to face her. "After Derek mentioned it." His voice creeps into a higher register. "He was the most important person in your life. His death must have been the worst moment you could have ever imagined, and yet you didn't think of sharing it with me."

"He's the past . . . like Smita."

"No, you hold a torch for a dead person. That's exactly what I *don't* want anymore."

Victoria looks towards the mantel, and there is Smita, smiling.

"She's not here." He places his hand at the base of his neck. "That's why I could tell you everything about her. All these months I just assumed I knew—maybe not everything, but—all the important things about you."

"You do, it's not important," she says in a neutral voice.

"That's not true, or maybe you can't even see how important it is. Kola is untouchable, infallible. No wonder you could ramble on about Kenya . . . the detail . . . Now that I know, I can see it in what you say and do. It's the tough part of you."

She knows he's speaking the truth. "I didn't want to complicate things for you," she says, feebly.

"No, you didn't want to complicate things for *you*. You haven't let go."

He's right. She's embarrassed. Kola was an ordinary man. She softens. "I wanted to at the beginning, but then I didn't. Then later it seemed . . . too late."

He sits back on the sofa, slightly calmer now. She doesn't join him. "I realized, in France, that you might not want what I want: a family again. I thought I'd made a huge mistake. But, worse, I thought you might think we're inappropriate . . . and maybe we are . . . there *is* something false about it." He crosses his legs and runs his hand through his hair again, his fingers digging into his scalp. "But I don't think it comes from me," he says finally and looks at her. "I'm trying to live with what's in front of me, Victoria."

"I'm sorry," she mutters, seeing how vulnerable he's been all along—how his gadgets protect him, ground him. Otherwise he'd just float up and up and up . . .

"Do you see me as another young thing you have to protect?" he adds finally.

"No. No," she says, horrified that all this time she's been trying to be as young as him, and now she sees it: "I was ashamed of having been a child myself for so long."

He looks into his hands. "It was a shock, that's all. I lost my confidence when you cut me off, and I've lost my stride a bit. It's as though there was a lie. I need to readjust."

"What can I do?" she asks, feeling like every word she says is suspect.

"It'll take time, that's all," he says and reaches for her hands and rubs them in his.

Victoria relishes the satiny roughness of his fingers.

The rain has stopped but everything is still dripping. The roses along Marlborough Place are glistening in the determined moonlight. She turns down Carleton Hill, deciding she'll take the shortcut through Blenheim Passage. She's weary. The walk is draining; there's no life in her step. A sound up ahead startles her. She catches sight of three young people near the passage. Two of them are in hooded sweatshirts, with the hoods drawn tightly around their faces. From the back they are indistinguishable; the ubiquitous hood of the teenage boy stretches from crown to shoulder, weighed down by hands and objects in the pockets. The third is a girl, Victoria thinks, as she catches sight of flowing hair just before the three of them turn into the passageway.

She feels nervous as she turns down the lane. They're just

children, she tells herself. The girl laughs. Suddenly, Victoria feels sick. She speeds up to try to get closer to the threesome. The boy on the outside spits, and pushes the one in the middle, who bumps into the girl. As Victoria tries to catch up to them, she sees the boy in the middle—that boy—pick up a plastic recycling box that has been left out for collection. He looks into the bin. She hears his voice. Hears him say, "Oh well," in happy resignation as he dips his hand in, takes out a single bottle from the bin, and dashes it against the pavement. The bottle doesn't break. He kicks it, and it rolls down the passage. Victoria swallows, speeds up. The three figures stop again as the girl rifles through another recycling bin full of newspapers. Victoria is close enough now to hear them:

"So, what's your problem with that? She's cool," says the boy on the outside.

"It's a bore!" There's no mistaking Kendra's voice. "She's there all the time now, or, well, it feels like that 'cause I can't bear her around. She thinks she can get back with him just because she spent one night. She's a witch. I hate her."

An iron rod of pain lodges between Victoria's shoulders, and she finds it hard to breathe. The first thing she feels is relief that she's not the subject of Kendra's conversation, and that she is not the witch. But the second, third, and fourth thoughts rush in after that: the who, when, and what now? The iron rod won't let go of her neck.

"Why's she round in the first place?" This is Derek.

"She can smell it from Richmond when Dad's unhappy; she's done it for years," Kendra says as she rifles through the discarded newspapers, apparently looking for something in particular. "She showed up when Mom died, showed up again after his first girl-friend, shit, I've forgotten her name . . . and then last week. She's got radar." She continues to hunt through the papers; the other two watch.

"I like her hair." Derek's voice is dreamy in the way reserved for stories or his mother.

"Her hair's shit. You think that's real? No way. She's bleached."

Victoria pictures Christine's hands holding car keys, the metal entwined by her confident fingers. After meeting Alexander and Christine, it was these hands that made her wonder what kind of woman Alexander would love. But then Alexander kissed her, and she thought it all became clear. Suddenly he is a stranger again, and the thought of his touch feels like a violation.

"Look," Kendra shouts as she holds up a magazine.

"Aaww, great tits," exclaims the other boy.

"I told you, the guy's a perv." She flings the magazine at a wall in the lane. They giggle. Derek kicks over the bin; the newspapers and magazines go sliding across the pavement. He kicks them again, scattering them as he walks. They laugh again and Derek starts to run. The others peel off after him.

Victoria cannot move. She tries to breathe deeply, but it's difficult. She's done everything wrong. She has failed her sister; it's all she can think of at the moment. And all she can see are Christine's confident hands. She's lost. Derek is no longer a little boy. She's not equipped for this, not here, not London. Not now.

By the time Victoria turns onto Blenheim Terrace the three children are sitting on the steps of the house. When she gets up close she sees that the other boy is Rory.

"I think your father's expecting you now," she says to Kendra coldly. Kendra gets up obediently and salutes the three of them, and then she's off. "Rory, time for you to go home now too." Victoria stares at Derek. Nothing comes to her. There's nothing to say to him. This is all her fault. She's been a child, she's been a child.

"Let's go up," she says finally.

The room smells musty. She doesn't put on the light but undresses slowly and puts on a nightgown she has not worn in over a year. She doesn't check her image in the mirror, nor does she brush her hair. She sits on the edge of the bed and waits for Derek to finish in the bathroom. When the door to his room clicks shut, she is relieved. Without brushing her teeth or washing her face, she slides into bed. It will be a cool night, but she doesn't have the will to fetch the duvet from the cupboard. She pulls the cotton sheet up to her chin.

When she opens her eyes, she feels like laundry straight out of the wash, tangled and moist, starched of soul. She drags herself out of bed. It is barely dawn, Sunday. Derek is not yet awake. There is no baking to be done today, but she feels the urgency of the morning just the same. For a moment, she stands at Derek's door making a decision. She opens the door a crack, sees a leg hanging over the side of the bed. The rest of him is a lump under the sheet and blanket.

Entering, she leaves the door ajar so that the light rising from the south window seeps into the room. She walks gingerly to his desk, sits down, and pushes the power button on the computer. The monitor illuminates the corner of the room. She waits for everything to click into place. A minute later she is online.

---

www.lastminute.com

Flights

click

Holiday Packages
Car Rentals
Entertainment

She selects the destination. Proceeding through the booking process one careful step at a time, she chooses the earliest possible departure date and the latest return before the start of school. Everything clicks into place with the mouse; she's amazed how easy it is.

By the time Derek stirs and pulls the sheet from his head, they are booked; she just needs to enter her credit card number.

Derek opens his eyes and props himself up in bed. "What's going on?"

Victoria stands up, heading out of the room to fetch the credit card in her purse. "We're going home, love, two days' time."

PART III

CHAPTER FOURTEEN

Bandy Legs

Last call for passengers on VIRGIN ATLANTIC FLIGHT 096 to Barbados, now boarding at gate 16.

"Here, hold this a moment, please love." Victoria hands Derek her purse and gets their boarding cards and passports ready to present. They've spent the last two hours juggling things between them: the passports, the boarding cards, the carry-on luggage, the few gift souvenirs Victoria bought at duty free for God knows whom. She knows no one in Georgetown anymore, but it wouldn't have seemed right to arrive somewhere one has called home without a gift or two. Money is flowing out of her account at an alarming rate.

The taxi fare from Blenheim Terrace to Victoria Station, from where they caught the Gatwick Express, was higher than she had expected due to the early morning traffic. She watched anxiously as the 10p increments ticked over. As they idled near Hyde Park Corner, she looked over at Derek, who was gazing drowsily out of the window at the statue of a woman on a chariot. She touched his sleepy head.

"Boudicca," he said quietly.

"Pardon love?"

He pointed up towards the chariot. "Boudicca fought the Romans . . . she was the only one who stood up against them, but the Romans threw javelins and the Britons had no armour. She poisoned herself when they lost," he concluded, and then yawned as though the story had taken too much out of him. He closed his eyes as the taxi inched along in traffic. Victoria kept her eyes on Boudicca, amazed at the things she still doesn't know, and with conflicting feelings of pride and worry for Derek. He is teaching her things. Boudicca's horses are unruly, the woman herself triumphant. Victoria liked the statue.

Derek is finally alert and gazing about the departure hall as though the world is pouring into his eyes. He holds the purse slightly away from himself with awkward elegance.

"There, now, you ready?" Victoria asks as she takes the bag from him. He nods. Since the night in Blenheim Passage, she's been brusque with him, wondering if this is really the boy she knows. But it occurs to her that he might be frightened. He hasn't been home in four years, and for a child that's as much as a lifetime. The two of them will have at least that in common when they arrive.

In the middle seat of row 32 in the airplane, the click of his seatbelt beside her coincides with a deep sinking of her heart. She feels like a stranger. From Derek. From Alexander. Even from Lenny, who lent her the money and is taking on her work so that Victoria can make this trip to Guyana. Settled in between Derek and a young Bajan man with long legs, she misses Alexander more than she can bear. "I don't want you to go," he said when he called that morning, and she felt her resolve yielding to his voice. But it was too late. The escape was in progress. And now the whole universe of escape is hers to bear like a passport. "True and like resemblance to the bearer," as it states on the back of the photo. Escape as a mark of who she is.

Even before he reaches the door he can smell it. The plane is on the tarmac at Grantley Adams International Airport in Barbados, and although it's not home, Derek can smell his mother. She's in the blast of heat and spice that hits him at the top of the stairs. His knees go weak, but he thinks it's because he's been sitting so long on the plane. He walks down the stairs towards the tarmac, followed by his aunt, from whom he hears gasps of, "Oh my God," every few steps. "Oh my God" or "Oh good God," as though she's testing out which one is better suited as a greeting for this assault of indescribably coddling air.

The departure lounge makes Derek restless again as they await their connection to Georgetown. His bobbing knee has taken over, and it's just a matter of time before Auntie Vic will tell him to stop. Usually she notices before he does, but now he's playing a game with his knee, trying to count the bounces, up, down, up, down.

"Stop that, Derek," Victoria says.

He gets up and wanders over to a kiosk selling flying fish in a box. He heard of flying fish from his mother, but he's never actually seen one. The fish in these photos do look like birds, with their long winglike fins.

"You tek one home wid you, son?" asks the thin bald man behind the counter. But Derek hears, "You take me home with you, son?" and immediately looks down at his feet in embarrassment. Why has the man asked such a question? Does everyone see his bristling need to be fathered? He concentrates on being big, looks up into the man's face and smiles.

"No, thanks," Derek says and returns to sit beside Victoria. His knee starts to bob again. "My mom told me Bajans were standoffish," he says to his aunt.

"Is that right? How did she know?"

"She came here with Robert," he says, the name effortlessly pulled from a group portrait in his memory. Robert was a genius in mathematics, his mother told him.

"You shouldn't say things like that; you should know better than that by now. It's not right to generalize about people."

But generalize is just what he wasn't doing. He was going to tell her that the flying-fish vendor had opened up his heart to him and was anything but standoffish. Derek doesn't say a word more. His aunt is full of suspicion. When she was with Alexander it seemed to disappear, but now it's back: he saw it again in her face that night in front of the house with Rory and Kendra.

When they board the twenty-seater air coach, Flight 201 to Georgetown, Derek feels that tingle of dread he associates with punishment. He stares out the small oval window. It is at moments like this he misses Kendra and her frank practicality: "Don't be daft," she would say now. It's barely a plane, he thinks, looking up at the ventilator button above him. He makes sure his seatbelt is fastened. He sits up straight and looks behind him towards the rows of black faces. Auntie Vic looks straight ahead; her face now looks more like his mother's, and less like the face of someone out of place. He notices large pores in her skin. His hands seem big and bony. They both seem to have expanded in the heat and humidity of their three-hour stopover in the Barbados airport. Derek is thirsty again. He was allowed a Coke in the departure lounge, which he downed quickly, but he knows not to push his luck with Auntie Vic and ask for another.

After less than half an hour in the air, the captain's voice comes over the loudspeaker to tell the passengers to prepare for landing. "We're almost there," Victoria says quietly, looking across Derek out the window. He looks out on the point in the sea where the aquamarine turns brown in the spill and churn of the Demerara River. *Whey de land o' mud, sista . . . whey dat? Dat's me home . . .* he remembers, but he's not sure he has the right tune to the song they used to sing in the playground in Kitty. Guyana is the land of mud. Spilling out from the rivers, the mud is washed back by the tides and baked by the sun into a mighty bank where people live. What a place to be born. He doesn't remember this view of the land when he left Guyana, but then again he doesn't remember much of anything about that time.

The plane tilts and he loses sight of the brown sea gate. "Who's meeting us?" he asks Victoria, the idea flowing out of a memory of his mother saying it was important to be met at the airport, or else you feel sad. He didn't know then that she had been referring to how she felt arriving back in Georgetown after her trips to Miami to make a baby.

"No one is meeting us, we'll take a taxi to the Pegasus and make our way after that," his aunt answers. The dread rises again and he has to swallow. Kendra, too, would insist on being met at the airport. But she'd like the idea of staying in a hotel; he doesn't. Derek remembers his grandmother's grumbling and under-the-breath cursing directed towards the woman who cleaned at the Pegasus Hotel, the woman she called a "bandy-legged bitch." He's afraid of the bandy-legged bitch, though he has no idea why.

The air is rank with bush. Although it has been cut back to make way for the Timehri Road that now connects Georgetown to Cheddi Jagan International Airport, Victoria feels the bush watching her like a panther.

The taxi driver blows his horn and shouts "damn fool" as a minibus with Bombay schmaltz blasting out of its windows overtakes them. Shack shops dot the spaces between stifled banana groves along the road. The taxi driver, not to be outdone, overtakes a donkey cart carrying barrels of fresh water, which has also just been passed by a bicyclist. Then a Range Rover overtakes the taxi. Everything at its own top speed. The sign for Marietta's Peas and Rice is hand-printed, and the slant of its letters is the only slow thing along this road.

Frank's Tyre and Auto, Vishnu Cleaners. None of this is familiar to her. The road is dull with progress, and Victoria frowns. She sees a world made crass and encumbered by speed. A long road. She swallows the feeling that must have been born in the bush, something that wants to spring out of the car and rage and tear and then recede like a sated predator into the night. After forty years away, this paved highway is her welcome, and it embarrasses her. These shops, those encroaching trees, and even the town that will appear at the end of it, surely these too feel embarrassed by the road.

In town they pass the Seasons NightClub, where she had her first dance. On the knotted, pitted wood floor, a sense of life's possibilities took shape in a beat, in the moment she first decided to leave home. The building is boarded up now. St. George's Cathedral, lofty wood and cracking paint, still stands as a testament to her Christian name, *I baptize you, Victoria, in the name of the Father* . . .

Booker-McConnell's department store, with its imports and delicacies, is humming with shoppers, still. Men and women, black faces, brown, saris, sandals—people make way for one another on the crowded pavement.

At first, Victoria had imagined staying at the Belair, a hotel from her day for elite tourists, but when they pass the spot where it used to stand, she sees an office building for a foreign bank. The seawall is dull just beyond it. There is no sound of the militia band that used to play there every Saturday.

Arriving at the Pegasus Hotel, a complex that at some point in the last twenty years must have been chic and full of promise, she feels disoriented. There is the smell of rotting limes in the air. The ironwork at the gate is rusted; the hotel's exterior walls are in need of paint. Lizards swarm the pavement through a haphazard garden gone almost wild. Georgetown is a ruined house.

Their room is clean and proper enough. The porter puts their suitcases down and turns to leave, then looks back at her. Their eyes meet. Victoria sits on the bed to cushion herself from his appraising stare. "Thank you," she says, uncomfortably, trying to hold on to all the Britishness she knows, but it seems to have escaped her wide-open pores in the heat. With no tip forthcoming he gives her an accusatory look and turns to leave. Derek passes the porter in the doorway as he enters from the hall, having remained downstairs to examine the pool.

"It's not like the one in France," he mumbles disappointedly as he shuffles in and throws himself on the other twin bed. The two of them sit in silence as the sounds of Georgetown—a quiet buzz of insects, traffic, and the distant pulse of the sea—wash into the room, covering them with deep, inexplicable sadness. A gecko climbs the wall between the beds. Slowly.

Victoria searches for something to ground her. If she came here for anything it was to gather them up, not to unravel. If only she could rally the forces of all she ever was before Toronto and London, and before that moment in France, the Victoria that first left this place in defiance, and to whom the world was a wide plain of opportunity. After overhearing Kendra speak about Christine and watching Derek defiantly scatter the pile of newspapers, she felt the only place that might fit them was this country. Where they began. Here she would gather herself the way she might the stretched-out waistline of a garment—by drawing a string that would ruffle and pucker delicately. She needs to fit herself again.

She makes plans. They will visit Berbice. They'll look in on Mommy's old friend who was ailing. Mavis has written Victoria a few times in the last few years, asking after Derek and offering condolences for the loss of her mother and sister. Victoria can sense, through the shaky handwriting, that Mavis's sentiments are full of guilt, as it was to her home that the two women were travelling that day. Mavis's hand scratches out the details of her recent ailments, but Victoria thinks that the ailing Mavis might well outlive them all.

As for Derek, she will help him look up school friends and neighbours, guide him in reconnecting with his southern self. He will put aside Kendra's foolish ideas and be happy for the simplicity of this place, his birthplace. He will remember his mother and forget the search for his father, because what does a father bring anyway, but too many women into your life to make you feel . . . what? How does Kendra feel? Victoria pictures Christine's theatrical face, with all its slippery gestures portraying attitudes of appropriateness or approval. Then she sees the legs of other women—those in the tomato patch, and other shapely legs in the press of bodies in Stabroek Market as her mother dragged her by the hand. Everywhere there were women's legs. What did fathers bring? Children. More and more children, through women's splayed-open legs, and wasn't Derek happy he never had to put up with that?

Derek slaps his leg again as the dawn light creeps into the room. His stomach feels queasy from the curried chicken they ate in the hotel restaurant before bed, and now he's irritable with the heat.

He sits up quickly, feeling like the site of a battle, pricked and gouged by airborne enemies throughout the night. His arm is full of welts from mosquito bites. He needs to scratch. There are more on his face. He gets up and walks to the mirror.

"Blimey," he says quietly to himself. The word sounds odd here. Victoria stirs and sits up in her bed. "What're you doing?"

"I've been eaten alive," he says and turns towards her. His stomach churns; he releases wind.

"Good God," she says, throwing off her sheet. She approaches with panic and holds his face in her hands. With his brown hair standing on end, he looks like a blistered troll.

"Nothing on earth like the mosquitoes here. They murder you. I would have thought you still had a bit of immunity. They didn't touch me," she says. "I smell the blood of an Englishman," she teases, and tries to make him laugh. He smiles reluctantly.

"Come on, let's get going and find a chemist. Calamine lotion."

In the front lobby, as Victoria arranges for a car to take them around for the day, Derek looks at pamphlets advertising excursions to the interior, to Kaieteur Falls, and a trip up the Essequibo River. His mother always talked of taking him to Kaieteur, saying that one day he'd see the falls with the sheerest drop in the world.

And the rivers, she continued, nowhere in the world are there rivers like the ones in this country. We'll go. You, my darling, are born of rivers; you flow through the world. But their summer holidays were spent at home with his granny, staring in idleness, day after day, or playing rounders with Thomas. His mother would look sad and wander about the house, painting her nails or listening to music. Until she met Robert. Then Gwen and Robert would go to Barbados or St. Lucia, and leave Derek with Granny, to stare and wait for her to come back and return the joy to the house. One day they would go to Kaieteur, she continued to promise.

Derek made sure to mention the falls to his aunt at the airport.

He looks up to see what is taking so long. His aunt is still in conversation with the man behind the reception desk. Derek's eyes make a tour of the lobby and fall on a woman at the far end pushing a bucket on wheels and mopping the floor. The woman is old, older than his aunt. Her widely bowed legs cause her to lurch from side to side. As she moves across the room, Derek notices that her face is lined, hard, and cross. *Bandy-legged bitch.* It's his granny's voice. *Come here again and I'll. . . .*

The woman looks up to see Derek watching her. Her fretful face makes him look away. Other voices come to him: his mother on the telephone to Robert telling him that Granny is crying again. It's the same every month. She's weeping because the bandy-legged bitch, who has a son by Granddad, wants some more of their money. He looks back at the woman, who is staring at him. He stares back, frowning to match her expression, unable to take his eyes from her.

She returns to her mopping.

PEPPERPOT

2 pounds of pork
2 pounds of cow heel
1 pound of stewing beef
1 slice of salt beef or 1 pound of pigtails
4–5 tablespoons of thick casareep
2 tablespoons brown sugar
In a net bag: one bunch of thyme, 4 medium onions, 4 hot peppers
Salt to taste

Clean and cut the meat into small pieces. Place the meat into a large conaree or casserole pot; cover with plenty of water.

When the meat is halfway boiled, add the net bag, thick casareep, brown sugar, and salt. Let it boil down until the meat is tender and saturated through with the casareep. Remove the net bag. Ready to serve.

NB The pepperpot should be warmed every day, or it will become sour. Be sure to use a clean spoon. Fresh meat may be added from time to time. The meat must be unseasoned, and add nothing starchy or the pepperpot will turn sour.

She can almost taste it. Food the way it used to be. Basic, filling, preservable over days and days of hot weather. Pepperpot stayed on the stove for a week at a time. Once a day, it was heated up to boiling point and served in the evening, with fresh meat added throughout the week. It was her mother's speciality, passed down from her great-grandmother, an Amerindian woman who made her own casareep, a thick, black syrup made from boiling down the juice of the cassava. It's the stickiness of the dish Victoria remembers the most—the beef and cow heel stewed for days to create a gelatinous soup. Sweet, sour, and peppery in one. She would sit on their front porch with a bowl in her lap and wipe up the last traces of gravy with her mother's home-baked white bread, as tough as a shoe. *Bread is for needing . . .*

As they wait in the hotel lobby, she smells something stewing—beef, and possibly pork, and wonders if it could be a pepperpot. After eating a full English breakfast in the hotel's restaurant, she feels pleasantly full. Since moving to London she has rarely eaten eggs and sausages, and she doubts that any of this meal was organically raised, but she was ravenous, and pork seemed to suit the surroundings.

The taxi pulls up. The car is modern enough, Victoria thinks, but its tailpipe is held up with string, its boot is smashed on one side, and the handle on the back door is hanging loose. The paint is redone in patches so it looks like it's been decorated with mosaics. It's a car that has been driven at reckless speeds, and taken on overland trips that have proved it less than a jeep. Their driver introduces himself as Ravinder, and they set off towards the main road. Ravinder adjusts the volume on the car stereo. Hip hop music comes blaring from the speakers behind Victoria's head. She holds her ears.

"Excuse me," she says loudly. No response. "Excuse me," she says again, even louder. Ravinder glances into his rear-view mirror for the perceived voice. "Could you turn it down a bit please?" He nods at her and turns down the volume.

Air-conditioning blasts throughout the car, chilling Victoria, but she doesn't want to complain a second time to Ravinder, who is singing quietly to himself to compensate for the music stolen from him. The drive through town is devoid of outside sounds, and Victoria looks longingly at a passing scene of a man arguing with another in a casual eruption of passion. This is not England.

The East Coast Road arrives like a murmur. Images are muffled in forty years of forgetfulness, and Victoria feels she must look carefully and thoroughly at the world going by. They will visit

Mavis, who must be ninety-five years old. Alive. While those who had planned to bring her pepperpot that day four years ago are dead. Victoria's mother would be getting near ninety herself had she lived to see her eldest daughter return after all this time.

The seawall appears on their left and an envelope of memory is opened: during a Saturday-night militia-band concert, a twelve-year-old Victoria sneaks up along the wall, behind the audience, to watch the band play, so that no one in the crowd will see her, because she is too young to be out so late.

As the sea takes over on the left and they leave the town, she becomes excited. She remembers the trips with her father to the countryside, sitting on the handlebars of his bicycle. The trip would take them an entire day, including the rides on the occasional lorry that would carve miles off their hot and tiring journey to Mavis's house. But she loved those trips, alone with her father and the rough road.

She looks over at Derek, who stares out the window. Boys run wild and barefoot on the road. Does he see them the way she does? She touches his hair and smoothes it back from his forehead.

The old woman has no teeth whatsoever, he notices, as she stands up with a grimace of effort. Derek is sitting on the mesh seat of a rickety, stained, and blackened mahogany parlour chair. The chair wobbles from side to side, and he resists riding it and tempting its collapse, knowing his aunt will shoot him one of her disapproving looks.

Photographs are pasted on walls about the room. Faces watch him, so he stays still. The photographs are of Mavis's family—the mixed colours of her children, grandchildren, and great grandchildren at various life stages and occasions, at home and abroad. Graduation ceremonies, Christmas mornings, and lunches. Presents. Houses. Newborns. Some snapshots are dull and yellowed, showing pre-automobile streets. Others are bright and fresh in colour. Photographs of nearly a century. Brothers and sisters growing old together over a century. He misses Kendra.

Auntie Vic has gone back to the kitchen to help Auntie Mavis prepare tea; Derek hopes he'll get a soft drink. He hears them talking, Auntie Vic especially loud because of Mavis's bad hearing.

"You're doing very well, Auntie May."

"No, no . . . no, thank you . . . not just at the moment, perhaps later," Mavis answers. His aunt does not correct the misunderstanding.

When they return to the sitting room, Mavis slumps into her rocking chair, relieved not to be standing anymore. Victoria hands her a cup of tea, but Mavis waves it away. The woman's eyes are almost invisible, sinking into her dark face like pebbles into mud. She has only a few white wispy strands of hair standing up on her head.

Suddenly there's a rush of liquid on the floor under her wooden rocking chair. At first, Derek thinks she has spilled her tea, but remembers she refused her cup, and realizes that Mavis has lost control of her bladder. He holds his breath.

His granny used to complain about Auntie Mavis, saying she was bothersome, but when Mavis fell ill, it was always Granny who was the first at her side. He looks up at the faces in the photographs. They accuse him. *I slay thee* . . . His throat constricts. He leaps out of the armchair and walks out onto the porch. Suddenly he is dizzy and his stomach lurches. A shot rises up through his chest and he vomits onto the tottery porch. He stairs at the chunks of sausage and egg from breakfast. Spilled, just like everything that has ever gone wrong.

He walks out into the yard and sits under a lime tree. He surveys the garden. Lime trees, guinep and guava trees; all fruits he used to love. He dares not remember what they taste like. Different, he's sure, because compared to the one in his bones, this Guyana is like a smudged comic book print, the colours running outside the lines. Which would he defend now? London or Guyana? Richard the Truck used to tease him about fruit when he'd mention them as favourite tastes. "Guineps. Sounds like gimps, and you are that for sure," Richard had said, shoving a fistful of crisps into his own mouth. Now that he thinks about it, the word does seem odd.

His stomach lurches again, but he holds down the eruption. He pictures his aunt, last night in the hotel restaurant, sucking on the bones of her curried goat and licking her fingers. "Good God," she said, "I taste home," while he nibbled on his chicken, which he didn't finish.

"What in God's name, Derek?" she shouts from the porch, seeing the vomit on the steps. God's name, God's name, what, what, he thinks. He never learned God's name, he thinks, and now he's so hot his head is spinning. His mother said never to use God's name in vain, but Derek can't remember ever learning it. He closes his eyes and tries to picture the letters that might form it.

When he opens one heavy eyelid, he is in the back seat of Ravinder's car, which is parked by the side of the East Coast Road on the way back to Georgetown. His aunt is standing just outside the car, examining the ground. Ravinder is sitting silently in the front seat. Derek's mind feels foggy, and he can't understand why they've stopped. He lifts his head and spies in the distance the muddy expanse of the seashore.

His aunt turns to see him awake. "Darling," is all she says at first, staring at him and then looking back at the ground. Derek opens his other eye and tries to see what she's looking at, but a wave of nausea forces him to lean his head back against the seat. His aunt comes back to the car. "It was here, I think. Must have been. This part of the road is tricky, cars pulling out of there"—she points to an intersection— "can't see the traffic coming. The minibus was loaded, as well. That would account for a lot."

It dawns on him she's talking about his mother and Granny's accident and that they are on the spot where their car hit the fuel lorry head on. He lifts his head again, much too quickly, and is dizzy with every feeling of guilt and responsibility he's had over the last four years. He wonders if it will be here, now, that he'll truly be punished. When he can focus, he examines the paved shoulder of the road to see if there is anything that might belong to his mother. Of course not. Years have passed. The area over which his aunt's eyes roam is nothing but asphalt and tar. Unmarked. Silent. No sign of explosion, fire, twisted metal. No sign of death. Or blame. Merely hot, indifferent pavement.

This blankness is the seat of mystery.

He closes his eyes again. A few minutes later the car starts.

"Derek, come along, come and let's get you into bed. We're here." He opens his eyes and eases himself out of the car.

"I'm going to make a few phone calls. We don't want to stay in this hotel. It's time we really go home."

He is confused. Their flight isn't for another week. But at least he will get to see Kendra.

"Your mommy would have wanted us to stay in the house," Auntie Vic continues, and Derek realizes she means the house where he was born and lived for seven and a half years. His stomach rumbles.

The decrepit wooden house is built on low stilts to raise it above the rush of mud in the rainy season. Now the mud is caked against the stilts and sculpted by wind to resemble a cracked topographical map of volcanic formations. For a split second Victoria thinks she sees Manfred, her father's mad cousin, lying under the house. Manfred used to howl at the full moon and would compete with Manu, his one and only friend, on Saturday nights, when Manu would get falling-down drunk. Manu had gody, his testicles hung almost to his knees, swollen and as large as grapefruits. A slide show of memory cascades through Victoria's mind as she walks towards the small house where she grew up. She sees herself giving Manu a bowl of rice at the back door. "Miss is kind, thank you miss," he'd say, demure when sober, shy in her presence.

She walks up the front steps and opens the door to the house. The smell of damp wood and spiders emerges as she enters. Derek follows closely on her heels. Small skittering sounds precede them through the rooms, and Victoria tries to hold back her disgust. She puts her hand on the boy's shoulder. Entering the kitchen, she flicks the breaker in the fuse box as the electricity company instructed, and she takes up a broom leaning between the cooker and the wall.

"Here, we'll need to clean up," she says as she hands him the broom. It will be good for him to do something. She decides that he'll sleep in her mother's room, while she will take the sofa in the sitting room, the only piece of furniture that doesn't seem too damp or fragile.

By evening the slatted floor is swept, the furniture dusted, and the main part of the house is almost liveable. Victoria joins Derek on the porch, where he is writing something in the notebook she bought him at Gatwick airport. She catches a few words over his shoulder:

The boy pulled his cloak tighter and moved off into the forest. Suddenly, on his back he felt a glow and heard the crackle of flames . . .

"What are you writing?"

"Just a story," he answers, placing his arm over the page.

The boy is still a puzzle to her, even after all this time. She sits beside him. "How does it feel to be here?" she finally dares ask.

Derek puts his pen inside the notebook and folds it closed. "Different," he says solemnly.

"How so?"

He shrugs and looks down at his feet. "Just different, I don't know . . ."

"I used to hate it here," she confesses at last, and the air between them feels suddenly damp, saturated, and Derek wonders if the sky might just cry. "I wanted to run away my whole life." She points to a boarded-up house next door. "There used to be a man who lived over there . . . His name was Harold, and he told me he'd take me away, that he was going to fly a plane and pick me up to take me away. He never liked my daddy, but to me, and later, to your mom, he was very kind. He spoiled us, but Daddy drove him away by being unfriendly. Daddy bought his house when he moved, rented it out to someone else, and expanded his front garden, just so, all the way across the front of both houses. Daddy liked Harold's wife, but Harold kept her away from him and she and Mummy used to fight—" She breaks off, weakened by the memory. "I just wanted to get away." She looks at him. "And now we're back."

Derek hugs his notebook.

During the next two days, Victoria and Derek keep to themselves amidst the everyday activities of their neighbours. They clean and clear out the house, and Victoria cooks. She experiments with food from the past. She sets medallions of pork to marinate in vinegar, garlic, and thyme, layered in a jar like a parfait of flavours that will insinuate themselves into the meat over the course of a few days. She makes pepperpot, then black pudding and souse. Derek hates them, but that doesn't seem to stop her. On the third day, she fries the medallions of pork for breakfast, which brings Christmas to the house. Derek remembers his mother's Christmas-morning garlic pork, so this taste he welcomes, and he eats the meat with buttered toast.

After breakfast Victoria digs and hoes in the wild and over-grown front garden. She doesn't plant a thing, just digs, weeds, and hoes as if the land is begging her. Pausing before starting another row, she looks at Derek watching the world from the shade of the porch. He looks around him, absorbs a colour or smell, then returns to writing in his notebook. After about an hour she looks up again and sees him wander over to the neighbouring house. He knocks on the door, and following an exchange with the woman who opens it, he is let into the house. In a few minutes, Derek and a boy his age, who must be his friend Thomas, come running out and begin to play with sticks in the yard. Another boy joins them, and Victoria notices that soon Derek becomes awkward, shuffling his feet on the periphery as the two boys engage in a game of rounders with pots standing in for posts.

"Inkland," she hears him say to them at one point as they sit on the ground under a tree, pelting pebbles into space. She watches as he tells them a story, the details of which she can't make out. The boys listen, captivated, as though the words are rising up within themselves rather than coming from Derek. Thomas—Derek's age but with a mother who is in her twenties—stops pelting stones and doesn't move a muscle; his jaw opens slightly. The other boy lies on his back and stares at the sky while he listens. Victoria feels proud.

At midday Derek returns to the house to write in his notebook. Victoria's stewed chicken with lime is simmering on the cooker for lunch. She stirs and tastes it. Ready.

"I'm going back over to Thomas's," Derek says after lunch. He rushes out in his bare feet. Maybe he prefers it here, she thinks. Wild and free and warm, with boys next door who don't encourage him to behave badly. She, on the other hand, suddenly misses the slender pods of the catalpa outside her window on Blenheim Terrace. She goes into the sitting room, not sure of what to do with herself. She sits on the green velveteen armchair with springs protruding from the seat and stares at the room's dank walls. The light is changing quickly as the afternoon sun shifts, and she watches the shadow of the tamarind tree outside the window elongate on the mould-dappled wall.

Victoria is alone with the house. The house is alone with her. Neither is particularly at ease. The house creaks and whines with decay. She gets up and moves into the bedroom she used to share with Gwen. The linen is still on the beds, now yellowed, crisp, and smelling of ammonia. She turns, leaves quickly, and darts from room to room. She tidies, dusts, and rearranges furniture to control it, to prevent it from moving her. Finally she collapses in her father's Berbice chair and cries.

What a fool. Victoria, you fool, you fool, she thinks, as the tears stream. Her hands rest on the mahogany arms of the chair. Her tears wet her white cotton blouse, the one she bought at the market in Lorgues with Alexander, while Derek and Kendra explored the stalls of olives and their oils, cheeses, wild game, and confitures. This French shirt, here, soaked by these South American tears.

She stares at the ceiling, its wood rotted and bored by termites, spotted with angry mildew. Victoria's mother used to complain about the mildew as though it was a pesty neighbour: "Do something about it, nuh, Henry? How can you let it go on like that. It's not decent." And then she'd look up at it: "A lotta nerve, I tell ya," and Henry would head outside to his garden, while her mother was left in the room with the spotted ceiling.

This is what she's from. This loss. Even with Kola as its antidote, loss found her again. If she keeps running from loss it will always catch up with her, that's its nature. But Kola left her with his fairness. Fairness is possible, isn't it? Perhaps that's all her mother was asking for. She needed Henry to share. Sharing is fair. Alexander knows as much. You build family, you don't lose it.

"Oh, Mum," Victoria whispers.

"Ya think you can just come back here and go on like that, well I neva, you stupidy, funny-face boy."

The voice arrives first. Then the woman. Looming in the doorway. She is a silhouette of anger, with the late sun behind her, the darkening, mildewy room before her. She is big and burly, barely dressed, in a singlet and wrap-around skirt to her knees. Her rippling black skin jiggles under her gesticulating arm, finger aimed at Victoria like a pointer in the hand of the headmistress at the convent. This woman, perhaps not as old as Victoria, is so far removed from received taste across the Atlantic that Victoria feels a kind of conditioned repulsion for the smells she knows will enter the room with her.

Victoria stands up, feeling ashamed of her thoughts, and walks towards the front door.

"You . . . you ta answa for the rudeness of dis boy, if dat's who raise he like a bad pig fa market." Thomas's grandmother rails on as she enters, and her silhouette hardens into wide flesh. For an instant Victoria notices a slant in the woman's eyes, and, in a horrible flash that must have been her mother gasping through her, she wonders if the woman is perhaps a bastard sister . . .

"Ya tink we some kind a savages, nuh? All this shite about Kanaima. Where the hell de boy get dis?"

Victoria faces the woman now, while Thomas stands cowering behind her looking fearfully at Derek, who is still in the doorway, his head lowered but not defeated. He seems amused. "What is the problem?" Victoria asks, and it dawns on her who the woman must be—Gerty's, Gertrude's daughter . . . what's her name? Just a young girl when Victoria would have seen her last. The family was very poor. Gerty was the washer woman who collected the clothes of the mulatto families in the neighbouring compound, and returned the washed, pressed, and folded laundry on a tray she carried on her head. Gerty was batty and confused most of the time, calling even the young children Master and Mistress: "Master Wayne, Mistress Gwen." Gerty's husband raised bees and collected honey. Gerty's daughter grew wild, climbing fruit trees and playing in mud. And here she is.

"Your grandson," Gerty's daughter says angrily as she steps closer.

"He's my nephew."

"Well, chance bruck you up den . . . your nephew is tellin' my Thomas jumbie tales that is makin' him fright."

"What do you mean?"

"He goin' on about nonsense buck stories about Kanaima and such shite as if he one a dem heself. I don' wan' more a dat in me house."

"Derek?" Victoria calls out and looks around the girth of the woman to find him. "What's going on?"

Derek looks up, a calm, knowing look on his face. "It's nothing, just some stories I thought he knew."

"He asked me stupidy questions," sulks Thomas. "And told me jumbie foolishness . . ."

The boy's grandmother sucks her teeth long and hard.

"Derek, I think you should explain," Victoria says, knowing the woman is not about to leave.

"He asked me if I knew about Hogwarts, and I told him it was shite—" Victoria and Gerty's daughter have no idea what he's talking about. "Never mind," says Derek.

"Don't you use that language," Victoria warns him.

"It is shite, not wizardry: stupid brooms and spells, and potions. I was talking about real magic, like the Kanaima. I told him to hit me, and I'd hit him back. I wasn't really going to—he should've known that. I was going to show him something I could do—" Derek breaks off, doubting if the experiment of staring Thomas down and making him feel the violence in his eyes would have worked anyway. "He doesn't get it. I won't apologize, because I did nothing wrong." He feels the words in his mouth, and they sound British. Words that give him strength the way they did when he first met Richard Lorry. Words are his weapon of choice.

Victoria walks around Gerty's daughter and moves towards her nephew. She stands in front of him. Holding his chin in her palm, she lifts his face so that their eyes meet. She sees the part of him he's trying to hold on to desperately—the part that knows truth like a mother knows her child. He has the weight of two deaths in his eyes, and she sees how much he wants to relieve it.

"It was I who told you those stories when you first came to London, Derek, you remember? I did it to frighten you from lying. It's a lot of stupid, old-fashioned tales my mommy used to tell."

He looks at her and doesn't blink. "No, it's not," he says calmly, then looks away, his chin still cupped in Victoria's hand. He knows what he's talking about. He feels a snake-fang bite, or even more, a bomb, inside him and knows their potential. What he doesn't know yet is what to do with the power. It's this feeling he's been trying to tap into and guide, to draw upon in the way a spliced atom can power a generator to light a house. He bangs up against opportunities to test his control, but he's not always successful. Victoria releases him and turns to Gerty's daughter, who is now shaking her head and waving her arms about, as though whatever Victoria has just done is inadequate. The woman is speechless. Her face begins to look even more familiar to Victoria, who realizes she will never be certain if or how they are related.

"He's right, he's done nothing wrong," she says to Gerty's daughter.

"Well, I neva. You gwon' to allow he to go around frightenin' other children? Is that what England people do—give children airs and tell them to frighten? He told Thomas he set off a bomb in a market." Victoria flinches, but keeps her eyes on Gerty's daughter. "He's bullyin' my grandson—would you like that to happen to him?" The woman's nostrils open wide with fury. Victoria remembers how her mother would roar at her father in this house, and suddenly she wants to embrace Gerty's daughter.

"He won't frighten Thomas again, I'll see to that. I'm sorry," she says, these last two words coming out in an almost jubilant tone.

The woman opens her mouth to speak, but the apology has her stymied. She shifts her weight. Her large hip swooshes to the right and suddenly she's all hip and thigh, and Victoria notices something she hadn't before—Gerty's daughter bears a vague resemblance to the Bluebird of Piccadilly. What's more, it could easily have been Victoria here, in Gerty's daughter's place, still in Guyana with a brood of children to look after and not a lone traveller on a quest for fairness in London. So, here they all are. These women, like an opening, peeling, double-helix strand in replication. All of them born with the fury, the searching, and the awe in the presence of tiny moments that erupt like a sprout. These belong to the look of no one woman in particular. Perhaps this is as related as one gets.

"Just a minute," Victoria says, and puts her hand on Gerty's daughter's back to stop her before she heads out the door, dragging Thomas by the arm. She signals for the woman to wait, then she turns and walks quickly to the corner of the room to find her purse. She opens it. Inside it she retrieves her wallet and takes out the pounds sterling she has been keeping for her return to London. She counts, £20, £40, £60, £100, £200—some of this is the rent due when she gets back. When Gerty had fractured her arm and couldn't work, she'd asked Victoria's mother for money, but Mary never had any money to give. The difference between Victoria and Gerty's daughter is the accident of privilege. She folds the bills in half, holds them tightly in her palm, and puts the purse back.

At the front door, Derek feels taller than a few minutes ago. Thomas and his grandmother stare at him, but he doesn't mind. He is in his power and wants to declare it in his chest, so he puffs it out conspicuously, so obviously that Thomas giggles, but that doesn't faze Derek. He thinks of Richard, Stephen, Rory, Kendra, and what they've taught him. He thinks of the lies he's had to tell his aunt, but he's not lying now. The lines between good and bad have blurred. Convinced he's on a deeper path than that dichotomy allows, he moves between their extremes. He looks spitefully at Thomas and mouths the word KANAIMA!

"You see, you see, Granny," cries Thomas, tapping his grandmother's enormous hip to alert her to the present evils of this boy from Inkland with the bush in his soul.

"Look, you'd betta—"

"Well, I think that's about all, then," Victoria says, cutting off her tirade. As she approaches Gerty's daughter, she holds out her arms as though inviting her for a hug. The woman steps back toward the door, but Victoria isn't deterred. She moves forward, hugs her, and lightly slips the folded bills of sterling into the pocket of the woman's skirt. It's like giving to a sister. "Thanks for coming, and I'll clear all this up, won't I?" she suggests with a smile as she steps back. Gerty's daughter is breathing heavily. She and Thomas walk out the door onto the porch and down the steps.

"You check pockets before you do washing, don't you, just like your mommy, I'm sure. She was the best at cleaning clothes we ever knew," Victoria calls out before she closes the door. She turns to face Derek.

"I want to go home, child," she says softly.

Derek is confused by the word. How many places can home be? He quickly realizes she means London and, although he's eager to see Kendra and Stephen, he's not ready to leave just yet. The Kanaima and the Druids are coming together. He has more to do here, more to learn. "But not before we see the falls. You said we could go to the falls."

Victoria sits on the Berbice chair. "That's for rich people. I should never have suggested it. I need to find a phone. My heart hurts," she says and puts her hand to her chest.

"What do you mean?" he asks, and comes quickly over to her chair.

"I'm fine. It's just a manner of speaking. I ache, here." She points to the left side of her breast.

She raises her hand towards Derek, who grasps it tentatively. "Alexander is a good father," she tells him. Sure, yes, I suppose he is, he thinks, but what does that matter? None of that really matters, now. It's too late.

"Go where love is, Derek, not where it's not. We need to leave this place."

"But we just got here." He drops her hand and gives her a look of frustration.

"You can't really be trusted unless you trust people yourself." She looks him in the eye. "No one ever gave me that . . . let's go . . ."

"But our tickets . . ." Suddenly he is the adult reminding the dreaming child about reality.

"We could change them. What do you say?" She touches his shoulder. The birthmark around his eye is barely visible against his tanned skin. "Everything is an accident," she says as she rubs his shoulder absent-mindedly.

"What?" He pulls back from her hand.

"Come with me," she says finally, and gets out of the chair.

She leads him to the garden that runs along the front of the house. The small patch of land she's been tending for the last few days is now free of weeds. She had thought of planting seeds there, perhaps courgettes, aubergine, or mustard greens, but who would eat them? Perhaps Gerty's daughter, her daughter, and Thomas. Or just anyone who passes by.

She sits down in the dirt of one of her furrows and feels the earth taking her in with a slight give. "Sit down with me."

He does as she asks, but looks at her suspiciously. When he's set-tled, she pats his leg. She turns to look straight out into the field, and he follows her gaze. Finally. These are the thoughts she's been wanting to say to him all along. Finally, she is giving them voice.

"It's not so important to have a father." Blunt but tender in one.

The boy doesn't turn towards her, and it's as though they're both watching the same movie out in the ready patch of earth.

"Why did you tell Thomas you set off the Dalton bomb?"

"Because I did."

She turns to look at him briefly, but quickly turns back to face the field. "What do you mean?"

"I did. I wanted everything to blow up, and it did," he says, thinking of the thrill of being tossed across the road against the wall of the pub.

Good God, she thinks, and is tempted to run through the litany of things she's done wrong for the boy to make him think such things, but she's too tired; she refuses to feel guilty. "You've got a good imagination, son."

Derek shifts his weight and brings his knees up to his chest.

"And the Kanaima, you know, it's just a story people made up to make sense of what they felt, to understand their fear, and you shouldn't use it against anyone."

Derek sighs and grips his knees tighter.

"We make everything up. We believe what we have to believe . . . and it seems like magic, because then everything you see through it makes sense." She looks at him. He tucks his chin between his knees and stares straight ahead. She picks up some dirt in her fingers. "You could make up a lot of stories in a place like this that teems with rivers. I was always afraid of the rivers, but now the idea of a river rushing just over there"—she turns slightly and signals in the general direction of the steadfast Demerara—"feels good." She lets a few seconds be heard, ticking.

"Maybe we're made up of all the water in the place we're born . . . like somewhere to go . . ." She fingers the dirt, then lets it run out of her hand. Derek rocks slightly, back and forth. She knows he's restless and doesn't want to sit listening to the foolishness of this old lady. But she has more.

"My daddy had other children, ones I knew of but never met, same as your daddy, I suppose. I used to wonder if he loved all those woman he brought out here, but now, you know, I'm not sure it mattered. Maybe Mommy didn't have any love left in her after she lost her first boy. Maybe all she could be was frightened that she'd lose someone else. And what you fear is what you get," she says emphatically. She shifts slightly and turns towards him. "You know, you probably have some uncles or aunts around this town we don't even know." Derek goes rigid. "Maybe Gerty's daughter . . . and if so, then you and Thomas . . ." Derek's shoulders rise up a notch. He stares at a small patch of earth in front of him, his chin locked between his knees, his arms around them tightly. "Cousins . . . they're close enough," she concludes.

He releases his knees and paws at some small stones under the reddish earth.

"Kola was shot in the head," she says, like the blank in her own gun. Derek quickly looks at her. They share a look of rippling knowledge. He turns back to face the field. He holds tightly onto the dirt in his fingers.

"We do what we have to do, don't we. Everyone's part of that, everything has a consequence." She looks around her as though seeking out the river. "Go where the love is, not where it's not." The repetition of this new mandate is like opening and closing, again and again, a newly discovered door. Like finding a new room in a house she's lived in all her life. She turns to Derek. "We could come back, someday soon—go to the falls."

With that thought he brightens. He doesn't want to live here, but a part of himself has come alive again. If he could just put this feeling—this one his mother gave him—together with the thrill of everything in London, if he could just show it to Richard, Stephen, Rory . . . to Lenny, Alexander, but mostly to Kendra. If he could put his finger on it, then he'd be big. After examining the blank asphalt on the highway, he knows now that blame has no bearing on any of it. It's about being big, he thinks. It must be. Being outside of the tiny self that is Derek Layne. Seeing everything from a higher vantage point. He wishes his mother had told him the secret, but without knowing it he's growing resigned to the fact that loss is the father of his imagination. Everything changes. To keep changing: that's perfection.

"OK," he says as he pelts down the earth in his hands.

"Go and ask Thomas if we can use their telephone, will you? I want to call London. Tell him I'll reverse the charges. It'll be OK. Go on . . ."

Derek stands up. Victoria taps his leg with her finger and lifts her arms towards him. "But first help this old lady to her feet."

She turns the key in the wooden door, securing the house now from a squatter or robber, despite its forsaken state. She picks up her heavy suitcase. The taxi driver has offered no help, so she drags it—filled with guavas, limes, cassava, and bottles of casareep—to the edge of the veranda. She leaves the souvenirs of London there, beside the door, hoping that an intruder might be satisfied with these spare offerings from *over there*. She turns to take a look at the garden she hoed and watered one last time this morning. The light over the field is like the shimmer in a painting by a mad impressionist: there's brown fire in the air, mud splattered into heat, and a tinge of blue, a distant refraction of the sea. She's pleased by the sight of the ordered, bare rows. Clean. Untainted. Unseeded.

She is perspiring from dragging the heavy case. The driver finally gets out of the car and comes towards her. Derek wanders back from Thomas's house, dawdling, kicking his feet along the path as though he's got nothing pressing.

"Derek, we're leaving," Victoria says breathlessly as she lifts the suitcase into the driver's hands. "Get in." He continues to dawdle, takes a final look at the house, and walks to the car.

As they sit together in the back seat of the taxi, Victoria can feel Derek's confusion. Or is it her own? "I want you to come back," Alexander said on the telephone. So, she's going. She's going to stop running.

As they pass through town, Victoria and Derek both catch sight of the bandy-legged woman making her way toward Stabroek Market after her morning shift at the Pegasus. Derek stares at her as they pass, craning his neck to watch her list back and forth along the pavement, her handbag in one hand, and in the other a plastic bag loaded with what looks like work clothes, the toes of a pair of trainers sticking out at the top. The woman's grey hair is pressed flat against her head with oil or sweat.

"What?" Victoria asks Derek, trying to find out what he's thinking. She restrains herself, as she's said enough for now, but what she'd really like to say is my daddy loved that woman! He loved her, and she's not why we're leaving now, but she's why I left here before, so I wouldn't walk burdened like that in this goddamn heat!

"How many days can we stay on the beach?" asks Derek. The last-minute change to their plane tickets has meant an unexpected stopover in Barbados.

"Two and a half. The only flight we could get on, but it's worked out well. You'll like Barbados. The beaches . . . Our flight leaves on Friday afternoon."

"Mommy used to be worried I'd drown," he adds. Still in the habit of withholding his deeper confidences from his aunt, he doesn't tell her what's really running through his head—the litany of warnings he has suddenly remembered at the sight of the bandy-legged woman walking down the road. *You'll drown if you swim after eating . . . Don' fall asleep with your face open to the moon, it'll get twist up . . . People with bandy legs were forced to walk too soon by their mothers. I neva did that, son, I carried you all the time . . .*

CHAPTER FIFTEEN

Stone

ᠥᠳᠥ

He's surprised at how light he feels floating on his back, his arms like the flapping seaweed that eddies among rocks at low tide. The sea is flat and carries him. The sky above is cloudless, but, to the left, ledges of white cirrus are heading towards the land. Seagulls dot the cyan firmament. He pretends he's a dead person, having had to walk the plank of a pirate ship with mutiny on his conscience. The sun is hot on his face. He closes his eyes to block it out. The dead do not care about the sun.

This is the best country in the world, Victoria—a fair place, or at least doing its best to be so. But, in our next life, darling, let's make sure that Canada is nearer the equator . . .

That early letter from Kola was lighter in tone than the ones that came later. He joked about snow and seemed resigned towards Toronto. But wherever Kola is now, the sun doesn't matter. Derek concentrates on the weight of his limbs, the cessation of his heartbeat, but it flutters, just slightly, at the thought that now he can tell Richard and Stephen that he had a friend who was shot in the head.

He likes Kola's idea of putting countries where you'd prefer them rather than where they appear on a map. He would put Guyana and England side by side, somewhere near this island of

Barbados, so that he could have all three. And have this sea. He's not sure where he'd put Miami, but it's not far from here, so he might just keep that connection across the water. Because Miami is still important, no matter what his aunt says. Fathers do matter, he thinks, but not in the way his aunt is talking about. Fathers matter for their secrets. He feels the wake of a passing swimmer, the water lapping up just over his forehead. To think that a father is not so important is like a mutiny on a ship. He stiffens his arms and legs to perfect the deadman's float. He starts to count, but doesn't get further than 1, 2, because he remembers that 12 and 21 are magic numbers in Druid lore. 12, 21, 1 . . . 2 . . . ones and twos, like a binary secret shared by ancient people and computer programmers. Now, as for Ireland, where would he put that? He might just keep Ireland right where it is, because the Druids needed the rain, the dark, the mist—it wouldn't be magic without mist.

He starts to count again. He won't stop until five hundred, and by that time he'll have broken his own record for floating, because he's been floating now a long time even before counting. Yesterday he lost track at 368. He knows Auntie Vic is waiting for him, anxious to see the east coast of Barbados the way she did when she was young. Pico Tenerife, she kept saying, telling Derek she once climbed to the top of the cliff and from there felt the world was hers. She told him that it was on that day she had really danced, just once, in a rum shop in St. Philip, after the beach at Bathsheba and the climb to Pico, with a man she had met at her hotel. "I was good, you know," she said with a sly smile as they drove from the airport to their guest-house here on the south coast of the island. And last night, before bed, he thinks that in his sunstroke dizziness he witnessed her dancing in the bathroom as she examined herself in the mirror. She shuffled her feet and wiggled her hips while holding her hand over her tummy. With her lips folded together, she tossed out her buttocks in a chicken-like stance, back and forth. He tucked his feverish head under the pillow and could see shapes on his eyelids.

He had taken too much sun. As soon as they arrived at the

guesthouse near Sandy Beach, Derek rushed to the shore and plunged into the sea, while his aunt went in the opposite direction, towards the Scotia Bank on the corner of the main road, across from the nightclub and the roti shop. She stood on the pavement and looked in wonder at the cars that had taken over the island. Fetching Derek from the water and dragging him up towards the road, she seemed in a flap. "Insects," she said, "insects breed this fast. Where will they all end up? In the sea? When I was here, it was buses and donkey carts still." Derek hadn't noticed that there were a lot of cars. There were a lot of cars in London.

"And in the supermarket! Tamarinds from China, for fifteen dollars. Tamarinds from China? Pick them up off the ground, just over there!" She waved in the general direction of the countryside. "Food from England—Waitrose, imagine that—and Canada. Boxes of pasta and frozen, ready-cooked meals from Loblaws. And the price! Good God! The boys on the beach rent chairs and umbrellas when they could farm." She stopped for a breath and a thought. "Like London, I guess, the Japanese, Asian food. Where will it stop? Some people grow all the food; others import it. And the rest? They serve it, I suppose . . . Gosh," she said finally and seemed to have got something out of her system.

Derek didn't care about the number of cars or the new buses or the price of food or the exchange rate being tied to the U.S. dollar. He walked back to the beach and stayed in the water the whole afternoon, to the point that his shoulders and back had burned in the strong sun. Before going to bed, his aunt gently soaked his face and torso with Calamine lotion from the same bottle she had used on his mosquito bites. In the mirror, his rabbit scar had reasserted itself like a gleaming Disney animation over his eye. He slept a deep unconscious sleep, his adamant skin trying to repair itself in the night.

Today he is smothered in 30 SPF sunblock, and his exposed face as he plays deadman floating is warm, but not tingling with a burn. Pirates were lucky, he thinks. They wore very little—torn trousers, a vest, and never had to put on a cardigan or shoes. They belonged to the sea the way Druids belonged to the woods. Nothing came between them and the environment that sustained them. Even dead, they would float on the sea first, then peacefully sink to become part of it.

In the mutiny he's just imagined, the captain of the ship had decided the crew were all to wear uniforms and now be identified solely as the captain's men, not free agents. Nor were they any longer to fight other pirates for territory—to lay claim to land and sea they would rule. Surely this was enough for a mutiny—a pirate's existence is predicated on freedom and movement. So he had allowed the captain's faithfuls to blindfold him, lead him to the plank and . . .

"Arghhhh!" Derek screams and flails, bobbing out of the water at the touch of a cold hand on his forehead.

"You didn't hear me?" asks Victoria, who is standing beside him, up to her waist in the water.

"Ahh, Jesus," Derek says, gasping for air.

"I didn't mean to frighten you—I've been calling for the last ten minutes! Come out now. We've got to get going."

Derek gulps and swallows. His eyes follow his aunt's back with annoyance as she walks out of the sea to the beach. He wasn't finished yet. He follows silently in her trail, keeping an eye on the puckered skin at the back of her thighs.

The bus reminds Victoria of the first rickety 139 she ever took from Piccadilly Circus to Abbey Road. As it winds along the coast road past Oistins Fish Market, Victoria is smiling. "I like this bus," she says simply, gazing out the window past Derek to the blue sea. She is not entirely sure why she's so content, but she breathes in deeply: the diesel, the fish and spices in shopping bags, the gingery air that emanates from the press of bodies. There's nothing hesitant in these smells.

"Y'ah right den?" asks a voice behind her. Victoria turns to see a smiling man with silver, close-cropped, natty hair.

"Yes, yes, thank you," she answers and faces front again.

"Ya come from far, people should treat ya pleasant. They ain't so pleasant no more."

Victoria smiles and half turns, wanting to acknowledge the man's friendly overtures but not interested in pursuing conversation. This is not what Alexander would have done, she thinks; he would have talked to the man, shared something of his life, found a common interest. She is disappointed in herself. As the bus pulls into the next stop and the man gets up to exit, she makes an effort: "Been a long, long time since I've been here," she says through a smile.

"And we've been waiting fa ya like a child for Fatha Christmas," he replies, revealing a gorge of broken teeth.

She recoils at the sight of the damage time has meted out to this man, who must be roughly her age. Her smile fades ever so slightly. When the door closes and the man hobbles towards a rum shop, she puts her arm around Derek's shoulders.

In the next forty-five minutes the island unfolds itself like a wrinkled map from her memory: remodelled plantation estates; dilapidated windmills and a renovated, functioning one; an old sugar factory; towering rows of palm trees; multicoloured chattel houses; and staggering glimpses of the sea and its white froth of surf. At the age of twenty she had been running. It was her first-ever escape, and this ragged coast felt like an outpost to the rest of the world.

The bus gradually disgorges passengers in the interminable stops through the countryside. Derek nods off between the jerking stops and starts; his head falls to his chin. Victoria gently guides it to her shoulder. It's another half an hour before they reach the small village of mainly wooden shacks. The woman at the Chinese restaurant in town told her that if they walked to the edge of this village, they would reach the foot of the rocks at Pico Tenerife. "At Pico ya gwan see somethin'," the man she had met on the beach told her as they drove these once-rough roads long ago. It is the one name she has remembered from Barbados after all these years.

"Derek, wake up, love, we're here. Come on. That's it." The boy frowns and rubs his forehead, pulls his hand down over his entire face quickly to revive himself.

The bus doors open at a small grocery shop—a shack with a metre-high Banks Beer sign in the front and, hanging on the inside of the door, a Ting poster with a bikini beauty holding up a bottle of Ting soft drink. The photograph is faded, the woman's now-diaphanous bikini creating the effect of invisible female genitalia being gradually revealed.

Victoria and Derek look about the shop, examining the display of tinned corned beef, beans, sweetened condensed milk, bottles of pepper sauce, and rolls of lavatory paper. They step back into the road expecting someone or something to appear from one of the chattel houses further along, but they all seem deserted. There are no clues as to which direction to take to the Pico rocks. This is not a tourist attraction, there are no signs, and Victoria cannot remember the way. She can see the peak in the distance.

A young girl of about seven, her hair in three flat plaits with bobbles at the end of each—like a trinity of black woollen dolls—comes out of the back room of the shop sucking on an ice lolly.

"Your mommy here?" Victoria asks, her accent suddenly slippery.

The little girl shakes her head no.

"Your daddy?"

No again.

"You alone here?"

No, once more. Then a nod, yes, then no, each indefinite.

"What ya'll need?" the girl asks finally, taking the rainbow-coloured ice from her mouth.

"We don't want to buy anything, we want to know how to get to the rocks . . . Pico . . ." Victoria points up towards the hill.

The girl's face lights up, and she almost smiles. "I'll show you," she says proudly. She runs off toward a small road at the side of the shop. She stops, looks to see if they are following, then turns and continues to run. Derek follows her quickly to the road. Victoria hurries after him. The road leads to the edge of a pasture, where the girl stops again and waves them on. The land rises toward a ridge, at the top of which black-bellied sheep graze. Derek runs and catches up with her and they head into the field. Victoria looks back towards the shop but sees no one. She continues to follow the girl.

At the top of the grassy hill, the pounding ocean comes into view beyond a pasture leading to piled rock that marks a sharp cliff. The pasture is distinctly literary, as though written into the island by an early visitor longing for something to resemble home in this strange territory. In the light of the afternoon sun, this patch of earth seems out of place in the Caribbean. The pasture dips and rises gently; the long grass is breeze-swayed, the land dotted by crumbling stone walls. The stone comes out of nowhere. Victoria doesn't remember this landscape at all, and feels she could be back in the English countryside with its traces of Roman wall running like a hot spring under a new civilization. She realizes that the walls are remnants of dwellings that likely were slave huts or shelter for freed slaves waiting here on the windy coast for boats to take them . . . back. But there are also traces of a low wall marking a farmer's pasture, leading to a valley, then a wood.

The girl walks confidently through the pasture, to a path along the edge of the wall. The path leads to the woods at the foot of the rocks called Pico. She disappears among the birch gum trees with their coppery peeling bark, the wild cinnamon, and the whitewood trees. When Victoria reaches the opening to the wood she recognizes a small Bread-and-cheese tree, with branches leaning over the path. She takes a wide berth around its prickly branches.

She is taken aback when she sees that the girl has stopped a few metres ahead and is examining a curved pod on another Bread-and-cheese. The pod has split and its black seeds, half-covered in white, fleshy rind, protrude from their cradle. The girl breaks off the pod and extracts a seed. She sucks on the fleshy rind of one, spits it out, then takes another. Her puckered mouth sucks on the flesh as though on a sweet. Derek watches her like an initiate into a sprite circle. The otherworldly presence on this ridge is palpable.

When she's sucked the white flesh off several seeds, the girl drops the pod and continues through the bushes. When she reaches the foot of the piled rock, the girl stops suddenly.

"Here is where you can go, but is all up rocks and you ain't suppose to do dat." The girl's voice is slow and deeper than it should be, Victoria thinks.

"Why not?" she asks her, slightly out of breath from the pace of the trek in the ringing heat.

"Mommy doesn't let me," the girl answers.

Victoria looks up at the steep climb they will have to make over rocks to get to the edge of the cliff. The rock face forms two distinct levels—one a few meters up, then the far peak of Pico Tenerife itself, another ten metres after that. She looks at Derek, who is still staring at the little girl. She looks down at her feet, regretting the flimsy thongs she chose to wear on this outing, and then considers what Alexander might do. Of course, he'd explore.

"I think we could try, ah Derek?"

He looks up towards the peak. The strong breeze makes him squint, and his eyes go sleek and sharp. He nods quickly. With great intent he begins to climb up the first ridge of rock, but stops and turns to the girl still on the path. "You coming?" he asks gently.

"Ya'll mad as shite," she says and turns on her heels, running off through the birch gum trees towards the pasture.

Victoria laughs and walks towards Derek. She hikes the leg of her khaki shorts up high on her thigh and places her sandalled foot onto the first flat rock surface. She pulls herself up onto the rock.

The breeze seems to hold her. Derek waits for her on the first ledge.

By the time she reaches him, she's panting and sweating. She holds out her hand for him to help her up onto the ledge. The moment she's up, she is overwhelmed by sound: the crash of the Atlantic. A gust of wind strikes her face and chest, and she stumbles back slightly. Derek grabs her arm above the wrist and steadies her. She notices how big his hands are getting, how almost manly they are, his wrists ripening with strength. They both stand and look. Below them are tiny coral-rock islands, out of the centre of which rise coral spirals like a tiny city of skyscrapers. The surf washes around them, unrelentingly. In the distance, the ocean appears deceptively inert, like a vast cobalt tundra. But a more concentrated gaze can detect its heaving from great depths, the regular swells and breaking whitecaps wheezing its seditious fury.

"Let's rest," Victoria suggests, and finds a flat wedge of rock to sit on.

Derek climbs up behind her and crouches down. He picks small pebbles from the crevice between his rock and his aunt's and pelts them down the steep jagged rock face into the crashing waves below. The pebbles make no mark, no sound; they just disappear.

Victoria and Derek give in to the snore of the ocean.

She feels his knee up against her shoulder and is pricked with love. She turns and looks up at him.

"Bear with me, son."

He puts his hand on her shoulder and presses his fingers into the flesh and muscle. "Maybe we should bring Alexander and Kendra here," he says boldly—his attempt to contribute to her spirits, his effort to tell her that he will fix everything. He doesn't know how, exactly, but he feels he has a role to play in his aunt's happiness. *A wizard lives everywhere, is cut off from nothing, and is as connected as the air* . . .

A sudden rustling above them pries the moment open. Derek

looks up quickly to see the hind legs of a goat scrambling up the rock.

"Huhhah!" he gasps with glee as he springs up.

"What is it?"

"Animals."

"What?"

"I saw legs, two sets of legs." He stands on his toes to see what else he can make out.

"Surely not," Victoria says, but she also stands up to look. Out of the scrubland above the Bread-and-cheese trees, another animal scampers up the rock. A feral goat, not like anything farmed on the island or the black-bellied sheep they saw on the way up from the road.

"I'm going," Derek shouts, and starts to climb up the rock to the next ledge.

"No! Derek, it's dangerous," Victoria calls after him, but he hasn't heard, or hasn't listened. She steps up on the next rock to call again, but he has already scrambled far ahead. She starts to follow him, then stops to rest. To her right lie the pasture and the mysterious rocks that line the field. Stone fences like England. She climbs on, with coral at her feet. Bending over, she grabs the rock with her hands to help pull herself up. The rock is precarious. Piles of it rise and dip before her, as though thrown up by the sea in Poseidon's juggling act. Derek is up near the top. She spots the perky tail of one of the goats scrambling back down the right side of the cliff. Where is this now? Greece? It could be Chile from the photos she's seen. Or New Zealand. It resembles even the coastal path in Wales. Or is it France? Is this rock so indistinct as to be everywhere? With all the moving, place to place, everything starts to blur. She steps once more and slips. Her foot slides between two boulders, and the ankle is wrenched in the crack. A gasp of pain; the shock of it puts her off balance. She falls to the rock, bracing herself with her hand. But the hand takes too much weight, and it too begins to throb. She shakes it like a thermometer, trying to reverse the flow of pain.

Damn, she thinks, and feels ridiculous at the thought of this happening now. She breathes deeply, trying to hold back the throbbing. The pain is too much if she tries to ease herself up on to her foot, so she sits again. Should she call Derek for help? She doesn't want to alarm him. Would he even hear her over the crashing of the waves? The boy is visible among the turreting of rocks above. He resembles a sentry in a fort. He holds his arms out straight from his sides, as though he's about to take off. She panics. She tries to put weight on her foot again, but no . . . Shite, damn, shite . . . as she sits back down and rocks gently back and forth to calm herself.

Derek feels the wind lift his arms. He tests his weight, pushing himself up onto his toes, and feels the rise of his shoulders. Maybe he could do it, he thinks. Fly. He watches a gull soar out over the waves. He tilts his outstretched arms and imagines he's soaring with the frigate bird towards the whitecaps. The sea looks darker now as the sun has begun to descend behind them in the west, dipping toward the hills in the middle of the island. Below him to the right is a coral protrusion that resembles a giant, sculpted dog. He soars for a moment longer but notices that with the dying sun the wind is calming. The seabirds seem to glide more gently. He lowers his arms slightly, and turns left with the gull as it gets closer to the cliff. Out of the corner of his eye he catches a glimpse of his aunt sitting curled up on the rock ledge below him. Something about her doesn't seem right. He drops his arms and hurries down to her, stepping carefully over loose rocks.

"What happened?" he asks, alarmed by the sight of her holding her ankle, which appears to be swelling. She looks up at him, trying to appear normal, as though the pain is not vying for her attention and making her breathe in measured puffs.

"Auntie Vic?"

"My ankle," she says, then breathes deeply again. "It's sprained, maybe broken, but I don't think so. I hope not. It'll be fine. We'll go down now, but I have to rest for just a minute."

"But . . ." Derek's arms go heavy, and his neck muscles tighten.

He looks around and notices that the sun is much lower, and here in the crag behind the ridge there is no direct light. The sky is mauve above the ocean. He crouches down beside his aunt's shoulder. Victoria takes a deep breath to hold the pain in. She looks at Derek's soft face in the dusk light. His eyes glitter with concern.

"What were you doing up there?" she asks him. Her voice is gentle. The wind is softer and there is no need to shout.

"Nothing," he answers, still staring worriedly at her. The breeze ruffles his hair.

"It didn't look like nothing," she says, but shudders again with pain, trying to minimize the sound of her gasp.

Derek sits beside her and reaches towards her ankle. He touches it gently, carefully, not wanting to hurt her.

"I was silly to wear these slippers, really! It'll be fine, I think . . . but," she looks around and notices the diminishing light, "we should get going." She starts to put weight on her other foot and to lift herself up. "Ooff," she says, shaking her head back and forth and looking towards the pasture beyond the rock, wondering how she'll make it.

"Auntie Vic," he starts. He wants her to stop moving. He holds her shoulders and steadies her on the rock.

"Blimey," she whispers, "you might have to lower me on a hook, like a carcass in an abattoir." She hopes the joke will make everything seem manageable.

Derek isn't paying attention to what she's saying. He keeps staring at her foot, and has something burning in him to say to her. He gathers his courage. "You know, Auntie Vic . . ."

"Yes, son."

"You know, I'm going to be quite clever."

She looks into his face, wondering if the gap between his teeth isn't smaller these days. She smiles, but this is not the moment for any of that. "I know," she says, holding on to the rock to readjust her weight. She tries to stand again. Derek watches her in alarm, as his thoughts rush about. He hasn't said exactly what he means, not what he was thinking up there at the peak. What he wanted to tell her was that he'd learn to be as wise as a wizard, but it didn't come out right. Finally he has the urge to tell his aunt something, to strip back the husk of his wariness with her and to let her in on a secret. He wants to tell her about the things stirring in him these last few months.

"A wizard," he says, trying again, as Victoria lifts herself up on her hands and manages to put the weight on her left side. She hears him, but doesn't answer. The only image that flashes into her mind is of Dorothy, Toto, and a journey to Oz, but she's losing her hold on her pain and her temper, and doesn't understand why he's brought this up now. She tries to stand. "Ooff," she breathes out again.

Derek panics and stands in front of her. "No, don't move." He holds her shoulder again and forces her to sit back on the rock. "I have a plan," he announces.

"Look, Derek, we don't have time for this. Let's get going."

"But you can't, Auntie Vic, even I can see that. You're foot's not going anywhere down this cliff," he says forcefully.

Victoria shakes her head and wonders if she should take off her T-shirt in order to use it as a bandage to secure the ankle.

"I know what. I'll go down and fetch someone to help me help you. Someone strong, to get you down. Back at that little shop—"

"Oh, no, I don't think—"

"Yes," he says, cutting her off sharply. "You can't make it, and the sun is going down. What if you fall or something? I'll get someone." He pauses for a moment, making further plans in his head, feeling the confidence that will become the man in him, with or without a father. "And they can bring a jeep over the pasture. That's the only way." He appears to make a few more mental notes, then he tucks his shirt into his shorts and prepares to move off.

"Wait, Derek," his aunt protests, but then, looking around her again, concedes that the boy might have the right idea. She sees the new certainty in his dusk-lit face. There's no denying it. "OK," she says, adding, "but hurry, and be careful yourself."

Derek heads down the ledge of rock and leaves her.

The wind drops even more and elongates the seconds she takes to reposition herself to face the sea. A mauve-and-amber light is wrapping itself around the rock. She knows it doesn't take long for the sky to get dark in the tropics. It happens suddenly, blackness moving in like sleep. She laughs, feeling ridiculous here alone on the rock at the mercy of her foot. But she's surprisingly unafraid. Could this be her moment to defy all the bogeys and invisible things she's picked up along the way? Should she raise herself up on one leg to do a little jig in honour of what she knows? She knows, deep down, that this is as much as we have: this body, this air.

Looking out towards the now calmer ocean, she notices that the sinking sun has drawn up the moon. It is faint but emerging in the distance to her right. As her eyes scan the horizon, she realizes that from here there is no landmass until Africa. Senegal, Gambia, Sierra Leone . . . nothing that blocks her from that place that became a chant in her heart after Kola left.

A delicate seabird flies low to the rock, humming past her shoulder. It startles her. She reaches for her ankle again. The pain has generalized; she's dizzy with it. She looks up. Other birds are circling, and the sight of them causes just a moment of panic. The Ethiopian vulture that dives down on carcasses to suck marrow out of broken bones comes to mind. But this is not Africa, even in this moment of disorienting pain. She breathes deeply and concentrates on easing the throbbing.

When she called Alexander from Gerty's daughter's phone in Kitty he said something that has occupied her thoughts these last two days. After his warm entreaty for her to come home, for them to meet and talk again, there was silence down the line before his static-dotted voice said, "I miss you." After a quick breath, she dared ask, "Which part?" Joking to try to cover up her uncertainty. The long pause over the crackling distance was disconcerting. She adjusted her blouse. "Every part I see," he answered finally, and she knew he meant, *only if you let me,* and knew she had been guilty of carrying injustice in her as though it was hers alone. Her mother's, Kola's—injustice hardened her. The real question, she thinks, is not what is right, but what can I give?

She is still making discoveries. Ancient things arrive in the body through the trajectory of others who came before it. Things we must absorb and interpret, in order to move ahead. But move ahead to where? Into love, she concedes. Alexander, or someone else. Because her body is made for love.

The throbbing in her ankle feels no less acute than anywhere else in her now, so she puts a hand down on a flat rock and pushes herself up slowly. She uses the other hand to pull up on the rock behind her and raise herself onto her uninjured foot. She tests the strength of the sprained one, thinking she'll try to make it down the ridge before it gets dark. *Eoeouwww!* The pain curdles her and she slouches forward. Straightening up, she stands on one foot looking out to the blackening sea.

She's worried about Derek. How will he find his way back without light? Will she be stranded here until the morning? She will need shelter. A few ledges down, the crook of a boulder creates a sheltered hollow. She drags herself towards it using her hands, sliding down and bracing herself with one leg. As she works she feels stronger. Finally, she positions herself in the curve of the rock and feels protected.

The sky has darkened. She crosses her legs, not quite Buddha-like, resting the injured ankle on her other calf. She looks up. The first stars have appeared. She gazes at them and visualizes herself aligned in position with them, becoming a point on a constellation. Like the buckle on Orion's belt, she becomes a connecting sparkle, creating the whole picture for an observer lying on his back, pointing up, drawing out meaning between Georgetown,

Toronto, London, and this rock. She sits straight, leans forward slightly, out over the edge, holding the boulder to steady herself. She brings her best glow forward. There's still time yet for this body, she thinks. Before it calcifies with the wash of salt air . . . *In loving memory, this stone commemorates . . .* still time for touch. And if that is as much as there is, well . . . *feel me . . .*

A brother. As far away as Georgetown or Miami. A brother would help now. Someone to show up and help him retrace his steps to the ridge. Someone to help him reach his aunt on the ledge and carry her down, to a hospital, to the hotel, back home. It would feel right to have one here. Now.

As Derek reaches the pasture and finds his way in the receding light over the field and broken stones, towards the road to the village, he worries about finding his way back, either alone or leading someone else. He wishes Thomas were here, or Stephen, or Kendra, or better yet, Richard, who'd be strong enough to do just about anything. A younger brother wouldn't do, not now, but would serve at other times. A younger brother he could talk to, and to whom he could teach the things he knows about wizardry, about circles and magic groves. A younger brother would listen. Perhaps one day he'll meet the grandson of the bandy-legged woman and tell him these things. Or he will go to Miami, where another brother might be found, and teach him the power of the wind, of rain, of fire. But he has much to do yet. Much more learning. He makes a mental note to look on the Web for a site that lists Merlin's mortal children.

As he finds his way down the hill along the path near the black-bellied sheep, then through the farmer's rickety gate towards the village shop and the little girl, he contemplates the lack of skill, the insufficiency he feels—his frustrated ambition in obtaining something he can articulate at this point in his life only as magic. He knows he is not a wizard yet.

And it's true. He is getting along, but he is not so powerful yet to be able to know that he will indeed make his way to the Ting shack belonging to the little girl and her single mother, who, along with help from a neighbouring dressmaker, keeps the girl's hair plaited, as the one remaining sign that she is not forsaken and left to run wild in the streets like an unwanted pet.

It will be a good hour before the woman returns from her day cleaning in a hotel on the west coast, so he will sit and wait on the side of the road with the little girl as she sings songs and he pulls up long blades of grass. When her mother returns, they secure the help of two hefty men for his aunt, who is found many hours later, in the blackness, on the edge of consciousness, muttering words that sound like condolences in a foreign language. They carry her safely, but with much fumbling and difficulty, to a nearby chattel house to be tended to, revived, and then driven to a hospital in Bridgetown, where the smell of fish frying in the street below her ward window wakens her, and she looks into the hopeful face of her nephew.

He cannot know how she will feel seeing his soft hazel eyes on her. She instructs him to call Alexander, to ask him to meet them at Gatwick airport the day after next. He makes the call with the help of the kind nurse on the ward.

Alexander will greet them, alone. As the arrival gate opens, he will be standing, timidly, looking shorter than Derek remembered him, and he will move towards Auntie Vic with tender reserve. He hugs her, then approaches Derek, who finds himself giving in to the sinewy feel of his arms—a texture that claims him. He likes that. Then Alexander will hand him the comic book sent by Kendra as a welcome-home gift. The three of them will return to Blenheim Terrace, where Alexander and Victoria will talk, Derek will see them kiss, but jetlag will overtake him as he sits in the armchair trying to read the comic. While Derek is deep in sleep, Alexander and Victoria fumble their way through the first moments of reconciliation.

Over the next few weeks he witnesses them becoming closer and lighter with each other, until the comfortable family insouciance that first surfaced before their trip to France returns. He sets no store by what feels like the growing solidity of a unit, because the more steeped he is in the invisible, the more wary he is of anything that appears permanent. In November, his aunt and Alexander throw a small party to celebrate his twelfth birthday, to which Stephen and Kendra are invited, but bring no gifts. Victoria, on the other hand, presents him with a new and sufficiently sonorous acoustic guitar. He takes a few guitar lessons but doesn't like his teacher, who has hands that resemble a wrench. He nevertheless practises with passion every evening alone in his room.

He will carry out three more deliveries for Richard Lorry, obediently, automatically, as though watching how to cast a spell, until at one scheduled appointment Richard doesn't show up, and Derek learns later from Kendra that rumour has it Richard has been taken into juvenile detention. Derek tries to understand just how wizardry has had a part in this, but he can justify no real connection.

As the summer takes its feeble hold on the country, he notices his aunt growing softer and wider—not a return to the attic woman he arrived to in London, but settling into a kind of winsome acceptance. He learns to confide in her, and as he becomes more steeped in the invisible, she, by contrast, absorbs his fantasies as though they are falls, listening to them with her whole body. When she embraces him, she feels like a reliable cushion set out before him. This loosening within her continues to be detectable during the periodic parting and reuniting that she and Alexander go through over the next few years, but is later apparent even when Alexander is no longer often around.

Later that year, another bomb will explode in the heart of London, but Derek and Victoria will be nowhere near the site. Responsibility for the bomb will be claimed by a terrorist group that no one, to that point, has ever heard of.

Derek will help Max and Monica as they learn to read, while his own studies will continue uneventfully, unevenly into senior school, where he is still most comfortable in the world of words on the page or the screen, manipulating fact and fantasy, fuelling his aspirations as a writer. His musical abilities develop slowly, while his tastes swivel like a divining rod over trends and whiffs of genius. In a casual exchange with Stephen, he will finally understand the persistent striding of tourists over a particular zebra crossing on Abbey Road.

He will develop much like any adolescent in the Swiss Cottage area, sometimes bored and other times pumped up with such a vigilant disrespect for the physical existence of things over which he has no control that he lashes out and causes others discomfort and even harm. Lenny will shepherd him through disagreements with his aunt, and it will be Lenny who first lets him behind the steering wheel of a car.

Kendra will see him through a private education in mystery and sensuality, always one level and many, many touches beyond him. He stands aside while she gives herself up to pleasure with a college boy she meets in the lilac spring of their second-last school year. Derek listens, not unmoved, to her descriptions of flesh and rhythm, and he fights the rising swell of betrayal in his throat. He tells her he worries about her, but this isn't entirely the truth, because there is nothing in life that Derek believes Kendra cannot conquer.

Left more and more to his own devices, he will search for his father in the eyes of girls in his fifth form and those in the streets, but also in the acceptance of other boys and the cruel discipline of a gang. And one Tuesday evening in April, when the sky is orange with promise, two policemen will arrive at the door to their home on Blenheim Terrace to question him about his involvement in the vandalism of a shop window on Finchley Road. Victoria listens in horror to the suspicions the police have regarding Derek's behaviour. She is given a warning to keep him under control, and is propelled into devising months of restrictions on his privileges. But Derek remains peaceful in the knowledge that everything he does, he also watches, and in that distance is the eye of the wizard.

Even so, he will not have arrived. His efforts will take a lifetime. He will look into the faces of some and see himself. In the faces of others he will see nothing.

Then, one day in the autumn before he begins studies in literature at a university in the centre of London, he will be walking along the south bank of the Thames River near Blackfriars Bridge. He bends down to pick up a piece of cloth that resembles something he has forgotten by the time the cloth is in his hands. As he straightens up, he tries to remember the thing in mind, but his glance slips out toward the water, where the tide is low, and rubbish and flotsam line the bank of the dirty river he has come to love. In that glance he is infused with an inkling he will carry with him his whole life: an itching, sparking, igniting sensation that being born means I have this body, and that dying means, simply, that I leave this body, and there's more.

Acknowledgements

Many books have informed this novel, but I would like to mention the following in particular: Koigi wa Wamwere, *I Refuse to Die: My Journey for Freedom* and *Conscience on Trial: Why I Was Detained: Notes of a Political Prisoner in Kenya*; Deepak Chopra, *The Way of the Wizard*; John Berger, *To the Wedding*; and case studies of fieldwork by Dr. Mike Meegan at ICROSS.

The quotations from Sir Thomas Malory's *The Death of King Arthur* are from the Penguin 60s Classics edition. The poem excerpt on page 36 is from Robert Browning's "Home-Thoughts, from Abroad." The quotation on page 157 is from Isabel Allende's *Aphrodite: A Memoir of the Senses*. Thanks to Carolina Aivars for the Spanish translation of *Dum pudeo, pereo*, from the *Epigrammata* of Valerius Aedituus, inspired by an English reading of this line in Anne Carson's *Plainwater*.

I am very grateful for the existence and generous support of the Canada Council for the Arts.

I'd like to thank the many people who have made this book possible: My family, especially the inspiration of my mother, Cicely, and my nephew, Sean. And my new family at Blenheim Terrace: the Ruhemanns, in particular Phillip Ruhemann for important walks in France, and the Ruhemann-Bridghams, especially Lotte and Otto.

I'm grateful for the gracious generosity and friendship of Andrew Ruhemann. To Simon Freakley, my loving gratitude for friendship and for making possible inspiring periods of work in London and the south of France. Similarly, my life in London would not have been possible without the supportive friendship of Richard Morris, Ronan Bennett, and Richard Kwietniowski. Many thanks to other friends who helped in the process of the novel: Jackie Kaiser, Suzanne Smith, Charlotte Thompson, Tony Brown, Lennie DaSilva (for her pepperpot recipe), and Sean Carrington (for giving me Pico).

I feel particularly fortunate to be represented by Stephanie Cabot, and to have had Virginia Barber as my agent in New York. In addition, Attila Berki's editorial acuity and friendship have been invaluable to me for many years now.

Deepest thanks to everyone at HarperCollins, especially Iris Tupholme for her insight and enthusiasm.

Finally, there's no way to appropriately thank Stephanie Young, except to say, "I sat with my back facing the window."